Dark
Secret

❧

Also by Elizabeth Atkins Bowman
from Tom Doherty Associates

WHITE CHOCOLATE

Dark
Secret

Elizabeth
Atkins
Bowman

A Tom Doherty Associates Book

New York

DARK SECRET

Copyright © 2000 by Elizabeth Atkins Bowman

A Forge Book
Published by Tom Doherty Associates, LLC
175 Fifth Avenue
New York, NY 10010

www.tor.com

Forge® is a registered trademark of Tom Doherty Associates, LLC.

Design by Lisa Pifher

Library of Congress Cataloging-in-Publication Data

Bowman, Elizabeth Atkins.
    Dark secret / Elizabeth Atkins Bowman.—1st ed.
      p. cm.
    "A Tom Doherty Associates Book."
    ISBN 0-312-86806-5
    1. Racially mixed people—Fiction. 2. Mothers and daughters—Fiction. 3. Passing (Identity)—Fiction.
4. Detroit (Mich.)—Fiction. 5. Sisters—Fiction. I. Title.

PS3552.O8757114 D37 2000
813'.54—dc21   00-028835

First Edition: July 2000

Printed in the United States of America

0 9 8 7 6 5 4 3 2 1

This story is for Alexander: May you always follow your heart and dreams, then celebrate the fulfillment of your accomplishments.

An enormous thank-you to my mother,
Marylin Atkins...for everything!
You are truly the greatest. And thank you,
Thomas Atkins, aka Daddy, for watching over us
and inspiring us to reach for the stars.

Merci beaucoup to my Lavender Love, Victor Bowman.

Ma soeur...mia sorella... Catherine Atkins, I cherish
your words of wisdom and creative counsel. Here's to
your own literary achievement!

Wilhelmena "Mimi" Horton: Your help during crunch
time was a huge blessing.

And always, Walter and Jeanette Bowman, we are
grateful for your love and support.

A special thank-you to Darnell Jackson,
financial consultant extraordinaire,
for sharing your expertise and enthusiasm.

Of course, my wonderful editor, Natalia Aponte—
your nurturance is a gift from the literary gods.

To my very cool agent, Susan Crawford...
I treasure your exuberance and faith that writing
wishes do come true!

And always, immense appreciation
to Jeff Wardford.

Dark Secret

❧

1

Camille Morgan shuddered as her backside touched the curving crystal wall of the enormous shower. She clawed Jeff's rippling shoulders, squeezed her legs around his waist.

"Harder," she purred, pressing her breasts into his chest. Jeff plunged deeper, causing droplets to rain from his sandy-blond hair.

Camille savored the dazzling image, behind her closed eyelids, of herself and Jeff turning to liquid gold. As if the white-hot intensity of their passion was melding their skin and blood, burning away all she wanted to forget. Especially today.

"My Lady Godiva." Jeff's deep, enraptured voice vibrated through her; his long fingers kneaded her thighs as he spun her under double shower heads. A *pouf* sound mixed with the patter of water on marble as he stepped on a heap of lavender-scented suds. "Can't ever get enough of you."

Lust glowed on the angular planes of Jeff's face and his straight nose, sun-pinkened from the previous day of sailing around Manhattan on Uncle John's yacht. That made his eyes even more blue, especially when he looked as if he were put on Earth for the sole purpose of pleasing her.

I have to keep him like this. Forever. Even though his parents hate me.

Camille's stomach cramped. She danced her French manicure over Jeff's figure-eight-shaped lips. He sucked her fingers as her five-carat oval diamond ring glimmered in the August sunshine pouring through two tall windows above. Then he held her against the bronze wall, where she glimpsed the golden pretzel that was their tangled limbs, in the huge, gilt-framed mirror across the bathroom. Her cheeks lifted as she watched a rainbow dance in the mist around them. As if it were mocking the tempest that she anticipated in just a few hours at his parent's mansion.

"Tell me how much you love me," she murmured, wishing Jeff had turned off the annoying drone of the TV in the cabinets. But the remote was between the crystal, rose-shaped sinks under the mirror. She longed to hit MUTE and kill any chance of news reports stealing his attention for days, even weeks.

"I love you more than the ocean is wide," Jeff purred back, lust thickening his Virginia accent. "More than anything in life."

Trembling on the verge of orgasm, Camille slid to her feet, turning to face the shower wall. She pressed her cheek and palms against the etched glass image of a naked woman on a horse, her long tresses flowing in the wind. But as Jeff, behind her, intensified his pace, her fingernails made a chalkboardish scrape that made her envision his mother's eyes raking over her, his father puffing a cigar, radiating superiority.

Have to make them adore me as much as they love that debutante snob Tabitha Lucas. I will . . .

"Honey," Jeff moaned over the solemn music signaling the top-of-the-hour report on Global News Network. His fingers combed long, wet hair off her shoulder; he sank his teeth into her skin. "Oh, honey—"

The news anchor's voice boomed into the shower: "A controversial Virginia senator coming under fire this morning, accused of denying a black executive membership into his country club."

"Shit!" Jeff stiffened, raised his head. Camille spun to see his eyes sharpen. He pulled away. Then he flung open the shower door, grabbed a towel, focused on the TV. His jaw muscles flexed; he was grinding his teeth.

Camille glared at his dripping-wet backside as he stepped closer to the screen. Neither of them had climaxed. And she was still aching for him to douse the blaze between her legs. But his nude reflection in the mirror revealed he was no longer in any condition to do that.

I can't believe he'd rather watch the news than make love. Camille slapped crystal levers to stop the hissing shower. She stepped out and wrapped a thick white towel around herself, then plunked onto the settee, covered in gold shantung, at the center of the room by the fireplace and chandelier. There she watched video of Jeff's father, a lean pillar of navy blue topped by a striking silver coif, as he talked at the podium on the Senate floor.

The anchor said, "Republican Senator Monty Stone now being named in a civil rights complaint filed by the CEO of a software company in Richmond. A lawyer for Gordon Williams says Stone sabotaged his application to the exclusive Rolling Hills Country Club because Williams is African-American."

Jeff pitched the towel onto the counter. "Pop's gonna be furious."

Then a sound bite from the lawyer: "Monty Stone's racial allegiance is no secret. That man still lives in the three-hundred-year-old plantation house where his great-grandfather owned slaves." More video showing White Pines, a white-columned mansion shrouded by wispy pines and magnolias.

"But Senator Stone," the anchor continued, "a former segregationist, denies race was the reason that Williams was refused membership."

A sound bite from Jeff's father in front of the U.S. Capitol: "It's been decided," Senator Stone nodded, "that Rolling Hills will stand by what gentlemen in the Old Dominion call tradition. Because we Virginians do value tradition."

Camille could not look away from his wolflike gray eyes. There was something enchanting about them that made her want to believe and support everything he said. Even though she couldn't remember him ever saying a nice word to her in the three years since she'd lured Jeff from Tabitha.

"Now understand, a nouveau riche Yankee," Senator Stone said with his deep, melodic drawl, "a miner's son from Pittsburgh, has no place with us. Our committee believes his needs can be better served at a country club of," he nodded, "another sort."

The anchor came back on camera: "Senator Stone, heir to a tobacco fortune, tells GNN he believes Williams is, quote, 'slinging mud' because black Democrat Marcus Jones is challenging his seat in Congress in the upcoming election. But a lawyer for—"

"Shit!" Jeff jabbed the OFF button. "Pop doesn't need this now. Those black militants! Making up lies, trying to bring him down."

Annoyance prickled Camille's damp skin. Jeff's mind was far, far away from her, from making love, from thinking about the exact words he would use this afternoon to ask his parents' approval to get married. And if this little scandal was anything like the last, Jeff would be distracted for months.

No! I won't let anything get in the way of the wedding. I've worked too hard to get here, and I'm going to stay. Have to make him focus . . .

Camille stood up, let the towel drop to the floor. She pressed her stiff nipples into his back, running the tip of her tongue up the firm valley of muscles along his spine. He let out a deep moan as she fanned her fingers up and down his flat stomach, down to where his spongy softness stiffened to attention.

"Baby," she purred, pressing her lips into his clean-shaven neck. She slid in front of him, running her fingertips over full, milky breasts, the creamy triangle below her belly button, and her gym-toned behind. Her skin felt extra soft today, thanks to that new herbal wrap she and Ginger had had at the spa this week. "Why don't you check out my tan lines."

Jeff's eyes brightened. His lips parted, pushing up dimples, revealing big, bright teeth. "Boy, all that sun yesterday. Mmm-hmm. Like a hot Puerto Rican chick up in Spanish Harlem. Makes me want to—"

"Tango." She pulled him toward the settee, where she lay on a cape of damp hair. Jeff's hot lips on her mouth, and his hardness pressing into her thigh, made her head swirl. *Yes, we can forget the news, his parents, our trip . . .*

"Baby Boy!" The maid sounded frantic on the other side of the door.

Jeff bolted up, wrapping a towel around his waist.

"Baby Boy, the car is here," Ida Mae said, swinging open the door just as Camille covered herself with a towel. "Your daddy's plane gon' leave without us if you don't get some clothes on. I tol' you, nine o'clock."

"You told us ten-thirty," Camille shot at the maid, whose face looked like a smooth, chocolate-brown heart centered by a button mushroom of a nose. Her hair was pulled back in a bun that resembled a black ball of yarn pinned to a white lace doily.

"I tol' you nine. And I want to get there just as fast as you do." Ida Mae ran her hands over the white apron of her starched gray uniform. Then she looked at Jeff. "Your daddy say he need the plane soon as it drop us off. 'Cause Davis in Atlanta. An' Mr. Monty gon' be in a tizzy if we late—"

"Enough." Jeff dashed into the bedroom.

Camille darted to the counter, grabbed a comb, and began taming the honey-colored waves hanging to her waist. In the mirror, her blue eyes, shaped like a cat's, were wide with worry, her full lips tight. They had to get down to White Pines before everyone arrived for Dixie's birthday party. Otherwise, there wouldn't be time to meet with his parents, because Mr. and Mrs. Stone would never be so *downright rude* as to leave their posts as southern host and hostess just to talk to Jeff about his girlfriend.

And if Jeff didn't ask them today, they wouldn't see them for two months. In October, when Mr. and Mrs. Stone were coming up to New York for some banquet celebrating Stone & Sons Tobacco for its philanthropy.

We can't wait that long. I want to get this ball rolling now. Today.

Camille took a deep breath to stifle a prickly wave of panic. A deep breath, without even a whisper of a wheeze. That in itself helped her relax for a second. But only a second. Because Ida Mae had tossed her into another trap. Camille glared at her, still standing in the doorway. "You told us the wrong time on purpose."

"No, Miss Camille. You got it mixed up in your own head. And you know Miss Millie gon' be mad, too."

"I can't believe you," Camille said, moussing her hair. "Last night when we got home, you said ten-thirty. Not nine."

Camille remembered distinctly: Ida Mae had greeted them in the foyer after dinner at Le Cirque 2000, where Jeff's uncle had given him a package of bearer bonds with a market value of a million dollars. All to celebrate his being named junior partner at the century-old law firm. Ida Mae said they'd leave at ten-thirty this morning, and Jeff had said good, that would give him time to take the bonds to the safe deposit box before they left.

"Believe what you want," Ida Mae said, glaring. She hurried into the bedroom after Jeff.

Camille started to follow, but dashed back to the counter. From a small drawer by her sink she pulled a pink plastic box, popped out a pill, and downed it with a glass of water. With the gulp came the memory of Aunt Ruby, telling those scary Jeremiah tales, reminding Camille she never, ever wanted to get pregnant. Just in case genetics really could play such a cruel and deadly trick.

Hurrying into the bedroom, Camille saw Jeff's black leather garment bag on their Italian Renaissance–style canopy bed, with its ornately carved and platinum-glazed woodwork, the lush folds of silvery satin secured with tassel ropes at the posts.

"Where are my things?" Camille rushed into the dressing room, where Jeff was pulling on white briefs and a crew-neck undershirt. She scanned the ceiling–high cabinets of shoe boxes and sweaters. No, she wouldn't need anything from the rows of gowns and blouses, or any of the tailored suits she'd gotten at Ginger's boutique for her new, wonderful job with Judge Mannington. There, the row of dresses— only those were worthy of Mrs. Stone's scrutiny.

"Miss Camille, I didn't know if you wanted them Ferragamo pumps or the Dior sandals with the skinny straps, so they both there." Ida Mae pointed toward a brass rack where, in the soft light of recessed bulbs, hung an ivory linen dress, tags still on, with a beige lace bra-panty set.

Camille hated the accusatory tone in Ida Mae's voice. *She even talks about my shoes as if I've done something wrong. Just like Mother used to.*

"Thanks," Camille said, slipping into her panties. But Ida Mae did not look up. She was too busy helping Jeff into his dark blue suit pants and starched white shirt. She inserted his gold cuff links with the Virginia Military Institute logo. And as Jeff pulled on polished loafers and a matching belt, Ida Mae combed, blow-dried, and spritzed his hair. It almost looked as if Ida Mae was an extension of Jeff that he barely acknowledged yet depended on like his right hand.

He looked Camille's way as she fastened the bra clasp between her breasts. "Honey, we can't be late." The urgency and seriousness in Jeff's eyes bunched raw nerves in her stomach.

She smiled. "I'll be perfect. I promise."

Her life was so different now, she would do anything to stay worlds away from the time and place when she was a sad little girl named Sharlene.

2

Sharlene Bradley tried to suck air into her closed-up, rattling lungs. But another mouthful of secondhand cigarette smoke made her gag so hard her chest and pink ruffled shirt slammed the edge of the kitchen table, her sweaty legs rubbed against the scratchy vinyl chair. Dingy walls and bluish air and rusty metal cupboards whirled, as if she'd done too many cartwheels. Beyond the fuzzy whiteness of her hand, raised to catch her cough, Karen and Mother were brown blurs.

"Mother, can you put that out? I can't bre—"

"Shut up, ghost baby. And finish them chicken livers." Gray clouds shot from Mother's flat triangle of a nose. Her full, chestnut face tightened; thick eyelashes became black slits. With the cigarette between her fingers, she smoothed dark strands popping from her ponytail. "And stop that nonsense about you can't breathe." Mother rose in a flash of orange, her T-shirt and shorts sticking in sweat spots to her thick body. One step to the stove, and she creaked its door open. "Ain't got nothin' to do with if I want to smoke. You see it don't bother Karen or nobody else."

Mother pointed toward the dim living room, where Aunt Ruby lay moaning on the old green couch. Ruby's hair was a giant black cotton ball around her face, usually a mirror image of Mother's but now all twisted up. In front of her, LaDawn kneeled on the wood floor, two braids bouncing as she scrubbed throw-up from her mother's orange shirt.

"Motherfuckers!" Ruby's boyfriend James shouted into the phone. At his feet, his pit bull terrier chewed Sharlene's Barbie.

The crash of dishes in the sink made Sharlene's head spin. Mother slammed the hot pan on the counter; roaches raced up the wall.

"Sweet praline, you want some cobbler?"

"Yeah!" Karen's big brown eyes sparkled; she kicked the table leg.

"Stop!"

Karen made the cold meat on Sharlene's plate jiggle again.

"I said stop!" A wheeze punctuated her words.

"Hush!" Mother glanced at Ruby who was moaning loudly. "James—"

"Them motherfuckers at nine-one-one act like Helen Street ain't on the map!" James wiped his freckled face on his beige muffler-shop shirt. His mean eyes reminded Sharlene how much she hated him living there, always hogging the TV and drinking beer. He wasn't her father. He wasn't even LaDawn's father.

Sharlene found it more pleasant to let her mouth water as glistening slices of cinnamon-speckled peaches rose on Karen's fork.

"Like it, sweet praline?" Mother balanced a spoonful at her own mouth.

Karen smiled, picking golden-brown crust the same color as her fingers. She popped it into her mouth. "Mmmm! Too bad *you* can't have any!"

Sharlene raised her gaze to Mother. "Can I?"

"Hell no. That on your plate's all we got 'til my check come."

"I hate liver!" Sharlene said, her throat burning.

Mother threw her spoon into the sink. "Damn ghost baby! Lookin' just like your daddy when you mad. I wish for one day you was like Karen. Just one damn day of my life!" She lit another cigarette.

Struggling to breathe, Sharlene crossed her arms, clamped her teeth. She was sure she would tumble to the floor, roaches creeping over her like raisins on cream of wheat. Itching, she fingered the honey mop of waves sticking to her sweaty forehead.

"And just for gettin' on my nerves, scrub them pans after you eat."

Sharlene glanced to the window, its splintered wood frame propped open by a beer bottle, letting in the sweet-sourness from the incinerator that her teacher said burned all of Detroit's garbage.

Mother will make me stay in here 'til I die. But if I live to have my own little girl, I'll hug her and never let anyone be mean to her. No matter who her father is.

The only way Sharlene would make it to her eighth birthday was to go outside and watch for Daddy, so he could take her away. He'd left after dinner one night to buy diapers, so he would come back around this time, too. Tonight.

She shot up, took two steps toward the living room—

Mother pinched her arm, pulled her back into the seat.

"I want to go!" But Daddy was never going to come. She was stuck.

Soon as I'm old enough, I'm going far away with people who love me.

On the porch, Karen was shaking as hard as when she and Sharlene would sit on the washing machines at the Laundromat.

"Ohlordhammercy!" Mama cried, holding Ruby's head in her lap on the splintered gray porch boards. "Twenty-four years old, dyin' like a dog in the street! And don't nobody care!" Beside her, LaDawn screamed.

Karen thought it was all happening so fast, it didn't seem real . . . Ruby screaming, running out into the sirens and flashing red lights . . . dropping on the porch. The ambulance drivers rushing up . . . James screaming. "Y'awl motherfuckers killed her!"

Kneeling beside Mama, Karen gripped Ruby's shoulder, shaking her.

"Don't die!" How could she? Ruby was so happy, always braiding Karen's hair, doing the latest dances. And why was the ambulance man staring up at James, looking as scared as Sharlene over there on the railing? The neighbors cramming the dusty yard were acting like this was a party. Even old Mrs. Hayes, who served free dinners in the church basement when Mama's check ran out, just stood there, saying, "My cousin died like that. Say that appendix just blowed up like a bomb. Poison inside'll kill you in a minute. And it hurt like nobody's business."

Karen ran to the driver, yanking his hand. "Don't let her die!"

He started to move. But James pulled a gun.

People screamed, ducking behind the red and white ambulance, trees, and a rusty car on cement blocks in the next driveway.

Karen froze. He waved the gun just inches from Mama's head.

"Sit your ass down, James!" Mama yelled. "They can't help Ruby if you up here actin' crazy!" It looked like Mama was holding a big mirror, because she and Aunt Ruby had the same cheeks that rose up like little apples when they smiled. The same "Indian hair" from Aunt Bertha. They even wore matching outfits Gramma had sent up from Mississippi.

Looks like Mama is laying there dead. No! She can't ever die!

Karen's dinner rose in her throat. Without Mama there would be no one to climb into bed with when she had a bad dream. No one to run a warm hand over her forehead and feed her soup when she caught the flu. And no one to make her feel wanted, since their father was never coming back.

"Please!" Karen pulled the ambulance man's hand even harder. More sirens . . . red and blue lights . . . screeching cars.

"Drop your weapon!" Officers pointing guns ran up on the porch. Mama crouched over Ruby. "Ohlordhammercy!"

In a blur, an officer's hot-dog-sized fingers pinched Karen's elbow. Her knee scraped the steps. LaDawn and Sharlene were being pulled, too. "Mama!" Karen dug her toes in the dirt. "Where are you taking us? Stop!"

The officer put them in the backseat of a police car on the street. He closed the door, scrunching Karen's shoulder against Sharlene in the middle, LaDawn by the other door. "No! Get my mama!" But the windows were rolled up, and plastic separated them from the officer using the radio up front.

"Let us out!" Karen clawed the door, but found no latch. More cops ran onto the porch, aiming at James and her mother.

Now Mama and Ruby are gonna die at the same time. They can't!

Karen banged the window. She had to run and help Mama. But

the sound of Sharlene's rattly lungs made Karen put her arm around her sister. She wished she hadn't kicked the table and teased Sharlene about not getting dessert. "Sharlene, we'll be okay."

"No, we won't!" Her blue eyes had a look that was as hard as an ice cube.

Karen withdrew her arm, bursting into tears. Why couldn't Sharlene always be as nice as this afternoon when they played *The Love Boat?* Sharlene was cruise director Julie McCoy, while Karen played a Hollywood actress looking for love. Ginger from across the street was there, too, as a fashion designer reuniting with a lost husband. But just as Julie showed her guests to the luxurious cabin and pointed out the rich, eligible bachelors by the pool, LaDawn screamed that welfare people don't take cruises.

"My mama dead!" LaDawn cried. "What they doin'?"

Mama was standing on the porch, her face twisted up and wet, with all those guns around her. Karen was sure her heart would explode, it was pounding so hard. After this, she would make her mother eat healthier, too, so she wouldn't get worse sugar and need shots like Gramma. But Mama was always saying, "Hush, girl. I don't need no white doctor tellin' me what to eat. A little cobbler won't kill me."

Crack! Crack!

Cops and people ran across the yard, between the houses.

Mama dashed off the porch. It sounded like a million firecrackers. "Hurry, Mama!"

There was an orange blur. And Mama tumbled to the ground.

3

Karen Bradley sped into the small gravel lot beside her mother's bakery. The peach-painted clapboard house, with its dark green shutters, flowers blooming in the window boxes, and wooden BISCUITS 'N HONEY sign on the lawn, looked deceptively cheerful in the Saturday morning sunshine.

No hint of the crisis inside. Yet.

Through her open car window, Karen could smell the hazelnut coffee and cinnamon rolls that were still luring a steady stream of customers from the crowded sidewalk, where folks were heading a few blocks down traffic-clogged Woodward Avenue to an early afternoon Tigers game at Detroit's new baseball stadium.

I gotta take care of whatever's going on in there before it hurts business. Or shuts this place down altogether. Karen gripped the steering wheel, remembering Betty's panicked voice over the phone just ten minutes ago. So much for her plan to spend Saturday in the office, getting caught up on the riverfront project press kits. She had to get them done, even though she'd been up late arguing with Franklin about how his business liaisons were souring their relationship. In the office *and* the bedroom. Now this, whatever was happening at Mama's bakery, was the last thing she felt like dealing with.

As Karen parked, she caught a glimpse in the rearview mirror of her worried, brown, cat-shaped eyes and her tense, caramel complexion framed by a clipped-up spray of dark corkscrew curls. She stepped out of her car as angry voices shot from the screen door. Daddy and Betty were at it again. The door swung open. Out stomped Andrea, one of the cooks. She ripped off her white apron, threw it on the grass between the cement porch and the green fence hiding the Dumpster.

"I'm through!" Andrea stormed toward the sidewalk.

Karen bolted inside. An alarm on one of the stainless-steel ovens lining the walls was blaring, but her father and Betty were just standing there.

"What—" Something squished under Karen's tennis shoes. Looking down, she froze. On the green tiled floor lay boulders of chocolate cake and a river of white frosting. A bride-and-groom ornament protruded as if half swallowed by an avalanche. A few inches away, frosting dotted Daddy's brown loafers and Levi's.

"What happened?" Karen demanded. At the same time, at the white, vine-covered trellis separating the crowded café and cashier counter up front, several customers were peering through the diamond-shaped holes.

"Christ." Exasperation filled her father's blue eyes. He ran a hand over his short, neatly trimmed beard and crew cut, the bristles alternately brown and gray, like a mix of brown and white sugar against his chalky complexion. "Betty dropped the cake."

"Hmmmph!" Betty wiped frosting from her brown fingers onto the white apron around her pillowy hips. "If they'da cleaned this place like they was supposed to, it wouldn'a been no grease on the floor."

Daddy shook his head, eyes closed. "I tried to catch it, but—"

"What time is the cake supposed to be delivered?" Karen asked.

"An hour ago," Betty snapped over the still-buzzing oven alarm. She leaned on the long, stainless-steel table centering the kitchen, inspecting her frosted shoes.

"We'll send another cake instead," Karen said.

"Can't," Betty said. "We outta flour. We spent all the money on them new ovens. And they won't deliver no more flour 'til we pay the old bill."

Karen dashed past the big table and the ceiling rack holding dozens of pots and pans. At the ovens, she slapped a red button to quiet the buzzer, then quickly donned oven mitts. Pulling four trays from the face-searing heat, she noticed they were way past golden brown. A minute longer and they would've been hockey pucks for the Red Wings.

"Lucky we got Joel up runnin' the register," Betty said.

"What about Mama?"

Her father tilted his head toward the office. "Doesn't feel good again."

Panic exploded inside Karen. Her mind spun in a thousand directions, just like at yesterday's press conference when the reporters were shouting questions at Franklin all at once. Now she felt enraged that everything was going wrong at the bakery. Terrified that Mama's health was getting worse. And she felt overwhelmed by the urgent need to find emergency money for the bakery's bank account and make a wedding cake appear out of nowhere. On top of that, her heart ached for the man she thought was her soul mate.

Stay cool. Take things one at a time. Starting with the cash crisis.

"Daddy, can you please take care of these muffins?" She yanked off the oven mitts, then hurried into the office, which had been a small bedroom before they converted the house into Biscuits 'n Honey. A quilt lay crumpled on the peach-colored couch. Next to it, the closed bathroom door and sounds of running water signaled Mama's whereabouts. Karen slipped into the desk chair, scanning a list of numbers posted on the corkboard before her.

"Here it is." She quickly dialed a hot line while scanning the framed newspaper article on the wall. The headline said: FROM WELFARE TO WEDDING CAKES—CITY COUNCIL PRESIDENT HELPS DETROIT WOMAN LIVE DELICIOUS DREAMS.

Below the headline was a picture of Mama smiling with Franklin in front of Biscuits 'n Honey when it had opened two years ago. The article described how Franklin Daniels had attracted state and federal money to help women like Mama secure small business loans and get training to become entrepreneurs. The program had even drawn praise from the governor.

"We're sorry," a recording said. "Due to recent legislation, inquiries for Welfare-to-Work Loans are being directed to your local Social Services office. We apologize for the inconve—"

Karen slammed down the phone. "Recent legislation?" Then she remembered: the Republicans on Capitol Hill, led by Monty Stone of Virginia, had slashed funding for the program that had started Biscuits 'n Honey. So she couldn't get emergency cash, as she had so many times, to cover today's crisis.

The bathroom door swung open. Mama balanced on the doorknob as if it were a cane. Her full face looked as gray as her long, flowered dress.

Karen shot to her feet. "Mama?"

"Ohlordhammercy. Can't take this headache much longer."

Karen helped her lie on the couch. She dashed into the bathroom and rifled through the deep, knotty-pine cabinets. There, a bottle of Tylenol. She took two tablets and a glass of water to Mama, then knelt before her on the rug. "I think we should go to the doctor, Mama."

"Hush, sweet praline. That dialysis yesterday, it takes a lot out of me. Just need some rest."

Karen tucked a tendril back into the thick French braid coiled around the top of Mama's head like a crown. "But you—"

"Go on. Sound like Mack and Betty 'bout to—" Mama closed her eyes.

Karen's throat burned as she stroked her mother's forehead. Every month, it seemed, Mama had some new complication from her diabetes. First the out-of-control blood sugar that had landed her in the hospital on the verge of a coma. Then the insulin shots. Kidney problems. Dialysis three times a week.

God, please make her well. She's the only person in my life who's never let me down. And now she's living her dream, but she's too sick to enjoy it.

Karen kissed her forehead. "Rest, Mama. I'll take care of business."

Somehow, some way, she would get cash and buy flour. Otherwise, they'd have to shut down for the afternoon rush after the game, and the Fox Theater crowd in the evening. Or, she thought with a pang of dread, shut down for good if Mama got too sick or the money problems worsened.

Karen hurried back into the kitchen, where Betty was tending to the ovens. Her father dashed to answer the ringing phone.

Yeah, run away, Daddy. Again. Just like you dodged the Vietnam draft and ran off with that woman in Canada. Leaving your babies in the ghetto.

Karen watched him on the phone, probably talking to one of the people he sponsored for Gamblers Anonymous or getting his weekly schedule for meals-on-wheels deliveries to homebound senior citizens. Daddy had changed so much, yet seventeen years of rage over his absence prickled just under Karen's skin, threatening to erupt at the slightest trouble.

"Karen, more coffee!" Joel yelled through the waist-high window from the cash register. She rushed through the half-door into the sunny, lace-curtained café. A good dozen people stood in line, while all six tables were full of folks in Tigers caps and T-shirts. And the bells on the door kept ringing, signaling more customers. At the counter behind the register, Karen quickly filled the coffeemakers with freshly ground vanilla- and amaretto-flavored beans.

"Hey, what kinda place is this," a man called. "All sold out."

Karen spun around. On the other side of the glass case of cakes and pies, a man was scowling at the row of baskets that now held crumbs.

"More's coming out of the ovens as we speak," Karen said. She leaned over the half-door to the kitchen. "Betty, hurry up with those muffins, please."

Behind her, another man's voice: "Excuse me, ma'am. I've got a taste for something sweet."

Karen rolled her eyes and broke into a smile all at once. Franklin. She turned around. But her smile withered when she saw his "consultant."

"This isn't a good time," Karen said, as another annoyed customer commented about the empty baskets. She glanced back at Betty, moving in slow motion as she removed muffins from the trays. *Hurry up!* Karen grabbed the empty baskets, rushed into the kitchen. Franklin and his "friend" followed.

"Here!" Karen filled the baskets herself, ignoring Betty.

"Darling," Franklin said, "I have urgent business."

"So do I."

He held out a leather folder, which she ignored. "I amended your press release. I want it faxed to the papers immediately—"

Karen looked up at his piercing eyes, framed by crinkled brown skin. His cap of salt-and-pepper waves matched a day's worth of growth at his narrow jaw and under his nose, except for the silver zigzag at the edge of his lip. Back in fifth grade, a boy who lived next door had smashed a pop bottle in Franklin's face while mocking his good grades and his status as teacher's pet. But when Franklin joined the city council, he tracked the guy down and helped him get a job. But lately, since getting involved with the Wish Master proposal to revitalize the riverfront, it seemed Franklin had no time to help the people who needed him most. In fact, the former bully had called about a month ago, but Franklin ignored his calls, saying he was too busy with Wish Master to deal with "that hoodlum."

"If you didn't notice," Karen said, "I have a crisis here."

He held her stare, saying nothing.

"I'll get to faxing after I find a couple grand to keep this place open. *After* I figure out why Mama is so sick. Okay?!" Karen's neck tilted slightly to punctuate that last word.

Franklin placed his large hands on her shoulders. "Darling, come here."

Karen dashed to place the muffins out for the customers.

"Darling, slow down."

Karen crossed her arms, glaring at him. His friend, with his hand always in a front pants pocket, kept looking around like a damn Secret Service agent.

"What are you looking for?" Karen snapped.

"Never been in a bakery before." He avoided her eyes. "Just curious."

"Darling," Franklin said, holding out the folder, "I need this done this morning. It's for Wish Master."

His friend grinned. "Yeah, soon we'll be poppin' champagne corks."

Karen took the folder. "I wish you'd both stop counting your eggs before they hatch." She hated how Franklin assumed that just because he and Otis Isaac had been friends since third grade, the mayor would pick Franklin's choice of development proposals for the riverfront. Nine other companies were bidding to build restaurants, a boardwalk, an amusement park, even casinos there. "Mayor Isaac might not think the Wish Master plan is solid—"

Franklin let out an arrogant laugh. "He will."

"He better," the friend said with a sinister chuckle.

Dark Secret

"Another thing, Franklin. If you don't start spending more time campaigning," she said, "you won't have to worry about Wish Master. Because you'll be out of a job. You and me both."

"Darling—"

Betty shouted near the office: "Don't tell me to pick up the pace!"

"Christ, Betty, if you need some caffeine, I'll get you a cup of coffee," Mack said. "Slow motion doesn't get anything done around here."

Karen stormed toward them. "Quiet down! Mama is trying to rest."

Franklin followed. He shook her father's hand. "Mack, what's up?"

"Christ, this cash flow crunch has everybody all worked up—"

"So you need some dough." Franklin pulled a wad of hundred-dollar bills from his pocket. He peeled off a thick stack, handed it to Karen. "Here."

Karen knitted her brows. "Franklin, where'd you get all that—"

He cast an omnipotent look down at her. "Just let me do this."

Karen pushed back Franklin's fistful of cash. "I don't know where you got that. Or why." She glared at his friend. Maybe that was how Franklin had financed his new bathroom with the Jacuzzi and the gourmet kitchen.

"I insist. You know this place is my pride and joy. This"—Franklin looked around—"Mama Ernestine's dream, is what I'm all about."

"What you used to be—" Karen watched her mother step toward them.

"Here I am." Mama sounded hoarse. She leaned on the steel table.

Franklin kissed Mama's ashen cheek.

"Feel better?" Karen stroked her back. "Mama?"

Her mother closed her eyes, turning grayer and teetering. "Oh Lord . . . hammercy. Feel so sick—"

Franklin caught Mama; they guided her back to the office couch.

Panic slithered through Karen, reminding her of that terrifying night when she thought Mama had gotten shot, when really she'd just tripped on a stump in the yard. Then, as now, Karen vowed to do whatever it took to make her mother safe and healthy. Starting with a call for an ambulance.

4

Camille Morgan's stomach did another somersault as she navigated ivory stiletto sandals down the steps of the Gulfstream. She gripped the silver rail with trembling fingers as hot, pine-scented wind tangled her eyelashes, whipped her hair into a honey-colored cloud.

Behind her, Ida Mae snapped, "Go on down."

Camille fanned her other hand on the navy-blue expanse of Jeff's shoulder. This flight down to Virginia was her most terrifying ever, even worse than that stomach-flipping plunge last year as they were coming back from the Four Seasons in Bali. Still, the second she felt her heel tap the asphalt, Camille wished she could fast-forward about thirty-six hours, when they'd be stepping right back into the humming beige-and-blue-striped jet. Yes, back home to New York, with Jeff's parents' blessing to get married.

"C'mon, honey!" Jeff grabbed her hand, forcing her to jog alongside him several yards toward a taupe Jeep Cherokee. The roiling sky seemed to frown on her; the thick woodland around the landing strip swayed and rustled like a Shakespearean chorus chanting a message she refused to hear. She tilted her chin higher as a black man in a gray uniform helped her into the vehicle. In the front seat, Jeff told the driver, "Make it quick, Len."

Camille gripped the door handle as the Jeep lurched onto a gravel road through the woods. She could feel the glare of Ida Mae, now wearing beige slacks and a white blouse, who shared the backseat.

"Baby Boy, your daddy gon' be in a tizzy 'cause Miss Camille so slow—"

"Ida Mae." Jeff's hard tone smashed the stuffy air like a gavel. He did not turn around, but Camille could see his jaw flexing as he checked his silver Swiss watch again. She couldn't believe how much attitude Ida Mae had toward her and everyone else. As if being Jeff's nanny since birth gave her the authority to sass everyone she pleased.

Minutes later, Camille's pulse quickened as the Jeep pulled into the circular driveway, just in front of the three-story white columns. Among the half-dozen employees waiting to greet them and take their bags, a young black man opened her door. She grasped his white-gloved hand and stepped out.

"Miss Camille," he said, smiling, "welcome home to White Pines."

"Looks like rain," Camille answered, hurrying alongside Jeff to the porch.

He took her hands in his damp palms, gazed down. "You okay?" Tenderness radiated from his eyes despite the tension tightening those tiny lines that showed where he squinted while sailing.

Camille's mouth curled upward a bit. Until something bumped her hip. She looked down; it was Ida Mae's Louis Vuitton duffel bag. And peeking through the brass zipper: a big teddy bear with a pink satin ribbon around its neck. That was odd, since they were there to celebrate Dixie's turning twenty-one, not five. Maybe Ida Mae was planning to visit a child in her own family in nearby Williamsburg before the three of them returned to New York. Good. A break from her would be more than welcome.

"Comb your hair, Baby Boy, before you see your mama." Ida Mae brushed between Camille and Jeff. Then, without speaking, she took a glass of lemonade from a young black maid holding a silver tray, headed past the spiral topiaries, and through the open double doors.

Camille stood on tiptoes to finger-comb Jeff's hair back into place. Just past his shoulder, she could feel the woman with the lemonade staring.

"How're you today, Sarah?"

The maid beamed, holding the tray closer to her pregnant belly. Camille smiled back. *They have no idea. And they never will.*

"Let's do this," Jeff said.

Camille's heels clicked on the gleaming white marble floor as she and Jeff entered the two-story foyer, its domed ceiling painted with the Michelangelesque image of a godlike man amongst voluptuous women with flowing hair and harps.

"Mr. Jeff, welcome home."

"Hey, Silas." Jeff nodded at the butler, whose bright blue eyes and snow-white hair looked eerie against his smooth but ancient licorice-toned skin. The sight of him always provoked a sort of *Twilight Zone* flutter in Camille's gut, as if she were in the episode where you could step through a mirror into another place and time. And he had a way of standing perfectly still, blending in with the huge urns of aromatic lilies on the twin Louis XIV tables in the curves of the double staircases, where other employees were toting their bags up royal-blue-carpeted steps. Near each staircase were white double doors, one set leading to the salon, the other to the library.

"Mornin', Miss Camille, Mr. Jeff." Hortense, the head house-keeper, appeared from the hallway leading under the stairs to the back of the house. "Your parents been waitin' awhile now, and they ain't happy about it." She swung open the salon doors.

Camille's heart leaped to her throat. Then she remembered one of her acting coaches at New York College saying, *Project from your mind; your body will follow.* Imagining herself cool and confident, Camille squared her shoulders. She stepped alongside Jeff into the room, its ceiling so high, its shiny walnut floor so vast, it made her feel as is she'd taken a shrink pill in *Alice in Wonderland.*

"Well, I'll be damned." Senator Stone's deep voice shot toward them like a cannon. He stood up from where he and Mrs. Stone were sitting at one of several rose-and-cream arrangements of eighteenth-century French furniture. "What the devil kinda clocks you got up there in New York?"

Camille stopped because Jeff did; he stood straight as a rod. "I'm sorry, Pop. We had a mix-up and the flight was—"

"My gracious, Jeff!" Mrs. Stone floated across the Persian rug, gold bangles jangling on her wrist as she raised cupped hands to Jeff's cheeks.

In her beige Dior pantsuit, she was as stick-thin as a praying mantis. "If you weren't so handsome, I'd be downright mad you're late."

Jeff flashed bright teeth and dimples as she trained beige-glossed fingernails on an invisible piece of lint on his lapel. Her diamond-shaped face softened into that I-would-give-you-my-last-breath look that mothers are supposed to show their children.

Someday she'll look at me like that. Then I'll finally have a mother who loves me. Someday . . .

"Hello, Mrs. Stone." Camille maintained her practiced good posture as Mrs. Stone's blue eyes, sharpened by a black, Cleoptraesque line at her lashes, raked her hair, her dress, her metallic bronze pedicure. "Do tell me you're not wearing *that* to the party."

"No, I've got a new St. John suit that you'll love." Camille smiled. "It's robin's-egg blue and—"

"Son, don't just stand there," Senator Stone called across the room. A silk-draped window, revealing a two-story swath of gray sky churning over the James River, framed him. "Let's get to talking."

"Yes, gracious, the guests." Mrs. Stone hurried back toward her husband. Jeff's palm felt hot and sweaty as he led Camille to a couch facing his parents. On the table was a silver tea service engraved with the family crest, along with a crystal bell and a three-tiered pastry stand stacked with fancy cookies. Camille's mouth watered. But she didn't dare indulge in front of Mrs. Stone. No, she'd lost thirty pounds since coming to New York, and had to exercise and eat lots of salad to stay size six. Even though Mother used to say a big, round butt was a blessing because it was "something for a man to squeeze."

Well, guess what, Mother, that's a black thing. White women have flat butts, and rich white women have none at all.

"My gracious, Jeff, what's so important?" Mrs. Stone perched next to him, her yellow hair poufed up and back on top, then swooped in a curl above her collar, like the back of a duck. Her thin face had a golden, end-of-summer glow. Helped, no doubt, by the chemical peels and facials Dixie said she got to maintain the Miss Virginia looks that had stolen the heart of a young politician named Monty Stone at a parade in her hometown of Charlottesville.

Jeff glanced up at her, then his father. "We saw the news this—"

"Hell, that's not the half of it." The wrinkle down the center of

Senator Stone's forehead deepened as he furled black brows, naturally arched to the same perfection Camille paid to have waxed that way at the salon.

Jeff bristled. "What?"

"The feminist war drums, they're beating loud," Senator Stone said. "Come sunrise, you'll see. The papers are running with it."

"Gracious, it's Vivian. She's suing for—" Mrs. Stone's eyelids lowered.

"Goddamn sexual harassment!" The words came like a wad of spit through Senator Stone's lips, which always looked ruby red, as if stained by the juice of fresh berries. "Lies! A big hornet's nest of lies!"

Jeff shot to his feet, joined his father near the fireplace. "She can't—"

"Son, she can! She is! And it's your fault."

Jeff stood like a deer stunned in the beam of his father's gray eyes. "You can't blame everything on me and Tabitha—"

"This"—Senator Stone squinted at Jeff—"I can. I'd bet my Purple Heart her father is paying Vivian's lawyer. To bring me down."

Jeff stepped closer to his father, scowling. "Pop, you don't—"

"You dropped one of your own kind for *that!*" Senator Stone pointed down at Camille. "Yankee T and A! And I'm paying the price!"

Mrs. Stone wedged between them. "Boys." But they kept arguing.

Camille's stomach cramped. Anger prickled through her like a million hot needles. But she would not budge. She would make Jeff's parents like her, love her, adore her, if it killed her. And she could start by steering the conversation down a more pleasant path, so they could talk about the wedding. *Their* wedding, not the one in which Jeff had left Tabitha at the altar, southern blue-blood pedigree and all.

Camille stood, reached to the tea service. She grabbed the crystal bell, rang it. The bickering stopped. Instantly. Jeff and his parents faced her.

She smiled. "Mr. and Mrs. Stone, Jeff and I need to talk to you. About something important."

Mrs. Stone snatched the bell. "This is for calling the maid. *Not* the master and mistress of the house."

In seconds, Hortense appeared. "What y'awl need?"

"Lemon," Mrs. Stone said. "For my tea."

Jeff stepped to Camille's side with a quick, shocked glare. He joined her on the couch. "She's right," he said, facing his parents. "We need to talk."

"Gracious," his mother sighed, taking a chair.

"Well, out with it." Standing by the fireplace, Senator Stone pulled a cigar from his breast pocket. He ran it under his nose.

Jeff inhaled as if he were about to speak, but Camille jumped in: "First, Senator Stone, I want to thank you. Judge Mannington says the brief I wrote for the Ashbury case was outstanding."

He tapped his right hand on the white marble mantle, making a soft clink with his VMI class ring. "Sugar, I got you that job to make my son look good. Had nothing to do with you."

She forced a smile to lift her cheeks. "Well, I've made it my goal to make *you* look good. By dazzling the judge with legal brilliance."

Mrs. Stone clattered her teacup in its saucer. "My gracious. That's a lofty ambition for someone three months out of school. Why, you don't even know if you've passed the bar—"

"Mom, give Camille a chance."

"A chance to what? Embarrass us down the road? When you realize she's an outsider humiliating the family? Poor Phyllis. If you knew what—"

"Camille's not your friend's daughter-in-law, Mom. Whatever you read about that divorce—"

"That California bimbo is dragging them to hell and back," Senator Stone added. "That's why you need a girl like us, like Tabitha."

"Listen." Jeff put his arm around Camille. "We came here to—"

Camille kept her eyes locked on Jeff, even though she could feel his parents glaring a hole in her cheek.

"—tell you we're engaged. We want to get married."

Camille tensed as the words seemed to freeze in midair, like water droplets turning to ice. Moments felt like an eternity as Jeff's father lit his cigar. His mother fingered the locket she always wore with her triple strand of pearls. Daisy-shaped with white and yellow enamel lacquered over gold, Jeff said it held a picture of her grandchild.

Mrs. Stone still hasn't gotten over losing the baby. Camille remembered that horrible morning last year: Mrs. Stone screaming, running down the upstairs hall, blue-lipped Baby Monty in her arms. Jeff performing CPR. Calling his brother Jackson and sister-in-law Sue Ann in Majorca to tell them.

"Marriage," Senator Stone said flatly behind a veil of smoke.

Camille dreaded the moment when the pungent odor would hit her. The asthma medication she'd been taking since coming to New York could control wheezing provoked by tense situations like this, but it was no defense against gasp-on-contact cigar smoke. And dashing upstairs to grab her inhaler from her purse was not an option until their business was done here in the parlor.

It would look like I was trying to run away. But I won't. Ever.

"We want your blessing," Jeff said.

"Hell no!" Senator Stone shouted.

Jeff reddened. He bolted toward his father. "Pop! Why?"

"Tabitha! Mend fences with her now, or watch Lucas and that nigger Marcus Jones run me out of Washington!"

"Pop! If you knew about Tabitha, you'd have another heart attack!"

Senator Stone sucked on the brown shaft of his cigar, the tip glowing red, the plume disappearing toward the flowers and vines molded on the white ceiling. Then, within seconds, the smoke reached down like a brutal claw around Camille's chest. She coughed.

Jeff cast a gentle look at her, then his father. "Pop, smoke irritates Camille's asthma."

"Son, don't tell me I can't enjoy the very thing that *made* this family!"

Mrs. Stone pinched glossy beige fingernails on invisible lint on her knee.

His father took another puff. "Son, look at the big picture here. You need a girl with the posture of"—he nodded—"a certain *class* of people."

His mother took his hands. "Jeff, think what's at stake. Your father's chance to live the legacy stolen from his own father. To be president."

"This is not fair!" Jeff shouted. He strode back to the couch, raised Camille's diamond. "See this? It means we're getting married. Whether you like it or not."

Dark Secret

"Gracious, I taught you more respect. Lower your voice or march out of here."

Senator Stone stormed toward them. He pointed down with his cigar, those silver eyes making Camille feel as if her heart had stopped. "Sugar, I don't know what kinda choke hold you got on my son's heart," he puffed, squinting in the smoke. "But keep it up, you'll both be buying your next meal with that pretty ring."

Camille coughed, feeling as if the smoke was a vacuum tube over her mouth, sucking away her breath. Jeff stood over her, a hand on her shoulder.

"Pop! Don't talk to her like that! You couldn't possibly mean—"

"I could, son. I could."

5

Karen Bradley pulled the pale blue hospital gown up around Mama's neck to combat the icy air conditioning. She was stroking her mother's forehead, humming "Ev'ry Time I feel the Spirit," and praying that whatever was wrong could be cured right away. But the sound of her father clipping his fingernails by the window in the cramped room made her pause. "Daddy!"

He looked up. "What now, Karen?"

"That noise. Will you please stop. Mama's headache—"

Daddy put the clipper in his pocket as he approached the bed, gazing down at Mama. "You'll be all right, Ernestine."

Mama opened her eyes for a second, cracking a faint smile up at him.

Daddy's gentle gaze did not stop Karen from wondering just how many of Mama's health problems were rooted in the heartbreak of his long absence. Or, after he returned, coping with his now-in-remission gambling addiction.

"What's taking the doctor so long?" She glanced at the closed door. They'd locked the bakery for the day, but that didn't mean they wanted to spend the night here. "It shouldn't take six hours to figure out what's wrong."

"You always want everything done now. Just hold your horses and wait."

Dark Secret

Karen kept stroking Mama's forehead. "Yeah, like I waited seventeen years to meet my father." She spoke just above a whisper.

"I wish you could see that I've changed, Karen."

Karen rolled her eyes. She couldn't deny, though, how happy Mama was having him back, at least when she felt good. Mama was always baking him lemon cake and her melt-in-your-mouth dinner rolls. Laughing and smiling while they watched TV or the evening news to see if Karen was on with Franklin. And taking him to church.

"Daddy, will you please go see what's taking the doctor so long?"

As he left the room, a foreboding sense of déjà vu cramped Karen's stomach. She kept remembering that day when she was seven, when Aunt Ruby died of appendicitis. Ever since, Karen had hated going to the doctor, for herself or anyone else. She never trusted them. Never felt like they were telling the truth or prescribing the right medicine.

"Here he is," her father said, coming back in, the doctor in tow.

Karen probed the doctor's eyes through his gray-tinted glasses. "Did you get the test re—"

"Let me do the talking here," her father said, stepping toward the doctor.

"Don't tell me when to speak," Karen said through tight lips.

"Hush. Let the doctor talk." Mama did not open her eyes.

"I am afraid I have bad news." The fortyish doctor faced them in his white lab coat, a clipboard against his thigh.

"Christ!" Her father ran his hand over his beard, then fanned his palms over the copper rivets of his jeans.

Karen steadied herself by resting a hand on Mama's shoulder. She tried to project a stoic face as dread pumped through her limbs like ice water.

"Your mother's kidneys are no longer working," the doctor said. "Even the dialysis is failing to cleanse the toxins from her blood. The vomiting, the delirium, the fainting. That is the result."

Karen tried to ignore the words that immediately popped into her head, blaring at a deafening pitch: kidney failure. No, that couldn't be what the doctor was saying. There had to be something else, something curable, that was making Mama sick. "So what's the treatment for that?"

Mack stroked Ernestine's forehead. "What do you do when dialysis stops working?"

Sorrow radiated from the doctor's eyes. "Mrs. Bradley needs a kidney transplant. Without a new kidney, she cannot last more than a few months."

Karen held his gaze, shaking her head. "We have to save her."

The doctor nodded. "We'll certainly try our hardest. I've placed your mother on the transplant register for a new kidney. Should one become available—"

Karen crossed her arms. "Should one become available?"

"Unfortunately, far more people are waiting for organs than what is available," the doctor said. "It sometimes takes years—"

Karen glared at him. "We don't have years to wait!" And if they did, donor organs most often went to young, white patients. At least according to an article her best friend Freida Miller had written for the *Washington News*.

The doctor stepped next to her father to examine Mama's puffy hand. "Until a kidney becomes available—"

"Get real! Chances are, a forty-four-year-old black woman from Detroit just won't make the top of the list in time."

The doctor cast a sympathetic look her way. "If this were my mother, I would try my hardest to find a family donor. That could save her. But even if we found a match, there are no guarantees her body would accept the organ."

Karen's throat burned. She glanced at Mama, whose eyes were closed as Daddy stroked her cheek. "I wish I could—"

"We can make an appointment to test you," the doctor said.

"No," Karen said softly. "I only have one kidney. I was born that way."

"Any siblings?"

Karen pursed her lips.

"Sharlene," Mama whispered, half opening her eyes.

The name hung in the air like a bad odor. The sound of it, not spoken for years, made Karen ball her fists so hard, her fingernails pierced her palms.

Damn Sharlene! Karen blinked hard to wipe away images of her older sister, bolting out the front door of their flat ten years ago, with nothing but a battered suitcase and a head full of dreams. And delusions. *Not one phone call, one letter to let us know where she is. Nothing!*

Sharlene was just like Daddy. Walking away without so much as a glance back at the people who needed her. Especially now.

"We'll track her down," Mack said softly to Mama. "If that's what it takes to make you better, that's what we'll do."

Karen glared at him. He wouldn't have the first clue about how to find her sister. And if he had stuck around in the first place, maybe Sharlene wouldn't have followed his bad example of disappearing without a trace.

"My baby," Mama whispered.

Karen saw a white-hot flash. Felt something scalding bubble up through her skin. "I'll find Sharlene. She has to come home now. For Mama."

6

Camille clenched a fistful of burgundy velvet framing open French doors to the back veranda. Squinting in the haze, she watched Jeff below, jogging the stone path around the swimming pool and the ivy-covered guest cottages, over the rolling emerald lawn, down to the boats bobbing at the dock.

"Jeff, come back," she whispered. Camille couldn't believe he'd just left her here with that painting of Victoria Stone staring down from above the flower-carved mahogany dressing table. On it, antique perfume bottles gave off the scent of lilacs, strong even across the acre-wide Oriental rug. Camille surveyed Jeff's clothes, strewn over the fringed damask bench at the foot of the huge, wine-velvet bed. She shifted, causing the dark, shiny wood floor to creak. Or was that the ceiling? She could only imagine what apparitions might be roaming the attic.

I hate being alone in this room. Releasing the drapery, she hugged herself and ran fingertips over goose bumps on her bare arms. Now Jeff was on the deck of his thirty-five-foot sailboat, *Miss Serenity,* bringing in the bumpers. No, he couldn't go sailing. She had to get him back up here to dress, so they wouldn't further enrage his parents by missing the party.

Already in her pale blue skirt ensemble, Camille hurried downstairs, outside, past dozens of people milling about the vast patio, to the dock. She dropped her shoes on the grass; the white planks were warm and sandpapery under her bare feet. On deck, Jeff was running the main line to unfurl the sail, his bronzed back rippling in the dim sunshine. She tiptoed toward him, kneaded his damp shoulders from behind. "Baby, don't you want to get ready for Dixie's party?"

"This is Mom and Pop's party," he said, pulling harder.

"We shouldn't miss it, even though—"

Jeff spun around, his blue eyes aglow with affection and anger. "Honey, I'm not in the mood. My parents are furious and—"

"Shhh. Let's just fake it 'til we make it," she said, nuzzling his cheek with her nose. "Give it a little time. They'll see how much you love me—"

"Love has nothing to do with it." He pulled away to run the jib lines. "Why don't you go find Dixie in the stable. She's dying to see you."

Camille stuck out her jaw. She hated it when he turned his back. After his parents' verbal slap in the face, he should be caressing her, kissing her, reminding her how much he loved her. But was Jeff mulling over their threat to disown him if he married her? Was he taking it seriously enough to call off the engagement? No, he couldn't be. Maybe if she caught up with Dixie about her premed classes at the University of Virginia, Jeff would have time to cool off.

"Okay, baby." She kissed his cheek. "I'll go see your sister."

Barefoot, Camille hurried back up the path. At the cottages—she never let herself acknowledge they were actually slave cabins, expanded and modernized—she veered north toward the redbrick stable. In the tack room, amongst bridles, saddles, and brushes, she slipped on boots. She loved that sawdust-hay-leather smell and the sounds of horses sneezing or clomping around. And she knew just where to find Dixie. In the stall with her prizewinning mare, Charity, who was recovering from a broken leg.

Camille strode through the stable, but froze when she heard Mrs. Stone say, "Gracious, you will ask no more questions on the matter, Dixie."

"Mom!"

Camille could see nothing but long rows of dark wood and black iron bars on each side. But it sounded as if they were nearby, on the left. If Mrs. Stone saw her, surely she would accuse her of eavesdropping.

"I'm old enough to know," Dixie said. "Tell me!"

"It was resolved," Mrs. Stone said, "and need not be revisited."

"Just tell me their name, Mom."

"Millie, I tol' you she was gon' start askin' questions. We lucky Wilson act like it never happened. But you bes' never tell, Millie. Might get out."

Camille shrank toward a stall. That was definitely Ida Mae. But where was the "Miss" before "Millie"? And why wasn't Mrs. Stone upset about the maid's domineering tone?

"Mom, I hate how you think you can control everything!"

"You will march up to that house and greet our friends and family!"

Camille felt a hot gust of air. She turned slightly, seeing a huge glistening nostril and a giant black eye poking through the bars. She smiled, stroking Georgia's ivory muzzle; this beauty had helped her lure Jeff's love.

"You don't get it, Mom. Me, or anything. I don't want you spending obscene amounts of money on a party. I'd rather use it to help animals. Or poor people, or Rand's center—"

That reminded Camille of Dixie's birthday last year; as soon as she opened the tiny box of diamond-stud earrings from her parents, she had handed them to the housekeeper, Hortense, to pay her daughter's college tuition.

"Hush, girl," Ida Mae said. "Your mama been through so much. Ease up. She jus' tryin' to make you happy."

"She knows how, but she won't do it. She still doesn't understand, I'm not a windup doll who sings and curtsies on command. And—"

"Dixie Stone! Get out from under that horse and march up to the house. Our guests are expecting—"

"I *like* being under this horse!" Dixie shouted over the rustle of straw.

"I will not have my daughter sticking her arm up a pregnant mare's—"

"Millie! Both y'awl! Calm down."

Dark Secret

The stable door rumbled open. "I'll be back later, Charity," Dixie cooed.

Camille couldn't let them catch her listening. But there was no time for a silent, invisible escape. So she quickly strode toward their voices.

In seconds, Dixie rushed out in jeans, a denim shirt, and black boots. Her diamond-shaped face, framed by brown tendrils stuck to damp temples, appeared taut, but her golden-hazel eyes twinkled when she looked up.

"Camille!" Her figure-eight lips parted into a smile as her quick, long stride caused straw to fall from her elbows and knees. "So glad you made it down to the festive occasion." She cast an annoyed look back at her mother, in a lavender dress and boots, and Ida Mae, in her uniform.

Camille hoped to deflect their glares by basking in Dixie's sudden effervescence, nothing like the somber expression Dixie had had when Camille first met her at a barbecue here a few years ago. Then, Dixie was holding a tiny rabbit, feeding it with a doll's bottle, because the family's beloved hound, Jezebel, had chased its mother into an old well behind the barn. Then, desperation glowed in Dixie's eyes as if her own life depended on saving that animal.

But that image only intensified Camille's envious twinge as she wondered why God hadn't let *her* grow up in a mansion with parents who loved her and looked like her. Where she slept in a frilly yellow bed shaped like a butterfly with its wings spread and played with a stable of show horses. *Dixie is so lucky . . .*

"Camille," Mrs. Stone said, stepping close in a lemony cloud, "you have no place wandering the grounds without Jeff. Where is he?"

Ida Mae's dark eyes narrowed. "Millie, I tol' you she sneaky—"

"Quiet, Ida Mae." Mrs. Stone knitted her brows, picking hay from her sleeve. "I don't take kindly to those who slink around the shadows. In fact I'd rather you and Jeff head back to New York. Now."

Camille did not look away from the sharp, threatening look in Mrs. Stone's eyes. Even though panic was squeezing her chest and her mind was spinning a web of disappointment and regret that she hadn't walked away as soon as she heard their heated exchange. Camille was not going to cower. But what had they been talking about? And how did it give Ida Mae the gall to talk to Mrs. Stone as if they were bickering sisters? Regardless, Camille had to think of a way to nullify this sudden expulsion.

She kissed Dixie's cheek. "You know we wouldn't miss your birthday."

"Thought I wouldn't see you until I come up to New York for my Columbia interview," Dixie said, leading Camille outside. "Jeff told me the good news. My whole life with four brothers and now finally, I couldn't ask for a sweeter sister."

Camille beamed, even though she could feel hostile gusts blowing from Ida Mae and Mrs. Stone behind them.

7

Karen Bradley's fingers raced across the gray keyboard of her laptop computer. It was early afternoon, and her office in Detroit's city hall was quiet except for the hum of the fax machine as Franklin's press release transmitted to newsrooms across the city.

"Sharlene Monique Bradley," Karen said, typing into an Internet people finder. But a second later, a *beep!* jolted her as red letters flashed: "Sorry, no matches found."

"I have to find her!" She squinted, reaching up to close the horizontal blinds on large windows overlooking the blue expanse of the Detroit River thirteen stories below. That stopped the light from reflecting off the nest of white paper that passed as her desk. But it reminded her of a half-hour ago when she'd closed the curtains in her parents' bedroom. Mama was tucked under the handmade quilt, with Daddy watching her from the tweed armchair nearby.

"Where is Sharlene?" She'd wanted to become an actress. Always talking with Ginger about going to New York or LA. "Ginger!" If she could find her sister's best friend, maybe she could locate Sharlene, too. Karen dialed directory assistance, getting a number for what she hoped was Ginger's parents in a Detroit suburb.

"I'm sorry to bother you," Karen said to the older woman who answered, "but do you have a daughter named Ginger?"

"Who are you?" The lady had an I-hate-phone-solicitors tone.

"Karen Bradley. My sister is Ginger's friend Sharlene."

"Oh dear, Ginger had so many friends."

"They went to Riverfront Academy of the Arts. She starred in the play—"

"Wait, there's something about her. When they moved to New York—"

Karen's hope surged. So Sharlene was in New York after all.

"She changed her name," the woman said. "Kerri? Carla? No, Camille."

Karen frowned. Why would she change her name?

"Mrs. Romanowski, would you mind giving me Ginger's number?"

"Dear no, she wouldn't be home. She's always at the store on Saturday."

"The store?"

"She's a designer. Got written up in *Vogue,* even, when things were better. On top of the world one minute, barely making ends meet the next."

That made Karen remember the troubles at the bakery, how she needed to call the bank for an emergency loan. "I would appreciate Ginger's number—"

"No, dear, she's not listed. And the world is such a crazy place. I don't know if you're really who you say you are."

Karen scowled. "Really, we lived across from your family on Helen Street. My mother, Ernestine Bradley, she made birthday cakes for Ginger."

"Oh dear, the house with the police shoot-out. I'm sorry, I—"

Karen remembered Ginger was never allowed to come over after James had shot himself amidst a hail of police gunfire. Sharlene always had to go across the street to their house to play, or out to Ginger's house in the suburbs once they got to high school.

"I'm sorry, I've got to go now."

"Mrs. Roman—"

"Good-bye."

"Damn!" Karen banged down the phone. Red-hot anger pumped through her. Ginger was the only person who might have Sharlene's number. Karen's fingers hit the computer keyboard, calling up *Vogue's*

Web site. Then, in the archives, she typed in Ginger's name. There! The article about her store, Mystique, appeared with a picture of Ginger in front of the store. With a quick prayer, Karen called New York's directory assistance.

"Mystique, may I help you?"

"Ginger?"

"Yes, how may I help you?"

"This is Karen Bradley. Sharlene's sister."

Silence.

"Ginger, I'm trying to get in touch with my sister." Karen stared at Ginger's image on the computer screen: petite, a straight, auburn bob on thin, bare shoulders, a brown minidress with knee-high boots. Milk-white skin.

After a pause, Ginger said, "I mean, nothing personal, Karen, but your sister would, like, strangle me if I talked to you. And I'm in a rush—"

"Ginger, this isn't a social call. Our mother needs a kidney or she'll die. And we need Sharlene's help."

"Your sister has a new life now," Ginger said, her speech fast and tense. "I mean, she's, like, erased her past in Detroit."

Karen was quiet for a second. But she couldn't let herself react to whatever twisted life path Sharlene had chosen. She could do that after she got her to agree to save Mama.

"Congratulations on your boutique." Karen made her voice smile. "I can still see Sharlene coming home in all those wild outfits you made in sewing class. Remember that funky see-through dress with the—"

Ginger laughed. "Feathers around the hem! Gawd! Scary!"

"So what do you sell at Mystique?" On the screen, Karen saw racks of slinky dresses through the corner store's huge plate-glass window.

"Suits, dresses, jeans." Ginger's voice deepened as if she were relaxing.

"Did Sharlene study acting?"

Ginger paused. "Yeah. I mean, for a while. She switched to law."

"Private practice?"

"No, she—Karen, I mean, I can't—"

"Ginger, don't you remember how our mother used to French-braid your hair? And give you extra frosting on your chocolate cake?"

"That was, like, the best cake ever."

"Ginger, what if your mother needed you to save her life?"

"Oh, I would do every—But this is, like, not the same—"

"Please."

"This is a bad time," Ginger said. "I'm supposed to be on a plane in an hour. Rand is coming and we're going down to see your sister in Virgi—" Ginger exhaled loudly. "Karen, I can't—"

"Sharlene lives in Virginia?"

"No, no, here in the city, but—"

"Ginger, please. I won't tell Sharlene you gave me—"

"Camille!" Ginger said sharply. "She's Camille Morgan now."

Karen closed her eyes. "Where is she?"

Ginger sighed. "She lives here, on the Upper East Side. But today she's with her fiancé's family in Virginia. Ever heard of Monty Stone? He's, like, a really powerful senator. Well, Camille is engaged to his son, Jeff."

Karen felt dizzy. *Sharlene couldn't have gone any whiter than that!*

As Ginger talked, Karen remembered meeting Monty Stone, when she and Franklin were in Washington for a nonpartisan conference on urban renewal. Stone had wowed the crowd with a speech about the entrepreneurial spirit that drove the nation's economy. Then, when she had chatted with him at a reception, she remembered the way he radiated power, in his eyes . . . his hand gestures . . . his expensive suit. *And he kept calling me sugar.*

Karen remembered Franklin telling her Stone had opposed integration and voted against civil rights legislation in the 1960s. Like that brief he'd written to the Supreme Court urging it not to strike down laws against interracial marriage in the case *Loving v. Virginia*. And a few years ago, he'd been all over TV arguing against a statue of tennis superstar Arthur Ashe alongside Civil War heroes on Monument Avenue in Richmond.

"Don't worry, Jeff is really cool," Ginger said. "Nothing like his father. I mean, rich, yes, but not so conservative."

Yeah, charging into the millennium by getting rid of programs that help women like Mama. Karen had also read, however, glowing reviews about Stone's institute that helped needy families find shelter, jobs, and health care.

Ginger said something about her sister working for a judge.

"Does Sharlene ever talk about us?" Karen asked.

Ginger exhaled loudly again. "Like I said, her new life is so real now, it's like you and your mother don't even exist."

Those words slapped Karen back to when she was nine at summer camp.

"Get away!" Sharlene shouted, snatching her arm from Karen, who was trying to give her a bracelet woven from a rainbow of string.

Karen cowered under the glare of her big sister—and the laughter of a half-dozen girls—in the arts-and-crafts cabin. She just wanted some comfort, being so far away from Mama at the exclusive camp in northern Michigan that she and Sharlene got to attend through a charity for inner-city kids.

"Your nanny's daughter thinks you're her sister!" The girl doubled over, two braids dancing across the floorboards. "As if you two could be related!"

And there stood Sharlene, surrounded by the girls, laughing with them. Karen figured the girls had seen Mama drop them off at the buses back in Detroit, where some of their own black nannies had left them. So now Sharlene was going right along with their misunderstanding, pretending to be rich and white like them. Acting like they weren't even sisters.

Karen tried to run for the door. But another girl blocked her way.

"Look, it's mud girl!"

Karen felt numb, locking eyes with that brat from the showers. The day before, Karen and her cabin mates had gone hiking, only to get caught in the rain. As a result, they had trudged through mud, becoming covered in the process. When they hit the showers, some girls called Karen "mud girl" because even when the mud washed off, her skin remained brown. Now, the girl pointed a finger in Sharlene's face.

"Mud girl! Mud girl!"

The other girls chanted along, repeating it over and over.

Karen shot a pleading look at Sharlene.

But Sharlene cast a silent, helpless glance, as if to say, "I'm on this side; you're not. And I'm staying. Too bad for you."

The girls finally let Karen run to her cabin, where she cried herself to sleep.

Now, Karen's heart ached even more; her sister really had crossed to the white side without caring about Karen or Mama or anybody but herself.

"They live in a twelve-million-dollar town house," Ginger gushed. "You should see it. I mean, East Eighty-second, right off Central Park. It was even in *Architectural Digest*—"

"Ginger." Karen's tone was hard. "Can I have Sharlene's number?"

"Camille! No one knows her as Sharlene."

I do. Mama does.

"Then, can you give me *Camille*'s phone number?" Her throat felt raw.

"She'd kill me! Absolutely kill me. Listen, Rand is here." She made a giddy laugh. "Funny I'm dating Jeff's brother, isn't it?"

Karen could sense her slipping away. "Ginger, wait! Can I have—"

"No, I just can't do it. But when I get down to White Pines, I'll tell her you called. Then she can decide if she wants to talk to you."

Karen gave Ginger her cellular phone number, then hung up.

Seconds later, the black plastic square chirped in her purse.

"I want to see you." Franklin's deep voice scraped across her nerves.

"Don't have time."

"You're trying to pull away, but I won't let you."

"Franklin, get real. We're through. If you need me to say that to your face, fine."

"I'll be waiting at home."

Karen rolled her eyes. Her troubles with Franklin were the last thing she felt like dealing with right now. All she could think about was Sharlene. And that made her shoulders feel heavy and liquid, as if she were melting under the pain of disappointment. If Sharlene had veered that far away from her roots, what chance was there that she'd help Mama? Chance enough. Karen straightened against the back of her chair, then dialed her best friend.

"*Washington News*, Freida Miller speaking." The sounds of ringing phones and loud voices echoed through the receiver.

"Freida, how you doin'?"

"Hey, girl. You know Saturdays are crazy when I have a big Sunday story to write. And let me tell you, my editor is on my back like a shadow."

Karen half smiled, picturing Freida, her bob of tiny braids framing her oval, cinnamon-brown face and curious ebony eyes. "Big story?"

"Yeah. Once Wade gets something in his head, he latches on like a leech and won't let go until he sucks all the blood out of me."

"I heard that." Karen glanced at the fax machine. A flashing red light made her bolt to her feet. It was jammed, so Franklin's faxes had not gotten out to the media yet. "Damn!" Karen hovered over the machine, jabbing buttons. "Listen, Freida, I need a phone number."

"Just a second." It sounded as if Freida was talking to a man.

Karen waited, wanting to take a baseball bat to the fax machine. But she knew she could count on Freida. She always could. Especially during her beans-and-rice days at Howard University, when scholarship money never seemed to cover all her books, tuition, and housing. Freida was always coming to the rescue with a check for whatever the amount. And she was willing to share not only her parents' money, but their beautiful home, too. Many a Thanksgiving dinner at their sprawling home in Prince Georges County, Maryland, had gotten Karen through otherwise bleak holidays when she couldn't afford to fly back to Mama and Daddy in Detroit.

"Sorry, girl, I told you," Freida said. "Whose number you need?"

"Monty Stone's."

"His home number?"

"Yeah."

"I can't give that out. And you wouldn't want to call now. I just did, and the man is highly pissed off about this lawsuit."

Karen frowned. She didn't want to tell Freida the whole drama about Mama and Sharlene. In fact, she'd never even told Freida she had a sister. No, by the time Karen met Freida, Sharlene had been gone a whole year. And that was time enough to convince Karen to cancel all referrals in her heart and mind to the person she had once loved as her sister.

"Freida, I really need the number. For Franklin. Stone is making life hard for folks on one of the welfare-to-work programs. So we want—"

"Franklin still giving you the blues?"

"Yeah, he scares me now," Karen said for the first time to herself or anyone else. She kept seeing the image of him with that fistful of money. "He's in deep with some shady characters over this riverfront project. Him now, and the way he used to be, only caring about helping the little people, it's like two different people."

"I'd watch that," Freida said. "I see it all the time. People tryin' to act one way to cover how they really are. Like this Senator Stone. Tries to be the perfect southern gentleman. But word is, he's a rapist."

Karen stiffened. "What?"

"Yeah, girl, some women filed a lawsuit. Say he attacked them at work."

"Ugh."

"I bet the Ethics Committee is gonna be on him like white on rice. Speaking of, I interviewed the new chairman. Your boy Jordan Kyles—"

"Oh, please don't bring him up."

Freida laughed. "Girl, the whole time I was with him, I couldn't stop thinking about that night on the Vineyard. How he held that lobster over your shoulder and," she laughed more, "let the butter drip down. Then he licked it off! Right there on the beach!"

Karen stifled a tingle at the memory of that steamy fling a few years ago. Before Franklin. "Now, why'd you have to remind me of him?"

"Just for fun," Freida said. "Girl, let me get back to work."

"Freida, I really need that number."

"You sure it can't wait 'til Monday when he's at the office?"

Karen thought of Mama's pallor. "No, it can't wait."

"Well, don't tell him you got it from me. Here."

Karen used a blue pen to scrawl jumbo digits over a white note pad.

"Only because you're my girl," Freida said. "It's hard enough covering him. And when he sees what I got for him tomorrow morning, I'll be at the top of his shit list. And I know Franklin won't tell where he got the number?"

Karen smiled. This was kind of like that time when they were both working summer internships in D.C. during college. Karen was working on the Hill for her Detroit congresswoman when she called Freida, an intern at *USA Today,* to give her a scoop about another lawmaker who was spending taxpayer money on lavish vacations. Freida's ensuing reports won her an award and a reporting position at the *News.* "Your secret is safe with me," Karen said.

Seconds later, she dialed Virginia. A maid answered; a few minutes later, Karen heard Sharlene say "Hello?" Karen's stomach fluttered. She was another step closer to saving Mama. And possibly reuniting with the stranger who shared her blood. "Sharlene, it's Karen."

She could hear excitement in her own voice. But silence on the line.

"Sharlene? I have to talk to you—"

"Yes."

"Mama is—"

"Great," Sharlene said. "Then we'll be watching for you. Drive safely."

Click! The dial tone buzzed in Karen's ear.

8

On the sprawling stone patio of White Pines, Camille focused on placing one light-blue skinny heel in front of the other with the sway she had learned from models at Ginger's fashion shows. Hips forward, shoulders back, eyes dancing with mirth. She imagined herself as carefree as the marble goddesses and cherubs spouting water into the huge swimming pool to her right. And she pictured herself as beloved to the Stone family as the uncles laughing in the smoke as they speared meat on long forks on the enormous barbecue grill by the cabana. Or the aunts and cousins, chatting and clinking silver on china under a dozen flowered-umbrella tables.

No sudden phone call, or the anxiety squeezing her chest, was going to interfere with becoming a legal part of all this luxury and love. Now all she had to do was charm the suspicion off the faces of Jeff and his family, and she could get back to work on changing their minds about the wedding.

As she returned to their table, phone in hand, two of Jeff's brothers, Davis and Jackson, scanned her clingy blue knit skirt and camisole. Next to Jackson was the chair abandoned a few minutes ago by his red-eyed wife. Then Dixie, followed by Jeff, who stood to pull out Camille's chair. She slinked close, smiling up at his eyes hard with questions in the hazy sunshine. Fortunately, Jeff had dressed for the party and apparently told his mother they would not leave. Sinking into the cushion as he pushed her in next to Mrs. Stone, Camille placed the phone on a tray held out by Ida Mae.

"Who on earth would be calling you here?" Mrs. Stone reached for her iced tea, causing her bracelets to slide. "During our meal, of all times."

Camille noticed two purple spots, like flat grapes, on the underside of Mrs. Stone's wrist. Bruises? Camille met her icy stare. "It was Ginger. She and Rand will be here in time for cake and ice cream."

Jeff took his seat. "Ginger doesn't breathe without checking with you first." His voice was sharp with annoyance. "I don't know what Rand sees in her. Or what Rand sees in a lot of things, for that matter."

"Hmmph, didn't sound like Ginger to me," said Ida Mae. "Ginger got a voice like a bird. This girl, deep and smooth, like Lena Horne way back when."

Camille wanted to tell her to shut up and go away. But she half smiled, gently pushing her fork into the golden-brown crust of one of Hortense's crab cakes. "Ida Mae, I can't believe your imagination."

Senator Stone, on the other side of Jeff's mother, looked up from his plate piled high with ham, ribs, and corn on the cob. "Get that phone away from here, Ida Mae. If one more reporter calls, I'll have Virginia Bell disconnect the lines for the entire eastern seaboard."

"Yes, sir."

"My gracious, Camille, if it wasn't Ginger, who was it?"

"Mom." Dixie set down a gravy-soaked biscuit; the irritation in her eyes seemed more dramatic with her hair swept back into a gold barrette matching her blouse and slacks. "She said it was Ginger, Mom. Why the third degree?"

"Dixie," Jackson said, making the word sound like an order with the same authority as Jeff and their father. An executive at the tobacco company's offices in Richmond, Jackson was as bland as the slice of store-bought white bread he'd requested instead of one of Hortense's melt-in-your-mouth buttermilk biscuits. He usually showed indifference toward Camille, but now the edge in his voice, and the sharpness pinching his diamond-shaped face, made it clear he wouldn't be sharing wedding well-wishes anytime soon.

"Now that you're a full-fledged adult," Jackson said, "it's safe to date."

Dixie wrinkled her straight nose. "Cripe, Jackson. Why don't you try taking my premed classes, see how much time *isn't* left to waste on dating."

"Excuses, excuses," Jackson said. "No one told you to take summer courses and play Dr. Doolittle at that farm."

Camille had never seen Dixie with a man, even though there was nothing about her to signal she might be gay. And as much as she loved animals and wanted to become a vet, she had lamented on several occasions that her parents refused to pay for vet school, saying that was beneath her.

"Pop, tell her she needs a nice man on her arm," Jackson said.

"Leave me alone, Jackson. It's my birthday."

Senator Stone's glance across the table at Jackson could have frozen any object on contact. "Back off, son." Then he bathed Dixie in a fatherly gaze that made Camille's heart pound. "You make me damn proud today, sugar."

Dixie's eyes sparkled at her father.

"Now let Camille answer Mom's question," Jackson said, his sandy hair and beige polo shirt a boring blur in Camille's peripheral vision. She didn't want to interrupt the deliciousness of her buttery biscuit by looking at him. Instead, she thought about doing extra laps in the pool.

"She already did answer," Jeff said.

"If she's going to join the family," Jackson said, "she should know we don't tell lies here."

Next to him, Davis's shock of prematurely gray hair swayed in the breeze like the coral-reef plants Camille and Jeff had seen while snorkeling in the Bahamas. He rolled his gray eyes and wiped barbecue sauce from the drapey sleeve of his white poet's shirt. Then he whispered, "Fucking hypocrites."

The crease on Senator Stone's forehead deepened. "What the hell did you say?" His eyes locked on Davis, who glared right back.

"Davis, if you can't show Mom more respect," Jackson said, "then I suggest you jet right back to your Russian Mafia friends—"

"Stop, you guys," Dixie said. "It's my birthday."

Davis pulled a tiny black phone from his pocket, hit one button, and started speaking German. As opposed to Japanese or Spanish, as he did other times for his work as a venture capitalist. Whatever that meant. Not once had he given Camille a straight answer about what exactly he did while jetting around the world. Jeff couldn't tell her either. All that mystery reminded her of someone she used to know who could make anything happen for a price.

"Camille, it's not polite to make people wait for an answer," Mrs. Stone said, dabbing her mouth with a linen napkin embroidered with the family crest.

Jeff's father shifted his eyes, so full of rage that they made the hairs on the back of Camille's neck stand, from Davis to Mrs. Stone. "Millie! Leave the girl alone. I wouldn't give a damn if that was Marcus Jones calling. She'll join this family when hell freezes over."

"Pop! You disrespect Camille, you disrespect me." Jeff put his arm around her. His palm felt like an iron shooting steam on her shoulder.

For a second, Camille sank deeper into the chair. Though she'd sucked down some medication from her yellow plastic inhaler after their meeting with his parents and it had relieved her of cigar suffo-cation, her lungs were clamping up again. From the shock of hearing Karen's voice for the first time in a decade.

I can't believe she found me. Especially here. And the maelstrom of questions whipping through her mind only compounded her fear that Mr. Stone's threat to cut Jeff off from the family fortune might make him reconsider the idea of marriage altogether.

No! He couldn't, not after yesterday on the yacht. When he'd gotten on his knee on the shiny teak deck and cracked open that little blue Tiffany's box. "Lady Godiva, marry me," he'd said, his eyes as gentle as the water around them as she melted like a stick of butter in the sunshine. But why couldn't she make his family love her, too? *I will! Just have to think of a new plan.*

Camille launched another brainstorm as Sue Ann returned, weighting the air with gloom. Her nose was red.

"My gracious, I wish this day would end," Mrs. Stone said.

"Worst year of our lives," Jackson said, pushing in his wife's chair.

"Sue Ann," Dixie said softly. "I understand if you'd rather stay inside."

Camille remembered: Baby Monty had died one year ago today. No wonder Sue Ann was more upset than usual. Jeff grasped Camille's shoulder more tightly; she bowed her head. In her lap, her ring sparkled, making her ponder how to expedite the process of having Jeff slide a wedding band next to it. A matching platinum one, with baguettes, like she'd seen in *Town & Country*.

"Gracious, that beautiful boy." Mrs. Stone fingered her locket.

Like a reflex, Camille stroked Mrs. Stone's back, running her palm in circles over the lavender silk of her dress. Camille had never touched her, and her stomach flipped when Mrs. Stone cast a glance of appreciation her way.

Ida Mae came hurrying back, phone in hand. "Mr. Monty, it's a reporter talkin' about you losin' a poll with Marcus Jones."

"Goddammit!" The iron chair screeched as he stood. "Jeff, take the call. Direct them to Rollins." Senator Stone paced, cussing softly.

Camille glanced up at the house, with its center rectangle and huge glass-domed conservatory flanked by two balconied wings. The Victoria Suite, where she'd watched Jeff earlier, was in the south wing; Jeff had said the upstairs of the north wing was locked and unused. But the curtain in one of the windows was swaying. And . . . what was that dark beige oval? A face? No, it was gone. Had one of the employees unlocked the north wing and let their kid play up there? Mrs. Stone would never allow that. Maybe it was just a reflection.

"Miss Camille." Ida Mae came into focus, staring down. "Don't you know starin' into the sun ain't good for your eyes?"

"Can't figure out this weather," Camille said, "sunny one minute, hazy the next." A few minutes later, after Ida Mae had retreated into the house and everyone else at the table excused themselves, Jeff hung up. Camille whispered, "Jeff, does anyone use the upstairs of the north wing?"

"No, it's locked," he said, sipping iced tea. "Why?"

"I think I saw someone in the window," she said, leaning close.

"Impossible. *I* don't even know how to get in there. As kids we found a way through the attic, but—" Jeff laughed. "Must've been a reflection, honey."

Camille shrugged, noticing a cluster of ladies in big hats around Mrs. Stone. Suddenly they started shrieking. Camille looked toward the lawn: Jezebel was chasing a skunk. Behind her came three more dogs. But within minutes, one of the brown-uniformed groundskeepers herded the canines away and netted the skunk. As the odor wafted to the patio, the hat ladies looked down pinched noses at Ginger, approaching in a blue micro-minidress.

"How appropriate," Jeff said with an annoyed twang as Ginger flitted toward them, holding hands with Rand and two kids from his community center in Harlem.

"There's a TV crew camped outside the gate," Ginger said. "I mean, they, like, shoved their cameras in the car window!"

Camille swept out of her chair to hug Ginger. "You called a while ago," Camille whispered, as Rand dwarfed Mrs. Stone in a hug, his brown ponytail swinging over the back of his olive-green mock turtleneck that matched his trousers.

"Hi, Camille!" The Puerto Rican girl who liked to sit on Camille's lap as she read to the kids every week pointed to her mouth. "I got a new tooth."

Camille smiled. "I'll have to talk to the tooth fairy about that."

"Mom, Pop, this is Devin and Esmerelda," Rand said, holding the cocoa-brown boy's hand. "Brought them down for horseback riding, if that's okay."

Senator Stone patted Rand's back. "Where's the photographer? Let's get shots for the brochures for my inner-city literacy program."

Dixie and her mother stared at Esmerelda. "My gracious, you are cute as a button." Then Mrs. Stone said to Devin, "Don't look scared. We don't bite."

"He's just shy," Ginger said, her straight auburn hair skimming pale, bony shoulders. "Hello, everyone." A nervous glint in Ginger's eyes made Camille wonder if her store's financial problems were getting worse.

Ida Mae took the kids' hands. "Let's get hamburgers off the grill."

"Let go!" the boy shouted. The girl shrieked. They clung to Rand's legs.

"It's okay," Rand said softly. An aura of gentleness, radiating from his hazel eyes and broad shoulders, cast an immediate calm over them. "Ida Mae is a nice lady. Aren't you hungry after that long trip?"

They nodded, then followed Ida Mae across the patio.

"Camille." Affection glimmered in Rand's eyes as he bent to peck her cheek. He raised her left hand, examining the ring. "He doesn't deserve a lifetime of you." Rand glared over her shoulder at Jeff, whose chair screeched.

"Back off, little brother," Jeff said.

Mrs. Stone stepped between them, flicking imaginary lint from Rand's chest. "Randolph, you could have come faster in your daddy's jet."

"Mom, you know I despise being called Randolph. Me and that slave owner who stole land from the Indians, we have nothing in common."

"You sure as hell do," Senator Stone said, putting his arm around Rand. "It's called power and pull. And that's why you'll find out next week, you got that Golden Hope grant for your center."

Rand's shoulder twitched. "Dad! How do you know about—"

"Don't be naive, Rand," Jeff said.

"You told!" Rand glared at Jeff, eye-to-eye. They shared strong jawlines and noses like George Washington's profile on a quarter.

Jeff shrugged. "Didn't want to leave anything to chance."

Rand narrowed his eyes at Jeff and his father. "I could have won it on my own merit. Not because my name is Stone!"

"Hell," Senator Stone said. "Use the money for whatever you need at your kids' place—"

"It hasn't been announced yet," Rand said with an accusing tone.

"My announcement is all the final word you need, son." Senator Stone flashed an omnipotent smile. "And buy that girl a whole dress," he said, glancing at Ginger, whose cheeks reddened.

"Pop!"

"Lower your voice, Randolph," Mrs. Stone said.

"And if you come telling me you want to marry a Yankee trollop, too," Senator Stone said, "the answer is just like I told your brother. Hell no."

Camille ached all over, and her lungs were tightening into a full-fledged wheeze. But her mind kept spinning. She had to draw out the softer sides of Jeff's parents, but how? It seemed every passing minute, something new was piquing their ire. Soft sides . . . tender spots . . . Mrs. Stone upset about the baby . . . Senator Stone, slipping in the polls against his black opponent.

Yes! A two-pronged plan jelled in Camille's mind. Something daring and bold that would make Jeff's parents dote on her as if she were the belle of the debutante ball.

9

Karen brushed past Franklin in the foyer of his three-story colonial in the historic Indian Village section of Detroit. The dark wood
floor creaked as she hurried through a doorway on the right, into his
sleek gray office. Under her arm was the folder containing his press
release, which she thought had permanently jammed the fax machine
at city hall.

She rushed to the silver table behind his desk, where her fingertips
raced across beige buttons. The paper finally hummed its way toward
newsrooms.

Karen couldn't wait to get this done—and tell Franklin, once and
for all, that their affair was history—so she could hurry back to Mama's
house, check on her, and try calling Sharlene again. Maybe when that
party at the plantation was over, Karen could reach her in private,
where Sharlene would talk. If not, Karen would just hop a plane to
New York, confront her face-to-face. And beg if necessary.

"Don't I get a kiss?" Franklin clinked the bolt on the front door.
Electronic beeps rang out.

Karen rolled her eyes. "Why are you setting the alarm during the
day?"

He came to her side in yellow cotton shorts and a tank top em-
blazoned with the University of Michigan logo. He checked the window locks, drew the blinds, and turned on the track lights.

Karen crossed her arms over her ankle-length, brown sheath dress. Goose bumps rose on her bare arms. "Franklin, why are you acting like ninjas are about to jump through the windows and blow us away?"

"Break-ins in the neighborhood. Can't be too careful." He scanned the desk, piled high with glossy blue folders. Then he looked across the room at the wooden shelves built into the wall. Along with books and pictures of his eighteen-year-old daughter who lived with his ex-wife in New Mexico were African masks and sculptures he'd bought during his trip to South Africa when Nelson Mandela was elected president. The shelves also held the hammered-brass chest lined with red satin that Karen had given him last year after picking it up at one of the ethnic festivals downtown in Hart Plaza.

"Franklin, I hate it when you won't look in my eyes."

He met her stare.

"I meant what I said last night. It's over."

He slipped his hands around her waist. "Darling, don't do this to me."

Karen twisted away. "Do what?"

"Mess up what we have together," he said softly.

Karen rolled her eyes. "Get real. This is your own fault."

Fear flashed in Franklin's eyes. "I expected you to be mature enough to understand what I'm going through. The international scope of this. The magnitude of promises I've made, the money—"

"That's all you care about!"

"But, Karen, think of what Wish Master can do for our city. Riverfront restaurants, casinos—"

"The numbers man coming to Mama's door was all the one-armed bandit I ever needed to see!" Karen remembered wondering why Mama had handed over money to that man in the leather baseball cap, when she and Sharlene needed winter coats and boots. "Not to mention my father—"

Franklin pressed his lips to her mouth. Hot, soft, comforting.

She pushed him away. "Stop! I fell in love when you were someone else. The man who cried when that little boy said if you hadn't helped open the swimming pool in his neighborhood, he would've spent the summer selling drugs. Not—"

The tenderness in Franklin's eyes hardened. "What is your point?"

"That! You have no patience for the people. You're all about the power."

Franklin glanced at the brass box again, then took her hand. "Darling, let's go away for a while. Forget about this riverfront stuff."

Karen squinted at him. "Go away? As in *run* away? You obviously haven't seen your schedule. We've got the Grand Prix parties—"

"I don't care," he said. "None of that matters if I don't have you."

Franklin kissed her again. The scent of fresh-cut grass lingered on his skin from his eighteen holes of golf that morning. And the warmth of his broad chest made her want to lose herself in the passion they used to share.

"I'm leaving." She headed for the door. But something sticking out of the brass box on the shelf made her stop. Stepping closer, the shelf almost bumping her chin, she saw it was a dark blue velvet bag. Something black and metal poked out. "What's that?"

"Don't—"

Oh, my God! Karen reached up. Opened the folds of fabric along the drawstring. Out fell a gun and a shower of diamonds, bouncing off the gray Berber carpet. "Franklin! What the—"

He dove beside her, grasping the gun, putting it on a low shelf.

"You're taking a bribe."

"Darling, no—"

She looked down, eyes wide, as he scrambled around her woven brown leather sandals, putting the diamonds into the bag, one by one. He even plucked a stone that scraped between her toes. This was hardly the way she had hoped Franklin would give her a diamond one day.

"You weren't supposed to see this." His calm tone made her shudder.

"Was I supposed to read about it in the paper when you get indicted?"

He glanced up with hurting eyes. "Darling, I don't want you involved. It's too dangerous. But I can explain—"

"No! Don't tell me a damn thing!"

With a trembling hand, she grabbed her purse. Then, on wobbly legs, she ran out of the house.

10

Camille Morgan couldn't type fast enough to keep up with the legal terms and concepts ticking and turning in her mind as smoothly as the interlocking parts inside a fine watch.

"The court found a father is precluded from parental rights—" she said aloud over the tap of the keyboard. Alone in her small office in the federal courthouse in lower Manhattan, she ignored her gurgling stomach and the ringing phone. It probably wasn't Jeff; he was in trial and wouldn't be home until late. But it could be Ginger, who had sounded so upset earlier. Camille had promised to swing by the store after work, to help iron out her finances. And it was her night to read to the children at Rand's center. *Too much to do . . .*

A quick glance at the small crystal clock on her desk showed she had just two more hours to weave three pertinent cases into the brief. Judge Mannington wanted to take it home tonight to review for tomorrow's trial. All last week he'd been asking for progress reports, reminding her this unusual case was sure to draw a small army of reporters to his courtroom.

"—when abuse and neglect—" Camille's right hand skidded to the right, hitting that annoying F9 key. A bright green HELP menu popped up.

"I can't believe I keep doing that!" Camille pressed ESCAPE, making the blue background and black text reappear. She hit SAVE just in case.

"Now . . ." She skimmed a week's worth of research, cases printed off Westlaw on the Internet, fanning both sides of the beige computer. There, that big yellow-highlighted paragraph was just what she needed to prove her point.

Perfect. Can't wait to show Jeff . . . he'll be so proud. And he'll tell his father what a good job I did. She leaned closer, typing as she read the papers. But her finger slipped again. She glanced at the keyboard, ready to hit ESCAPE. No, something was different. The screen was orange. And blank!

"No!" She ran the cursor up and down. Hit that handy little UNDO TYPING button the computer technician had shown her. Still nothing.

Her chest tightened. Rage and frustration prickled under her white silk blouse, her navy-blue skirt suit, and panty hose. She kicked off her pumps, making them smash into the wall under the desk.

There was no way she could rewrite twenty pages by five o'clock. It had taken most of last week to write what she had. Turning it in late wasn't an option. No, she would look incompetent and give the judge something negative to tell Jeff's father. And she hadn't made any backup copies. But perhaps the hard drive had. Maybe the computer guy could come retrieve her brief somehow. Camille snatched up the phone.

"Miss Morgan?" Judge Mannington's black robe and the shiny dome of his head, ringed by gray curls, reflected on the blank screen.

Her heart leaped to her throat. She pushed a button to make her screen saver flash flowers. Then, spinning her tweed chair to face him in the doorway, she made her eyes dance as she looked up at him.

"Judge. Senator Stone told me to tell you, start your target practice now. He's got his sights set on being hunt master this year."

The judge's round belly shook as he laughed. "Let him dream." He tossed a newspaper on the desk. "Take a read. They're clobbering him today."

Camille lifted the paper, scanning the headline. Something about the sexual harassment lawsuit, but her mind was spinning, searching for a way to get the judge out of her office so she could call the technician ASAP.

The computer beeped behind her.

"Everything okay?" he asked.

"Of course. I'm glad you came in. I needed a quick breather. Spell-checking can be so tedious."

"Ah, then you're done." His face reminded her of a pear with dark seeds for eyes, a small lump of a nose, a slit for a mouth.

Camille smiled. "It'll be in your hand at five o'clock." She glanced down at the article. "I can't believe how reporters print accusations form the senator's enemies without bothering to get proof."

The judge chuckled. "Then they wouldn't have a story. They certainly do walk a fine line beside reckless disregard for the truth. Anything for a buck."

Camille ignored the beeping computer. She had no idea what that was, but it was definitely bad. "But it's so wrong that after they dismiss Vivian's lawsuit for lack of evidence, people will still remember the lurid allegations."

The judge squinted at her computer. "That's the name of the game. Mud-slinging makes for sexier headlines than the cleanup job." He stepped closer to the screen. "Sounds like it's about to take off."

Camille spun her chair, clicked the mouse. "No, it always does that when I interrupt spell-check."

"Here, let me try." He squeezed past her, hit a few F keys. The screen went black. The little green "on" lights extinguished.

Camille's heart exploded. The computer was completely dead! No chance of finding her brief now. Her chest tightened, rising and falling with panic.

"There, now turn it back on. Rebooting should solve your problem."

She wanted to shout, *Just get out of here and let me handle this!*

"Thank you, Judge Mannington. I'd better get back to work."

"Turn it back on," he said. "Show me I was right."

The phone rang. Camille hoped that would send the judge on his way, but he stepped around her to pick up the mouse and examine it.

She reached with her left hand, glimpsing her ring as she picked up the phone. Earlier, she had mailed engagement announcements to

Dark Secret

papers in Virginia, New York, and Washington. That would get Jeff's parents showered with congratulations and help them get used to the idea that she was going to marry their oldest son. "Good afternoon, this is Camille Morgan."

"Sharlene—"

Camille froze. "I'm afraid there's no one here by that name. I'll transfer you to the—"

"Get real. I'm your sister and you know it."

For a second, Camille felt a twinge of longing to hear about Karen's life. Had she gone to college? Married? Had kids? But Camille didn't dare. Not in front of the judge. Or in the midst of computer meltdown.

"Who exactly are you trying to reach?" Camille asked.

"You! Sharlene Bradley. Oh, excuse me. Camille Morgan."

Karen's voice flipped on a mental slide projector of images that had gotten Camille from a wide-eyed nobody, stepping off a bus in Penn Station with seventy-five dollars to her name, to a lawyer engaged to a sexy millionaire. Like sharing that apartment on the Lower East Side with Ginger, four other girls, and rats so bold they would stick their little pink noses in your Ramen noodles if you left your bowl unattended. Or taking off her clothes to do unspeakable things with Nick Parker in exchange for his services.

"Sharlene?"

No, I'm someone else now.

"I suggest," Camille said, "you check the number—"

"Sharlene, if you don't talk to me I'll be on the next plane to New York—"

"I'm terribly sorry I couldn't help." Camille hung up. "I wish the operator would be more careful about transferring random calls up here."

"Happens all the time," the judge said. The computer chimed, the tiny green lights came on, and the screen lit up. "There." He glanced at his watch. "Now you can print, and I'll see you in my office in about an hour."

11

Nick Parker's gaze tripped over a familiar face smiling up from
the newspaper. Yeah, it was definitely her, hugged up with some
clean-cut rich dude named Jeff Stone. The paper whooshed as Nick
snatched it off the table in the Starbucks near his Manhattan penthouse.
He had to take a closer look.

"Sharlene, baby!" Nick said, skimming the caption under the engagement announcement. Jefferson Stone, oldest son of Senator Montgomery "Monty" Stone of Virginia.

"Holy shit!" Nick had a pack of Stones in his pocket right now.
Miss Motown is gettin' hitched to goddamn Fort Knox!

He gulped his double espresso. The bitter flavor made him grimace
as he studied the chick he had banged more times than he could count.
That bitch would be nothing without me. I made her!

Nick focused on Camille as he pressed onto the crowded sidewalk
and the chaos of honking cabs, buses belching exhaust, people talking
on cell phones. He broke a sweat striding in the soupy heat past heaps
of reeking black garbage bags and boxes on the curb and storefronts.
He let himself into the locked nightclub, which would reopen when
he ditched the bill collectors.

"Has it been ten years?" He strutted past the round booth where
he had found lust at first sight, not just because Sharlene looked so
good in that skintight jumpsuit and come-fuck-me boots. She'd come

for a private party for a socialite with her designer friend. No, it was the tough glint in those big blue cat eyes. Vulnerable, mysterious. And hungry. This chick was starving for all the wealth and luxury New York had to offer. Just like himself, after coming to the Big Apple from the wrong side of the tracks in Milwaukee.

"Have some more champagne," he'd said, filling Sharlene's glass as techno-beat blasted over a throng of bodies on the dance floor. At first she shot an annoyed stare his way. But she cracked a smile after learning he owned Pseudo, one of the hottest spots in town. It had a way of impressing women like Sharlene Bradley and her designer friend, Ginger.

That night when all three of us got freaky together . . . It was sweltering in here without the air conditioning. He leaned on the acrylic bar, remembering how he had fucked Sharlene there, while long neon tubes inside it flashed continuously, changing from blue to yellow to pink, then lavender and lime. That made for pretty psychedelic sex as every few seconds the lights cast a new color across Sharlene's creamy skin. And oh how desperately she had wanted to turn a knob to change her own color. *Camille the chameleon.*

Nick headed for his office at the back of the club. Right away he noticed the blinking light on the answering machine. He pushed PLAY, hearing a deep voice: "You got a date with an ass-kicking if you don't pay up pronto."

Nick slammed the newspaper on the desk. "Shit, man, where am I gonna get all that dough?" His gaze fell on Sharlene's happy-in-love grin.

That's where. She owes me.

12

In the giant windows of her clothing store, Ginger paced behind opalescent mannequins in pastel crochet dresses, watching for Camille's chauffeured black Lincoln Town Car. A renowned fashion photographer and two models dashed from the trendy restaurant across the street, sidestepping a red puddle from Beef Bazaar next door. Rush-hour traffic clogged the street. But what was taking Camille so long?

Finally, Ginger dashed to the door. In black oval sunglasses, Camille swayed across the sidewalk between a man in a bloodstained smock and the chichi florist two doors down who kept his parrot on his shoulder. He stopped in front of Camille, making an exaggerated bow and hand roll. She smiled, hurrying in with a blast reeking of exhaust and rotting flesh that always seemed stronger on hot days here in the meatpacking district, between the Village and the Hudson River.

"I'm, like, such a mess today," Ginger said. "I got an eviction notice. And the lady at the bank was a total bitch. She goes, 'Miss Romanowski, I'm sorry, but you've exhausted your line of credit.' "

Camille kissed her cheek and put warm palms on her bare shoulders. "Ginger, slow down. Whatever the problem, we'll find a solution."

The solution was getting a big chunk of cash to pay two months' rent. Ginger hated borrowing money, especially from Camille. So after that bitch at the bank blew her off, she'd called Nick Parker, even though she hadn't spoken to him in years. But she was desperate and wanted to deplete all options before asking Camille. Rand had already written her a more-than-generous check, but a hungry pile of overdue bills had chewed it up right away. And Nick said when she figured out how to raise a lot of cash in a hurry, to give *him* a call. She'd wanted to talk to Camille about it more at White Pines, but they never got a minute alone. So she never told her about Karen's call, which had provoked nasty guilt pangs all day.

"Ginger, you look terrible. How can I help? We need to make this the hottest place outside Paris. Then we'll throw a big party. Like the old days."

"I wish." Ginger led Camille past circular racks where Lisa, the clerk, was rearranging her trademark satin stretch second-skin jeans, then past the men's section and the brick cashier's counter.

"And once my wedding dress is in all the papers and *Town and Country,* brides will be *begging* Ginger Roman to design their gowns."

Ginger stopped just inside the softly lit dressing room. "They said yes?"

"They will."

"Camille, I'm, like, so impressed with how you can act calm and confident, no matter what. Like Saturday when Jeff's dad was being a total ass. I wanted to *die*. But you—"

Camille laughed, tossing her head back, her hair dancing over the giant purple mushroom stool as she sat down. "If you knew what I just went through at work! I can't believe it worked out, thanks to the computer guy. I'm ready for anything now."

"Including a little game of loan officer?" Ginger asked softly. She hated that Camille was on the verge of securing her dream while her own life goal was unraveling like a gauzy skirt without a hem.

Camille raised her brows. "How much?"

Ginger told her, keeping her back to the two walls of mirrors, not wanting to see the reflection of herself doing this.

Camille flipped open her designer purse, which cost about a month's rent, pulled out a monogrammed leather wallet, and wrote a check on her crossed leg. The perforated ripping sound, and the love in Camille's eyes as she held out the beige slip of paper, made Ginger's throat burn.

"You're the best," she whispered. She took the check, then looked at it. "My God, Camille, this is, like, twice what I need."

Camille shrugged, leaned back on her palms. "You need it all. When I get home I'll check the accounts and see what else I can do."

Ginger closed her eyes, envisioning Karen storming into the dressing room at the Riverfront Academy of the Arts after opening night of *A Streetcar Named Desire*, shouting at Camille for trying to hide her race.

"I have to tell you something," Ginger said quietly. "I, like, feel terrible about it, and I meant to tell you down in Virginia. But—"

Camille straightened, uncrossed her leg. "What is it?"

"Karen."

Camille's suntanned face blanched. "What about her?"

"She called here. Saturday, before I left. My mom said she called her, too. Wanted to know where you are. But I wouldn't give your number."

Camille bolted up. "What *did* you tell her?"

She seemed extra tall, staring down like that. Ginger stepped back. "I—"

"Did you tell her where I was?" Camille almost shouted, her eyes wide. "I can't believe you talked to her at all! If Bill called me asking about you, I'd slam the phone in his ear! In a heartbeat!"

Bill. Ginger's crazy high school boyfriend who had threatened to kill her when she said she was moving away to become a designer instead of marrying him. The restraining order hadn't kept him away, but the anonymity of New York, and his fear of leaving Detroit, had. Thank God.

Ginger flitted toward the purple armoire overflowing with measuring tapes and swatches of fabric. In the mirror, she hated the frightened glint in her blue-green eyes and the new crop of freckles exploding on her tiny nose since the horseback ride yesterday with Rand and the kids. And why did she wear these yellow capri pants today? They made her legs look like sausages, even with the spiky yellow mules. "Camille, I'm, like, so sorry. I didn't tell her anything! But she said your mom is dying, and I—"

Dark Secret

"I don't care what she said!" Camille's chest rose and fell; her lips tightened. She had not raised her voice like that, to Ginger's knowledge, since their high school graduation day. The memory was crystal-clear: Ginger waiting in the cab in front of Camille's house on Helen Street, only to hear Camille scream at the skinny man on the porch claiming to be her father: "I hate you for leaving me here!" Camille had climbed into the taxi, trembling and sobbing all the way to the bus station.

"Camille, please don't be mad at me."

Camille turned her back, crossed her arms. Her shoulders kept rising and falling under that big flow of waves. "Karen called me at White Pines. During Dixie's party. Spoke to Ida Mae, of all people. And today she threatened to come—"

"It's not my fault!"

Camille spun to face her, eyes sharp. "How else would she have known to call me there? And how'd she get the number? The Stones aren't exactly listed in the phone book."

"You have to believe me," Ginger said.

"What did you tell her?"

"Just . . . that you're getting married. To Jeff. And that you're a lawyer."

Camille was making her ring flash dots of light on the wall. Her long, slightly rounded nose flared. She shouted, "Are you crazy?"

Ginger cringed. She balled her fists to stop her fingers from trembling. The sound of the check crumpling reminded her it was there. She wanted to stomp her feet in frustration, to scream at the top of her lungs that Camille had it all wrong. But how could she make Camille believe she hadn't given Karen the phone number? And how could she make her forget about this and mend the most important relationship in her life? It was as if Camille's anger had gouged a chunk of flesh. She had to stitch it up, or bleed to death.

Ginger stepped close to her friend, took her damp hand.

"You have to believe me, Camille. I think you're overreacting because, I mean, you're so stressed out about the wedding, and the bar exam."

Camille snatched back her hand. "I'm not overreacting. What

Karen will do under the guise of 'helping' our mother is anyone's guess."

"Listen!" Ginger said. "I've got your back. Always have, always will."

Camille glanced down at the check. "No, I've got *your* back. But you just stabbed me in mine."

13

Camille smiled as she read to the dozen little faces circling her. In the bookshelf-lined reading corner of Hugs and Hope, the children's community center run by Jeff's brother in Harlem, she was holding up a book about a boy's adventures in an enchanted forest.

"But when he arrived," Camille said, her voice echoing off the huge loft's shiny wood floor, "the fire-breathing boar jumped into his path."

Esmerelda, the girl Rand had brought to Dixie's party, shifted in Camille's lap while a funky beat pounded from a far corner where older girls practiced a dance routine. Camille finally finished the book. Heavy with exhaustion, she just wanted to get home to an already late dinner with Jeff.

"Read us more!" shouted Devin from a red beanbag chair a few feet away. His bright eyes and grin reminded Camille why she loved spending time with these kids; the first time she saw him, after his parents had gone to prison for larceny, his gaze never left the floor and he mumbled.

"I'll read extra stories next week," she said. "But I have to go now."

"More! More!" Rand stood behind one of the waist-high book-shelves around the red rug, his hazel eyes fixed on Camille with a gleam that made her feel she should look away. But there was something so genuine and comforting about him in his jeans, dark ponytail, and beige T-shirt with the Hugs and Hope insignia: two hugging teddy bears framed by a rainbow. "Don't leave so soon," he said, his words blending with the scent of pizza being served at a nearby table. Behind him, streetlights flickered outside the warehouse-style paned windows.

Camille stood, telling the kids, "I promise. A reading marathon next week." Esmerelda gripped her hand as Camille approached Rand. He was illuminated by one of countless industrial-style lights hanging like silver bells amongst exposed ceiling pipes painted blue and yellow. Following her toward the door, he picked up a smock, tossed it over an easel.

"Camille," he said, "you're like two different people, you know."

She raised her brows. "No, I don't know."

"There's Camille with Jeff. And Camille without. Here you're relaxed and down-to-earth. With him, I see something else in your eyes. As if you're trying so hard to please him, you lose yourself."

She bent down. "Esmerelda, honey, remember to practice reading."

"Thanks for talking to the tooth fairy." Her little face lit up; her long ponytail bounced as she ran to the other kids.

Rand stood closer as Camille straightened. "Wait a few; Dixie's coming after her Columbia interview and dinner with a friend. She'd love to see—"

Camille glared up at him. "Keep your relationship analysis to yourself."

"I speak the truth." His voice was raspy, and he took his time talking. "You're special, Camille. And I don't want to see you spinning your wheels—"

"I'm not," she said, hating the warmth she felt when his gaze enveloped her with the softness and comfort of her oversized pashmina wrap. "And my relationship with Jeff is not your business. Now, I enjoy coming up here, but—"

"I'll keep my opinions quiet," Rand almost whispered.

But the affection in his unblinking eyes made Camille lower her lashes toward burning cheeks. Jeff's brother shouldn't be looking at her like that, and she shouldn't be putting herself in situations where he could. He was her best friend's boyfriend, her future brother-in-law. But this visceral affinity for him . . . he just looked so much like Jeff, that was all. She didn't want to stop coming here; she knew better than anyone just how desperately these children needed role models. In fact, it reminded her of escaping Mother's smoke and scorn at the branch library to hear Mrs. Williams's Saturday story time. Camille would just have to deflect Rand on a gaze-by-gaze basis. "Rand, I—"

The door swung open. In blew Dixie, in a black pantsuit, her curled-under shoulder bob framing her smile. "Camille, I knew it was you when I saw your driver smoking outside." She kissed Camille's cheek, then Rand's. "This would be super if I get into Columbia's med school. Just a few minutes away."

Rand grinned. "Got my fingers crossed for you."

"Your other brother has a message," Camille said, putting her arm around Dixie. "There's a hunky new lawyer at the firm who was made for you."

Dixie pursed her lips; her eyes narrowed. "Not you, too."

Her tone stung Camille. "Pardon?"

"Don't gang up with them. I'm not interested in the dating game."

Rand stroked her shoulder. "Hey, Dixie, relax."

Dixie stepped back. "I know you mean well, Camille, but no thanks."

The door opened again; in came Esmerelda's mother. With a high black ponytail, glossed lips, and a tube top, she looked all of twenty. She held a baby carrier; lacy blankets framed a tiny face and jet curls.

In seconds, Dixie was on her knees, staring with glazed eyes at the infant. "May I?" She glanced up at the mother, who nodded. Dixie lifted the baby, her plump legs wriggling in a pink jumper and booties.

"You're so lucky," Dixie whispered, cradling her. "She's beautiful."

"No, she is always crying," the mother said with a Spanish accent and sad eyes. "So am I. Since Miguel went back to San Juan without us."

Camille dropped an imaginary steel door over her heart and mind; she would not feel or see or relate to the pain and fear . . . young mother, two babies, no money, no father . . . no! And why was Dixie acting as if she'd never seen a baby? Rand said something about what Esmerelda had done today, but Camille wasn't hearing it. She had to get out of here, away from reminders of what she'd escaped and confusing messages from Rand.

"Dixie, stop by later if you get a chance," Camille said. "Rand, see you next week."

Camille hurried to the chauffeured car that would shuttle her back to the luxurious town house where she could change into a silky night-gown and revel in the mind-numbing adoration of the man she loved.

14

Camille loved when Jeff kissed her like this in the elevator of their town house. With its dark, shiny wood and beveled glass, it made her feel as if she was on the set of some old movie, stealing a passionate moment with a man she wasn't supposed to be with. She combed her fingernails through his hair as his hot mouth made her head whirl.

"Keep those lips hot, Counselor," Jeff whispered as the doors opened onto his third-floor study. He had to review some deposition testimony to prepare for cross-examination of a key witness in the morning. In his hand: his briefcase and a stack of mail. "I want dessert when I come up."

Camille smiled as the elevator ascended to their master suite, the entire fourth floor. Comfortably full from a late dinner of salad and baked chicken down in the dining room, Camille flipped open her laptop computer on the writing desk that matched their bed. She connected to their brokerage firm's Web site, hoping to figure out how she could help Ginger resuscitate her store.

I can't believe I overreacted like that. As soon as she got home, Camille had called Ginger to apologize, blaming her outburst on worry about whether the wedding would happen. She didn't mention Rand's gaze to either Ginger or Jeff; maybe she was reading more into it than Rand intended.

Camille scrolled several accounts. "Now, let's see . . ." She glanced back to make sure the bedroom doors were closed and all was silent. The last time Jeff found out she had given money to Ginger, he raced his Ferrari down to Washington to hang out with his best friend Dillon Saxton at his father's apartment. As she scribbled calculations, she remembered working with one of their brokers, Ms. Eaton, to make a nice profit when an Internet company offered its stocks to the public. It had made Camille realize how much Jeff had taught her about money and investments.

I've come so far since my cash-stuffed shoe box back in Detroit . . .

The ringing phone drew her attention. Jeff never answered while preparing for trial. But where was Ida Mae? Camille dashed to answer it on the night stand.

"Miss Motown!" The voice was deep. Sinister. Familiar.

My God. How did he find me?

"Sharlene, baby. Saw you in the paper with Rich Boy. Congrats on the upcoming nuptials. I see all my hard work is payin' off in a big way!"

The static of rushing blood filled her ears.

"Sharlene, baby, talk to me."

"I'm sorry," she said softly. "You must have the wrong number."

She set the receiver in its cradle. "He has no right to call now."

Anger prickled under her white cotton drawstring pants and T-shirt. What was this, call-and-harass-Sharlene day? Was there some connection between Karen and Nick hunting her down at the same time? Yes, a big loud warning from fate that it was time to secure her position as Jeff's wife ASAP. Before anyone could jeopardize it. And she had the perfect plan to make his parents think she was the best thing since tobacco. It would relate to his mother's yearning for a grandchild, and his father's obsession with getting reelected. But Camille needed more time to work out the details.

Suddenly an acute craving struck, to savor the luxury around her. She'd lived here three years and never taken it for granted. But Nick's voice and Karen's calls made her remember how far she'd come. And how much she could lose.

In the dressing room, she pulled a large white box from an upper shelf. From the crinkle of tissue paper, she withdrew a satin nightgown so soft, so shimmery, it was like cream pouring into a puddle as it slipped between her fingers. She'd wear it Friday night, when she whisked Jeff away in a limousine for a surprise night at a bed-and-breakfast in Connecticut and a day of bike riding in the country. She knelt, caressing her cheek with the gown, feeling like Daisy in *The Great Gatsby* when she sobbed into Gatsby's silk shirts.

"Camille!" Jeff's voice shot into the dressing room, grabbing her throat.

No! He heard it all. Nick's call.

She swayed into the bedroom, pulling her hair back, letting it tumble around her shoulders. She said softly, "What is it, baby?"

By the elevator, Jeff was surveying the room, with its silver-bronze sponge-textured walls, the billowy drapes on tall windows flanking the desk, and the cherubs-and-fruit-carved fireplace mantel.

"What the hell, Camille!" Shoulders forward, he marched toward her.

"Jeff, baby, relax. If your trial is stressing you out this much—"

"You can't cover this one up!"

Camille's chest tightened.

He raised his hand, waving a fan of small blue papers. "You shop like I can print up hundred-dollar bills in the attic!"

Camille stood close, pouting as she gazed up at him. "Jeff? Remember that little strapless dress I wore to your father's banquet last month?"

Jeff's jaw muscles flexed as he glared down at her.

She ran her palms under his white T-shirt. "You know, the one with the tiny buttons that you unhooked, one by one, when we got home?"

His gaze softened.

"And those strappy sandals? The ones you said made my legs look extra long? Made my calf muscles flex just so?"

Jeff's dimples began to form. "Lady Godiva. What'll I do with you?"

Camille locked her fingers around his neck, stared into his eyes. "I know you haven't forgotten that evening coat, with the feathers I tickled you—"

"Yeah, yeah." His eyes darkened. "Goddammit, honey. I'm gonna send you to a twelve-step program for shop-aholism."

Camille stroked his back, crushed her breasts into him.

"I see what Mom means about people who don't come from money."

It would've hurt less if he'd whacked her cheek. "Jeff!"

"It's true."

"I saw your mom's beige pantsuit at Saks. The price would make you—"

"Mom has her own money from when Grandpa Smith died. You don't. And another thing."

Camille raised her brows. *The phone call. He heard it . . .*

"When Rand calls, don't flirt for ten minutes before I find out he's on the line." Something menacing flashed in his eyes. "Did he just call?"

"Rand?"

"Yes."

"No, that was a crank. But Rand called earlier because he wanted to know why Ginger was so upset."

Jeff pulled away. "So you did your best coquette act! Ida Mae says this is a routine thing."

Camille scowled. *The Spy.* "Why does she make it her business to watch me all the time? Do you tell her to?"

"Should I?"

Camille ran her thumb over her ring. "I can't believe we're having this conversation. Why are you lashing out at me?" She sank into the bed, letting a curtain of hair fall around her. She let out a soft sob.

"I'm sorry, honey." Jeff nuzzled her ear. "You know how I get about money. And I don't want Rand muscling in on you."

"Never." Camille traced his lips with her tongue.

Jeff laid her across the bed, devouring her neck as if she were a giant ice cream cone. His fiery mouth sent tiny shock waves of lust rolling toward a burning throb between her legs.

"Lady Godiva," he whispered, stroking her hair into a sunburst. "Sometimes I think I would curl up and die without you."

Camille touched a fingertip to his lips. "Shhh. Make love to me."

15

In the backseat of a yellow taxi, Karen scanned the town houses along East Eighty-second Street: a beige limestone one, another with red brick and a rounded bay window. But so far, no sign of the six stories of mauve stone and fancy black wrought iron around the windows and double doors.

If I have to knock on every door on this street, I'm going to find Sharlene and talk to her face-to-face about Mama. Then she'll help . . .

Karen had the right street, thanks to Ginger. And the five-year-old copy of *Architectural Digest* open on her lap showed glossy images of Sharlene's town house, inside and out, as well as a picture of Senator Stone and his wife. They were standing in front of some ridiculously expensive painting in the dining room. And the caption said their family had built the eight-thousand-square-foot showplace a hundred years ago when their law firm opened its Manhattan branch.

The hot, still air and all the town houses whizzing past in the blazing morning sun made Karen dizzy. "Can you slow down, please?"

"You need an address," the driver barked over his shoulder.

"Well, I don't have one. Just this." She shoved the magazine through the scratched Plexiglas window between the seats. Images of her frantic search through the Detroit Public Library for that edition blurred with helping Franklin prepare for the mayor's riverfront press conference. Not to mention securing an emergency bank loan for the bakery while Daddy kept the place running and took Mama to dialysis.

Karen's head snapped back as the cab sped up, then screeched to a stop.

"There it is." The driver exchanged the magazine for her fare.

Trembling, Karen adjusted her straw hat as she stepped into the choking heat. A bead of sweat rolled from the top of her thick braid at the base of her neck into her beige knit top. Her linen pantsuit felt damp, and her black sunglasses slipped on her nose as she closed the cab door.

"Good morning." Karen turned to see a fortyish man in a blue seersucker suit, smiling as he strode past. With him, a svelte woman in a flowered hat, and a brood of kids in dresses and ribbons, suits, and bow ties. One of the boys was talking into a cell phone about going to the park after church.

A far cry from Helen Street.

Karen rang the doorbell, staring down two stone lions flanking Sharlene's front door. After a second ring, a sky-blue form shimmered in the beveled glass beyond the black wrought-iron gates. The door opened. Sharlene's eyes—yes, that was her!—grew enormous. Slam!

Anger exploded inside Karen like a red flare. How could she convince Sharlene to help Mama through a closed door? She had to stay calm, like when she talked to Ginger.

"Camille," she said cheerfully, "I just dropped by for a visit."

The door opened. "What do you want?"

"Can you open this gate, please?"

Sharlene stepped out, unlocked the wrought iron, swung it open.

But Karen's feet would not lift. No, not while she looked into Sharlene's eyes, the same shape as Mama's, the identical color as Daddy's. They looked bigger now. And was that a flash of curiosity, even affection, behind the fury?

"Can I come in?"

Sharlene glanced behind her shoulder. "Ten minutes."

Karen followed her into the coolness of a large entrance hall. Soft lights illuminated a stone statue of a Greek goddess towering next to a staircase whose banister matched the front gates. Karen pulled off her sunglasses. Something welled inside her, pushed her toward her sister, arms outstretched.

Dark Secret

But Sharlene stepped back. "This isn't the time for a reunion." She crossed her arms, resting her perfect manicure on the ice-blue satin sleeves of her pajamas that matched her slippers. Eye-popping diamonds glistened on her finger, in her ears, in the hollow at the base of her very thin neck.

"I see you're living quite the glamorous life this Sunday morning." Sharlene's stare made Karen's cheeks feel hot.

"Don't look so evil, Sharlene."

"My name is Camille." She raised her arched brows. "Stop laughing!"

"Sorry," Karen said playfully. "But I think you should have gone with Krystle. As in Krystle Carrington from *Dynasty*." Karen hummed the song from the show that used to draw them to the TV every Wednesday night.

Sharlene walked—no, she moved like liquid, as if you could pour her into a mold and she'd freeze there. At a table next to the goddess, she flipped through the *New York Times,* the *Washington News*, and a stack of paper with yellow highlights. "Don't ever call me that. I can't believe Mother named me after that woman in Mississippi, with chickens in her house, no running water—"

"Gramma Bradley died four years ago. From diabetes." Karen stepped closer to Sharlene. "Now Mama is sick."

Sharlene faced her with an expression as unfeeling as the beige tile floor.

"Her kidneys," Karen said over a hot lump in her throat. "She needs a transplant. And you're our only hope."

Sharlene wrinkled her brow. "Hope for what?"

"To save Mama. You could donate a kidney and—"

Camille's shrill laugh echoed off the ivory taffeta walls. "That's why you've been calling? To get a vital organ from me?"

"Sharlene, please—"

"I don't believe this." Sharlene cupped her hair into a ponytail, then let it tumble. "I suppose you've got scissors in your purse! So you can just snip it out. The way Mother used to pin me down and cut off my hair. Making me feel like the ugliest little—"

"Did you hear me?" Karen grabbed her sister's arms. "Mama is dying!"

Sharlene twisted away, smoothing her sleeves. "Loud and clear. It's the most ridiculous thing I've ever heard."

Karen's pulse hammered in her ears. She felt numb and jittery. Panic made her breathe faster. But no, she had to make Sharlene understand that Mama needed her, that you're supposed to help your own blood. What could she say to make Sharlene understand her desperation? Or realize what a dangerous thing she was doing, pretending to be someone else? Karen had to convince her Mama was different, that she deserved help.

"We've got a bakery now," Karen said softly. "Biscuits 'n Honey."

A rustling sound down the hallway, on the other side of the statue, made Sharlene glance back. "No wonder she's sick. All those sweets—"

Karen stepped closer. "Daddy is home, too, trying to make up for—"

"Mention him again and I won't listen to another word." Sharlene crossed her arms once more, her gaze cold and hard. It was the same way she had looked at Daddy when they saw him the first time. That awful day when Karen felt the exhilaration of gaining a father and the devastation of losing a sister.

"If they hadn't been so irresponsible, bringing two interracial babies into the world, she wouldn't be in this mess."

The words slammed Karen in the chest.

"Don't look so shocked, *sweet praline*." Sharlene cocked her head. "She didn't care about *ghost baby*. So I left. And I'm happy. No thanks to her."

Karen's eyes burned with tears she refused to release. "Please—"

"She never got too worked up over *my* health problems," Sharlene said. "Listen." She breathed deeply, closing her eyes as her pillowy lips curled up in the corners. Her curiously larger chest rose and fell.

A guessing game was about the last thing Karen wanted. "What?"

"My lungs used to make more noise than the wind section of the Detroit Symphony Orchestra. Because Mother always had a cigarette dangling from her lips. Just to torment me."

"Get real! Mama was always taking you to the clinic or rubbing Vicks on your chest at night."

Sharlene raised her brows.

Dark Secret

"And if you hated her smoking so much, why are you joining a family that got rich with tobacco, using slaves? Pretty hypocritical—"

"Shut up!" Sharlene whispered loudly. "I will not explain myself anymore to you. Now leave."

Karen was trembling with frustration. And the thought of walking out on that street, going back to Detroit, without her sister's agreement to help Mama, well, it was not a choice. She had to try harder.

"Please just get tested," Karen said softly. "And if there's a match, the surgery is a lot safer. They make a small incision—"

"Impossible."

"You'd be back on your feet in a few days. And we could keep it secret—"

"Your ten minutes are up." Sharlene was doing that trick, like when she was little and something was making her feel bad. Her face looked like a crumpled white blouse being ironed. It was like you could see the muscles relaxing, her eyes almost glazing. She had always done it when Aunt Ruby stared her down, telling her if she ever denied who she was, she'd end up dead.

"You can't pretend forever, Sharlene."

"Watch me."

"That's what Uncle Jeremiah thought," Karen said.

"Aunt Ruby was a liar."

"You saw the pictures." Karen envisioned the dusty crate Ruby had pulled from Gramma Bradley's closet. The tattered photos were burned into her memory: a white couple in wedding finery. A caramel-skinned boy. Orphaned at birth by the mob that lynched his father as his mother slit her throat.

"Just wait 'til you and Jeffie-poo have a little brown baby."

Sharlene tilted her chin upward. "Impossible."

"Take *that* to your new family down on the plantation!"

"Shut up. I want you to leave now."

A fiftyish black woman in a gray uniform came rushing from the hallway. "Didn't know you was expectin' company, Miss Camille." The woman had a southern accent. She was breathing hard and sweating, as if she'd just run up a flight of stairs. "I woulda gone to the grocery store later on. Just got back. Whew, hot as blazes out there."

Karen couldn't help staring. The housekeeper was checking her out, too. As if she'd never seen anything darker than Sharlene walk through the door.

"Ida Mae, don't worry about it." Sharlene's voice was smooth and soft. "This is a friend from court, dropping off some research for a case."

The woman looked at Karen's hands. "I don't see no research."

Sharlene pointed to the highlighted papers on the table. "Over there."

"You gals sit down. I'll get some lemonade and cookies."

Sharlene stepped toward the door. "No, Ida Mae. She was just leaving."

"Uh-huh." The woman eyeballed Karen, then headed into the hallway.

Karen followed Sharlene. "I won't even comment on that Scarlett O'Hara scenario, *Miss Camille*. All I want is your help. For Mama."

"Sorry." Sharlene swung open the door.

"But you might as well whip out a pen and sign her death certificate—"

Sharlene was squinting in the hot sunshine. And smiling.

Karen put on her sunglasses. Just outside the door was a tall, thirty-fiveish man in jogging shorts, a sweat-stained University of Virginia T-shirt, and running shoes. He flashed a pearly smile with boyish dimples.

"Hey, honey." His sandy-blond hair bounced as he stepped through to the door. Red roses jutted from under his arm. "Got company?"

Sharlene grinned.

And Karen's heart split in half.

She doesn't give a damn that Mama is dying.

16

In Detroit, Franklin Daniels struggled to pedal his mountain bike up Woodward Avenue, his gut aching as if he'd downed too much coffee. Every time his leg pumped down, another fistful of tiny needles shot through him.

Man, I need a bathroom, fast. As he passed the quiet baseball stadium, the wooden sign on the lawn of Biscuits 'n Honey looked ten miles away. But he had to make it there and talk to Karen. He had to lose himself in the glow of her flawless caramel complexion, stare at her sensuous lips and bright smile. Then he'd decide how to unload the package in his pocket, in case things didn't go his way tomorrow. The Wish Master party was set for his house, and his future would sparkle if Otis saw things his way. But if not . . .

Franklin pedaled faster, grimacing. As he'd done for the twenty-minute ride from the other side of downtown—he was more incognito on his bike than in his black Lexus, especially in the Lions cap and ski shades—he glanced around. Had to make sure no one had their eye on him for too long.

Man, how'd I get caught up in this shit?

It was costing him Karen. His peace of mind. His reputation. Putting them in danger. Granddad had raised him to reach back and pull others along to a better place, not take Mr. Charlie's money and forget his roots. Finally, he propped his bike against the fence in back.

He tried not to breathe the nauseating sweetness wafting toward him as he knocked.

"Karen didn't tell you she left?" Ernestine asked through the screen.

"No, ma'am. Where'd she go?"

"Family business." She had a don't-do-my-daughter-wrong glare.

"Mama Ernestine, can I get some water?"

She swung open the door. Why had Karen left town, and would she be back for the press conference? All week, she'd passed messages through his secretary and cut him looks with those feline brown eyes that made his spirit dance. But she couldn't blow off the biggest night of his career. Karen just wouldn't *do* that. Franklin's need for a bathroom became more urgent.

"Mack, baby, get him some water." Ernestine headed to the giant silver mixer on the long table. Mack nodded, then took a glass to the sink.

Franklin slipped into the bathroom, locked the door. Peach potpourri in a bowl on the vanity made him want to heave. The knotty-pine cabinets blurred as he made his way to the toilet.

That old O'Jays song about money kept playing in his head. Franklin thought he loved it. And the power. But he loved Karen more. And buying stuff for himself, it just didn't bring the same rush as helping somebody with nothing get somewhere in life. Besides, the mysterious edicts from Wish Master were making him feel like a puppet. And he had no name, no face, for the very rich wizard behind the curtain. *Man, after tomorrow, come rain or shine with Wish Master, I'm gonna nip this shit in the bud. No more . . .*

17

"So who was the black chick?" Jeff's bare, glistening chest bulged as he pressed up red grips on the weight machine. Ten-pound blocks clinked as he grunted. Sunlight intensified the curious glow in his eyes and highlighted the golden hairs on his legs as he straddled the red leather bench.

Camille kept breathing in rhythm with the cross-trainers hitting the black conveyor belt. The green digits on the panel showed she'd burned 386 calories so far. But that wasn't enough to intercept those syrup-soaked pancakes yesterday at the bed-and-breakfast before they glommed onto her butt. Nor had she worked off a single pang of shock over seeing Karen next to Jeff downstairs. And she wouldn't even ponder what Ida Mae was thinking.

"She works for Judge Jenkins." Camille pushed the incline arrow upward. "Had some cases I needed for the Dickerson brief, which I need to work on today." She wanted to change the subject and get on to more important things that would put a "Mrs." in front of her name right away.

The weight machine clanged. Jeff stood, adjusting his waistband. "Couldn't see much under the hat and glasses. But something about her—"

Camille pumped her legs faster, gripping the yellow inhaler. One puff before her workout was all she needed to keep her airways open.

And the pulmonologist said exercise would keep her lungs strong.

"You're just a sucker for pretty women. Admit it."

Jeff lay on the red padded floor. "She reminded me of Sally Hemings."

"Who?"

"Fifty, fifty-one." Jeff's laced fingers behind his head guided his upper body toward the sloped ceiling. "The slave. Remember our visit to Monticello?"

The hard ridges on his stomach made something hot tingle behind Camille's belly button. "God, I love watching you do that."

"Ninety-two, ninety-three. Honey, Thomas Jefferson's mistress."

Camille chugged cold bottled water, letting a few drops dribble onto her black sports bra. "You and your history! Speaking of, what'd your dad say this morning?" She had skimmed the front-page article about Marcus Jones making headway in the polls by running those TV commercials of Jeff's father, back in the sixties, leading a rally to oppose school integration in Richmond.

"Nothing I can repeat to a woman. I thought the phone would melt in my hand, he was so steamed. Fifteen, sixteen."

"Jeff, I think I can help." Camille described her idea to shoot mud right back at Jones.

Jeff sat up, looking at her as if she was speaking Swahili. "Hell no."

"But I want to do this."

He shot to his feet. "Too dangerous. Besides, those black militants would never trust a white person."

Camille knitted her brows. "It would be a cakewalk to play a liberal Democrat—"

"A nigger lover."

Camille maintained her pace. "I can't believe you don't like my idea."

"Enough." Jeff grabbed her water bottle from the holder on the treadmill's control panel. Then he took a jump rope from a hook on the mirrored wall. It made a slicing sound as Jeff, his jaw tight and eyes straight ahead on the wooden sauna door, whipped it into an ellipse in front of her.

Camille stuck out her jaw, ignoring the stitch in her side. All this anger and adrenaline made her feel as if she could run until Christmas. How dare Karen come here! Camille still couldn't believe her sister had gotten the phone number *and* address. Was Ginger to blame for that, too? Regardless, the feeling of being under siege by her sister made it urgent that she retreat behind the security of a marriage license. But why didn't Jeff like her idea?

I'll do it anyway. Then his father will see what an asset this little orphan from Cleveland can be for his blue-blood empire. As for Jeff's mother . . .

She purred, "Baby, don't be upset. I'm just trying to help."

He whipped the rope without looking at her. "That's not your place."

"Then let's talk about the wedding."

"Huh! I mentioned it to Pop this morning. His voice alone knocked me into the bedroom wall." The rope caught on Jeff's sneaker, but he resumed the rhythm in seconds.

"I think we'll have better luck with your mother," Camille said. "When we ask her to dust off Baby Monty's bassinet."

The rope snaked at Jeff's feet. He had no expression as he looked at her.

Camille tapped her flat stomach. "By April thirtieth, to be exact."

18

The brown box of press kits was so heavy, Karen wobbled and bumped the metal doorway to the reception area outside her and Franklin's offices in Detroit's city hall. It was too early in the morning to sweat like this, or to feel as if she could just lean against the wall and go to sleep.

"Darling, give me that." Franklin came from behind. She hoped the dark circles under her own eyes weren't as ghastly as his; at least she had concealer.

"I don't need help." She trudged toward her office. All she wanted was to get through the riverfront press conference this evening, then go home and update her résumé. And for now, staying as far away from Franklin as possible. The disappointment yesterday of seeing how her sister was living, so untrue to herself and her family, reminded Karen of the importance of using your talents in righteous pursuits. As she used to do with Franklin, channeling Uncle Sam's money into programs to improve people's lives.

"Darling, today is too important to spend in the ER with a sprained back." Franklin grasped the bottom of the box, yanking it toward his crisp peach shirt and shimmery tie, the gray pin-striped trousers. His spicy cologne had a sort of nervous-sweat edge. "And it's time for a truce."

Karen attempted to straighten her cramped fingers. Dust smudged her caramel hands; the clear polish on her nails, just long enough to arc over her fingertips, had almost rubbed off. Franklin's secretary, in her yellow suit and flawless black French roll, was typing at her desk just a few feet away, facing them but staring at the screen.

"Look at me, Karen. Talk to me. Not Renée. We're adults here. Not pouting schoolgirls on the playground."

An explosion of expletives vibrated on the tip of Karen's tongue. Anything she said was sure to get blabbed down at the snack shop during Renée's morning popcorn break. Like when she had walked in on Karen and Franklin kissing in his office, before their affair became known; an aide called later asking if Karen really was fucking her boss on the windowsill.

"Come into my office," Franklin said.

Karen followed, closing the door. Wish Master jumped from every angle: teal yard signs against the desk; a black leather coat embroidered with the logo on the coat tree with Franklin's suit jacket.

"Karen, come here." He plunked the box on the ledge overlooking the river.

She crossed her arms. "What."

"Tomorrow will be different."

"You got that right." Of all the brass-framed pictures on the wall, she focused on the one of herself smiling with Franklin and the president at the Congressional Black Caucus last year in Washington.

"Darling, I've been in the fast lane with blinders on. But I'm pulling the emergency brake."

Karen rolled her eyes.

"I don't like what Wish Master is doing to me. To us."

"The damage is done."

"I'll do whatever it takes to fix it."

"You can't just squeeze some superglue on yourself and think your integrity is back together," Karen said.

The heels of Franklin's black wing tips made three ominous hits in the short beige carpet as he came close. Something in his eyes reached down and tugged at her soul. His right hand cupped the side of her head, pulling her cheek to his chest; his racing heart echoed in her ear. Karen wrapped her arms around his waist, holding tight as Franklin sobbed into the top of her head.

Karen hated that she felt sorry for him; he'd got himself into this mysterious mess. And while she wanted no part of the diamonds, the gun, the paranoia, she could not abandon Franklin in such a fragile state. And what if he was sincere about wanting to change? Didn't Mama always say it's okay to make a mistake once, just don't repeat it? So maybe Franklin deserved a second chance. Maybe. Regardless, Karen would at least see him through tonight for the mayor's announcement of whether Wish Master was in or out.

"I'm here for you," she whispered. She guided him to the couch, swatting Wish Master bumper stickers to the floor to clear a spot to sit. Then she laid his head on her lap, stroking his forehead and humming a hymn.

That evening, Karen tested the microphone while scores of people gathered before her in the shadow of a crumbling brick warehouse whose broken-out windows looked like missing teeth on a sad face.

"It's working," she said over the scream of seagulls dipping toward the river. She pointed to several folding chairs lying on the weed-clumped dirt around the podium. "We need someone to set these up. Ten minutes ago!"

One of the mayor's aides shouted commands to the crew as Karen hurried to the skirted refreshment table for more coffee. Tending to Mama's late-night vomiting had left her with three hours of sleep plagued by images of Sharlene saying no. But that had set off a brainstorm for Plan B . . . something else that might inspire Sharlene to help Mama. Now, if Karen could just get through the evening without shouting at the dozen or so Wish Master people smiling in Franklin's face over there by all the TV cameras.

"Excellent idea, Karen." The mayor's voice made her turn around. "Having the press conference here." He raised a hand toward a pile of tires and concrete slabs. "The symbolism, the potential, it's very rags-to-riches."

That phrase burned like the coffee passing her lips. Rags-to-riches for Sharlene and Franklin carried a sell-your-soul-to-the-devil price tag.

"I just want what's best for the city." Her cheeks were stiff and hot.

A few minutes later, Franklin introduced Mayor Isaac, then took a seat with the rest of the council flanking the podium. Every few minutes, he locked smiling eyes with the Wish Master folks in the front row.

" 'Arduous' does not begin to describe the task of choosing just one proposal from ten stellar blueprints for urban revival," Mayor Isaac told the buzzing crowd. "But after careful consideration, I am delighted to announce—"

Karen rested a hand on the table as the crowd became quiet.

"—that Starlight Enterprises will break ground on this very parcel of land, before winter. Starlight presented the most compelling proposal," the mayor said, "with the financial backing to build a boardwalk with restaurants, a marina, and an amusement park—"

The crowd exploded with applause and rumbles of disappointment. Franklin joined the city council in applause. But he was as gray as his suit.

About an hour later, at Franklin's house, panic quickened Karen's pulse as she stopped by the buffet of jumbo shrimp and oysters in the dining room to shake hands with the mayor and his wife. They were clinking champagne flutes with Starlight Enterprises' CEO and supporters by the doors opening onto the bustling patio, where a jazz quartet made it hard to hear anyone talking.

"Mayor Isaac, have you seen Franklin?" Karen almost shouted.

"As a matter of fact, no. But tell him to find me later. We'll talk."

Karen wove past people of all races and ages, including several women with big hair and tight dresses. No sign of Franklin in the sleek, red kitchen, or the backyard. But she had to find him, to comfort him, tell him this was probably a blessing in disguise, so he could break away from Wish Master. She rushed to the upstairs hallway, past a line of people outside the bathroom. Passing them, Karen knocked on the door to the master bedroom. "Franklin?"

She opened the door. The room was dark and reeked of fruity

cologne. Had one of those hoochie mommas at the bar down in the basement lured some guy upstairs for sex? A strip of light glowed under the bathroom door. It sounded as if the whirlpool tub was running. And water was seeping from the white floor onto the bedroom carpet.

Pink water.

His name squeaked from her mouth.

She wrapped trembling fingers around the doorknob. Turned, pushed.

Blood bubbled in the overflowing Jacuzzi.

On the floor, water washed over the handgun she had seen with the diamonds. And Franklin slumped lifeless in the steam, part of his head splattered on the jade ceramic wall.

19

Jeff Stone fanned his fingers across Camille's bare stomach, pulling her backside into his chest and slightly bent knees. Her warmth, along with the vanilla scent of her hair and skin, made him feel as mellow and languid as if he'd tossed back a couple shots of Jack Daniel's.

"I'm sorry, honey," he whispered. All week, he'd left before dawn, spending days in court, evenings at the office consulting with Uncle John about how to handle curve balls from the defense. Then he'd come home, slipping under the covers and holding Camille as she feigned sleep. Now he was ready to talk about how a baby would change things. And he wanted to tell her how they should proceed. "Mrs. Andrews took the stand today," he said. "Said her accident made her realize what's important in life."

Camille lifted his hand from her stomach and pushed it back.

"Honey, listen. It made me think about you and the baby."

Balancing on an elbow, he stared at the cascade of hair and the still curve of Camille's hip under the satiny bedspread.

"Camille." He gently pulled her shoulder, making her lie back on the pillows, looking at him with wet eyes. "Oh, honey, don't cry."

"You don't want the baby!"

Jeff pulled her close enough to feel her hot breath on his neck. "Ssshh. Yes, I want you to know—"

"I haven't missed a pill. But Dr. Bryant said sometimes you can still—"

"Honey, ssshhh." Her back muscles trembled under his palms.

"Today she said," Camille whispered, "she said I can make arrangements to take care of it if you're that opposed—"

Jeff sat up, grabbing her elbows to pull her up, too. "You will not!"

Her eyes glistened behind a wild tangle of hair. "But you don't—"

"I'm trying to tell you!" He stared into her eyes. "Pop's threat and Mom's reaction to the engagement. I kinda freaked when you told me. But now I think it can work to our advantage." He pushed her hair over her shoulders and said, "We should tell them in person. This weekend. I think Mom will—"

Camille shook her head. "No, Jeff. You still haven't said you *want* the baby. That you're happy about it."

Jeff cupped her jaw. "Lady Godiva, listen to me. I love you more than anything in life. Anything. Anybody. And our child growing inside you is beautiful evidence of that."

Camille's face was smooth, but something flashed in her eyes. "Why did it take you four days to say that?"

"I'm sorry, honey. I was still smarting from the way Pop looked at us and kept talking about Tabitha. So it floored me when you—"

"Floored? What about me? All week you've been gone. And I could've done without your little five-minute phone calls at work because your mind was obviously elsewhere. I can't believe you're hurting me like this, Jeff."

"No, I never want to hurt you. Ever."

"And if this is how you deal with heavy news, then maybe marriage isn't such a good idea. Is that how your dad was? Gone and unavailable?"

"Enough!" An unspeakable urge pulsed through him. A compulsion Pop could never control. An impulse that Jeff hoped never to act out, especially with Camille. But how dare she bring Pop into this discussion! Why couldn't she understand he just needed some time to think about it all? That he would give his right leg if she needed it? And there was a lot to ponder, especially Pop's threat. Would he really deny him the family fortune for marrying down?

Dark Secret

Jeff hated the hypocrisy of his parents teaching him and the other kids to value a person for their heart and accomplishments while encouraging them to stick to their own kind. Jackson had. But Davis and his mysterious business dealings, and those Asian chicks he liked, and Rand with his community center in Harlem, they were basically telling Mom and Pop to screw it. So was Dixie, with her refusal to conform to Mom's southern belle expectations. What all this meant, after days of processing, was that Jeff would marry Camille and have the baby, and make his parents happy about it.

He picked up the phone.

Camille's eyes widened. "What are you doing?"

"Calling my parents. We'll go down Saturday, tell them the good news."

20

Karen's knees threatened to buckle as she approached Franklin's closed casket at the altar of the huge Baptist church in Detroit. Elaborate flower arrangements became dizzying kaleidoscopes; the low buzz of thousands of people packing the aisle and pews behind her made it hard to focus.

But she had to stay composed and make it through the funeral. Too many people were watching and whispering for her to throw herself on the gleaming black coffin and scream, "Why, Franklin? What could have been so bad to make you do that? And let *me* find you?"

Karen held a clump of tissues to her nose. She wished her parents had come, but Mama couldn't reschedule or miss her dialysis. And Daddy had to take her on the twenty-minute drive to the clinic, where for several hours she would sit reading the Bible or cookbooks while her blood pumped through a tube to a cleaning machine, then back into her body. Without dialysis, Mama would end up just like Franklin.

No! Never! Sharlene has got to help . . .

Something hot and numbing made Karen feel disconnected from her body, walking to a front pew. Her thick braid pressed into her back as she sat by the center aisle, focusing on damp tissues on the lap of her black dress.

"That ain't what I heard," a woman passing by said. "My friend at police headquarters said she the only one who coulda shot him from that angle. Even though they officially callin' it a suicide."

The other woman sucked her teeth. "Serve that girl right. Switchin' through city hall like she in a rap video with that hair down her back."

"You know Franklin's ex-wife was dark-skinned," the first woman said. "And his daughter hate Karen Bradley 'cause she so young and—"

Through swollen eyes, Karen glanced up at the women. In their forties, they were vaguely familiar from the halls of the Coleman A. Young Municipal Center. Karen said flatly, "I think Franklin would have preferred you not come to show your *dis*respect." She cut her eyes back down to her fidgety fingers as the women shuffled forward. Then a black dress in her peripheral vision made her look up and say, "Zora, I'm so sorry—"

Hostility pinched her wet, brown face. Franklin's daughter curved over Karen like a tree branch. "Bitch! You killed my daddy!"

The crowd hushed; heads turned.

Karen stood. "Zora, calm down. Your father—"

Zora crossed her arms. "Don't tell me—"

Franklin's ex, the same height and size and also in black, pulled Zora away. "It's not her fault." She said "her" with the corners of her mouth turned down, the word coming out like a poison dart.

Malice burned in Zora's eyes. "My daddy shoulda been arrested for bein' with a high yellow sack-chaser like you. You killed him!"

Her mother dragged her away. But the curious stares of strangers, the city council, and the mayor who was seated with dignitaries near the altar, made Karen want to disappear. How could people say and think such horrible things about her? And what could she do to set the record straight? She'd spent most of Monday night, after Franklin died, at police headquarters, answering the same questions over and over. She told investigators about the gun, the diamonds, the fruity smell in the bedroom. But when she led them to the brass box in Franklin's home office, it was empty. And the jewels were gone.

Somehow, everything Karen told the police ended up in the next day's *Detroit Free Press* with a picture of her and Franklin dancing at the mayor's inaugural ball. And every day since, the papers and TV stations had run reports about whether his death was linked to the riverfront project.

Somber organ music played; Karen concentrated on stiffening her face and lips to hold back a hot wave of sobs. But her shoulders trembled, her limbs ached. Only after she let it spew forth could she calm down and maybe endure the funeral. So she bolted down the aisle, to a back hallway, into the women's lounge. She darted into a stall, not locking the door. Instead she leaned against the pink metal wall, taking deep breaths. The tap of two pairs of high heels on the tile floor grew louder.

"You know Franklin was up to his ass in Wish Master." That was Franklin's secretary, going into a stall, locking it. "I wouldn't put it past Karen to do it 'cause she was so pissed off he lost a deal for all that dough."

Someone else popped open a compact. "She doesn't strike me as that type." This voice was proper, unfamiliar. "Actually, neither did he—"

"Well, her mother is sick," Renée said. "A big reason to go off."

Karen could hear a brush going through hair and Renée's tinkle.

"I heard her father is white," the other woman said.

"Franklin liked a lot of cream in his coffee. Wouldn't give me the time of day if he wasn't asking me to type something or get somebody on the phone."

The proper woman chuckled. "Sounds like the green-eyed monster has got you. The only time I met Karen, she spent fifteen minutes explaining the new antidrug program in the schools. I could tell she really cared about it."

Renée flushed. "Can't stand pretty bitches like her. Things come too easy for them. But now she's gettin' her due."

Karen's whole body stung. Red-hot rage punched down her sobs. Easy? No, it seemed life was getting harder by the minute. No way could she go back into that church; she wanted to go home, tell Mama she loved her, that she would do anything to keep her here. But first, she had to clear the air with Renée.

Karen bolted from the stall, staring into Renée's venomous eyes, saying, "I feel sorry for you. Being that angry all the time, lashing out

Dark Secret

at people who've been nothing but polite and professional toward you."

Karen hurried through the long, Gothic-arched hallway, lit by the glow of stained glass on one side. Shoving her hand into her brown leather purse, her forearm disappeared in search of car keys. Distant organ music made her think of Franklin's body in a casket. She remembered the horror frozen on what was left of his face in the Jacuzzi. A chill quickened her pace.

"Cutie pie." The hard, gravelly voice shot from the shadows. An arm, too. Someone yanked her up the stone steps of a narrow stairwell.

"What—"

It was a lanky man whose onyx eyes took her breath away.

"Where's the loot?" He pulled her close to his charcoal face, so smooth it shone in the shadows. His black hair was molded into finger waves.

Karen's throat felt like sandpaper.

He pinched her arm harder, pulled her into his electric-blue suit. "Show me the diamonds, cutie pie!"

Karen gasped. That fruity cologne . . .

She tried to pry his skinny fingers from her arm. "Let go!"

He pinched harder.

A scream lodged in her throat.

He shoved her into the wall. Her head thudded into the stone.

"Find the loot, cutie pie. Or you a dead bitch."

21

Camille followed Jeff into the two-story solarium, lit by the moon and lights shooting up into the trees and lush plants. Mrs. Stone was curled up under a reading lamp in an oversized white wicker chair with daisy print cushions. She was reading *Fortune*. That reminded Camille of Senator Stone and her plan to woo his affection. She had already rented the apartment in Richmond and gotten acquainted with Marcus Jones's campaign manager. Hopefully the rest would fall into place.

"Mom," Jeff said, "when is Pop coming back? It's already nine o'clock."

She removed mother-of-pearl glasses. "My gracious, Jeff. You know when your father is campaigning, he loses all track of time."

"We need to talk to both of you," he said. "Urgently." Camille joined him on the white wicker love seat.

Mrs. Stone, her eyes bloodshot and puffy, picked lint from the knee of her heather-gray lounging pants. "We've had a talk. You know how we feel."

Camille wished Dixie were home from school in Charlottesville for the weekend. Judging by her reaction to the baby at Rand's center, Dixie would be thrilled over the idea of a little niece or nephew. Camille would call her in the morning; her enthusiasm could no doubt inspire acceptance from Mrs. Stone.

"That's why we came down today," Jeff said. "Pop knew—" He held Camille's hand where their bare legs touched. "Mom, something has changed."

"What now, pray tell?" Mrs. Stone set her magazine on an ottoman.

"You're going to be a grandmother again."

Mrs. Stone's diamond-shaped face, her blue eyes, showed as much reaction as the large green leaves around them. Until she fingered her locket, and shifted her gaze to Camille. "Are you sure?"

"Yes," Camille said softly. "My doctor says I'm six weeks along."

"Gracious."

"The proper thing to do," Jeff said softly, "is to get married right away."

Mrs. Stone's head drew back ever so slightly. "The proper thing to do would be to avoid this situation altogether. In my day, young lady, you would be sent away, and the baby would be kept under wraps."

The circular brick pattern on the floor danced; Camille's cheeks burned.

"Mom, we want a wedding here. Next month. In the gardens, just like you and Pop." The softness in his voice made Camille's stomach flutter.

But Mrs. Stone's eyes made her feel frozen stiff.

"If, in fact, you are carrying the next generation, then of course you will legitimize it. But I will only talk to your father about this"— she cast a quick look at Jeff, then Camille—"after a pregnancy test. I'll send Ida Mae or Hortense to the pharmacy now. You'll take it first thing in the morning."

Mrs. Stone picked up the phone on the glass-topped wicker table to her right. She punched two numbers and said, "Ida Mae, come to the solarium."

Camille could feel a gale-force brainstorm being churned up by Mrs. Stone's sharp gaze. Why wasn't Jeff challenging his mother? Did he not believe her, either? Or was he afraid? Regardless, Camille had about twelve hours to jump through this seemingly impossible hoop without a scratch.

Ida Mae hurried down the back stairs, toward them, her face taut.

Wringing hands in her apron, she flashed a panicky look at Mrs. Stone. "Gracious—" Mrs. Stone bolted toward Ida Mae.

The maid stood on tiptoes to face Mrs. Stone's ear. Her black bun moved up and down, back and forth as she whispered.

Camille strained to hear, picking up Ida Mae's murmur of "Dr. Zane" and "she" several times and "the fever."

"My gracious," Mrs. Stone said softly. "It can't happen again."

Jeff stood, knitting his brows. "Mom, why is Dr. Zane here?"

Mrs. Stone, eyes aglow with alarm, sandwiched Ida Mae's hand with her own palms; they laced clenched fingers. Her bracelets jangled as they hurried toward the white marble hallway, then up the staircase.

Jeff's quick strides slapped the brick floor; his mother turned back. Her stern expression made him stop and grind his teeth.

Camille stood, hooking his arm. "Maybe that maid, Sarah, is in labor."

"Then we call an ambulance, not our family doctor. Besides, the servants' quarters are downstairs. Sue Ann and Jackson are in Savannah—"

Camille pulled him toward the kitchen. "Who knows, Jeff. Let's go watch a movie or something." The clandestine house call—and Mrs. Stone and Ida Mae's shared concern—were bizarre. Could it have anything to do with that face Camille saw in the window during Dixie's party? Or did Senator Stone have some crazy first wife hidden away in the attic, like Rochester did in *Jane Eyre?* Regardless, Camille needed to spend her brain energy on treating a medical emergency of her own: Mrs. Stone's pop pregnancy quiz.

22

The blue digits on Karen's clock blinked 12:05 A.M. She craved the peace of sleep, if only she could still the torturous troop of worries about Sharlene hanging up on her, Mama getting sicker, and that man threatening her at the funeral. Karen slipped out of bed, hoping a glass of milk and some peanut butter cookies from Biscuits 'n Honey might help her fall asleep. She stepped down the spiral staircase to her living room, silent except for traffic noises on Jefferson Avenue and the humming refrigerator. She crept through bluish shadows cast by streetlights through multipaned windows.

Scritch-scratch! It sounded like metal scraping metal, like a screwdriver on the doorknob out in the apartment building's hallway. Heart pounding, Karen crept across the carpet, toward the phone in the open kitchen.

Tiny strips of light framed the dark door, except for the inch-wide bolt and the hinges. And two dark spots on the floor. The space was large enough for her to see feet. Large ones.

The door shook against its frame. The men's boots shifted.

Karen tiptoed closer to the door, into the kitchen. With a shaking hand she pried the cordless phone from its cradle on the small island. She pointed an index finger at the greenish keypad, but froze.

The door stopped rattling. Metal clinked. Was the bolt opening?

Karen crept into the walk-in coat closet just in front of the door.

Slipped into knee-high boots, ducked behind coats. Her damp fingers hit the 9 and 1 buttons, just as she heard the apartment door swing open.

Her throat was dry as dust. "Someone's in my apartment."

"Are you alone, ma'am?" The operator's voice seemed so loud.

"Please," she whispered. "I think—"

He was ransacking kitchen cupboards, knocking CDs off the rack, getting closer to the closet.

23

Camille let tears roll down her burning cheeks. She sank deeper
into the plush red couch, under Jeff's arm. Watching *Jefferson in Paris*
here in the media room of White Pines was not her idea of a relaxing
Saturday night. It was bad enough mulling over how to pass Mrs.
Stone's pregnancy test in the morning. But now, after Jeff had overruled her choice of the romantic comedy *You've Got Mail*, Camille
just wanted to end this cinematic foray into the scurrilous liaisons between masters and slaves.

"Where I'm gon' go?" Sally Hemings's pretty face crumpled into
a sob. She was larger than life on the huge screen as Thomas Jefferson
talked about freedom. But Sally knew only slavery and love for the
man who *owned* her.

Jeff dabbed Camille's face with a tissue. "Honey, it's only a
movie," he whispered, then scooped a handful of popcorn from the
bowl in his lap. "See, slavery had its tender moments. But all those
militant blacks, they want you to think the slaves were mistreated—"

"They were *property*," Camille said, more forcefully than she intended. "Beaten, raped, forced to do grueling work without getting
paid—"

"Hey, whose side are you on?" Jeff asked, scooping more popcorn.

"I'm not on a side. But that romantic view of slavery is not accurate."

"It was accurate at Monticello. And right here at White Pines." He stood, leading her by the hand into the long, tiled hallway. "I admit, my"—Jeff moved his finger in the air as if he was counting—"great-great-great-great-great-grandfather found his daughter messing with a house nigger who was her half-brother. That boy found himself at the wrong end of a rope."

Sourness bubbled from Camille's gut. She wanted to clamp palms over her ears. "Hung his own child?"

"The boy was a slave, like his mom."

The hairs on the back of Camille's neck rose as they passed the huge, pitch-black dining room. The room where Jeff's ancestor had taken his meals, might have even decided to kill his half-black son. From the vaulted, ceiling-beamed kitchen, a twangy voice said, "You coloreds don't do anything right anymore!"

Camille tensed. It was Grandma Stone, standing by the granite-topped island in her robe as the young maid, Sarah, put a lemon wedge in a steaming cup. She waddled to the stainless-steel gourmet stove. There, under the shiny copper hood, Sarah paused, grasping her huge belly straining the white buttons on her gray uniform. Camille asked, "Sarah, you feel all right?"

The maid's dewy face lit up. "Just slow. Got a couple weeks yet."

"Come sit down for a minute." Camille guided Sarah to the long wooden table under a wall of windows overlooking the lighted patio. Perhaps she'd just found the answer to her pregnancy test dilemma. "I'll get you some water."

As Camille retrieved a glass and headed to the refrigerator, Grandma Stone held her arms out to Jeff. "Dear Jefferson. Kiss me good night."

Jeff bent toward her forehead, as wrinkled as if someone had crumpled a white paper bag into a tight ball, then stretched it over her skull. Her knot of white hair accentuated caved-in cheeks as she glared at Camille.

I bet she'll die without saying one word to me. Jeff had said his grand-mother distrusted Yankees, especially those without a blue-blood pedigree. But maybe she had some southern matron's black blood detector that was beeping now.

Jeff stepped toward the carved walnut cupboards. He lifted a glass dome from a pastry plate, cut himself a piece of pecan pie. He strode past a breakfront displaying a copper still used for making corn whiskey and brandy in colonial times, then sat on the huge hearth whose field-stone pattern covered an entire wall. The twelve-foot fireplace, Jeff had said once, was big enough to roast a whole ox in the old days. And above the firewood cubbyholes were two bluish oval stones above a pinkish triangle—like a face that had witnessed centuries of mistresses and slaves, whites and blacks, on this original brick floor. "Grandma, I'd like you to cozy up to Camille. We're getting married."

The old woman clanged her spoon against the china, looking at the tops of the cabinets, where sprays of dried sage perfumed the room when Hortense wasn't whipping up her melt-in-your-mouth butter-fried chicken or crab stew.

"Should stick to your own kind," Grandma Stone whispered.

Camille gave Sarah the water. "Take it easy. I'll check on you later."

Bewilderment flashed in Sarah's eyes; she gulped the water and nodded.

Jeff set his plate on the island, then took Camille's hand. He led her into the foyer, whose shiny opulence always brought to mind the image of Mother blasting eerie blue flames on the stove when the heat was cut off. And how she and Karen would drag their dingy mattress onto the kitchen floor, so the February freeze in their bedroom wouldn't kill them. Fighting off roaches all night. Not sleeping for fear the house would burn down.

Stop! That's not my life anymore. This is . . .

Camille followed Jeff into the library.

"Honey, let's take a peek at the past," Jeff said, flipping open one of several leather-bound books on the huge mahogany desk.

Camille walked past the burgundy leather couch and two wing chairs facing a fireplace as tall as Jeff. "What's that?"

"My granddaddy's journals and Bibles. Pop's using them to re-search his book, with all those boxes over there. But you wouldn't believe the juicy shit inside them." Jeff sank into the desk chair, his eyes aglow with mischief. "Honey, close the doors. Listen, Randolph Stone the Fourth wrote this in 1725. The year he got his wife and a slave pregnant at the same time." Jeff read:

"Many months ago, Victoria learned that Lucy was my con-
cubine. Little does she know our relations began long before
we married in the garden of White Pines. For my love for the
mulatto daughter of a slave named Tess blossomed long before
I ever met my wife."

Camille, heading toward the door framed in bookshelves so high
there was a wooden ladder on a track around the room, said, "Jeff, I
can't believe—"

"Honey, listen." He read:

"Perhaps I felt empathy for the poor girl, knowing that her
conception began in a drunken rage, when my uncle stole
Tess's maidenhead on the muddy slope by the river. Lucy's
sunny disposition, with her black plaits bouncing as she
skipped toward me in the yard, prevented her from believing
this. Especially when we frolicked in the pond. And I, enraptured by her yellow skin as radiant as the brightest star—"

Camille closed the doors, remembering not to look up at the glass-
covered brand that had sizzled black flesh, or the tattered Confederate
flag that one of Jeff's ancestors had gripped as he bled to death on some
Civil War battlefield not far from here. "Jeff, I really don't want to—"

"Just listen."

Camille crossed her arms, catching a glimpse of the gilt-framed
painting of Randolph Stone, its plate at the bottom saying "1609–
1667." He was tall, lean, and dressed in formal colonial clothes. And
with his pointed nose and full head of silver hair, it seemed his gray
eyes were X-raying her very soul.

Repulsion zigzagged through her. And she thought of Mother.
*Some slave owner wouldn't have to sell me up the river, away from my mother
and father and sister. I'm doing it myself.*

Numbing sadness crept through her. The woman who had given
her life needed her now. Simple as that. But here she was, spending
the night in a racial house of horrors, wishing this family with its
repulsive past would love her as one of their own. Yet she had no
recollection of love from Mother. None. Just the image of Mother

squinting through smoke spiraling from a cigarette between her lips, saying, "Ghost baby, mop that floor."

"Honey, are you listening?"

Camille met Jeff's gaze. Yes, the look that wrapped her sad heart in a cashmere cocoon of love and affection, shielding her from all that had hurt her in the past. And for that, a few hours of secretly nursing her throbbing racial nerve was a paltry price to pay.

She hurried toward him, perching on the arm of his chair. "Yes, baby. Read on." She glanced at the chicken-scratch writing on brittle yellow pages. "Don't let me get close to all that dust and mildew. My lungs couldn't take it."

Jeff pushed it farther up on the desk and kept reading:

> "Lucy ripened like a peach before my very eyes. She beamed with gaiety, and her gentle hands could massage away the nastiest of riding injuries. One particular time, when I first tasted her lips, I was drunken and worthless for days. Quite naturally, I lost my mind, my virginity, and my heart to her voluptuous flesh. For that reason, perhaps Victoria could see in my eyes the affection I harbored for the slave girl who was my true love. And when she saw that Lucy's belly swelled at a rate identical to her own, Victoria lashed me with her tongue. But that did not stop me from retiring to Lucy's bed where she held me close to her warm hills of flesh until I fell into an infantlike slumber. Never could I escape the sultry allure of my fair Lucy's bosom, as smooth and sweet as butter-cream."

Jeff put Camille's hand in his lap. A huge erection bulged his jeans. "I can't believe you're getting turned on by this stuff."

"Forbidden lust." He licked her ear. Then continued:

> "However, a few weeks later, I was informed that Lucy had run away with a rebellious buck called Molasses Joe for his slow manner of speech. Overnight, my wife became the gay, witty woman I knew as my bride. But quite naturally, I felt enraged for losing such valuable property—for Lucy was

handy in the kitchen, and Joe could plow like no other—and betrayed by the slave girl who had pledged her love to me, and who carried my growing seed. Without hesitation, I ordered them hunted down. Joe was never found. But, two years later, Lucy was discovered in a small coastal town, married to a silversmith with two babies. And living as a free white woman. It was my privilege to have her walked back to White Pines, our baby in her arms, where I unleashed the wrath of her abandonment and deception under my cracking whip. I can still hear her flesh bursting, the thin cotton of her dress ripping as her crimson blood seeped—"

"That's enough, Jeff."

"Wait." He dashed toward one of the boxes on the floor. He rifled through it, pulling out a lock of dark, curly hair and a grayish lump of fabric. As he held it up, light shone through its shredded, stained back.

"Oh, Jeff, please don't tell me that's—"

"Lucy's dress. And her hair! Ida Mae told me it was here somewhere, because my family never gets rid of anything."

Camille coughed. "I'm afraid to ask what happened to Lucy."

Jeff returned to the journal, skimmed several pages. "She died. The baby became the servant to his first child with Victoria." He ran his fingers over the dusty page. "Victoria confessed . . . she had sent Lucy away to marry the silversmith. Just to get her away from Randolph."

Camille felt ill, her chest getting tighter. *Need my inhaler . . .*

But before she could speak, Jeff pulled her onto his lap, slurping her neck. He squeezed her breasts through her sleeveless white blouse, stroked her thighs bared by white denim shorts. She grasped his hands. "Your parents!"

"They're sleeping." He planted his hot, open mouth on her lips.

Erotic tingles rippled through her, igniting a throb between her legs.

"I want you now," Jeff panted. Something ravenous glinted in his eyes.

"Tell me how much you love me," she said.

"More than Randolph Stone loved Lucy."

Camille slid to her feet. "Not here."

"I said I want you now." Jeff grasped the back of her head, yanked her close for a roguish kiss that sucked away her breath.

She had to get away from those dusty books that made it hard to inhale. Camille pulled back a few inches, staring into his eyes. Then she stuck her tongue way out. Licked the side of his face, from jaw to sweaty hairline.

"You wanna fuck me right here?" She trained her voice to sound like a kitten purring. "Right on top of your granddaddy's scandal sheets?"

A lusty grunt escaped Jeff's parted, glistening lips.

She traced his figure-eight-shaped mouth with a fingernail. "Then you gotta take it."

Jeff stood, yanked open his jeans. He ripped down her shorts and panties. Shoved her cheek-down onto the desk. Rammed her from the back.

Camille gasped. Her face crushed against a dusty page of the journal. Jeff snatched off her barrette, letting her hair pour over the desk.

The sound of skin slapping skin, pages crinkling beneath her, blocked the soft whistle of her chest. *I'll use my inhaler when we go upstairs.*

"Yes," she moaned. "Do me like that." Jeff hadn't felt this huge and diamond-hard since the time she had given him a blow job in the pantry of that fancy Fifth Avenue apartment, during that wake-me-when-it's-over dinner with clients. That was a close second to the night she had made a necklace of herself in that Jamaican bungalow, her tanned thighs the chain, her lacy black thong the pendant. *No, I won't think about what got him this turned on. I can't . . .*

Maybe they could go swimming in the morning. After she passed the pregnancy test, hopefully with the maid's secret help. Then Mrs. Stone would all but whip out the latest edition of *Martha Stewart Weddings . . .*

"Honey, you never felt so good." His voice had an animal bass pitch as he dug his fingertips into the flesh on her hips. Hurting her.

"Stop!" She tried to pry off his grip. His face glistened. Hair stuck up in wet tufts. "Jeff! You're hurting me!"

But he stared straight ahead, as if watching a movie or reading a book behind the glaze in his eyes. And bruising her inside.

Camille coughed. Tried to twist away.

If I don't get my medicine soon, I'll pass out.

24

Karen's fear dissolved under a red cloud of anger as she surveyed white stuffing pouring from her black leather couch.

"He was definitely looking for something," the police officer said over the radio crackling at his hip. His partner was upstairs, where dresses, shoes, and purses carpeted the bedroom floor.

"Lieutenant Sykes, I told you. The Wish Master people think I took Franklin's diamonds." Karen crossed her arms over the sweats she'd thrown on over her tank top and boxer shorts. "I'm telling you, I think he killed Franklin."

The officer scribbled notes on a small pad, taking long strides, his face showing no reaction to the overturned chairs or the closet spilling coats like a gutted fish.

"Look, Miss Bradley, if I were you, I'd keep that wild shit about the diamonds to myself," he said. "Just between us, you're lucky you're not counting sheep in the Wayne County Jail tonight."

"Excuse me?"

"If Franklin Daniels's ex-wife had her way, you'd be *under* the jail."

"Get real." She inhaled loudly through her nose. "Can't you smell that? Like raspberry cough syrup. That man's cologne. It's the same—"

The officer stepped close. "Miss Bradley, calm down. You understand, now, that some might say you staged this tonight? Just to deflect suspicion—"

Karen rushed to the door. "If you're done with your noninvestigation, I need some sleep."

"I'd be careful if I were you," the officer said as he and his partner left.

Karen glared at the backs of their heads. "I'd be careful not to feel like an idiot when you find out I'm right." She slammed the door.

On the table was the program from Franklin's funeral. She grabbed it, ripped it to bits, let it snow toward the floor.

"Damn you, Franklin!"

But how could she stop gossip? How could she wash away the suspicion? And make that thug leave her alone?

She didn't know, but she would figure it out. After she got some rest at her parents' house. Karen snatched up her keys and fled into the night.

25

Jeff perched on the wine-velvet bench at the foot of the chiseled mahogany bed, pulling on white cotton pajamas. The only light in the Victoria Suite was the small fringed lamp on the vanity where Camille was brushing her hair. It cast a golden aura around her and glowed against the scarlet walls and endless folds of tasseled drapes over the French doors leading to the veranda.

But an electric current of female attitude wended from her plush stool past the dark armoire and dresser, the curtained archway to the sitting area and bathroom, over the vast burgundy rug crackling at Jeff's bare feet.

"Honey, explain why you're so upset."

Camille brushed so fast and hard, it made static popping sounds.

And even with her jaw stuck out, her eyes unwilling to meet his in the mirror, Camille was luscious beyond words. As if she had stepped right off the shiny pages of that tattered girlie magazine he and his best friend, Dillon, would pull from between the mattresses at boarding school: Lady Godiva, doing things atop the horse with any eleventh-century English villager, male or female, who dared join her in the town square, indulging Jeff in his first orgasm. It seemed those sweaty, trembling moments had seared her image to his psyche, turning his insides to grits every time he laid eyes on Camille.

Jeff strode toward her, wondering how tonight was any different from all those times back in their bedroom in New York, when she put on that black garter belt or her French maid's costume and read him X-rated letters in the *Penthouse* "Forum" as an erotic prelude to making love. Slow, fast, rough, gentle. Reciting from the journals was the same, except tonight's tale about Randolph and Lucy had been written centuries ago. And this time, Jeff had done the reading.

Now, with the same concentration as if he were sailing, trying to gauge the strength and direction of the wind on his cheeks, he wanted to understand why she was so upset, and what he could do to make it better. After all, tomorrow they'd have reason to celebrate. Towering over her, he ran a fingertip along the ivory satin strap of one of those shimmery nightgowns she was always wearing. "Honey," he whispered, "you like it rough."

She slammed down the silver brush. In the mirror, she glared at him. "You became someone else, Jeff."

Confusion flashed in her eyes as he traced her clavicle, stopping to finger the diamond in the hollow of her neck. "I was just horny," he said.

"You hurt me. And I couldn't breathe."

He exhaled. "I didn't realize—"

Camille grasped the hairbrush, pointing it at him. "You were possessed. Like you were having some kinky, interracial, slave days flashback."

Jeff placed his hand on hers, stilling the brush. "Honey, explain how tonight was any different than story time at home."

Camille raised her brows. "If I don't breathe, the baby doesn't breathe."

"So this is about being pregnant."

"Think what you want."

"I don't know what to think! Two days ago, when we did it after dinner, you said our sex life wouldn't change."

Camille scowled at him in the mirror. "Don't ever hurt me again."

"You can't possibly think I would." He glanced at her stomach, feeling something warm and proud gush inside at the thought of giving his parents the next generation. "Especially now."

Camille shot up, staring into his eyes as if looking for something. Then she swayed into the bathroom and slammed the door.

"Shit!" Jeff balled his fist, punched the hump of damask still warm from her bottom. He would never do the kinds of things Pop did. Never. But was this a hormonal mood swing? Would he have to deal with nine months of this? No, maybe tonight she was just upset that Mom wanted proof before saying yes to the wedding. In the morning, Camille would be back to normal. Now it sounded like she was running a bath. And sobbing.

Jeff bolted to the bathroom door. But his knuckles stopped just short of the dark-stained wood. She needed time to cool off, to realize the irrationality of her outburst. So he turned off the light and climbed into bed.

But he couldn't shake the downright craving that made him want to devour Camille right now. The urge was as strong as the moment he had first seen her on the witness stand, in that 1896-style men's suit, her hair pulled back, during the NYC mock trials. He remembered every detail:

"And why is it, Mr. Plessy, that because you say you're one-eighth black," Jeff said, stepping close to the wooden witness box for dramatic effect for the jury and to look deeper into her unusually shaped eyes, "you should scoff at the law and ride in the whites-only train car? After all, this law isn't about pigment, it's about blood. Black blood."

She raised her chin, holding his stare. "That mixture of colored blood, sir, is so insignificant, I should be entitled to every right of the white race."

The courtroom, packed with her law school classmates and professors, was silent. Until Jeff laid out the law, just as the U.S. Supreme Court had, by convincing the jury that the 1890 Louisiana legislation requiring "equal but separate accommodations" for black and white railroad passengers did in fact apply to Mr. Plessy, despite his white appearance. So Mr. Plessy was still relegated to the black railroad car.

At a reception immediately following, where Camille wore a short skirt, her hair tumbling over her shoulders, Jeff did not think about his engagement to Tabitha and their upcoming wedding. All he wanted was to taste Camille's pillowy lips and bury his face in those breasts, as a sort of *sayonara* to bachelorhood. So he invited her to a nearby café for coffee.

"Thanks," she said, "but tonight I have to get deep into the briefs."

Jeff chuckled. "I assume you mean legal briefs?"

She gave him the once-over. "You're the big-time lawyer. You decide."

Then she pivoted on a high heel and sauntered away, leaving a breeze of perfume and the start of a hard-on in her wake. Then, and now. Jeff reached under the blankets to stroke himself. Maybe if he made love to her soft and slow, she'd forget whatever had made her mad down in the library.

The bathroom door swung open; Camille made her way through the dark, climbed onto the far edge of the bed.

"Honey, I was just thinking about the day we met," he whispered, sliding toward her. "And I love you more today than—"

"I can't believe you're going along with your mother's little mandate for a pregnancy test." Her harsh tone hung in the silence. The blankets ruffled as she wiggled away.

"Snap out of it, Camille! If that's what it takes for a yes on the wedding, then so be it." Jeff bolted into the sitting room. He hit the POWER button on the remote so hard, it slipped from his hand as a baseball game clicked on. So he picked it up again, threw it against the wall, where it rained in pieces, and the television went dark.

A teardrop spilled from Camille's eye as she studied the darkness while Jeff breathed heavily on his side of the bed. Her skin and muscles still burned from that near-boiling bath. But it had not washed away her newfound guilt about Mother dying. Karen pleading for help. Hearing the raw racial history of White Pines. Wanting so desperately to become part of it.

Now all she wanted was the oblivion of sleep. But as she closed her eyes, the ceiling creaked. Or was it the floor? Her heart pounded in her ears. The shadows remained still, yet she could feel something. Someone.

It's Lucy, warning me to end the masquerade.

Camille imagined the dead slave, telling her to go back to her own kin, because blood was more important than love and money. She could almost hear Lucy warning that if the genteel wife Victoria could get her killed, surely the husbands could do worse. Or maybe it was

Victoria coming from the grave, screaming, "You can't get away with this, you Nigra wench!"

"Yes, I can," Camille whispered. And just to make sure, she slipped out of bed, into a robe. It was time to check on Sarah down in the maid's quarters.

26

Karen stormed into her office, where Renée was tossing books, papers, and pens into a dusty box. "Stop!"

Renée snarled. "The mayor wants you out in an hour."

Karen called the mayor's secretary. "That is correct, Ms. Bradley. Remove your belongings by ten." She slammed down the phone.

"Renée, leave. I can do this myself." Alone, Karen surveyed the room where she'd spent so many satisfying days, evenings, weekends, doing important work that helped people.

Damn you, Franklin! I'm not leaving until I line up another job. I deserve better than this. Karen fished her Rolodex from a box on the floor. She called a half-dozen political contacts all over the country, made mostly during Democratic conferences with Franklin. They were always saying to call if she ever needed anything. Finally, she called Freida.

"What about your own PR firm?" Freida said over the tap of her keyboard. "You were always talking about that at school."

Karen wrapped a picture of herself and Franklin in newspaper, placed it in the box. "Starting a business? Maybe when Mama's better."

"Then I know a senator who's desperate for a press secretary."

"Republican?" Karen asked, putting plaques into a box.

"To say the least."

"Who?"

"Monty Stone. From Virginia."

The name slammed Karen's chest. "I saw him on the news," Karen said. "About his country club. Now, if he won't even let a black person join there, he certainly won't hire a woman of color. A Democrat at that? Get real, Freida."

"You never know," Freida said. "I'm covering his campaign. He'll charm your pants off—or jack you into next year."

"How?" Karen crumpled some Wish Master press releases, throwing them so hard her elbow made a snapping sound.

"There's a rumor . . . Stone got caught up in a love triangle with a secretary. She was also screwing a psychologist, so Stone had the IRS ruin the guy. Lost his practice, his house, and his mind."

Maybe leaving town would help her escape the rumors and threats. And perhaps a job with Stone might convince Sharlene to help Mama. Or what if she flat-out told the Stone family that Sharlene was an impostor?

No, it would only piss her off more.

"Freida, I'll think on—"

The other line buzzed.

"Let me call you back." She pushed the button for the other line.

"Karen, I'm at the hospital," her father said. "An ambulance brought your ma. She doesn't know up from down. Now the doctors are—"

"Is she okay?"

Static on the line grated her raw nerves.

"I said is Mama okay?"

"Christ! The doctors, they say we're getting to the end of the line."

Karen barely felt her feet touch the floor, or her hands grip the steering wheel, as she sped to the hospital. Within ten minutes, she was at her mother's side in the ER at Detroit General. The doctor, standing over Mama, said, "She's confused. The blood toxins can cloud the mind."

"Sharlene," Mama whispered.

The name sliced Karen's heart. She stepped into the hallway, whipping her cell phone from her purse. She had dialed her sister so many times, she knew the numbers by heart. In seconds, Sharlene was on the line at work.

"Mama is dying! Please, Sharlene. Save her. Please!" Karen heard a muffled sob. "Sharlene?"

"Karen, I can't believe this. There's just too much at stake."

"Mama's life is at stake!"

"But—" Sharlene sniffled. "Karen, I finally have the life that I've always wanted. I can't just let it go."

Karen wanted to jump through the phone and whack some sense into her sister. "But we can't just let Mama go, either. She—"

"Mother didn't love me. She didn't care that I couldn't breathe."

Karen's hand cramped around the phone. "Mama keeps saying your name over and over. She does love you!"

Sharlene blew her nose. "I'm sorry. I have too much . . . I just can't help."

27

Camille stuffed a few more envelopes as the last campaign workers left the storefront office in a black neighborhood in Richmond. It
was almost midnight. Almost time to make her move.

That loose vent flapping on the roof startled her again, making her
glance up at the glass window overlooking the leaf-blown street. A
painted image of Marcus Jones thrust his brown fist in the air next to
her reflection. Camille bit down a smile.

Jeff would never recognize me like this. Black. But he'll love the result.
And he would never know that her supposed visit to a sick relative
back in Cleveland was really a quick-change artist's fantasy.

"Sista Annette, you want this coffee?" Isis, the only other person
in the fluorescent-lit room, lifted the pot from the automatic coffee-
maker next to a long table of pamphlets depicting Senator Stone as the
pariah of civil rights.

"If not," Isis said, "I'm 'bout to throw it away." Her inky complexion glowed against a Hampton University sweatshirt as she stepped
closer.

"I'm straight," Camille said. With her newly caramel hands, thanks
to bottled self-tanner, she ran the yellow sponge bottle over the lip of
an envelope with the easy slowness she'd observed in a high school
classmate from New Orleans. "That caffeine would have me twistin'

like an ornery alligator 'til sunrise." The roof vent slammed again. She startled. "See, I'm wired as it is."

Isis dumped the coffee in the sink against the wall, a few feet away. She set down the pot, then cupped her mushroom of hair. "Who did your braids?"

Camille looked at a stray black braid resting on the sleeve of her mudcloth shirt. "It's a sista by my auntie's church. And she won't charge you an arm and a leg. Here." Camille reached down for her tattered red, black, and green cloth bag. Buttons saying AFRICAN QUEEN and POWER TO THE PEOPLE tapped the brown folding chair as she yanked it from the floor. Reaching in, she felt the microcassette tape that would surely rock Marcus Jones's world once the media got ahold of it. There, a pen. Camille pulled it out, scribbled a phone number. "Her name's Dee. Tell her I said to call."

Isis grasped the card. "Annette, you cool people. When I heard a Creole chick was comin' to work my shift, I was, like, she better not be siditty like some folks whose blood ain't all the way black."

Camille let out a silly laugh as she stuffed envelopes. "Honey, everybody knows if you got one drop, it spoils the stew. Like my mama makes some hot sauce so strong, one drop spices up the whole pot of gumbo."

In faded jeans, Isis sat on the table. "So both your parents is black?"

"You the third person here to pop me with a race quiz," Camille drawled. "First Darius Williams, askin' if I'm mixed. Then that bald dude, sayin' why did I leave the Big House to be with field Negroes. That shit is so tired."

Isis tilted her neck. "Relax, girlfriend. I was just askin'."

"All my life people been 'just askin'.'" Camille remembered black kids on Helen Street calling her whitey, while white kids at school invited her to swim or have lunch with them until Karen and Mother showed up to watch her in *Fiddler on the Roof*. Always a lose-lose situation. "I'm here, ain't I? If my heart wasn't in it I'd be there stuffin' envelopes for Monty Stone."

That flapping roof intensified Camille's annoyance. "As if I have to *prove* myself to my own people." She shoved envelopes in a box for the post office.

Isis slid to her feet. "See, sistas like you so quick to slap an attitude over they light skin. Make me sick." She snatched her jacket off a nearby chair, flipped off the lights, and dashed into the night.

Alone in the dark, Camille crept into the back office. For the past five nights, she'd observed that no one would return until morning. Still, her heart raced as she booted up the computer. Nervous sweat prickled under her arms as she inserted her disk into the hard drive.

Slam! Camille turned back toward the door. *Someone's here.*

No, it was only that roof vent slamming in the wind.

In the blue glow of the computer screen, her heartbeat pounded over the humming hard drive. She skimmed a list of files. *There.*

She clicked on EXPENSES. Scrolled down far enough to find PAY-ROLL.

Bingo! Camille copied the file onto her disk. She did the same with a file called GOLD STAR SUPPORTERS.

Slam! *I wish they'd fix that damn ceiling vent.*

Finally, she checked her disk to make sure the files had copied. Yes, but whose reflection was that in the glass of the computer monitor?

Over her shoulder stood Darius Williams, the campaign manager. *I'm busted.*

28

"What the fuck are you doing here?" Darius shouted, suspicion burning in his eyes. "Annette, you know this office is strictly—"

"Yes!" Camille shook raised fists as if she'd just won a race. "Darius, you got my page!" she drawled. "Why, finding you tonight has been like looking for a penny in a swamp. Didn't know what to do—"

"What's going on?!"

Camille leaned over the computer to close the window. "A precinct manager had an emergency. Needed to transfer some funds right away. And I of course didn't have authority, so I paged you. But I didn't hear back so—"

He flipped open his suit jacket to check the pager on his right hip, giving her just enough time to eject the disk and slip it into her sleeve.

"My pager is on, but no message from you. Or anyone else here."

Camille plastered confusion across her face. "Yes, sir, I sure did, frantic as I was. And my baby-sitter is gonna quit me. I'm two hours late." She shoved a piece of paper toward him. "Here. Doesn't matter how late you call, they said. Just call. Sounded like Marcus Jones will be up the creek if you don't take care of business."

He took the paper, his face twisted.

Camille grabbed her purse, looked back at him from the front door. She said, "And you'll all be up the creek when we get through with you!"

She tossed back her head, laughed, and ran into the night.

29

The FOR SALE sign in front of Biscuits 'n Honey made Karen's knuckles whiten on the steering wheel.

"Ohlordhammercy," her mother sighed from the passenger seat as they pulled into the lot. "This about to break my heart."

"No, Mama, I promise we'll figure out how to get it back." As Daddy helped her mother from the car, Karen blamed him for making them grow up in conditions that inspired Sharlene's disappearance. Monty Stone was guilty, too, for slamming the door on her mother's dream.

For now, they had to clean up and gather their belongings. For a second, Karen had thought losing her job would enable her to run Biscuits 'n Honey. But the bank officer had refused to stop the fore-closure, especially after playing twenty questions about her involve-ment in Franklin's death.

"A damn shame," Mama whispered as they entered the kitchen. An accordion of dirty loaf pans stretched from the sink. Flour dusted the table. Bits of dough dotted the floor.

Her father grabbed a broom and mop while Mama rested on a stool at the table. "Lord, if I ever needed a cigarette, it's right now."

"No, Mama, we'll clean up and come up with a plan." Karen put on a pair of yellow rubber gloves and filled the sink with hot sudsy water. She scrubbed the baked-on crumbs and stains from a pan so fast she broke a sweat. Then, steel wool in hand, she tackled the ovens.

"Sweet praline, you think your sister gon' come to her senses?" Mama clung to the stainless-steel handle on the jumbo refrigerators, taking stock of butter, eggs, and milk inside.

Karen backed out of the oven. "She needs a reality check. We sacrificed for her, but she seems to have memory loss."

She remembered that letter from the exclusive Riverfront Academy of the Arts. One scholarship. Two girls. And no money in the mason jar on Mama's dresser to send the other girl, too. Then, the silent treatment from Sharlene for days. Until Karen forfeited her acceptance.

"I went through hell for her," Karen said, scrubbing again. "Thugs in chemistry class stealing my backpack and making crude comments. People hating me because I use verbs in my sentences. If she only—"

"Baby, you don't have to tell me. I know."

A burnt-on spill from apple pie broke up under Karen's Brillo pad. So what if Sharlene had been handed their mutual dream of studying acting at the academy? Karen had excelled in her own way: as student body president, setting up a voter registration drive in the neighborhood. Coming home after college to work for a state representative who made it a priority to pass funding to keep libraries, community centers, and hot-lunch programs open for poor people. Then helping Franklin and the mayor rebuild a city scarred by decades of white flight and corporate abandonment.

Her father headed into the bathroom with the mop and bucket, while Mama slumped against the refrigerator door and said, "I wanna see my baby one more time before the Lord take me home."

Karen froze. "Mama, don't talk like that."

"I'm just tellin' you what I want."

"But you're not—"

"The doctor said it won't be long," Mama said. "And I can't change Sharlene's mind. So I just wanna see my baby once more."

Karen imagined Sharlene slamming her fancy town house gates in Mama's face. She peeled off her gloves and led her mother to the door.

"C'mon, Mama, we need to go buy you a new dress for Sharlene's wedding."

30

In the chandeliered ballroom of a hotel in Arlington, Camille strained to hear what Senator Stone was telling Jeff over the chatter of hundreds of people eating five-thousand-dollar plates of prime rib and garlic mashed potatoes.

"Lucas wants to skewer me on the devil's pitchfork," Stone said, the crease on his forehead deepening despite his practiced smile. "Son, it's not too late to take Tabitha back. For me."

Jeff squeezed Camille's hand, flexing his jaw muscles. His father was to his right, followed by Mrs. Stone, picking at her asparagus, and Jackson, tossing back a martini. Dixie, in a tailored blue pantsuit, was near the string quartet, her brow furrowed as she talked with poultry king Jake Frisian. A few minutes earlier, she had kissed both Camille's cheeks, telling her she was counting the days until she would become an aunt again.

"Otherwise," Senator Stone said, "I can feel it in my gut, Lucas will take me to hell and back before this election is over."

"Pop, no one could possibly believe those women. You've always gone above and beyond—"

In her lap, Camille ran her palm over the manila envelope. Her winning ticket to a real father. And something to negate all the damage those three women had done on the news today, joining Vivian's lawsuit. Former employees, they claimed Stone had groped them, offered gifts for sex, even threatened to blacklist them if they refused his advances.

As he huddled with Jeff, Senator Stone's aura made her feel warm inside, as did his whispered drawl and the masculine planes of his face.

"Sugar," he said, his silver-gray eyes making her stomach flutter, "didn't they tell you back in Cleveland it's not polite to stare?"

She raised the envelope. "This is for you. Marcus Jones will wish he'd never heard the words 'Capitol Hill.' "

Jeff wiped his mouth with a napkin. "Mom, Pop, Camille has been so upset about the polls, she did something about it. Can't say I approve in her condition, but I'm damn proud of her."

Senator Stone slipped on silver half-glasses to examine the papers he pulled from the envelope with the microcassette. Next to him, Mrs. Stone raised her gaze from the goods to Camille. In her eyes was the same softness that had glowed Sunday morning, when Camille held the white plastic stick with double pink stripes next to the box reading "two lines, pregnant." Mrs. Stone had even smiled before agreeing to call the wedding planner for an Indian summer ceremony in the gardens. All thanks to the pregnant maid who had happily shared a cup of hormone-rich urine for several hundred-dollar bills.

Now, Mrs. Stone donned her own reading glasses. "What on earth?"

Senator Stone focused on the columns of numbers.

"The tape," Jeff said, "is a conversation of Jones and a state rep, scheming to buy votes from ministers across the Commonwealth. Nothing but a big, fat scandal, Pop!"

Mrs. Stone removed her glasses. "Camille, did you steal this? Gracious, those people wouldn't let anyone even remotely associated with our family within a mile of their offices. Or any white person, for that matter."

Jackson laughed. "Mom, if it helps, who cares how she got it?"

"Son, get Rollins." He flipped pages, his forehead crease deepening.

Jeff leaned close to whisper, "I love you, Lady Godiva." Then he strode across the ballroom toward the bar.

Camille sipped milk, certain her stock value had just spiked. Until Senator Stone shoved everything back into the envelope. His eyes threatened to wither her like a leaf in the blazing sun. But she kept her spine straight, her shoulders square.

"Sugar, what the hell are you doing?"

"Just trying to help." She smiled over red–hot alarm searing her senses.

"You think I want Jones taking me to court, too?"

Camille pointed to the envelope. "A lot of people have access to those records. Give them to the right reporter and your name will be sterling again."

Senator Stone nodded, his stare raising goose bumps under her red knit suit. "Sugar, try as you might, you can't buy what you didn't get by birth. Not from me, anyway."

Camille concentrated on stopping a band of tension from squeezing her chest. She wanted Jeff to come back, to coerce some praise from his parents for her brave deed. To convince them she could make good things happen for the family. Just over his father's head, she saw him: at the bar, smiling down at Tabitha Lucas! In a snug skirt and blouse, she was tossing around that shampoo-commercial brunette hair, touching Jeff's shoulder. No! Neither of them had any idea how it felt. Having no father, no food. Wanting desperately to be someone else, somewhere else, to find love at any cost.

Camille's every cell exploded with rage.

"Excuse me," she said softly. A cough threatened to race up her throat, but she held it back. She would not let an asthma attack broadcast her bruised emotions. "I'm going to the ladies' room."

Camille held her head high, her shoulders straight, as she swayed past waiters serving trays of cheesecake. The cough ricocheted in her throat, back to her ever-tightening lungs. She turned a corner toward the bathroom, into a soft-lit alcove lined with brass public phones.

"Miss Motown!"

She froze. That voice scraped up a freak show of memories. Nick's striking dark hair, combed back, his piercing eyes and goatee and Armani suit, belied the sewers he would swim for a buck.

"I always said you'd clean up nice," he said, eyeballing her body.

"Excuse me." Camille pushed the bathroom door.

"Sharlene, this is the welcome I get? What about a hug?"

"What do you want, Nick?"

His brown eyes turned rock-hard. "Drop the bitchy attitude. Now."

Camille pointed. "Don't talk to me like that. Those days are over!"

Nick stepped closer. "Sharlene, I made you! I motherfuckin' made you! Without me, you wouldn't have Rich Boy out there waitin' to marry your mixed-up ass."

Camille crossed her arms to stifle a shiver. She hated the violence in his eyes. And his fists. "Your point is what?"

He twisted her left hand in the light to examine her engagement ring. "I did everything for you. The new Social Security number, even those tits! And don't forget the records at NYC. No one will ever know you used black scholarship money to wiggle out of that Detroit ghetto."

"And I paid you dearly for all that." Camille couldn't stop the dirty memories of her and Nick. "What I gave you was better than money!"

"But now you got it, and I want it," Nick said.

"You crazy motherfucker! I finished paying you off long ago."

He looked at her ring again, then threw her hand down. "I want five hundred grand."

A haughty laugh burst from Camille's throat so hard she coughed.

Nick pushed her into the bathroom. Forced her into a stall.

Her heart thundered.

He could kill me. Right here, right now. While Jeff grins in Tabitha's face.

Her rattling chest rose and fell as Nick shoved her to the wall. The cold toilet bowl bruised her shin. Her wrists ached under his grasp.

"I said I want five hundred grand."

She sucked in a cloud of cognac. "Never!"

Nick buried his face in her neck. "Then I'll go tell Rich Boy all about freaky-deaky Sharlene. Black Sharlene."

31

Jeff strode toward Camille as she headed back into the ballroom. She looked pale; maybe the dinner wasn't sitting well on her already queasy stomach. He would talk to Mom and Pop later about showing more enthusiasm for her efforts to please them. "Honey, I was worried about you."

As they walked past Pop, illuminated by a TV camera, the soft floral scent of her perfume put him at ease for a moment. Until she tilted her jaw upward, anger flashing in her eyes. "How's Tabitha?"

"She wouldn't leave me alone. You know I can't stand the sight of her." Jeff remembered coming home for lunch in the town house to find Tabitha, her milky limbs tangled in the arms and legs of her secretary. Her sweet mouth that he loved to kiss latched onto a big tit. Her red fingernails clawing the woman's tanned thigh. And lesbian sweat staining the very sheets where he and Tabitha had made love that morning.

Now, if Pop knew the truth, he'd get chest pains. But he'd never know, lest Jeff risk his father thinking he didn't have sound enough judgment to choose the right woman. And if one of their own could be so degenerate, then he would take his chances with Camille. After he made her smile.

"I can't believe you were looking at her like that," Camille said.

"Enough." He pulled out her chair at the table.

"Mrs. Stone, I just met a charming lady." Camille said, sitting. "She couldn't say enough about your work with the children's wing at the hospital."

Jeff took his seat, glad that Mom at least was insisting on coming to New York, once the baby was born, to help Camille.

Mom set down her coffee cup. "Oh? What was her name?"

"I want to say Mrs. Riley. Or was it Mrs. Robinson? To tell you the truth, she talked so fast and so long, I don't remember. She had white hair, a gold dress. From Alexandria, I think."

Mom's bracelets jangled as she picked a dot of lint from the satin cuff of her royal-blue dress. "That doesn't ring a bell."

"Well, she was charming all the—" Camille squinted.

A woman reporter shoved a microphone in her face; Camille raised her hand to block the light of the camera held by a man.

Hell no! Jeff bolted to his feet, sliding between Camille and the cute, thirtyish brunette he recognized from a Washington, D.C., network affiliate.

"Patricia." His tone made him sound as if he were greeting a long-lost friend. And he flashed that smile that Camille always said made her knees weak, something about his bright teeth and perfect lips and dimples. It masked the hostility pulsing through him at the mere thought of how the media treated Pop. "Good to see you. Saw your segment last week on campaign finance reform. Outstanding."

She smiled. "Thanks. Excuse me, but I'd like to interview your fiancée."

"You know, Pat, Camille's been wanting to talk to a reporter. About how my father's work can help the women of our generation. Come to think of it, you'd be perfect. And what I'd like to do, Pat, is set up something more structured, not just a hit-and-run sound bite."

Dixie returned, taking her seat.

"Maybe," Jeff said, pulling a business card from his suit jacket pocket, "you might even talk to my sister, too. Call me Monday, Pat. An exclusive just for you."

The reporter smiled. "Well, I wanted to talk to Camille tonight, but this sounds like a plan."

"Great." The reporter and cameraman retreated into the crowd.

"Jeff, I'm not doing an interview with her," Camille said.

Dixie wrinkled her nose. "Neither am I."

He stroked both their backs. "I know."

"Politics one-oh-one," Jackson said. "How to make a promise you never intend to keep." He raised his martini. "Here's to the same finesse that put a gag on Ben Reams."

Jeff stiffened. "Enough, Jackson."

"That snake got what he deserv—"

"I said drop it!" Ben Reams, that sneaky bastard. A fraternity brother, no less. Only the most depraved lowlife would make friends with somebody, get close to the family, steal private journals, then try to sell a scathing article about Pop—including pictures of him with a topless lobbyist on a yacht—to a news magazine just weeks before the last election.

"Boys," Mom said. "Your manners."

Jeff ground his teeth. It was Ben's deception that had cut most viciously. Nobody would ever know exactly why Ben decided to take a swim in the East River. Or who made him do it. The only thing cooling Jeff's still-smoldering rage was the thought of his flawless vengeance and how he had unleashed it before any damage could be done to Pop's image.

"My goodness," Camille said. "I can't believe how reporters leap out of nowhere when you're least expecting it."

Jeff vowed to always protect her, and their baby, from the rabid media and all the leeches in the world who wanted a piece of his family for their own personal gain.

"Brace yourself," Jackson said. "Once Dad runs for the White House, we'll all be under a microscope."

"Speak for yourself," Jeff said as Pop approached.

"They'll see," Pop said. "They can report all the vicious lies they want. You mark my words. The Oval Office will be mine."

Jeff grinned, until he saw the dread flashing in Camille's eyes.

32

In the dressing room of her store, Ginger pinned the white satin bodice tighter at Camille's waist. "Better?"

"Perfect." Camille ran her hands over the explosion of tulle cascading to the floor. "I can't believe it's actually happening in two days."

Ginger laughed. "Pregnant women are supposed to expand their waistlines, not take them in. By the way, I got the pills. Your brand. I mean, I told my doctor I was moving to Europe, so he gave me a year's worth."

Camille secured a ball of hair on top of her head with combs. "What would I do without you?"

Ginger secured more pins at her waist. "You mean, how would I keep this place open without *you?*" She still hadn't made amends for talking to Karen. But now Ginger was sure if she could just get Camille through the wedding without any kinks, perhaps that would ease the guilt and show her appreciation for all the money that had kept Mystique afloat. For now, Ginger had to do as much as she could to calm the anxiety churning in her friend's eyes.

"Okay, turn around." Ginger adjusted the looped satin buttons down the back. "Dixie called. Said she's so busy with school, I'll have to do her alterations at White Pines."

"Cool. I can't believe how beautiful the bridesmaids' dresses are."

"Thanks," Ginger said. "Any word from Karen?"

"No news is bad news in my book. At least when she was calling I knew what she was up to."

"And?"

"Either Mother died or Karen is scheming to get me."

Ginger snipped a thread under Camille's bare arm. "But I mean, how are you gonna wrap up this pregnancy thing?"

"Just when I'm supposed to start showing—"

"Camille, you should get pregnant for real, like on the honeymoon. And with Dixie and her mom so excited, nobody will suspect you—"

"No way. I'm not taking that risk."

"Ever?"

"Ginger, remember my uncle Jeremiah? The one who got lynched when they found out? If the baby has the slightest hint of brown, everything I've done for the past three years would be for nothing."

"I think you're being paranoid. Next issue: Nick. Heard from him?"

Camille let out a disgusted sigh. "No. Forget him, too."

That wouldn't be easy, not with him calling every day, even stopping by once, saying he could help her now. Funny how he had suddenly become generous the day after springing an extortion threat on Camille. Ginger had told him to get lost, but he just wasn't hearing her. "That thug better leave you alone."

"I can't believe he thinks I'd actually give him money. What an idiot—" Camille turned. "Do I hear Rand?"

Ginger felt light and tingly. Yes, that was Rand's deep voice, talking with the clerk out in the store. He must have come to pick up the costumes she had made for the kids' production of *Pocahontas* at Hugs and Hope.

As he knocked on the open door, Ginger smiled.

"Isn't this taboo or something?" he asked, bright teeth flashing.

Something about him was extra gorgeous today, but what? Ginger set her pincushion on the carpeted platform where Camille was standing. She flitted toward him for a kiss on those lips that would make any male model jealous. After a quick pull into his chest, Rand released her, then stared at Camille. "Look at you!"

Camille stepped down, smiling. "It's only taboo for Jeff to see me in my dress before the wedding. But you're fine."

Ginger wanted to jump through the magnetic force suddenly glowing between Camille and Rand. "You guys!" She waved a stiff palm. "Hello?"

Rand put his arm around her. "Ginger, your talent amazes me. Look at this creation."

Camille's eyes rolled up and down Rand's muscular length, in the taupe slim trousers and V-necked sweater bearing Ginger's label. "I was about to say the same thing," Camille said, taking Ginger's hand. "This is how Ginger Roman will splash back onto the fashion scene."

Ginger shrugged. "What?"

"Look at him!"

"I like to do that."

"Ginger, focus here. Rand. Men's clothes. You build up your menswear line, have a show, invite all the fashion media. I guarantee—"

Ginger crossed her arms, studying the simple yet flattering cut of Rand's outfit. Expand that for spring, in earth tones and shimmery pastels . . .

"Love it! I love your idea."

As Ginger surveyed him further, Rand smiled at Camille.

"I hope my brother appreciates what Cupid is doing for him."

Camille's eyes twinkled up at him.

And something blinding exploded inside Ginger. "You two! It isn't fair!"

Camille and Rand froze, turning toward her at the same time.

"Fashion is fickle," Camille said, taking her hand. "You knew that going in. But we can—"

Ginger yanked her hand back, then darted through the dressing room to the carpeted door. Into the shadowy stock area leading to the back alley.

Can't be jealous. They're like brother and sister, nothing more.

She hated that she was so anxious about her looks, about her talent. Was she suffering some kind of Othello vision, projecting her own insecurities onto the situation? No, Camille would never do her wrong. Ginger wanted to think she was just stressed out over finances.

But soon, with Camille's brilliant idea, the cash might start to flow again.

Ginger took a few deep breaths, smoothing down her sheath mini-dress. She would blame her mood swing on PMS or something, then enjoy the company of her two favorite people.

She pushed open the door to the dressing room. "You guys," she said cheerfully, "I'm sorry—"

They were gone.

33

Dashing from the store in jeans and a blouse, Camille couldn't believe Ginger was jealous of her and Rand. How ridiculous. She just wanted to get in her chauffeured car, waiting at the curb, go home, finish packing her trousseau, and let Ginger cool down. Rand, still inside, would talk some sense into her.

"Miss Motown!"

She turned. Nick Parker stood against the red brick, to the right of the door, holding a bottle of Coke. If she didn't know him, she would think he looked cool, even sexy, in snug jeans and a white T-shirt. Yellow cabs and dark cars in the late September sunshine flashed on his silver belt buckle.

"Just talked to Rich Boy." Nick swigged the soda. "Said you weren't home, so I figured I'd find you here with your freaky-deaky friend."

Camille stepped toward him. "You're such a loser."

Nick pitched the bottle into the gutter. "Maybe your own voice would be more convincing." He pulled a palm-sized tape recorder from his pocket, pushed PLAY: "Yeah, baby, bust me wide open. Pound my ass like that!"

It was her own voice. Camille seized the tape recorder, stomped it under the thick heel of her black loafers.

Nick squinted. "Got plenty more at home. How 'bout I play one at Rich Boy's bachelor party? I bet that'd get him off like—"

"What do you want, Nick?"

"I told you, half a mill. Then you'll never see me again."

Camille hated his malicious stare. However, she loathed more the thought of losing everything. How could she get that much money without Jeff noticing? She would have to figure something out. Fast. But tomorrow they'd be heading down to Virginia for the wedding, then the honeymoon. "I need some time," Camille said.

Nick nodded. "How much?"

"Give me 'til Halloween. I'll be in the atrium of that glass building with the red pillars down the street."

"I want cash money, Miss Motown." He pulled another tape from his pocket, holding it next to his grin. "Or Rich Boy will hear you sing."

34

"**What the devil are** you going to do now!" Monty Stone shouted at the image of Marcus Jones on the television in the library at White Pines. He glanced at Jeff, grinding his teeth at the other end of the leather couch.

"And while the Election Commission looks into allegations that Jones was buying votes from the clergy," the redheaded reporter said, standing in front of Jones's campaign headquarters in Richmond, "sources tell us Jones may be forced out of the contentious race to unseat veteran Senator Monty Stone."

"Yeah!" Jeff's deep voice echoed off the high ceiling as he shot to his feet.

Stone wrapped his lips around the damp cigar, sucking in a sweet pillow of smoke. He nodded toward Jeff. "Son, this dance with the devil has gotten me thinking. You could do a world of good for my campaign now. And gearing up for the White House."

Jeff, in khaki shorts and a polo shirt, crossed his arms. His gaze was as sharp as Randolph Stone's in the painting over the fireplace. "Move here?"

"You're quick, son."

Jeff shook his head. "Camille loves New York and her job. And I've got too many big cases coming up—"

"My bid for the presidency is the biggest case of our lives."

"That's why, when things heat up, Uncle John says I can take a few months off. That's not 'til next year."

"The time is now, son." Stone nodded toward the TV. "The niggers killed my daddy to keep him out of the Oval Office. Now Jones and his people are trying to assassinate my character."

"That may stop, thanks to Camille."

Stone remembered his sergeant in the army saying, as his platoon headed into enemy territory during the Korean War, "Trust no one but your own kind." That always came to mind when he thought of Camille, despite her miracle with the Jones camp.

"Son, what she did was only the start. I hear Lucas is about to sic the Election Commission on me, to find out who's footing my campaign bills."

Jeff flexed his jaw muscles. "Don't even say her name, Pop. Tabitha is history. And if you knew the truth, you'd gag on that cigar."

"My point, son, is that tomorrow, after the wedding, things will change. And with the baby coming, Camille won't work——"

Jeff chuckled. "I don't know about that."

Stone patted Jeff's back. "Son, the first time I held you, I vowed to become the man your grandfather could never be." Monty remembered waiting there at the hospital while Millie nearly died giving birth. All while his own mother sobbed over Daddy's bullet-riddled corpse at the morgue, after they had ambushed him in his hunting blind here at White Pines.

"I pledged on his grave, son, that his death would not be in vain."

"That was a different time, Pop. A lot was going on in the sixties. We can keep things static to a point, but——"

"To hell with your defeatist attitude! Think of your unborn child." Stone remembered how Daddy, standing before a sea of white faces, would never give in. Not while preaching the evils of integration as civil rights laws let blacks into schools, bathrooms, and restaurants. All to protect the sanctity and security of his family.

"Desegregation," he would say, "is like inviting black ants to your Sunday picnic. They'll leave filth on your fine blankets. Steal your food, terrify your children. Then scurry away, a stinking mess in their wake."

Stone puffed on his cigar, trying to vaporize the raw memories of being a political orphan, a state legislator at age thirty-five, navigating the typhoon whipped up by the likes of Martin Luther King, Jr.

"I'm sorry, Pop. I'm just not ready to leave law and get into politics."

Stone felt as if his insides were turning to scalding water. He needed Jeff around him. Jackson was too busy with the tobacco business. Rand's bleeding-heart liberal stance would never sync. And there were too many question marks and shadows around Davis's globe-hopping business deals. But how could he entice his oldest son to derail his legal career and hop on board the political train?

He nodded at Jeff. "The law will always be there, son. But I'm going on seventy. This window of opportunity is a one-shot deal, hear?"

35

The library doors burst open as Jeff pondered his father's proposal. In walked Davis, wearing baggy cargo pants, a denim shirt with
red Japanese letters, and a silver hoop earring. Jeff hugged him. "Glad
you could make it for the big day."

Davis shrugged. "I was in the States."

"Where do you live, anyway?" Jeff asked. He still was not exactly
sure what Davis did for a living. And his brother was just as strange
now as in boarding school. Hanging out with the foreign exchange
students, listening to that mind-numbing techno crap. Opting out of
polo to play Dungeons and Dragons with that kid who dyed his hair
maroon. And as a boy Davis would tie a squirrel to a fishing pole, dip
it into the river out back until it drowned, then burn it.

"Everywhere and nowhere in particular," Davis said, running a
hand through spiky gray hair. He leaned against the side of the tall
fireplace. "Got pads in New York, LA, London. And I can stay with
associates all—"

Pop stepped between them, glowering at Davis. "Take that thing
out of your ear in my house. You look like a goddamn faggot."

Davis shoved the earring into a hip pocket. "Nice to see you, too,
Pop."

"That's better. How's business, son?"

"It's there," Davis said, lighting a cigarette. "Just had a development deal go bad in the Midwest. Now I'm trying to mop up the bloody mess."

"Well, keep it clean, son. I don't want my friends at the CIA to come calling with any more pictures of you and money launderers in Cape Town."

Davis blew smoke, his silver-gray eyes dull. "Guess you were too busy bludgeoning me as a kid to school me on good business practices."

"Show some respect or get out!"

"I'll take respect for six hundred," Davis said. "Two out of four ain't bad, though, Pop. Jeff and Jackson, the perfect puppets. Me and Rand, black sheep. And Dixie—"

"Enough," Jeff said. "We're here for a wedding, not a funeral, Davis."

"That could be a good thing," he said, glaring at Pop, "or a bad thing, depending on who's dead."

Pop lunged, but Jeff caught him before his fist whacked Davis's chest.

36

In a lace-curtained inn near Colonial Williamsburg, Karen helped her father tuck Mama into a four-poster bed. How could Sharlene take one look at Mama's sad, ashen face tomorrow and not agree to help? She had to. But first, Karen needed to get their clothes ready, so they could talk their way into the wedding.

On the bedside table, Daddy placed Mama's pager from the hospital. The doctor would call immediately if a kidney became available.

"Christ, I wish that thing would beep right now." His eyes glazed with sadness. Along with taking Mama to church, delivering meals to seniors, and going to Gamblers Anonymous meetings, Daddy was working down at the marina to pay the mortgage. He even baked chicken and steamed broccoli or prepared whatever else Mama wanted for dinner. He hadn't gambled or had a drink in years, but Karen still feared he could slip up at any moment.

Daddy's hand over his beard made a bristly sound. "I don't know about this, Karen, showing up where we're not wanted—"

"Daddy, we have to try." Karen smoothed down the blankets, remembering the Internet Web site that said less than nine thousand cadaver kidneys were available for transplant last year. "Our choice is Sharlene or getting in the kidney line behind forty-three thousand other people."

Karen surveyed their wrinkled outfits, hanging in the open armoire. Why hadn't housekeeping delivered that iron yet? Just as she picked up the phone to call again, someone knocked. "It's about time." She opened the door.

A teenaged girl handed over an iron and ironing board.

"Thank you—" Karen froze. Raspberry syrup. The smell was strong in the hallway lit by electric candlestick sconces. "Are you wearing perfume?"

The girl wrinkled her pug nose. "Just cinnamon-stick shampoo, but—"

"No raspberry?" Karen peered out, seeing no one.

"There's a couple in the suite upstairs, but you're alone on this floor."

A few minutes later, Karen cradled her cell phone between her ear and shoulder while ironing Mama's dress. She'd sent Daddy out to look around while she called the Detroit police. "Lieutenant Sykes, I think the man who broke into my apartment followed me to Virginia," she said.

He exhaled. "Ms. Bradley, paranoia is a normal reaction to trauma—"

"I'm not paranoid."

"We have an update on the Daniels investigation. A source has information about an international company involved in diamond smuggling."

"Tell me something I haven't figured out myself."

"Ms. Bradley, we're trying to help you. The company was a major investor in the proposed Wish Master complex."

The iron hissed as she pushed the steam button. "Obviously."

After Daddy returned, she pushed a heavy table in front of the door. Until the police found the thug who had killed Franklin, she wouldn't be safe anywhere.

37

Camille shifted in the warm, aqua water. In a red maillot, she was sitting on the top step of the pool at White Pines, under the moon and stars. Despite the rectangles of yellow light glowing from the mansion and the guest cottages full of relatives in for the wedding, and Ginger and Dixie sipping champagne beside her, Camille was trying to quell a fist of anxiety pummeling her insides. She was hours from her dream, yet it could evaporate if the wrong person accessed the right people. That was why all she wanted tonight was to relax and savor the security of finally having a new family and a better life.

"Let's go skinny-dipping!" Ginger said, ripping off her bikini. In seconds, she was an auburn and white blur beneath lighted cherubs and goddesses.

Dixie's bathing suit became a wet heap on the patio; she dove in. But not before Camille saw a flash of silver zigzags across Dixie's stomach. Stretch marks? Or was the shimmering turquoise water reflecting off her skin? Was she once overweight? No, Mrs. Stone would never allow that. *How strange* . . . Camille slipped into the water.

"C'mon, Mrs. Stone!" Ginger splashed them, her bare breasts bouncing. "Dixie, what was it like growing up here? I mean, I feel like I'm at a resort."

Dixie treaded water near the fountain. "I thought it was normal 'til I was about fifteen. Then I visited a poor person's house. Cripe, when I saw kids without enough food, it upset me so much, I launched an all-out rebellion."

"Against who?" Camille asked.

Dixie glanced around. "This place, I guess. I'd sneak into town or to the country. Giving money to anyone who looked poor. And the staff here. My mom had so many fits! Especially when I pawned one of her necklaces—"

"The girl Robin Hood!" Ginger cheered.

"Yeah," Dixie said. "Rand came with me sometimes, if he was home. One time we drove up to these tiny shacks in Appalachia with holiday food baskets stuffed with cash. Mom was furious we went there alone."

"That's, like, so cool," Ginger said.

Camille imagined Dixie and Rand knocking on the door to the Detroit apartment, Mother reaching out to take whatever they offered. The thought evoked a warm glow deep down, a kinship with Dixie. She would be sympathetic to—not scornful of—Camille's sad but secret past.

Dixie wiped her eyes. "Hate to be a party pooper, but I have to get some studying done before the big day tomorrow. And I need to go down to the stables to check on Charity." She patted Camille's stomach under water. "Night-night, baby Stone."

Camille smiled, ignoring guilt pangs. A short time later, she and Ginger headed to the Victoria Suite, but Camille was as wired as if she'd chugged espresso. Jeff and Rand would probably be gone most of the night at the bachelor party at Dillon's mansion nearby. It was time for a midnight snack.

"This place is spooky," Ginger said as they walked the long upstairs hallway past another closed, white-painted door set in red-and-blue striped wallpaper. The chatter of guests and visiting relatives penetrated the walls. "I mean, all the black maids and butlers creep me out. How can you sleep here?"

"I try not to think about it," Camille said softly as a maid passed with a stack of linens. "And Jeff says if he decides to run for his dad's seat in Congress, we won't have to live here. Thank God."

"Hey," Ginger said. "I'm sorry about my little mood swing when

Rand saw you in the dress. It's just, like, sometimes I wonder what he sees in me."

Camille stopped, putting her hands on her friend's shoulders. "Ginger Roman. Rand and I have this sort of brother-sister bond, so he's told me how he feels. He's not the type to pretend; I *know* he adores you."

"I just feel, like, so boggled, Camille. I mean, even with your help, I keep sliding back into this money pit. And the other day I started feeling one of those dizzy spells I get when I'm really stressed."

"I told you, the men's line. After the wedding, we'll get to work on it." Camille led Ginger onto the royal-blue-carpeted landing. To the right was the double staircase leading down to the foyer. To the left, a cluster of furniture on a balcony overlooking the tree-filled solarium, and another staircase. And straight ahead . . . Camille did a double take: the door to the north wing was ajar. So it wasn't locked after all.

"C'mon." She led her friend down the dim hallway, trying all the brass doorknobs. Locked. Camille stopped in the area where she'd seen the face in the window. "Shh, listen." The tinkle of music came through a door.

"Sounds like a music box I used to have," Ginger whispered.

Camille tried the knob. But it wouldn't turn.

Ginger paled. "I don't even get this weirded out on Halloween. What if there's, like, an old uncle who's retarded so they keep him out of sight?"

"You've seen too many bad movies, Ginger. I wonder who's—"

"What you gals doin' up here?" Ida Mae came barreling out of nowhere. "Shoo away now. Ain't nobody supposed to be—"

"Who's in there?" Camille pointed at the door. How odd that Ida Mae was up here in jeans and a T-shirt, when the maid's quarters were downstairs, near the butler's pantry.

"Ain't nobody in this whole wing."

"Then what's—" The music had stopped.

"Y'awl better scoot, else I tell Miss Millie you was sneakin' around."

Camille and Ginger headed down to the kitchen. But Camille was determined to find out who, or what, was locked away in there.

38

In the sunny Victoria Suite, a silver breakfast tray in front of her, Camille vowed to do anything to preserve that tender expression in Mrs. Stone's eyes. It made her insides ooze like the river of butter on the hip-thickening grits that Hortense must have been crazy to think she would eat two hours before her wedding. *If I die this second, I felt the comfort of a mother's loving gaze.*

Mrs. Stone, in a damask chair, pushed the vase of red roses and the telephone across the wooden table butted against the wall between French doors to the veranda. She set an ancient wooden box on the table.

Camille nibbled melon, hoping her pounding heart was not making her ivory satin robe flutter.

"Gracious, Camille, I know it hasn't been easy, trying to get close to our family. You understand we are a very proud, and private, breed."

"Yes, of course."

"Well, Monty and I decided"—she glanced down—"because you're carrying our grandchild, we ought to accept you as one of our own."

Camille ignored nasty gales of shame and guilt whipping her conscience.

"Believe it or not, I was in your shoes once." Mrs. Stone dabbed Camille's eyes with a linen napkin.

Yeah, right. The corners of Camille's mouth turned up. She loved the lemony scent wafting from Mrs. Stone's draping white dressing gown.

"Marrying Monty wasn't easy. We weren't nearly as wealthy as the Stones. Gracious, no one was. Tell the truth, it was years before I felt a part of things here. So in my own way I was protecting you. Young, naive—"

Ha!

"—wanting so desperately to join a world you couldn't possibly understand. One that's not easy to leave once you see the inside." Mrs. Stone's gaze became sharp and glassy. This almost sounded like a warning, but her singsong accent made it hard to tell as she opened the old box.

Camille gasped. A tiara, sparkling in the sunshine.

"It's been in the family for three centuries," Mrs. Stone said, turning it.

Camille wondered if Victoria had worn it before having Lucy killed.

"Every bride, since Randolph Stone had it made in Paris in the 1600s, has worn it, including myself." She aimed a polished beige fingernail at the diamonds. "Those are for the fortune Randolph Stone was building. The emeralds—the lush Virginia land. Those aquamarines represent the ocean that our ancestors crossed from England to the New World."

"What about the rubies?" Camille said. "My birthstone."

"The purity of the Stone bloodline," she said.

Camille couldn't stop the hot tears stinging her eyes. "I don't know what to say." She felt so close to Mrs. Stone at that moment, as if—

As if she were my mother!

Mrs. Stone began securing the tiara on Camille's head with hairpins. "You just sit right here and I'll—"

Ida Mae hurried in. "Miss Millie, the guard down at the gate say he need to talk to you, in a hurry."

Camille could still feel Mrs. Stone behind the chair, fixing her hair. "My gracious, what could be so important? Put him on the speakerphone."

Ida Mae pushed a button on the phone on the table.

"This is Mrs. Stone."

"Uh, yeah, Mrs. Stone. I feel bad botherin' you and all, but—"

"What is it?" She pulled a few tendrils to fall around Camille's face.

"Well," the guard said, "I know we're supposed to watch for crazies tryin' to crash the wedding, like the senator's enemies and everything—"

"Get to the point, please!"

"Well, ma'am, there's a black lady down here with a white man, and a girl who's somewhere in between."

Camille's heart jumped to her throat. Fear coiled around her chest, squeezing like a boa constrictor. No! It couldn't be them!

Mrs. Stone turned Camille's shoulders and stood in front of her. She glanced at her watch but did not stop with the tiara. "It's still early, but if they're on the guest list, let them in. Don't call up here for that."

"Well, ma'am, they ain't on the list. I checked three times."

Mrs. Stone pulled a few hairs, making Camille's eyes water. "Then they're not invited and they can't come in. Simple enough." She held a silver hand mirror to show Camille what she'd done. Camille stared without seeing the fantasy image of herself looking back.

"But," the guard said, "these people say they're the bride's family."

39

Outside the spiked iron gates of White Pines, Ernestine Bradley felt as if she were wilting like a dying flower under the scorching September sun. Also making her slump were the state troopers milling around the little white house where that security guard was checking a list every time a car drove up.

Lord, this heat is 'bout to kill me. I feel so sick. She shifted in her wheelchair. Sweat glued her new pink dress to her skin.

"I don't care what the lady just told you," Mack said, standing at the guard's booth, where the young fellow had just gotten off the phone. "I'm the bride's father. Now, we're asking politely to go in-side."

Despite her fading hope that she would see Sharlene get married, Ernestine smiled. Karen was talking to the guard now, looking so pretty in her powder-blue suit, that pillbox hat with the net over her face, hair twisted up in a bun. But it was hard to hear, with TV trucks jamming the country road. They barely gave that Rolls-Royce space to wind up the drive to the mansion.

I couldn't live in a house like that if I had a dollar for every time I breathed.

Ernestine couldn't get over all those folks running around with microphones in their hands and big cameras on their shoulders. You'd think Princess Diana had come back for another wedding.

She swallowed a wave of nausea. Soon, Saint Peter and Saint Paul would greet her at the pearly gates and welcome her inside. Unlike those mean-looking state troopers guarding this entrance. And Mack was getting loud with the guard, who looked at him like he had a screw loose.

I oughta go slap some sense into that young boy.

Karen was doing her best to stay calm. "Like we told you, I am Camille Morgan's sister. This is her father. And her mother."

The guard laughed. "Yeah, and I'm Santa Claus!"

Ernestine's cheeks stung. "Young man, watch yourself."

Mack balled his fists. "Listen, man—"

"Daddy, let me handle this."

All that bickering get on my last nerve. Been arguin' since we left Detroit. But she would rather have that than Karen's big brown eyes clouding up. And Mack doing everything, as if she couldn't heat up her own damn can of soup.

Well, some days I feel so weak I can't think straight. Ernestine thanked the Lord for blessing her with two people who cared so deeply about her. Unlike Sharlene. But Ernestine had known from that first doctor's visit two months ago that her ghost baby was not about to come back to Detroit and have some doctor slice out part of her body.

Even for me. Ernestine just knew. Sharlene never did know how to share. Even as a baby, that girl would have a fit whenever Karen tried to play with her raggedy dolls. Hated doctors, too. Every time she took Sharlene to the clinic for her asthma, that girl would kick and scream into next week. Poor child. She talked different, had a look in her eye like her mind was far away, in another place with other people. White people.

The minute Sharlene was born, Ernestine just wanted to cry all the time. She knew that baby's life on the color line would be one long trail of tears.

"Why'd I let him knock me up?" she'd whispered in the delivery room. She loved Mack. Still did. But back in the late sixties and early seventies, she had bought into all that hippie talk about free love and civil rights. But the world was too caught up on black this, white that, to leave little mixed kids alone to laugh and play. She knew the black kids would make fun of her pale daughter. That white kids wouldn't think she was good enough. And her child might hate her own mother for bringing her into the world.

Ruby's probably twistin' and turnin' in her grave right now. Mama, too.

Her mother had been so disappointed, after she and Dad came up to Detroit to make a good living for their daughters by working at Ford. No wonder Mama was so mad. Both daughters got pregnant, dropped out of school, and got on welfare. Now, with the Lord calling her home, Ernestine would get to tell Mama and Ruby all about how Sharlene got herself a rich boy and tricked the whole clan into thinkin' she was white!

"I'm real sorry y'awl came all the way here," the guard said. "But if you don't leave, we'll have these officers escort you out."

If looks could kill, that man would be long gone with Karen staring like that. And Mack, you could almost see steam shooting from his ears as the guard held that damn list. *Oh Lord, he's gonna grab it and rip it to shreds.*

But a state trooper in mirrored sunglasses took the list. "Lemme see what I can do here to help y'awl out." The trooper started to dial a phone.

Ernestine straightened her back. *Lord, grant me this one last wish in life.*

40

Millie Stone burst into the bedroom where Jeff was pulling on tuxedo pants in front of a tall cherry dresser. She slammed the door.

"Mom! Can you knock?"

She stormed toward him. "Jefferson Stone!"

He froze, facing her. "What's wrong?"

"There's a colored woman down at the gate. Says she's Camille's mother! A white man and a mulatta . . . they're with her. I want an explanation!"

Jeff flashed that I'm-always-right expression that he'd inherited from Monty: his gaze sharpened, his nose flared a bit, his full bottom lip tightened. He tucked in his white shirt and fastened his pants.

"Mom, that's ridiculous." Jeff placed his hands on the sides of her arms. "Pop said someone would try to sabotage my wedding—"

Millie balled her trembling fingers. "My gracious, I knew there was more to that girl than meets the eye. But this—"

Jeff guided her to a floral-print chintz chair. Below, past the veranda railing, was the giant pink tent. But never would she allow this. Never!

"Mom, relax. Did you see the news this morning?" A few feet away, Jeff adjusted his striped ascot in the long mirror. "Some left-wing crackpot on the Ethics Committee wants an investigation about

Dark Secret

Pop's involvement with tobacco legislation. This is probably just—"

Something white-hot and primitive propelled Millie toward him, waving a finger. "Jeff, I will not have you humiliate this family by marrying a mulatta."

Jeff threw his tie on the dresser. "Mom! This is downright insulting! You couldn't possibly think I would—"

"My gracious, I don't know what to think anymore. You call off a wedding with the most desirable girl in the county. Then you shack up with a common Yankee. And get her *pregnant*. Now this."

Jeff shook his head. "Mom, my judgment is as clear as the blue sky. Pop ordered extra security today because he knew all kinds of kooks would show up. Not to mention the media camped out there."

Millie's mind spun like the old spindle at Grandmother's house in Charlottesville. She remembered hearing her mother and aunts talk about their former friend who had married a black cook at the hunt club.

"It's downright dirty," her mother had said, as the ladies sat in their Sunday summer finery under the shade of dogwoods while the men played croquet on the rolling bank of the James. "And it makes mutts of the children."

"Heaven knows we've had enough of that here in Virginia," Aunt Gloria had nearly whispered, glancing discreetly at one of the light-skinned black maids serving lemonade. "What with the rumors about Thomas Jefferson and Sally Hemings. My, my! If our girls ever so much as looked at a colored boy, I'd have their hides."

Her mother had chimed in, "Coloreds. They're inferior in every way. It's just not right to mix. Goes against nature."

And society. And everything I've been raised to represent. Private finishing school. Debutante balls. Marriage into the most prestigious family in the Tidewater region. A husband who by birthright would be president. And no scheming black Yankee would jeopardize that. Nor would Jeff's poor judgment, Davis's shady business deals, or Dixie's secret crisis. Thank goodness that had been kept under wraps. Gracious, five years. But could it go on forever? She would wither up and die of shame if it ever got out. And Monty would kill . . .

"Jefferson Stone, I will not be deceived."

"Mom, slow down. Think about this. There couldn't be a drop of black blood in Camille. Blond hair, blue eyes, skin whiter than mine in the winter."

"We'd say that about Sally Hemings and Lucy if they walked in this room. But they were still Negro. Still slaves."

Jeff's laughter only made her tremble harder. "I've heard of wedding day jitters, Mom, but this is ridiculous. And Pop's guys checked into her parents' plane crash, her being raised by her aunt and uncle in Cleveland. The social security number, everything was legitimate."

Millie picked a thread from his shoulder. "Identities can be created."

Jeff combed his hair. "Where's Ida Mae?" He laughed. "Camille, black. Whoever came up with that scheme to embarrass Pop is downright berserk."

Millie cupped his clean-shaven jaw, looked into the eyes whose gaze only a pure-blood woman deserved to enjoy. "I will not have you disgrace our family name by marrying a mulatta who has tricked us all! I will not!"

Jeff held her wrists. "Mom—"

"I want the wedding stopped until this can be checked out!"

Jeff threw her hands down. His eyes hardened. "Mom, you sound as crazy as those people down at the gate!"

Millie slapped Jeff across the cheek. The sound hung in the silence for long moments. In his eyes was as much shock as she felt widening her own. She had never struck her son.

"My gracious, Jeff, I apologize."

She reached up to embrace him. But he stepped back, holding his cheek.

"Mom," he said softly, turning his back, "if you have such a low opinion of me, go talk to these people yourself. I'd bet money they're on Marcus Jones's bankroll."

"I think I'll do that," she said. "After I call off the wedding."

41

Camille gripped her bouquet to stop the spinning. Dixie and Ginger were two blurs of fluttering cream chiffon. Jeff, Dillon, and Jackson, columns of black. The reverend, a big plum topped by a smaller beige circle.

She swayed. Until Ginger's thin fingers clamped her upper arm.

But the perfume of huge sprays of lilies was going to make her vomit, right here, in front of the politicians and business moguls and their waxed, coiffed, and bejeweled wives. Every strum on the harp scraped her nerves. And she was sure, any minute, Karen and Mother would step right up for a freak show here under the pink tent.

She tried to listen to the reverend, but all she could hear was the mental replay of Mrs. Stone saying, "No need to dress. I'm canceling the wedding until I can 'verify' a few things." And her eyes turning to ice. But why had Hortense come minutes later to say the wedding was in fact on?

"Will you present symbols of your devotion today?" the reverend asked.

Jeff motioned for his four-year-old cousin to come forward with the white satin pillow. Camille smiled up at him as he slipped a sparkling wedding band, the one she had chosen, onto her trembling finger. She wanted to savor the moment she had craved for as long as she could remember. But she was numb. Stop! It was a false alarm, or Mrs. Stone would have called off the wedding.

Still, Camille imagined Karen standing in the pink-petal-strewn aisle, between all the garland-draped and bowed white chairs, shouting that Camille was a black fraud. Jeff would slap her, call her racist names. Senator Stone would cuss himself into cardiac arrest. And Mrs. Stone would rip off the tiara with bloody clumps of hair. The guards would drag her white gown through the dirt. All while Karen and Mama looked on, eyes aglow with vengeance.

And I'd be back where I started. Unloved and unhappy.

Camille smiled at Jeff, wishing she could turn around, inspect the scene for herself. But then she'd see Mrs. Stone, whose glare could start a bonfire.

"If anyone here objects to the holy union of this man and this woman," the reverend said, "let them speak now or forever hold their peace."

Gasps and shrieks erupted from the crowd. Behind her, Camille heard the rustle of people moving. The sound of chairs tipping over on the grass.

Camille's heart raced, but her limbs froze.

A man shouted, "Somebody get her!"

More shrieking ladies. She could only imagine them scrambling in flowered hats and dresses that cost as much as a small car.

Jeff spun around. "Oh, shit!"

Why can't Karen and Mother just let me be happy? Why can't they leave me alone? Camille's face twitched. She would burst into tears at any moment.

"My gracious!" Mrs. Stone shrieked. "Heavens no, not now!"

Camille was trying to muster up the nerve to turn around.

Until she heard barking dogs. Just like hounds chasing runaway slaves.

A heave rose in Camille's throat. The barking was getting louder. So were the squeals and frenzied sounds from the guests.

Ginger gasped.

Dixie said, "We should've seen this coming."

Then Jeff, shouting, "Somebody do something!" Fury and disappointment burned in his eyes as he looked down at her.

Dark Secret

It's over. Camille pivoted on a beaded slipper. Three of the Stones' hounds were romping over laps, feet, and turned-over chairs. There was Jezebel, charging down the petal-dotted aisle. In her mouth: a dead skunk!

Yes! Camille almost grinned. For any other bride, the sight and smell would have been horrific. But Camille's insides felt like the cool gush of a just-opened bottle of champagne. She laughed. Tingled. Laughed some more.

Jeff's expression flattened; he stared at her for long moments. Until relief washed over his face. He laughed, too. "You're the best!"

A team of groundskeepers in brown uniforms closed in on the dogs. One, with a net on a pole, seized the dead skunk from Jezebel. In their wake hung a horrible stench. All the flowers in the world could not cover it up. But people straightened chairs and smoothed rumpled clothes.

"Shall we continue?" the reverend asked with smiling eyes.

"Yes, I don't want to spend another minute as a single man," Jeff said.

The audience cheered. And Camille finally became Mrs. Jefferson Stone.

42

Karen's every thought was like a firecracker spreading hot sparks through her body. She could barely think straight enough to answer when the guard in the glass lobby of the *Washington News* asked whom Karen wanted to see.

"Freida Miller." She contemplated telling her friend all about Sharlene, imagining a Sunday morning headline: RACIST SENATOR WELCOMES BLACK WOMAN HOME TO THE PLANTATION. That would end the honeymoon!

"Girl," Freida said, rushing down the steps, braids bouncing. "Why didn't you say you were coming to town? We could've had dinner tonight."

Karen frowned. "I'm just in and out for the day, with my parents."

"Too bad." Freida was a few inches shorter, wearing a denim dress over her not fat, not thin build. "I've been worried about you, girl. With Franklin and your mother—"

"Look at me. I'm fine." Karen had not spoken much to Freida about details of Franklin's death or the subsequent scandal. She preferred to draw the line between friendship and work in situations like this, lest she see an off-the-record detail wind up in print. Karen had enough problems with rumors and suspicion in Detroit.

She didn't need it splashed on a national scale. "Freida, can we talk?"

"I'm crazed, doing this page-one Sunday story. Marcus Jones says Monty Stone planted a spy in his camp, but I don't know—"

A reporter Karen had seen outside Sharlene's wedding hunched between them. In fact, he had spoken with her father and taken some notes.

"Steve," Freida said. "How's it going?"

"Shitty." He shoved a hand in a pocket. "I didn't come here to play the fuckin' society reporter, bakin' all day in Virginia. And did I get into the wedding? Hell no!"

Freida jumped back playfully. "Sorry I asked."

The reporter's angry demeanor stopped Karen from introducing herself. And she wasn't quite sure if she was ready to divulge the complicated saga of her sister's white masquerade and Mama's desperate need for a kidney. No, she had to think of Plan C first.

Steve bit into a Snickers bar. "Well, it wasn't a complete waste of time. I met a guy who said he was Camille Stone's father. And her mother is black!"

Freida pressed a hand to Steve's forehead. "Just how long were you out in the sun today?"

Steve chomped. "If it's true, this would be one honkin' scandal."

"Not a chance," Freida said. "Camille Stone is as white as your eyeballs."

Karen remembered that photographer taking their picture back at the mansion. A mistake. She didn't even know where she worked.

"Listen," Karen said. "Some crazy woman with a baby showed up at the mayor's inaugural ball back in Detroit. She told anyone who would listen that Otis was the father."

"Was he?" Freida asked.

"Of course not." Karen said. "Someone put her up to it, just to ruin his night. So those folks you saw at the wedding—"

"I don't care what you two say," Steve said, peeling down the wrapper. "I need a big story to show those bastards upstairs that I'm too important to send to fires and car wrecks. And if this is true, my career is *made*."

"Dream on, Steve!" Freida cried after him as he sprinted up the stairs.

Karen rolled her eyes. "You don't believe that BS, do you?"

Freida shrugged. "Never know. But I highly doubt it. There's not a drop of black anywhere near that chick. Now, what did you want to tell me?"

43

This is nirvana. Camille kept reminding herself it was real: warm waves lapping her legs, the hot sun tickling her nude body, her new husband drizzling pina colada on her. As he slurped it off, her nipples pointed toward the cloudless blue sky while the rest of her melted. He nibbled his way up from her toes, taking delicious detours in oh-so-sensitive places.

She was determined not to let any worries deflate her euphoria. Not Karen, not how she would handle the pregnancy issue or quell Mrs. Stone's suspicion about that wedding-day brush with blackness.

Camille moaned as Jeff flicked his tongue over the fiery velvet between her legs. But Nick came to mind again. All week, she'd been staring into her dazzling ring as if it were a crystal ball, hoping to envision the least risky way to get five hundred grand in a hurry. Without Jeff noticing.

She quivered. "Baby, you do that so good . . ." The bonds. The bearer bonds from Uncle John. In Jeff's safe deposit box. But Camille didn't have signature privileges to access it. Yet.

With that solution taking root, she could let go . . . allow her limbs to tingle in the warm ocean foam as Jeff worked his oral magic. A few minutes later, she savored a new sense of serenity as he scooped her up, splashed through knee-high waves, then playfully tossed her into the turquoise sea.

Camille swam toward him.

"Come here," he said, lowering his lashes, staring at her lips as he pulled her close. Then, in one shoulder-rippling instant, he speared her like a giant fish, spinning her as she tightened her legs around his waist. The huge salmon-colored house dominating the top of the island and the anchored yacht that had brought them here whizzed past. Camille shuddered, thinking for a split second to do something nice when they got home to thank the senator's best friend for this wedding gift: a week here, chef, masseur, and yacht crew included.

I'm killing her . . .

The thought burst out in a sob. Jeff stilled, his eyes aglow with concern.

"Honey?"

Tears streamed down her wet cheeks. "I . . . I'm just happy."

"Get used to it." Jeff placed salty lips on her mouth.

But could she get used to this heart-clawing guilt? Or the fear that if she gave in to sleazy Nick Parker's demand, Jeff might discover the bonds missing and learn the truth about her? Would she ever know peace of mind?

Yes. She would do everything possible to preserve her new position and keep the ugly truth about herself buried. Forever. So she moaned and kissed her new husband, until she thought of nothing but the erotic euphoria dancing through her flesh.

44

Karen gathered up the résumés, the ivory linen paper still warm from the copier at the downtown Detroit Kinko's. She carried the stack to a table by the floor-to-ceiling windows facing the street circling the mirrored-glass hotel-office towers of the Renaissance Center.

Plunking into a chair, she matched a résumé with the cover letter and envelope addressed to the head of public relations at Ford Motor Company in nearby Dearborn. She would have preferred to stay in politics, but right now, a job was a job. Sealing the manila envelope, she glanced at the next letter, for the Denver city councilwoman she'd met last year at a Democratic women's conference.

What a relief to finally have a few hours to do this, after a day of taking Mama to the doctor, then meeting with that loan officer who said they'd depleted all resources for getting the bakery back. It was almost midnight, but she could still get these in the mail tonight.

"Karen." A high voice, and a blue Kinko's smock, made her look up. "You left this on the counter."

"I'm not a scatterbrain, really," Karen said, smiling. "Just tonight."

"No problem." The clerk returned to customers at the register.

Karen took this as a sign she needed rest. But lately she was lucky to get two, three hours of sleep a night, even after her usually effective insomnia tonic of peanut butter cookies, warm milk, and the ever-growing stack of newsweekly magazines next to her bed.

"Senator Monty Stone. Should I, or shouldn't I?" Her thumbs, grasping each side of the letter, suddenly seemed darker as they pointed to his name. She'd written this about a week ago, right after getting home from Sharlene's wedding, thinking this might be Plan C. But something held her back.

She pulled her cell phone from her purse, speed-dialed Freida.

"Girl, it's late. And you sound like hell."

"Quick question. Does Stone still have a job opening?"

Freida yawned. " 'Gaping hole' or 'gorge' might be better words. With you on the case, my life would be a lot easier."

"I don't know," Karen said, stuffing an envelope for a government relations position at a small company in Chicago. "All this with Franklin. It's left me kinda jaded."

"All the better," Freida said. "Then you won't mind working for an ultraconservative. And you need to get out of town, girl. All those rumors—"

"I don't want to leave Mama."

"What is it, an hour to fly to Detroit? His chief of staff even told me they're looking for some brown window dressing at the Big House."

Karen laughed, raising an envelope to her mouth.

"Oh, girl, listen. My editor is all hot and bothered about this rumor that Stone's daughter-in-law is black!"

Karen's tongue stilled on the bitter glue strip.

"He almost had me cancel an interview with the head of the Ethics Committee—"

Sweet Jordan Kyles.

"Anyway," Freida said, "this tabloid has a mixed couple that says they're her parents."

"Yeah, and there's an alien baby starting kindergarten in Memphis," Karen said with a deep chuckle. That was all she could do to cool a hot gush of panic. No, she would not tell Freida that Camille Morgan Stone was her sister. Not yet, anyway. That was her trump card in this life-and-death game to save Mama. And she didn't want anyone else to play it.

But getting close to Freida and Stone might be the one-two punch Karen needed to make Sharlene change her mind.

"Go back to bed, Freida. My letter is going in the mail tonight."

About ten minutes later, sealed envelopes under her arm, Karen hurried onto the sidewalk, bundling the collar of her black leather jacket to her neck as the wind whipped her ponytail into her cheek. Fortunately the main post office on Fort Street was open all night, with its constant buzz of customers and people coming to or leaving work.

She would not allow fear to paralyze her. And since the mere scent of raspberry had clouded her senses with paranoia at that inn in Virginia, Karen had decided *No more*. She would carry on, let the police do their business, and hope that thug would finally realize she didn't have his damn diamonds.

Karen slid into her car, plopping her packets and purse on the passenger seat. Then, listening to that Luther Vandross song that made her think of Franklin and cry, she sped off to the post office. There, she pulled behind a truck at the meters near the well-lit door, dropped her keys in her lap, then leaned over the passenger seat for her envelopes. She vaguely noticed car lights and slamming doors behind her.

Until she turned to open her door. She pulled the black latch, but it wouldn't budge. And on the other side of the glass, a dark coat. She dove toward the passenger door. But there, too, was a green jacket, from hip to chest, and someone jiggling the handle. Back to the driver's-side door, the silver tip of a gun aimed right at her throat.

45

On Camille's first day back to work after the honeymoon, taking care of Nick was number one on her "to do" list. On her noontime break, she had her driver take her to her bank.

"I'm here for Jefferson Stone," Camille told the heavyset redhead working the safe-deposit boxes. The thin brunette normally there when Camille came with Jeff must have been at lunch. "He wants to add a name to the safe-deposit box signature card," Camille said.

"Sure," the woman said. "Take this card, have him and the new person sign it, and fill in the name of whoever he'd like to add."

Camille smiled. "Thank you."

The next morning, Camille returned to the bank, carrying the card with Jeff's signature authorizing her access to the safe-deposit box. She handed it to the usual brunette, who escorted Camille into the silver chamber, where she unloaded half the crisp green sheets into her black leather Chanel backpack.

Next, Camille called their broker's neighborhood office just down Fifth Avenue from the town house. She had to do this unbeknownst to their broker, Mr. Harris; the last time Camille had tried to get the limit raised on a credit card to accommodate a Barney's spree, he'd immediately reported her to Jeff.

"Mr. Harris, please," she said into her cell phone from the backseat of her chauffeured car, parked in front of the office. When he came on the line, she said, "Mr. Harris, this is security at the parking garage. Your alarm is going off, and it appears your vehicle has been vandalized." A minute later, he dashed down the street.

Inside, Camille was ushered into the office of Ms. Eaton, another broker, whose henna highlights glowed in the sunshine pouring through the blinds.

Camille set the bonds on the desk. "I need to deposit these into my account."

Ms. Eaton flipped through them. "Do you have a purchase receipt?"

Camille slumped, letting her face droop. "No, they're an inheritance from my father. I just—" She blinked away tears. "Sorry. The funeral—"

"I know what you're going through. Lost my mother to cancer last year."

"Oh no, I'm sorry," Camille said. "I want to sell them at the current market price and get a cashier's check. How long will that take?"

"Normally three days, but with you being a good client, we can short-settle, and get it to you today."

"Perfect," Camille said.

But as she hurried out of Ms. Eaton's office, Camille bumped right into Mr. Harris.

46

Jeff barely noticed the clunk of his briefcase hitting the table in the foyer. No, all he heard was Camille's laughter upstairs. And Rand's voice.

"Baby Boy, what you doin' home so early?" Ida Mae closed the front door and picked up his briefcase.

From the foot of the steps, Jeff could not make out what they were saying. "How long's he been here?"

"Not half an hour." Ida Mae ran her palms over her white apron.

"This ever happened before?"

"Not that I know of. But they was talkin' about money."

Jeff ground his teeth. His black wing tips took the stairs three at once as he loosened his tie and unfastened the top button of his English blue shirt. Mom and Pop owned this place, but that didn't give Rand carte blanche to come as he pleased. Or lay claim to the lady of the house.

My wife. Who suddenly needs five hundred grand without telling me.

In the upper hallway, Jeff paused under the chandelier. Pop's voice shot from his memory banks: "Son, never let them see you sweat." He could still see his parents retreating to the limousine under the brick portico at Foxbury Academy. Leaving him for twelve academic years, where Jeff learned to project confidence when nervous about a test. Calm when furious he'd lost a polo match. And indifference while wishing he were home in Mom's lap as she read *Robin Hood* or *The Three Musketeers.*

Now he painted a steely mask over the arrows of jealousy and suspicion shredding him inside. Rand had to leave, now.

"Hey, you guys," Jeff said, stepping into the cavernous salon Camille had had him pay a small fortune to decorate in golds and bronzes just after she took the bar exam in July. She was flashing way too much leg, on the couch next to Rand, who wore one of those mod outfits he no doubt got from Ginger.

"Hi, baby," she purred, standing to crush her breasts into his chest. God, why did she have to smell so good, her hair feel so soft as he touched his palms to her back? And why did her pillowy pink lips and cat eyes dazzle him so, turning those blaring questions to mere whispers in his mind?

"You're early," she said, poking an opalescent fingernail into the knot of his blue silk tie. Her rings sparkled in the soft evening light that filtered through the window sheers.

"My settlement conference let out sooner than expected." Jeff stared deeply into her eyes, looking for answers. He kept his back to his brother.

"Is that good news or bad news?" she asked.

"Good, for my client. I wanted to hold out for more, but Uncle John said grab the offer on the table and run with it."

Camille combed her fingers through his hair, smiling. "Then let's celebrate. I'll have Ida Mae bring up some champagne. Sparkling cider for the mother-to-be, of course." She patted her stomach as she swayed toward the door, where she turned back and smiled. "Jeff, let's order Thai and eat on the terrace. I have a craving like you wouldn't believe."

The glow in Rand's eyes only intensified Jeff's sour-stomach memory of the last time Camille had talked him into sampling that mouth-burning dish he couldn't pronounce from the Thai place over on Lexington.

"You can put your eyes back in your head now." Jeff shoved his right hand in his hip pocket. There was something about his brother, maybe all that hair flowing over his shoulders, or the self-assured smirk, that made Jeff want to whale on him. "This game is old, Rand. Time to grow up."

Rand laughed. "Looks like you're having a Suzanne Calhoun flashback."

"No, it seems you are." Jeff's pulse hammered in his veins as he remembered Rand trying to steal his girlfriend, kissing Suzanne in the cabana during Jeff's sixteenth birthday party. And wiping the shrimp sauce from Tabitha's low-cut dress at the Christmas party a few years back. "Little brother, you're out of luck this time. So take your 'sensitive guy' act back up to those hoodlums you're trying to save in Harlem. And stay there."

Rand stood, stretching his arms over his head, exhaling. "Camille needed a little advice today. Just wanted to help out the family." Those last two words came out with a snide twang.

"Seems you would've learned your lesson about butting into family matters where you're not needed." Jeff's tone hardened with the memory of Rand shielding Mom from Pop and having Dr. Zane stitch up his head in his room as a result.

Rand's shoulder twitched. "If there's even a split second of 'like father, like son' going on here—"

Jeff grabbed a handful of Rand's hair, twisted it so hard Rand's head snapped back. "Little brother, no need for you to call again."

Camille's footsteps in the hallway made Jeff release the fistful of hair.

She swayed into the room, her gaze moving back and forth between them. "Whoa. You could blow out the windows with all the testosterone in here."

"Rand was just leaving."

"No," Camille said. "One toast to you, baby."

Rand took a glass from Ida Mae's tray, his eyes full of defiance.

Jeff ground his teeth. The thought of Camille confiding in his brother seared him with sweat. Didn't she know that whatever the situation, he would always try to help? And if she needed the money for her aunt's medical bills back in Cleveland, he could work something out. Or was she trying to pay off her law school bills in one lump sum? But this was way more than that. Jeff would find out as soon as Rand left. He took the flute from Camille, holding it up alongside her and Rand's glasses.

"To my brilliant husband. Lawyer extraordinaire."

That word, rhyming with "millionaire," roused an uneasy pang in Jeff's gut as they sipped. Rand set his glass on the tray.

"Gotta go," he said, looking at his watch. "The kids have play rehearsal."

"Thanks, Rand," Camille called after him as he left.

Jeff fanned a hand on her back, guiding her to the plush couch. He pushed away the tasseled pillows taking up the sitting space, then sat her down, their knees touching. "Honey, is there anything you want to talk about?"

Camille's jaw stuck out a bit. "Actually, I'm really stumped on this brief I'm writing for—"

"No, about us."

She pulled her hair up, then let it tumble. "Like what?"

He hated to think she would ever deceive him. As Tabitha had. Using him as a front to her conservative family, wanting to get married as a cover for her muff-diving depravity. *No, Camille loves me for me.* But Mr. Harris had been banking with his family forever, and Jeff had never even heard him tell a joke. He wouldn't make a mistake about something this grave.

"Whatever you felt compelled to share with Rand," Jeff said.

"It's nothing," Camille whispered.

Jeff stroked her cheek, leaning closer. "Honey, you can tell me anything that runs through that pretty little head of yours. No secrets between us."

Camille stuck out her jaw a bit more. "Jeff, every case you touch turns to gold. But I have performance anxiety. I'm terrified of making a mistake."

Jeff wanted to believe that was the extent of it. "Honey, you're smarter than ninety-nine percent of the women lawyers out there. Judge Mannington's rave reviews are all the proof you need."

Camille laid her head on his shoulder, ran a hand around his waist. "Thanks, baby. I can't believe I was afraid to talk to you about this. But I thought you'd get sick of me yakking about whether I passed the bar."

Jeff kissed the top of her head. "Honey, I'm here for you. For-ever."

Camille purred, "You have no idea what that means to me."

Jeff bit down so hard, his jaw ached. He hesitated to ask Camille why she'd forged his name on the signature card for the safe-deposit box before stealing his bonds; she might clam up as she had after they'd read from the journals at White Pines. But how could he find out what was going on?

Dillon. A few hours later, Jeff called Saxton Investigations.

"Hey, sailor boy," Dillon said. "When are you and your pretty bride comin' back to the Commonwealth?"

"Don't know. But I need you to check somebody out for me."

"Sure, anything for you, sailor boy. Who'll it be?"

"My wife."

47

The deep rumble of the garage door opening downstairs made Karen bolt from the tweed armchair next to her parents' bed. Mama's face, framed by fluffy peach pillows and blankets, was smooth and peaceful, finally. Karen kissed her cheek, then turned out the light.

She bolted down the hallway, stopping to raise the thermostat against the blustery October evening. Past her bedroom—the break-in at her apartment, then the post office threats from the charcoal-skinned diamond thug, had convinced her to move in with her parents. And until she found another job, she was making meals and driving Mama to dialysis while Daddy was at work. But she suspected he'd been elsewhere tonight.

The slick bottoms of Karen's slippers, which looked like brown teddy bears in the front, helped her glide down the steps, through the dark living room, into the kitchen. An angel-shaped night light above the cane-backed dinette set cast an eerie glow on the yellow curtains and cupboards. Karen was going to tell her father this was not the time for a relapse.

"Don't look at me like that," he said, peering over the open re-frigerator door. "I've been at a Gamblers Anonymous meeting."

Karen slammed the door, sniffing for booze fumes. "Did Johnny Walker and Jack Daniel's happen to be the guest speakers? And was this the souvenir?" She snatched what she thought was a horse betting ticket from the breast pocket of his navy-blue work jacket. But it was a drugstore receipt.

He grabbed it. "For your ma's prescription." He pulled a white bag from his back pocket. "Here. And stop looking like I'm the fox who ate the hen."

For an instant, she wanted to remind him that if he gambled away the mortgage payment, she couldn't help this time, because she had no job. But while her mouth stayed quiet, she probed him with her eyes.

"Christ, Karen. I spent the day in court trying to get the deed to Phyllis's house. So I can use the money to get your ma's bakery back."

Karen crossed her arms. "I don't want to hear about those people!" Even though she knew the death of his wife and son in that fiery car-train crash outside Windsor was what had brought him home to her and Mama. But Karen could scarcely focus on her father's sad eyes when she thought about him teaching her half-brother to drive his boat or bait a fishhook out on Lake St. Clair. Never knowing his father had another family just across the water.

"You've hurt Mama enough!" She would not let the tears come. She had shed enough as a child. But why couldn't she trust her father? She always sensed he was building up her faith that he would do right, only to let it tumble like so many dominoes. Why did everything have to be so hard? Being a parent meant taking care of business, no matter what. And that was what Karen had to do. Whatever it took to put family first. Unlike her sister.

In the morning, she decided, she would make a follow-up call to Senator Stone's office. She had indeed mailed the letter and résumé to his office that night, after calling the police and giving a report right there in front of the post office, after the men ran away when a squad car patrolled past. At least now the police seemed to believe her. But that incident made her want all the more to get out of town. At least for a while. So tomorrow, she would also get her favorite power suit, the fitted russet one, from the cleaner's, in case she had to fly out for an interview. It was time for Plan C.

48

Jeff dashed into the bedroom, not bothering to take off his suit jacket before curling around Camille on the bed. She was like a red caterpillar in her thick bathrobe as he pulled her wet, puffy face into his chest. His pulse raced even faster as she sobbed and pressed a hand into her stomach.

"Honey? Is the baby—"

She burrowed deeper into his shirt and tie.

"I'll call an ambulance." Jeff reached for the phone on the night-stand.

"It's . . ." she whispered, "too late."

"No. It can't be. Ida Mae said you were sick. Not—"

Looking up, dark smudges ringed her eyes. "I already went to the doctor."

Jeff buried his face in her hair, where he couldn't smell the cleaning chemicals that had assaulted his nose when he entered the room. He could see his mother's face, disappointment clouding her eyes, finger-tips on the locket. No, this couldn't be right. Even though Camille had not been showing yet, their baby couldn't be dead. A healthy man like himself, from superior stock, should succeed at something so nat-ural. Especially with a woman physically fit and just twenty-eight. "But how?"

Camille let out a squeaky sob, a wheeze. "I'm so sorry, Jeff. Your mom and Dixie, they were so excited—"

"Your asthma?"

She shook her head. "The doctor said it was under control, didn't hurt the baby. It was just—"

"What?" Jeff found no answers in her eyes. What could possibly be going on? All in the middle of jury selection. But a medical emergency was just that, and fuck the judge if he didn't understand.

A rattling sound made him look at the bathroom door. Out came Ida Mae, carrying a bucket with yellow rubber gloves, a scrub brush, and several bottles of cleanser.

"Ida Mae, are you trying to kill us with those fumes? Do that later. When Camille feels better."

"Hmmph! I know you don't want to see the mess she made in there. Look like somebody slaughtered a hog—"

Camille let out a stuffy-nosed sigh.

"Ida Mae, just go," he said. She left the room and closed the door.

He stroked Camille's arm. "Honey, how could this happen?"

"Do you still love me?" she whispered.

The question was, did he trust her? And without trust, what was love? Immediately, though, he knew: yes, because love was the horrible sensation seeping through him at the mere thought that she was hurting, physically or emotionally. He pressed his forehead to hers. "Lady Godiva. I love you more than life." Still, he had to know how this could happen. After a few minutes, after her sobbing had quieted, he asked, "What about you being on the pill when you got pregnant? Could that—"

"No. Genetics, stress, even that Brie I ate over the weekend. There's this bacteria called Listeria that lives in soft cheese—"

Stress. Camille was under too much pressure from her job. She needed to relax. And Jeff would not, he just would not, fail at something that people on welfare did so easily. Jeff stroked her hair, looked into her eyes. "Honey, I think we'd have better luck starting a family at White Pines."

Camille held his gaze, her eyes and face freezing into a mask void of emotion. "Jeff, the town house. My job. The kids at the center. New York!"

Dark Secret

He scooped her into a sitting position, holding her back against his chest. "We can visit. But this way, I can help Pop. Losing his press secretary just shows he needs a strong team to get where he wants to go." Jeff rested his chin on her shoulder. "And you can focus on getting pregnant again."

Camille's shiny fingernails disappeared into the bunched robe over her gut. "I'm sorry. You just don't know—"

No, he didn't know a lot of things lately. But Dillon was going to help him find out just what secrets his Lady Godiva was keeping.

49

Monty Stone flung a stack of résumés and recommendation letters, causing a great flutter across his polished mahogany desk. He pulled off his silver half-glasses and tossed them so hard they clanged into the brass-framed picture of himself and his daddy, taken forty-some years ago on the steps of the governor's mansion.

"Hell, Rollins. When the ship is sinking, the captain doesn't think about hiring a new deck mate. Especially a colored one!"

"Monty," Rollins said, standing across the gold-star-patterned cobalt carpet, near the colonial-style blue couch and armchairs facing the fireplace. He touched the waist-high wooden stand around a brown globe. "The Election Commission is breathing down Jones's neck. The polls won't mean a thing—"

"Don't give me that broken-record bullshit. We've got one week!"

Rollins pulled a hankie from his pocket to shine his tortoiseshell glasses. "Our best bet? Get our ducks in order for the presidential—"

"Why the devil has it been so hard to find a new press secretary?" Those two words conjured up images of Vivian in a slinky negligee, luring him into her bedroom. Or tearfully accepting the money for her son's medical bills. Sashaying into his office at lunchtime for a quickie before he returned to the Senate floor. And now, accusing him of the worst kind of debauchery.

Dark Secret

"So I'm gun-shy." Monty fanned his fingers. Pretty hands that knew just how to make a woman squeal. But the polish was chipped, and a hangnail stung his left thumb. He pushed the intercom button on his phone. "Lucille, sugar, make me an appointment for my nails." Lifting the button, he looked at Rollins and said, "Now you want me to do something to make my daddy claw from the grave. Just to whip my tail."

Rollins furrowed his brow, checking the lenses several times against the light of the tall, gold-draped windows. With the glasses back on his prominent nose, under the side-parted chestnut hair that was in perpetual need of a good combing, he pulled a letter from his suit jacket. "Monty, there's one applicant in particular who stands out. Here's a positively glowing recommendation."

Stone bit off the hangnail. "Hell, don't tell me. It's from the NAACP."

Rollins chuckled, holding the letter closer. "No, sir, it's from a company in Atlanta called . . . Wish Master. Apparently had business in Detroit."

Monty scanned the framed maps of Virginia covering the white walls of his high-ceilinged office here on the fourth floor of the Russell Senate Building, just across from the Capitol. "I'd just as soon hire a lumberjack from Oregon than—"

"Monty, we received hundreds of résumés, but this girl does stand out. And if we play our cards right, she could work wonders."

Stone stood, pulling a cigar from the monogrammed humidor, a gift from the ambassador to England, on the credenza behind his desk. "The girl might have some secret left-wing agenda." Stone raised the unlit cigar. "Or some blasted feminist chip on her shoulder. And my standards—"

"Monty, there are quite a few astute blacks here on the Hill."

Stone watched Rollins read that letter again. True, Rollins had guided him through countless campaigns to win the state legislature and five terms in Congress. But this new idea, it just didn't taste right. Still, with the lawsuits and the Ethics Committee about to bite, maybe a bold new plan was the answer.

"Hell, Rollins. You got my go-ahead."

Rollins glanced at his watch. "Then we'd better head out. I've staged a sort of cattle call. At the Ritz, of course."

"Only a superstar will suffice." Stone slid his unlit cigar in his breast pocket as they headed for the door. A short time later, Stone followed Rollins into a meeting room, where dozens of people in suits greeted them with handshakes. A deep voice drew his attention to a crowd in the corner.

"You are the very definition of a sellout, Uncle Tom, house Negro," said a man in African garb with a hairdo reminiscent of Medusa. He was pointing down at a young woman. "Sista, black folks like you show nothing's changed since Willie Lynch. The high yellow ones always the first to sell out."

Stone nodded at Rollins, who immediately pulled out a cell phone. A foreboding twist in his gut reminded Stone this was a preposterous plan. Coloreds had no sense of decorum, no—

"It's called equal opportunity," the woman said. "I have the right to work for any person I so choose. Maybe I believe Senator Stone's position that black folks should wake up and stop taking handouts from the white man."

Stone stepped closer. What a beauty! She was all legs in a short, russet business suit, high heels, a cape of curly dark hair. Big brown Sophia Loren eyes with long, black lashes. Skin like golden-baked pie crust.

"If folks would just get on with the business of school and work and self-improvement," she said with squared shoulders, "maybe black America would be a different place."

The man snarled, "You're brainwashed, girl. Been listening to the devil so long, you're preaching his venom."

"Oh, that's right," the woman said, her gaze sharp. "Your group says white people like my father are the devil."

"You are a sad excuse for a black woman," the man shot back.

Stone felt a stirring somewhere deep down. She seemed to stand taller as she said, "Look around, see who holds the power. White men. And your separatist rhetoric won't change that. Or improve people's lives."

Several people applauded just as two security guards came to escort the man out. Those eyes sparkled as she approached. She smiled, her upper arm raising half her luscious bosom as she extended a dainty hand.

"Senator Stone." A voice like warm syrup. "Pleasure to see you again."

He grasped her fingers. He could just bite that cute little nose, spend a day or two sucking on the full lips pulling back in a bright smile. The chatter and movement of all the people around them blurred to a quiet gray, as if she were the Technicolor star in an old black-and-white film.

"Sugar, I'd remember meeting you. Do me a favor, jog my memory."

"It was at an urban renewal conference, here in D.C. Two years ago."

He leaned toward her shoulder. Perfume like butter cake. "Please—what is your name?"

"Karen Bradley. You gave a rousing speech about states' rights." She moved like liquid, heading to sit at a table with him and Rollins.

"Tell me, Miss Bradley, what makes you want—"

She crossed sheer-stockinged legs. He remembered the jaw-clamping lust and longing stirred while reading his forefathers' journals. *A mulatto mistress . . .*

"What makes you want to work for me?" He grasped the résumé as Rollins, to his right, slid it into his hands.

"I handled media for the city council president, back in Detroit." She hung a burgundy leather shoulder bag over the back of the chair.

Rollins whispered, "Mysterious suicide, scandal over a land deal."

A lens of suspicion dropped over Stone's gaze. "Tragic story. How were you involved?" He studied her. If she had one shifty glance, or nervous twitch, she would be last week's lunch. No troublemakers in Monty Stone's battalion. Too easy for enemies to entice her into becoming a saboteur.

"I became disillusioned with the Democratic party," she said with a riveting gaze. "Your message of self-determination is what I'm about."

Stone skimmed her résumé. "Howard. Three-point-nine GPA. Communications. Campus newspaper."

Her arched brows drew together. "Without my UNCF scholarship, it would have been impossible."

Rollins's phone rang. "Senator, it's Kurt back at the office. Says GNN is calling again, about the lawsuits."

"Blasted reporters."

Miss Bradley pulled a laptop computer from her attaché. "May I?" She started typing. "I'll prepare a statement. That reporter will wonder why they even bothered to call."

A smile almost parted Stone's lips. Eye candy with a brain to boot. Just what the consultants had ordered. But she was all wrong. Hell, she was colored. The people who stole his father had deprived America of a great leader. But how could he turn her away? A quick glance around the room, and she was the Hope diamond in a bucket of rocks. Still, he couldn't shake Daddy's voice: "If something seems too good to be true, boy, you can damn well be sure it is."

50

Just home from work, Camille balanced mail in her left hand, flipping envelopes with the glazed bronze nail on her right index finger. Under the yellow beam of a recessed light in the town house foyer, she came to a pink envelope addressed to Mrs. Jefferson Stone.

The letter had no return address, and the postmark was smudged. It was probably from Karen, sending a picture of Mother in an open casket or an obituary saying, "Daughter Sharlene preceded her in death." After all, she hadn't heard from her sister since the wedding a month ago.

Her chest tightened even more. *Relax. You can't stay this stressed out.*

Camille pulled out a card. On the outside, a cloudy pink border around a black-and-white image of a woman rocking a swaddled baby. Inside, in handwriting with *i*'s dotted with circles: *"Camille, I never had a sister to get me through the scary and sad times. But I feel your loss more intensely than I can say. I'm here for you. Call anytime. Hugs, Dixie."* What did Dixie know about loss? She did behave rather strangely when it came to babies, but she exhibited the same maternal instinct toward animals. Camille picked up the hall phone and dialed Dixie's apartment at the University of Virginia.

"Dixie, the card is sweet."

"My heart is just breaking for you. I know—" Was that a sob?

"Dixie, I'm okay. Sorry this is upsetting you so much."

Dixie exhaled. "I just don't want you to have to suffer."

Camille's eyes burned; guilt cramped her stomach. "Maybe Jeff and I will have good news by Christmas. You'll be home for the party, right?"

"Unfortunately," Dixie said. "The one time I tried to skip the party, Pop had two of his security guys find me at a friend's in Charlottesville and fly me to White Pines in time for a yuletide toast. And Mom had a fit. So I'll be there." Dixie had sulked at the past three holiday parties Camille had attended at White Pines. Yet it baffled Camille how anyone could be unhappy amidst such opulence and indulgence, even though she knew Dixie found it obscene to spend so much money on a gala when other people were starving and suffering.

A few minutes later, Camille scanned return addresses on the other envelopes. Still nothing from the State Bar of New York. What was taking so long? A simple letter, saying yes you passed or no you flunked, was all she wanted. Not that it mattered. In just two days, she couldn't believe she'd be walking away from the job that sent an envious rustle along the law school grapevine. Now, spending the rest of her life in that giant house where slaves had bled to death and spooky music played in empty rooms was not what she had in mind as Mrs. Jefferson Stone.

Nor was this level of anxiety. But with just forty-eight hours until she would put a crisp green muzzle on Nick, Camille's brain whizzed images and questions so fast it made her nauseous. She'd already cashed the cashier's check; her Chanel bag was hidden in the back of her closet, stuffed to the brim. She would not, however, let it erode her cool demeanor. No, she would get past these glitches, eventually convince Jeff to let her work as a lawyer in Washington, and somehow avoid the pregnancy issue. Somehow.

Camille tucked Dixie's card into her purse on the table. Next to it: an orange bag holding a naughty Halloween treat she had picked up during lunch for Jeff. Last year, she had worn ribbons on her pigtails, a ruffled minidress, lace bobby socks with red patent-leather pumps. All while Jeff flashed a lusty grin and said, "I've got a special lollipop just for you." This year Camille hoped to arouse an even more frenzied tryst.

Taking off her mink-collared ivory cashmere coat in the silence, she figured Jeff was still at the office, Ida Mae in the kitchen making what smelled like stuffed peppers for dinner. Camille stepped past the stairs to the closet, where she hung her coat. All those hulking wardrobe boxes, in the sitting room, were like warlocks watching from the darkness.

The doorbell rang. Stop! There would be no more cringing or startling or wondering. She would not live her life peering around every corner, every door, wondering if Karen were about to pounce. A quick glance down the hall revealed no sign of Ida Mae coming to answer the door. So Camille swayed to the vestibule, looking through one of the small, eye-level windows. She smiled and opened the door, letting in a cool gust from the lamp lit street.

"Dillon!" She tiptoed, even in her heels, to plant a loud kiss on his cold cheek. "What brings you to the Big Apple?"

"Business," he said, the word coming out like those globs of green-brown spit when he and Jeff chewed tobacco while watching football on TV whenever they were together.

"Does Jeff know you're in town?" Camille helped him remove his double-breasted brown leather jacket. That brought to mind how his linebacker thickness had dwarfed Ginger in the trendy downtown bar where the four of them were hanging out a few years ago, to make a Dillon-Ginger love connection. But Ginger said she'd be terrified to go to bed with him, lest he accidentally steamroll her in his sleep.

"Sure does." Dillon all but took out a jeweler's loupe to get a closer look in her eyes. What was his problem tonight? Was he working on a tough case? Not getting enough roughage? The parentheses etched around his dark mustache and thin lips appeared deeper; his eyes raked her beige windowpane pantsuit. He slid the leather cap off his shiny scalp. "Sailor boy home yet?"

"I'm not sure, but—"

"Hey, man." Jeff, in faded jeans and a blue crew-neck sweater, stopped midway down the stairs. "Come on up."

The steps creaked under Dillon's brown suede hiking boots.

"Baby," she said, smiling up at Jeff, who did not look away from Dillon, "I didn't know you were home."

"Tell Ida Mae to hold dinner, about forty-five minutes." Jeff disappeared back up the steps.

Camille kicked off her pumps. Her heels pounded the tiled hallway, past the elevator, past the lighted, shell-shaped niches in the bronze walls.

"Millie, you bes' not!" Ida Mae almost shouted, her back to the kitchen doorway. The gray cordless phone, cradled on her left shoulder, appeared connected to her stiff uniform as she stirred a steaming pot on the wide blue stove. "Boarding school, my foot—"

Camille stepped back, to hear without being seen. She couldn't believe Ida Mae's tone. And she was dropping the "Miss" before "Millie" again, as if *she* were the boss. "Don't matter how long it's been, Millie. Far as I'm concerned, things can stay as is. The world too messed up." Ida Mae exhaled.

Along with the rumble of boiling water and a pan rattling the wire rack in the oven came the rustle of paper. "The *People's Enquirer*. Yes, ma'am. It's a small picture of a black woman in a wheelchair, with a white man, and a girl. Can't make out her face, all that net from her hat—"

Camille sucked in air, lungs whistling. If that was what she thought—

"Millie, I done told you. They at the gate. It says 'Mack Campbell claims he was shut out of his own daughter's wedding at Senator—' "

Camille clamped her hand over her mouth. To hold back a cough, a sob, a gasp. They really had been there! Mother, Daddy, Karen . . . at White Pines. Trying to crash the wedding. And now in a tabloid, for Mrs. Stone and Ida Mae—and Jeff—to see. Camille's chest rose up and down, tightening, aching.

Need my inhaler . . . She dashed to the foyer, fished through her purse on the table. Exhaled as much as she could. Closed her lips around the yellow plastic tube, depressed the metal canister, sucked in the cool mist.

But her lungs were so tight, she coughed out the medication. Tried again. There, a little relief. She perched on the steps, closing her eyes, imagining her pinkish bronchial tubes opening, her limbs not trembling.

Just how much information was in that tabloid? And why was Jeff conferring with Dillon upstairs? Had he, too, seen that picture? On the flight to their honeymoon, he had joked about the incident, blaming political quacks.

She would do the same. Camille straightened her spine, finally took a deep breath. Yes, she would carry on as planned.

A short time later, after Dillon had left, Camille sat in her usual gold-skirted chair across the long table from Jeff. He did not look up from his salad. But she would find out what was bothering him, and make it better, before the first bite of what smelled like apple pie for dessert.

"Miss Camille, that's your nonfat vinaigrette." Ida Mae set a glass plate of mixed greens in front of her.

"Baby Boy, you want Coke or iced tea?"

"Jack Daniel's. No ice."

Camille speared arugula. She focused on Jeff's eyelids, his pupils trained on the clunky sandstone candlesticks they'd picked up in an open-air market in Egypt.

"Jeff, baby, how's Dillon?"

He crunched salad. Maybe he was just worried about his father. After all, the morning papers had interviews with the women suing Senator Stone. Camille couldn't believe one woman said he'd followed her into a small copy machine room, ripped off her skirt, and shoved himself inside her. At ten o'clock on a Monday morning! And, it said, the Ethics Committee was officially launching an investigation. This, less than a week before the election.

"I think it's good that you'll be helping out your dad," Camille said, looking into the bottom of his amber-filled glass, just delivered by Ida Mae. "Jeff, baby, please talk to me. I don't know what's—"

He slammed the glass on the table, his eyes fierce.

"All right, Camille. I'll talk to you." His right shoulder rose as he slid a hand into his front pocket. He shot a small pink disc across the table, hitting her hand like a hockey puck in a goalie's net. "Let's talk about that."

Camille drew her brows together, wrapping fingers around the birth control pills. "I thought I threw this away. Why'd you bring it to dinner?"

He stared at her, jaw muscles flexing.

"Jeff?"

"Ida Mae found it this morning. In your makeup drawer."

"And?"

"It was my understanding we were trying to get pregnant again."

"Let me set your mind at ease, baby." Camille popped open the container, pointed to the date on the prescription label. "Look. The day I found out I was pregnant. That was the last pill I took."

Jeff stared harder. "Ida Mae said you were trying to trick me."

"I can't believe you'd listen to that."

"She knows about Tabitha."

"Jeff, I thought after we got married, I wouldn't have to hear that name."

"She tricked me."

"I hate that Tabitha has a presence in our marriage, Jeff. I hate it."

"Listen! I found her in our bed. With a woman. She was using me, so no one would know she's a dyke. So her family—"

Camille wanted to let a face-cracking smile have free reign. Miss Perfection had a dark secret, too. *But no, I'm not like her. I'm with Jeff for the love and security I never had. We're soul mates.* She just had to keep him focused on that. And damn The Spy for blowing suspicion into Jeff's head.

"Oh, baby, no wonder you're upset." Still in her trousers and turtleneck, Camille slunk around the table, bending at Jeff's side to drape her arms around his shoulders. She kissed his cheek, then purred. "Ida Mae has the most bizarre imagination—"

"I'll tell you what, Camille." Jeff was stiff, staring straight ahead. "Throw me into a temptress trick-bag, and we'll be playing a whole new game of life."

Camille fought the urge to let her jaw stick out. Her skin prickled, as if her head, full of question marks, was piercing her flesh. One thing she did know, however: this heart-stopping brush with the birth control pills was the final scene in her Jeremiah pregnancy paranoia. If a baby was what Jeff and his family wanted, then she would deliver.

Anything to rekindle the tender glow in her husband's eyes. She'd worry about pigment later.

Laying a palm on his cheek, she turned his head to face her. She pressed her lips to his stiff mouth, running a hand down his chest, his stomach, and lower. No response. So she licked his neck.

Jeff reached around her, made a great clatter of stemware and china, then laid her across the table.

51

Freida Miller focused on the green letters on her computer screen, racing against the clock to meet her five o'clock deadline. She typed even faster as her editor tapped the top of her monitor. "You learn anything new about Stone's daughter-in-law?"

Freida finished a sentence before meeting his nicotine-and-caffeine-glazed eyes surrounded by dark, puckered skin. "I've done some work. But, Ward, I'm trying to do justice to these election stories. That *is* my beat, remember?"

"Get on it, now." He fingered his shaggy black beard; a splotch of coffee marked the collar of his blue oxford shirt. "Bob just asked me about it. I can easily tell the managing editor you're too lazy—"

She stood. "I got a packet today. But Vivian Newton just called—"

"If you'd spent more time in the trenches, you'd know—"

Freida crossed her arms. *What a jerk!*

"—the news value of hypocrisy. Stone won't let a black man join his country club, but a mulatto may be joining his family. Get on it." He bumped newspapers jutting from her visitor's chair as he trudged from the cubicle.

As she plunked into her seat, the words on the screen turned to alphabet soup. A pang of panic gripped her insides; the little box in the corner that said "375 files" dimmed. The last time that had happened, the computer ate all her stories and notes. Freida slapped its side; the numbers brightened.

If Camille Stone was black, so was Marilyn Monroe. Screw Ward. What a waste of time. And she hated his grudge. She couldn't help that she'd been hired at this journalistic zenith right out of school. Whether it was her parents' connections or her talent, it had nothing to do with Ward's twenty years of hopscotching papers from Mobile to Tucson to Gary and wherever else he'd honed his irritating skills. But she knew one thing: one day she would show jerks like him just how good a reporter she was. And if breaking the Camille Stone story was what it took, she'd get right on it.

She hit SEND, then opened a big envelope from New York College. Law school documents listed Camille's parents as Michael and Jane Morgan, deceased. Guardian: Ella McCormick, 1435 Waverly Drive, Cleveland. Siblings: none. Walnut Creek High School. GPA: 3.8. Race: Caucasian.

This is such a waste of time . . . Freida skimmed undergraduate scholarship application forms: ten thousand dollars from—

What? The Sojourner Truth Scholarship Fund. For black students.

But the line where Camille's name should have been was smeared gray and worn thin. Erased? And it listed the student's high school as the Riverfront Academy of the Arts in Detroit. Either the bursar had sent the wrong form or someone had tampered with the records, and not done a very neat job. Why hadn't anyone noticed? Freida knew of white students scamming scholarships by checking "Native American" on college forms. But it would be beyond coincidence if Stone's daughter-in-law had checked "black."

That tabloid article. Freida yanked it from an overflowing paper tray where her desk butted the corner. The fuzzy picture was no help. And the article named only one person: Mack Campbell.

Freida dialed the operator as the brown-uniformed janitor bent to pull her overflowing trash can from under her desk.

"Thank you," she told him as the operator said, "No listing in Detroit."

Even though it was after five, Freida called a source at Social Se-

Elizabeth Atkins Bowman

curity. But his records showed nothing on Mack Campbell since the draft in 1973.

Freida e-mailed Detroit's Riverfront Academy of the Arts as well as the Cleveland school to order yearbooks. She also contacted the Sojourner Truth Scholarship Fund.

If this story is true, my star is about to rise.

52

Camille grabbed the black leather bag from under her desk. It was her last day on the job, her last lunch break, her final few minutes of having to give Nick Parker another iota of brain energy.

The crystal clock on the desk said 12:20. Ten minutes was plenty of time to get to their meeting place. She couldn't be late; that bastard probably wouldn't waste a minute getting to Jeff's office for story time. And the way Jeff was acting lately, hardly speaking during their morning jog through Central Park, not even noticing the other runners in Halloween masks, she needed to take care of business and get on with making him happy.

She stepped toward her coat, hanging behind the door, but it opened.

"Judge," she said, smiling, gripping the bag over her shoulder.

"Wanted to bid you adieu," he said.

She extended a hand.

"You could've gone far," he said, squeezing her fingers. "But a young woman with babies on her mind, you've got other work to do. At home."

Camille smiled. "Well, I certainly didn't toil three years in law school to spend my life changing diapers. I'm hoping for a happy medium somewhere down the line. Maybe working part-time once children come."

The judge offered a plastic pumpkin full of treats.

"No, thanks."

"If I know Monty, he won't allow that," he said, munching candy corn. "Too old-fashioned. I suspect Jeff's a traditionalist at heart just the same."

Camille imagined Nick standing in the atrium, checking his watch, playing his tape recorder into a cell phone, her moans blaring in Jeff's ear. She waved toward her computer. "I've organized the files for my replacement—"

"A Harvard grad, top of his class. I passed him over when Monty called, so you might imagine his relief now. Well, Mrs. Stone, a job well done. But young Thad won't have to take his ovaries into consideration."

She chuckled, glancing at the clock. Five minutes was barely enough time, even if she ran.

"How about lunch?" the judge said. "It's the least I can do."

"Thank you, but I have errands. We're moving Sunday, you know."

The judge's eyes locked onto her bag. "Taking the law library with you?"

"No, I accumulated quite a collection of shoes, coffee cups, a big sweater. I'm taking it all home on my lunch break."

"Well, let me get someone to help you to the car."

She stepped past him, through the door. "No, no, I'm fine, really."

"Mrs. Stone, you're forgetting something."

She turned around. He held up her black wool coat.

She returned to the office, plunked her bag on the desk, slipped into her coat. Twelve-thirty. *Stay cool. Nick will wait five minutes. Or will he?*

"Thank you, Judge. I'll see you this afternoon."

Camille dashed through the reception area, down the stairs, to the crowded sidewalk. She navigated a river of men in beige trench coats, women bracing themselves against misty wind. Gripping both shoulder straps of the Chanel backpack, she cut through clusters of people at the corners for red lights. She dashed between moving cars, avoiding the prospect of telling a police officer some purse-snatcher had made off with half a million dollars in cash.

Dark Secret

Finally, the building where they were to meet came into view. She sprinted, wishing she'd used her inhaler to prevent this sudden wheezing. Shoving past people pouring through the glass doors, Camille scanned the lobby. Where was he? The clock over the information desk said 12:40.

One more scan: there, by the pebble-walled planter in the corner. The back of Nick's shearling coat and a tiny black antenna over his ear.

Camille took long strides, stopping at his side. "Nick."

He focused on the dirt. "Tell him Nick called. It's about his—"

Camille snatched the phone. "I'm here!"

"Lucky for you, Rich Boy is out to lunch." His eyes were brown marbles.

Camille twisted out of the backpack, shoved it into his waist. "I hope this buys you a one-way ticket to hell."

Nick slung it over his shoulder. "Yeah? I'll see you there."

53

"Follow him!" Jeff shouted from the passenger seat of the black van. The tall guy in the shearling coat and sunglasses, striding down the crowded sidewalk with Camille's bag over his shoulder, would not get away. Jeff pounded the dashboard. "Stay on him!"

Dillon's zoom-lens camera hit the steering wheel as he navigated the lane closest to the cars parallel-parked along the canyon of tall buildings. "Looks like blackmail to me, sailor boy," Dillon said, making the windshield wipers beat faster. "She must have one helluva skeleton in her closet." He revved the engine through a red light.

"It couldn't possibly be as bad as Tabitha. I would've helped Camille—"

"No, man. Sometimes it's better not to know. Could be a drug habit. Maybe she made skin flicks to pay for college. Frickin' traffic—"

A delivery truck pulled out of an alley.

"Shit!" Jeff shouted, grabbing the door latch. "I can't see him."

The truck moved. "There!" Dillon pointed, surging through a patchwork of honking yellow cabs, rumbling buses, and cars. A bicycle courier shot in front of the van; Dillon screeched.

The extortionist turned around, then took off past the purple-neon sign of a drugstore, a hot salad bar joint, buckets of roses and tables of vegetables at the Asian grocery on the corner. All while dodging a forest of umbrellas.

Dark Secret

"Don't lose him!" Jeff shouted. "The alley!"

But Dillon couldn't turn that fast. So Jeff, in his suit, trench coat, and loafers, hopped out, sprinting through the alley, past Dumpsters and windowless metal doors.

The guy was gone.

Jeff bit down, balled his fists. "I'll kill the lowlife who threatens my wife and takes my money. I'll kill him."

He had to find him first, though.

"Stay here," Dillon, who had parked the van, said over the noise of cars whizzing on the street abutting the alley. "I'll go around front, check the stores."

Ignoring the cold spray and wind, Jeff kept watch by a stinking pile of trash. But fifteen minutes later, Dillon returned, breathing hard and sweating. "Checked all three stores, man. Even the cellar. Nothing."

54

Ginger stared at the red numbers on her calculator.

"That can't be right," she whispered, standing at the cash register counter in her store. How could she still get a negative number by subtracting her bills from all the money Rand and Camille had given her?

"I am, like, so screwed right now."

She fingered her silver thumb ring, surveying full racks of clothes, then the counter. Sketches of her men's line taunted: "You can't even afford thread to stitch us up, much less a fashion show like Camille suggested."

And Camille had enough problems these days. She needed a loan officer herself, with that scumsucker Nick coming around. Right about now, in fact, she was finally getting him off her case. At least he'd stopped calling here. Ginger didn't want his dirty money, anyway. She yanked open the top drawer, flipped through a box of business cards. "Who can I call?"

The noise of tumbling boxes in the back storage area made her look up. Lisa was down the street, picking up some of that lentil-and-rice salad from the food bar. She wouldn't be coming in the locked back door, anyway.

Despite her pounding heart, Ginger crept through the dressing room, pushing open the carpeted door to the dark back room.

"Nick!"

His face glistened in the rectangle of light from the open door. Chest heaving, he shoved a wet bag into her hands. "Keep this. 'Til I come back."

Ginger clutched the straps. Camille's black leather Chanel backpack!

"Nick! What's—"

"Show me a way outta here." He glanced around.

"Are the cops—"

"You asked for it. Now shut the fuck up and tell me how to get out!"

For a second, she imagined depositing the money and writing a pile of checks, then launching the most fabulous men's line ever. She pointed to a door behind the mess of boxes. "That's a staircase up to my manufacturing area. Take the fire escape back down to the street."

Nick shot into the darkness; the door creaked.

With trembling hands, Ginger carried the bag into the dressing room. Set it on the purple mushroom seat. Unzipped the top.

"Oh, my God."

Bricks of hundred- and thousand-dollar bills.

Ginger felt dizzy. She plunked next to the bag, striking the crisp cash, letting that scent intoxicate her.

I have to call Camille. I mean, she's probably, like, such a mess right now.

But no, Camille was probably happy the curtain had finally fallen over her debacle with Nick. She wouldn't be looking for this cash, especially not with the big move coming up this weekend.

So if Nick got arrested or something, and I keep this, she'll never know . . .

55

Karen set a bowl of tomato soup and a chicken salad sandwich on the wooden tray in front of Mama, who was reading the Bible on the couch with one of Gramma Bradley's rainbow-knit blankets over her legs.

"An update now," a male reporter announced from the nearby TV, "on the neck-and-neck race for a city council seat left vacant by the tragic death of Franklin Daniels." Karen jabbed the power button. Her heart ached for Franklin and raced every time she thought about the sinister voice that had awakened her with phone calls the past three nights. The police had traced the calls to a pay phone downtown, but had not caught anyone.

She put a yellow napkin in Mama's lap.

"Sweet praline, you're too good to me."

"Just doing what I'm supposed to do until you get better. Need pepper?"

Mama's braided crown moved up and down as she bit into the sandwich.

In response, Karen padded in her teddy-bear slippers across the dark green carpet, which accented the leaves on the yellow-flowered armchairs and couch. She savored the coziness of the matching wall-paper and drapes, compared with the gloom out the front window.

And the clouds in her head. Why hadn't Rollins called? Today made one week since the interview. She'd done a good job evading questions about just how frightening the Franklin aftermath was; Stone probably wouldn't want to hire a stalking victim. But the more she thought about it, the more she liked the idea of getting out of town, away from the diamond thug, closer to Sharlene. After all, Plan C depended on it, and she had yet to conceive Plan D.

The flap of the brass mail slot on the front door made Karen stop.

"Don't tell me the trick-or-treaters are here already," she said, heading toward the door. The basket of mini candy bars was ready on the carpeted staircase and—

She picked up a white envelope from the green welcome mat. Out tumbled several snapshots of herself: paying the clerk at the nearby gas station, leading Mama from the doctor's office, talking with Senator Stone at the reception in Washington. *They're following me . . .*

Mama set down her sandwich. "Why you look so scared, girl?"

She shoved the pictures back into the envelope. "Junk mail."

The phone rang on the dark wooden TV cabinet. Was someone sitting in a car outside, watching? "Hello?"

"Ms. Bradley. Joe Rollins here."

Was it really?

"Hello?"

"Yes," Karen said. "Nice to hear from you again."

"Well, Senator Stone wants a second interview. Next Thursday." He chuckled. "Give us a few days to recover from the election."

Karen forced out a friendly laugh. "I know how exhausting that is."

"One thing," Rollins said. "How are things coming along in Detroit, with your political troubles? We don't want to proceed if your . . . entanglements . . . are still a problem."

Karen pinched the envelope and remembered the late-night calls. "No, things are back to normal. Please tell Senator Stone I'm looking forward to seeing him next week."

56

The sound of skidding tires on the nearby street set Jeff into overdrive.

"There he is!" Dillon shouted.

The guy was pushing off the hood of a red Cadillac, darting into a cloud of bus exhaust, about twenty yards away. Jeff and Dillon shot through traffic, cars screeching all around, to the other side of the street. They had to catch that motherfucker, find out what the hell he was doing.

But running in business attire on this urban obstacle course of strollers and dollies loaded with crates of cabbage and mounds of trash bags was nothing like the easy jog this morning with Camille.

"Right there!" Dillon yelled, as the guy traversed the meat district, with its vast brick buildings with no windows. The scent of death wafted from trucks and loading docks abuzz with men in bloody smocks handling huge slabs of meat.

"Got him!" Dillon pointed to the archway of a red building.

Jeff hopped onto the waist-high loading dock, into the dark building, just ahead of Dillon. A heavy sourness hung in the air. Giant metal hooks on chains dangled from the ceiling. Crimson light poured through painted windows near the four-story ceiling.

They followed the echo of the guy's feet on metal conveyor belts, wooden crates, then up a ladder to a catwalk, into a huge empty room.

Dark Secret

Dillon pulled a .357 magnum.

"Hey, dude, it's cool," the guy said, raising his hands.

Dillon shoved him down against a metal balcony railing.

Jeff kicked his leg. "Where the hell is my money?"

"Take it easy, sailor boy." Dillon sat on a wooden crate. "Let's find out what's goin' on."

Jeff ground his teeth. The thought of this lowlife touching his wife, even talking to her, made him spit. "I said, where's my money?"

The guy squinted. "I need a cigarette."

"Hey, buddy," Dillon said, "I'll shove a cigarette up your ass."

"Talk!" Jeff shouted, kicking his ribs.

The guy coughed. "It's wack, dude."

Dillon fired into the floor, inches from the guy's leg.

He jumped. "Easy, dude. She was at New York College. Needed a service."

"What kind of service?" Jeff asked.

"New Social Security number. A new identity. New name, passport, college records, the whole works."

"Liar!" Jeff stomped the guy's knee, making him cry out and grab it.

Dillon stroked the gun. "If you're bullshittin' my buddy here—"

"It's the truth, dude. Take it or leave it."

"Why'd my wife want this done?"

"You won't believe it," the guy said.

"Out with it!"

"Her real name is Sharlene Bradley. From Detroit. Grew up real poor on welfare, no dad. And her old lady is a nigger."

Jeff laughed. "You read that trash after our wedding. Try again."

The guy smirked. "I said you wouldn't believe it."

"Prove it," Jeff said.

"She's got asthma. Loves to get fucked hard—"

Jeff's loafer smashed the guy's other knee. He groaned, tried to get up.

Dillon shoved him back.

"That doesn't prove her mom's a nigger," Jeff said. "What about the plane crash? That a lie, too?"

"Hell yeah. She came to New York to be an actress. A white one."

Jeff squatted. "So then you come back on the scene to cash in on her good fortune? Dirty sack of shit!" Jeff spit on him.

The guy laughed. "Better that than a gold-digging whore like your wife."

Dillon pressed the gun into the guy's sprout of dark hair. "You got a death wish?"

"If you don't whack me, someone else will."

Jeff kicked his thigh.

"Hey, Rich Boy, aren't you gonna ask me about how your blushing bride paid for my services?"

Jeff glared at him.

"Endless installments of hot, wet pussy. Fucked me, sucked me, licked me on demand. Where do you think she got those big tits?" The guy laughed. "What will your old man say about a black slut in the family?"

"Where the fuck is my money?" Jeff screamed. His pulse was throbbing so hard at his temple, he felt his head would explode. And something primitive and hot surged through him. He threw off his coat and suit jacket, erupting with punches and kicks. He straddled the guy, grabbing fistfuls of hair, ramming his head against the rusty metal railing. Then Jeff stood, panting. The guy slumped back.

An ear-splitting crack echoed through the warehouse.

The rail ripped from the wall, bent in its base.

The guy tumbled backward, screaming. Then, a thud on metal. Silence.

"Shit, sailor boy." Dillon peered over the ledge. "You didn't have to kill him."

"Yes, I did." A white-hot veil of rage clouded Jeff's mind. His wife was an impostor, worse than Tabitha. Tricked again. The election was four days away, and if this got into the press, Pop would be the laughingstock of Virginia society, the Beltway, and the whole country. And if Jeff divorced Camille right now—no! How could this happen? Whoever she was, he loved her. He was crazy about his Lady Godiva. If he'd never met that nameless thug, if Camille had never paid him off, Jeff could have gone a lifetime not knowing the truth. And that would have been all right. But who was she? What should he do?

Jeff grabbed a two-by-four from the floor. He pounded a waist-high wooden crate. Deafening cracks joined the boots-on-metal clank of Dillon going down the catwalk.

Splinters sliced his hands; sweat soaked his shirt and pants.

That crate became a pile of twigs. And in his mind's eye, it was his wife.

57

In the candlelit bathroom of the town house, Camille wanted to soak in the huge, steaming bathtub all night. But even that wouldn't cleanse the grittiness chafing her soul. Money for Nick, a kidney for Karen. No, that just wasn't going to happen. Not after all this. Maybe Mother got a donor kidney, after all, and they wouldn't need to hassle her anymore. Yes, then she could move on with her new life at White Pines.

After a ghoulishly lustful evening here with Jeff.

The door burst open. The lavender-scented suds and water sloshed as Camille startled. She didn't expect him home for at least a half-hour; his farewell cocktail with Uncle John would give her plenty of time to get ready.

"Ida Mae, once Jeff gets home, don't come barging in on us."

She set a basket of towels on the long countertop. "Hmmph. You worried 'bout what else I might find up in here."

Camille stepped from the tub into a fluffy towel. "I'm sick of you trying to turn Jeff against me."

"Don't nothin' turn 'less it s'posed to." Ida Mae loaded towels into the cabinets under the television. "I got my eye on you, girl. And I won't stand for no lyin' hussy doin' my Baby Boy wrong."

"You act like he's your own son!"

"My own son, if I wasn't watchin' his tail, he'd a been dead years ago." She ran her palms over her apron. "So watch yo'self, girl."

Camille let her face twist into the thousand scowls she had held back in Jeff's presence when Ida Mae annoyed her. "I'm so sick of your spooky talk!"

Ida Mae glared right back, still humming as she'd been all week. Why did she have to move back to White Pines with them? Couldn't she just stay here, tend to the town house? But maybe, with Hortense in charge and the endless rooms down there, Camille would see less of Ida Mae.

"You ought not use that word." Ida Mae slammed the cabinet and left.

"I can't believe her," Camille said, slathering lotion on waxed legs. She slipped into black stockings, then from the orange bag retrieved a leopard-print bra and garter belt. She pinned matching ears into her loose hair, then attached the fur-tipped tail. Black patent leather pumps, and oh, whiskers. With a black makeup pencil from the drawer, she made six lines on her cheeks radiating from her nose. "Meow," she said to her reflection, smiling.

In the bedroom, in the warmth of the fireplace, Camille lit orange candles on the mantle, the desk, and the nightstands. At the first hum of the elevator, she turned on New Age music, then lay on her stomach on the bed. As soon as the beveled doors sparkled in the candlelight, Camille raised her torso, clawing the satiny bedspread. She would make it perfect, so she and Jeff could both slip into the oblivion of passion for a while.

"Pussycat wants to play." She arched. "Meow."

Wow, Jeff must've had one too many shots of Jack Daniel's at the office with Uncle John. His hair clumped in every direction. And when had he changed out of his suit into those jeans and the too-big flannel shirt? With glistening lips, he came toward her. Something in his eyes was different, ominous, but it was hard to discern in the candle-light. Had someone dropped an eleventh-hour bomb on his father's campaign? Or was he just putting on a Halloween act?

Jeff stopped at the edge of the bed, but a stinging whiff of whiskey didn't. He clawed his shirt, pulling so hard, a button struck her face. He yanked down his jeans—no underwear! Jeff never went without underwear.

"Baby, what—"

"Suck my dick." He raked her head into his crotch. She obliged, but something was wrong. Very wrong. After a few minutes, Jeff flipped her, pressed her flat on her stomach, dove onto her back. He yanked her thong underwear to the side, stabbing himself inside her.

"Yeah, Lucy," he whispered. "Fuck me like that."

Camille froze, eyes wide.

Jeff roared with laughter. Gathering her hair in his hands, he pulled it like reins on a horse. But what kind of erotic terrain was he galloping into?

Her brain went haywire, like an out-of-control radio tuner twisting past stations: . . . *the banker blabbed about the money . . . Karen called and exposed me . . . he's mad I talked to Rand this morning on the phone . . . Ida Mae showed him the tabloid . . . father had a heart attack . . . he's pretending he's Randolph Stone for Halloween . . . Nick took the money and told Jeff anyway, just to be the bastard that he is . . .*

Camille closed her eyes. Jeff's thrusting was causing her cheek to burn back and forth on the bedspread. She was drying up, aching down there. And she felt nauseous again, as she had on and off for the past several days, especially when her stomach was empty. It made her wonder if that ulcer she'd had during college was eroding her insides.

I have to find out what he's thinking, what he knows. But how?

She glanced back; he was spasming, his face glistening in the candlelight, his eyes glowing with something she'd never seen, something that chilled her soul.

58

Ginger pressed the phone to her ear for what must have been the twentieth ring.

"Pick up, Nick." Twisting her thumb ring on her left hand, she leaned back in the purple leather desk chair. That way, the Chanel bag blocked the crumpled sweats on the couch where she'd spent the night. Not really sleeping, or succeeding at sketching her new men's line, but listening, waiting for Nick to return. He *had* to come back for this money. It was dirty, and could potentially ruin Camille's marriage.

Ginger hung up, then dialed the club again. He couldn't have run off to some island without the cash. Or had he gotten out of town with the intention of calling her to say, take what you need and deposit the rest in a Caribbean account? Whatever. She just wanted to resolve this situation before Rand arrived for the ride up for a good-bye brunch with Camille and Jeff.

"Yeah." The voice was male, but not Nick's.

How strange. Pseudo was still closed, and she'd never heard anyone else answer the phone, especially on a Saturday morning. "Nick Parker?"

"You seen him?" Something sinister punctuated the guy's Bronx accent.

"No," she said. "I'm . . . his cousin in Milwaukee. Is he there?"

"I was gonna ask you the same thing, sweetheart." Another man in the background mumbled something with the words "ass kickin'."

Ginger hung up.

"Ah!" She jumped. "How'd you get in here?"

Rand smiled in the doorway, wearing faded jeans and a sweater with the Hugs and Hope insignia: two plump teddy bears embracing under a rainbow. "Still unnerved from Halloween? The kids and I missed you at the party."

"I wasn't feeling well. In fact . . ." The bag on the desk sat between them. Had she snapped the top? Could he see the cash? "I never made it home." Actually, she hadn't wanted to leave the money or risk carrying it anywhere.

Rand stepped closer, running knuckles over her cheek. "Talk to me, Ginger. If the store is still giving you problems, you know—"

"No, no, it's family," she said, the black bag doing a sort of double-vision dance. She closed her eyes, pressing Rand's palm to her cheek.

"Another argument with your mom?"

"I'd rather . . . I mean, it's not something I want to talk about."

"Then let's get to Camille and Jeff's. Ready?"

No, Ginger wasn't ready to leave. She couldn't just tell Lisa to hand over the money if Nick came calling. And where was she supposed to leave it? If she delivered it back to Camille, and Nick returned, she'd be jeopardizing their safety. Especially with thugs after Nick.

"Rand, let me freshen up in the bathroom. Can you tell Lisa to come back for, like, a split second?"

"Sure thing," he said, heading into the store.

Ginger lugged the bag to the dressing room, flipped the purple mushroom chair, shoved the bag into the hollow cylinder that was its base, then turned it back over. She tossed dresses and pants over it. No one would ever guess . . .

"You need something?" Lisa asked.

"Yeah. If someone named Nick calls or comes by, tell him to call my cell phone. I mean, *immediately*."

A short time later, in the town house foyer, the distress in Camille's eyes made Ginger get that ringing-ears-about-to-faint feeling. She clutched the banister as the floor tiles rotated around her pointed black ankle boots. She had to calm down and console her friend.

"Let's get you something to eat," Camille said, walking her down the hallway with Rand's help. How did Camille know she hadn't eaten dinner or lunch the previous day? Ginger couldn't even remember if she'd had anything to drink in the past twenty-four hours.

"Ida Mae's bean soup will cure whatever ails you," Camille said, leading her and Rand into the dining room.

"Where's my brother?" Rand took a seat facing them.

"Upstairs, working," Camille said as The Spy placed steaming blue china bowls before them. Ginger couldn't imagine, if she married Rand, having a scheming maid trying to pry them apart. Even though he'd grown up with a nanny, he was a master with everything from peanut butter on celery to pesto, and the sun-splashed wood floors in his Riverside Drive apartment were always spotless.

"Ida Mae," Camille said, "Ginger needs some juice. Right away, please."

"Yes, Miss Camille. How you doin', Rand, baby?" Ida Mae kissed his forehead, making him smile and squeeze her hand.

"I'd be better," Rand said, "if they weren't about to leave town."

Ginger took a spoonful of navy beans, onion, and cubed Virginia ham. But the soothing warmth of it sliding into her stomach soured; way too much tenderness glowed in Rand's eyes as he said, "Camille, we'll come to the rescue if life on the plantation gets too macabre—"

"It won't." Jeff strode in, taking the chair next to Rand. "This is a new beginning for both of us." The sparkle in his eyes, as his gaze shifted from Camille to Ginger, was like the glint of a silver knife blade.

It's my fault. I could make it all better by giving back the money. As Ginger pulled back the cardigan of her olive sweater set, the green number pad glowed on the phone hooked to the belt of her ankle-length black skirt. But why hadn't Nick called? That staticky sound returned. She whispered, "Camille, can we go upstairs for a minute? I mean—"

Camille stood in a split second. "We'll be upstairs," she told Jeff and Rand, whose body language reminded her of the repellent ends of two magnets.

"How'd it go with Nick?" Ginger asked over the hum inside the elevator.

Camille, her hair loose and framed by soft light and walnut paneling, said, "Fine, I guess. But I can't believe Jeff. He called me Lucy."

Ginger remembered Camille describing that horrible story time at White Pines. "Did The Spy show him the tabloid?"

"Probably, but he doesn't believe that stuff, since so many lies have been printed about his dad. Maybe Karen or Nick got to him."

Ginger held Camille's hand. "You should, like, forget about your problems here. Your sister has probably given up on you. And Nick, he's history now that you've . . . I mean, think of your new life of leisure."

"I'll go crazy down there. Promise you'll visit? Next week is the campaign victory party. If he wins, that is. And don't forget the Christmas party."

"I'm, like, *dying* to see what everyone will be wearing! But I think Rand is gonna miss you more than I will."

Camille's jaw stuck out. She crossed her arms over her thick cream sweater. "Not that again, Ginger."

Ginger glanced at her phone again. "I'm sorry, Camille. But you're leaving me all alone here. We haven't been apart since . . . ever."

Ginger wrapped her arms around Camille, her cheek nestled in a pillow of honey hair. There was nothing like the warmth of Camille's presence, the deep-rooted solidarity of shared secrets and dreams. It mellowed Ginger out, made her problems somehow seem smaller. She sobbed, certain the Oriental rug would get a new bean soup design; she feared she would get sick with grief here in the elevator.

I love Camille like a sister. How could I have even thought about keeping the money? Even for a second?

She couldn't. No. Nick had twenty-four hours to claim it. Otherwise, Ginger would be right back here to return it to Camille before she and Jeff hopped the Gulfstream to Virginia.

59

Jeff kissed Camille square on the lips in front of thousands of Pop's supporters and a cluster of TV cameras aimed up at the entire family, staffers, and campaign workers.

"Six more years!" The crowd's chanting shook the stage.

"Thanks to you," Pop thundered, standing between Jeff and Mom at the podium, "we can restore America to a glorious mountaintop of pride and respect, peace and prosperity."

Exactly. Jeff squeezed Camille's shoulder as they faced a sea of smiles.

"When my opponent conceded just moments ago," Pop shouted into a red, white, and blue squall of streamers and confetti, "I said, 'No hard feelings, Mr. Jones. But let's learn from the challenges we presented one another, and move on for the good of family, for the good of country.'"

That was just what Jeff intended to do. Remain the enamored husband to his Lady Lucy, play the dutiful son to guide his father toward the White House over the next two years. All while keeping the truth under wraps. No one would ever know. And the ending he envisioned would only work to his advantage, drawing sympathy to the family. But secrecy was imperative.

What the—

A woman in a green suit jumped onto the stage. Wild hair, crazed eyes. "You're a vile excuse of a man!" she screamed at Pop and the microphone.

Where was security? With the feminists and civil rights militants protesting outside, the plainclothes cops were supposed to be out in full force.

"You play with women's lives, then snuff them out like one of your cigars!" the woman shouted. "If your wife knew—"

Jeff pushed past Dixie and Mom to tackle the woman, just as two state troopers jumped her. In seconds, the cops escorted her through the stage door.

"Even George Washington had enemies!" Pop said, smiling as a woman in the crowd shouted, "We love you, Monty!"

Jeff wove past Jackson and Sue Ann to Camille's side. He cupped a hand around the belted waist of her ivory pantsuit, eliciting a smile.

"I can't believe that woman," she said.

"Just like the wedding," Jeff said. "Crazies crawl out of every nook and cranny in Virginia to ruin the day." Camille held his gaze, her eyes blue pools of empathy. Not a glimmer of anxiety. Jeff almost chuckled; Hollywood movie studios paid women millions to put on such Oscar-worthy performances.

"Senator Stone," a reporter asked, "what's the first thing you plan to do next term to protect Social Security?"

"I'm glad you asked that question," Pop said as the crowd quieted and red lights glowed on TV cameras adorned with symbols of the local and national news stations. Jeff glanced at his silver watch: one minute after eleven. Three reporters, their backs to Pop, were going live, right here, right now, telling the world that Pop was king of the Commonwealth once again.

"Protecting the financial well-being of our nation's seniors," Pop said, "is of utmost importance to me. That's why I propose a three-pronged attack on the forces threatening to—"

Why was that reporter staring at Camille like that? She might as well slice her apart and shove her under a microscope. Jeff wedged a shoulder forward, blocking the view. But the staring chick held up that tabloid story that Ida Mae had shown him right after the honeymoon. "Senator Stone, have you heard rumors that your new daughter-in-law is half black?"

Alarm exploded inside Jeff. No! Not on live television! Damn her for putting him and his family in this position. Jeff's jaw ached as he ground his teeth. Just like the rest of him ached over losing the woman whose very breath he yearned to breathe, whose skin was sweeter than the most succulent home-cooked meal, whose joie de vivre made his soul smile. Whose deception had the potential to humiliate and crush them.

"That's so ridiculous," Camille whispered. "I can't believe—"

Jeff's heart beat loudly enough to drown out the rest of whatever she said, along with the startled whispers from the crowd. He hated the curious and contemptuous expressions on the media crews, as if they would all come on themselves if they could prove this story true. No, he would show them, it was a bold-faced lie. Credit that slimeball Nick—if he had done a clever enough job changing her identity, there would be no trail of clues to the truth.

"Pop, if I could respond," Jeff said, moving toward the podium, pulling Camille by the hand. He cast a loving look at Mom, whose roiling eyes belied her practiced smile.

"Being the son of a prominent man," Jeff said, locking eyes with a white-haired lady in a calico dress, a balding man in a suit, a thirtyish woman in a pink blouse, "has brought its dark moments. So when I'd come home and ask Pop about the cruel rumors being spread about us, he'd say, 'Son, believe half of what you see, and none of what you hear.' "

He cast a tender gaze at his mother. "Because, ladies and gentlemen, while they say words will never hurt you, they can be as damaging as sticks and stones. So let's not throw any more."

The crowd thundered; Mom, Pop, and Camille swallowed him in a hug.

60

In the Victoria Suite at White Pines, Camille awoke to a brown face peering over her. She slid up, clutching blankets, her back cradled in the burgundy velvet folds of the headboard. "Ida Mae, I can't believe you!"

"I been callin' your name, sayin' wake up. Thought maybe you was dead."

"You'd like that." Camille's lips tightened. "What's the big urgency?"

"Miss Millie want you in the kitchen." Ida Mae looked down her button mushroom nose. "And don't tarry, girl." She left.

Good. Camille could smooth things over. Especially after the way Mrs. Stone had glared so hard in the limousine after the victory party the other night that Camille had felt nailed to the baby-soft leather seat. At least Camille had succeeded in avoiding her yesterday, after dismissing the employees so she could put her own clothes in the dressers and closets.

Camille hurried into the bathroom, past the claw-foot bathtub, into the shower. *I can't believe he just left me here.* She hoped Jeff wasn't intending to spend every weeknight at his father's apartment while she tossed until three under the creaking ceiling and thoughts of Lucy being whipped to death. Not to mention the instinct to search out that mysterious music in the north wing.

Dark Secret

In a long, cream angora dress and brown loafers, her hair loose, Camille speed-walked the royal-blue corridor, then down to the kitchen, where Ida Mae was arranging melon, toast, and eggs on a white wicker breakfast tray.

"My gracious, Camille, you're as pale as porcelain." Mrs. Stone, in creased hunter-green slacks and a slim-fitting sweater, sat at the island, laying out menus, guest lists, and sample invitation books for the Christmas party. "Which place card do you prefer?"

Camille pointed to one with engraved gold script. She sat on a high stool at a right angle to Jeff's mother. "That one. Simple, yet elegant."

Mrs. Stone pointed to a red card with silver block letters. "I was thinking of something more jazzy this year. Gracious, you're awfully pale." Her brushed-back yellow hair seemed extra high today; the ducktail swoop was motionless as she shifted her gaze from the cards to Camille.

"I didn't sleep much with Jeff away."

"Gracious, that doesn't faze me," Mrs. Stone said, bracelets jangling as she picked a tiny fuzz ball from her sleeve. "Call me a weekday widow. Some weekends, too. Monty's mother keeps to her room, so it's just me and the staff." She glanced at Ida Mae, hurrying out with the tray.

"Then who's that for?" Camille asked.

Mrs. Stone's gaze hardened. "Any inquisition here will begin with me, demanding answers from you."

Camille flipped the switch in her mind, raising that impenetrable shield that had deflected so many of Mother's glares and scoldings.

"But gracious, for now, I'll refrain." Mrs. Stone removed her pearl glasses, set them on the cards. "And to be blunt, young lady, your only saving grace here is your uterus." Yes, Mrs. Stone's carnation-pink lips did move outward and back to form that word. The "us" seemed to echo.

"Pardon me?"

Mrs. Stone glanced at the grandfather clock near the hearth. "In one hour, Dr. Zane is coming to give you a complete physical. If indeed you did have a miscarriage, I need to determine if your parts are in good working order."

"My parts?" Camille slid to her feet, crossing her arms.

Mrs. Stone stepped close, engulfing Camille in her lemony scent. "You have exactly twelve months to produce a baby for me. Should you fail, the marriage will be annulled on grounds of fraud."

For a second, Camille wanted to dash through the French doors, running until she reached . . . what? *I'm exactly where I wanted to be.* She remembered being ten, her stubbed toes throbbing and bleeding through church service, because she refused to wear the secondhand Mary Janes that pinched her feet. So Mother had forced her to walk the six blocks barefoot, only to whisper during the sermon, "You made this bed, ghost baby, now sleep in it."

Her chest tightened; the walnut cabinets, the sprays of sage, the beautiful stone wall over the fireplace seemed to spin. Sure, growing up, and when she had first moved to New York, it was her singular goal to live in a mansion with servants, swimming pools, and more money than she could fathom. But now, it seemed more farce than fantasy. Mrs. Stone's edict reminded her of that Margaret Atwood book she had read in college, *The Handmaid's Tale,* about a society in which military matrons enslaved young women to produce babies.

She squared her shoulders, kept her chin high. "Mrs. Stone, I have my own doctor. And Jeff and I are already trying for another baby."

Mrs. Stone cupped Camille's cheek. "Gracious, girl, have a bite of breakfast. You'll need to go up, undress. Dr. Zane is never late."

61

Freida was sure the picture in the high school yearbook was Camille Morgan Stone, albeit with short hair and thirty more pounds. She was standing on a stage in a dingy slip, playing Blanche in *A Streetcar Named Desire* with beefy Stanley in his trousers and sleeveless T-shirt.

Besides, the caption said Sharlene Bradley. And when Freida turned to the senior class pictures, there was no photo of either a Camille Morgan or a Sharlene Bradley. Then she glanced again at that tabloid article. The father's name was Campbell. It didn't make sense yet . . . but there had to be something to the fact that her college records listed a Cleveland high school, while the scholarship listed a Detroit high school.

Freida flipped to the page with names beginning with *B*, where Sharlene Bradley should have been pictured. Then she called directory assistance in Detroit and got a number for a black female classmate named Joan Brown.

"She die in a plane crash or something?" Joan asked.

"No, she's a lawyer," Freida said.

"Well, you might try this girl who was her Siamese twin," the woman said. "I saw her in *Vogue* a couple years ago. Ginger Romanowski. Has a store in New York called Boutique or Unique. Something like that."

"Thanks. Do you know if Sharlene was mixed—half black, half white?"

"Hmmm," Joan said. "Sharlene was too depressed to have a personality. But she could act. No, we're talkin' lily white here."

A short time later, Freida dialed Mystique and got Ginger on the line.

"I don't know anyone by that name," Ginger said before hanging up.

Then Freida reached Arthur Bolinger, who had played Stanley in the play.

"Oh yeah, Sharlene," he said. "Boy, was that girl strange. She hung out with that redheaded chick who designed costumes for our plays."

Freida typed notes as he talked.

"But Sharlene, she was a great actress, man," he said. "Had the whole auditorium on their feet after that play."

"Do you remember her being half black?" Freida asked.

Freida could hear Arthur turning down the volume on a TV set. "Yeah, okay, now I remember. Only a few people in school knew Sharlene was black. Or half black, anyway. It was her mom, I think. And her sister—"

"Her sister?"

"Yeah, Carrie or Carmen, I don't know," he said. "But she went to another school. Never saw them together. One girl looked white and the other one looked black. It was weird."

Freida smiled.

This story will rock Washington. Maybe I can get a book deal out of it . . .

62

Karen Bradley didn't like the way her brother-in-law was dissecting her with his eyes here in Senator Stone's office. Jeff was sitting on the couch facing her and the fireplace, in an impeccable navy-blue suit, his sandy hair military-short at the ears, but long enough on top to hint at orderly chaos.

Whereas his father, perched on the front edge of the desk to her left, having foreplay with his unlit cigar—smelling it, licking it with closed eyes—had flawless hair. Not a grain of stubble glistened on his neck or at the perfect shaved sideburn line to his ears. His almost feminine black eyebrows and lashes accentuated the jet strands in his side-parted coif, standing straight but swaying back with the grace of wind over a wheat field.

"Sugar, tell us about that hornet's nest you tripped into in Detroit."

Karen remained still, her stockinged legs crossed, shoulders square, eyes projecting confidence, she hoped. She almost smiled at the idea of telling Stone the situation was so terrifying, that someone might indeed have photographed her entering his office. No! She had to get this job. For Mama.

"I assure you, Senator Stone, that situation would not in any way shadow or hinder my performance here. The police back in Detroit—"

"What about those threats we read about?" Rollins asked from a chair to her right. He was polishing his glasses. "Sounded quite ominous."

"I admit the situation was unusual," Karen said. "But the misunderstanding that prompted the threat has been cleared."

Jeff's jaw muscles flexed. "I'm still not sold on why you jumped the Democratic ship." His voice had an accusatory edge.

Karen nodded slightly. "As I said, Jefferson—"

"Jeff."

"I thought I read," Karen said, "that you were a lawyer in New York."

"My wife and I, we just moved down. Pop needs me."

Karen smiled. So Camille was at the Big House now. "Were you named after Thomas Jefferson?"

The smooth skin around his mouth, full enough to make Karen wonder if one branch of the family tree might have a deeper hue than the rest, curved into dimples. "Depends who you ask. Mom says yes. But Pop, he'll say Jefferson Davis, president of the Confederate Congress."

Karen smiled. "I've been reading up on my history. Those passions and loyalties still run deep in Virginia."

"What exactly is your loyalty, Miss Bradley?" Jeff asked. "With you being . . . a black female—"

Karen remembered watching GNN on election night, seeing a quick sound bite from Stone's victory party. "Jeff, you yourself said, 'Believe half of what you see, none of what you hear.' And what I see"—she glanced at Stone—"is a man with profound vision. Vision to make America even greater."

Stone strode toward her and rested a hand on her shoulder. "Enough cross-examination, son. Let's get to telling Miss Bradley her first task. Rollins?"

"You're aware of the Ethics Committee investigation." He perched on the edge of his chair, elbows on knees wide apart, polishing his glasses with a plaid pocket square. "You may also know, the fellow in charge is Jordan Kyles. Democrat from Chicago who—"

Karen's stomach fluttered. Jordan. Sweet Jordan. The only other man she'd ever shared her body with. That summer three years ago, before Franklin, Mr. Smooth Talk had picked her up and put her down like the too-sweet cocktails they served at the beach party where they'd met. Forget him.

She tuned back into Rollins: "—got to stop this investigation in its tracks. Or at least slow it down, derail it."

Meanwhile, Senator Stone was moving about the office, adjusting his collar in the mirror over the fireplace, straightening a brass picture of himself and Mrs. Stone on the table next to the couch, turning the giant globe.

"We want you to cozy up to this Jordan Kyles fellow," Rollins said, his eyes falling briefly to the silky vee of her blouse. "Sweet-talk him. Convince him he's spinning his wheels trying to dig up dirt on Monty."

Stone caressed the North Pole as his gaze rolled over her loose hair, her legs, her high-heeled suede pumps, the same almond as her fitted suit. "Coming from you, sugar, the message will pack more punch."

Jeff strode toward her, looking down. "Remind Kyles that as chairman of the Finance Committee, Pop holds the purse strings for all his help-the-needy handouts. Nothing's free, so if he wants to take, he has to give."

Rollins checked his glasses against the chandelier and said, "Don't be afraid to do whatever you have to do to get the job done."

Karen had a sudden urge to take a shower. Getting pimped around Capitol Hill wasn't the kind of work she'd envisioned. And she wanted to heave with déjà vu; just as Franklin's dirty dealings had tarnished her image, the potential scandal of this could ruin her, too. But she'd only be here the few weeks or months it would take to change Sharlene's mind. And if bending the rules a bit would save Mama, then she was game.

"I'll set up a meeting with Senator Kyles right away," Karen said. "But I'll need a few carrots to dangle, some incentives."

Rollins held up a finger, then spent several minutes explaining what kind of tradeoffs Karen should offer Jordan Kyles.

Karen stood, feeling the men's eyes on her body. "Will do. Also, Senator Stone, I can help soften up Freida Miller at the *Washington News*. We were roommates at Howard."

Senator Stone slapped the globe. "Hell, that . . . that girl thinks I'm the devil incarnate. I'd bet she has a hot line just for people who want to smear me and get it into the paper."

"Pop, relax."

"You'll be happy to hear," Karen said, "Freida is doing a piece about how hiring me may quiet your critics."

The wrinkle on Stone's brow eased a bit.

"Miss Bradley, before you go," Rollins said. "Keep the first Friday of December open. We'll be formally presenting you to family and friends at the senator's Christmas party at his home."

She smiled. "I'll be there."

63

The creak of the door opening made Camille lurch off the bed, where she'd been crouching for hours. "Jeff, we have to go back to New York. Now."

He held out his arms. "Honey, what happened?"

She burrowed her hot, puffy face into his broad chest. "Just hold me."

He kissed her head. "Mmmm, I missed you."

She pulled back, never wanting to leave the tender glow in his eyes. "Baby, I'm serious. Let's go."

Jeff guided her to the bed. "I thought you understood the importance of me working with Pop—"

"I do, but—"

He placed a fingertip on her lips. "Ssshh. You're not used to the house, the country. The South, for that matter."

She shook her head. "That's not it." No, she would not let that burning bubble in her throat send her into yet another crying fit. She slowed her speech. "Jeff, let's get our own place, at the Watergate or something."

He held her close. "Honey, this is home. And when I'm at Pop's apartment, I'm just a helicopter ride away. I apologize for you being here alone. But Mom—"

"I'm not her!" Camille shot to her feet. Throwing off her robe, she wished the red marks hadn't faded from her wrists and ankles where they'd held her down. Without proof, Jeff would never believe what had gone on in the very spot where he was sitting. "I'm leaving, Jeff. I'm not staying here."

She charged toward the closets.

"Camille, honey," he said, "I talked to Pop. We'd like you to get involved in the institute. Give you something to do, attach your beautiful face to Pop's image to lure that professional young women's vote."

She bent to pull on brown leggings. "I'm not a campaign prop. And I'll only do it if we get our own place." Black wing tips appeared where her hair dangled on the floor. Straightening, she said, "I can't believe you—"

"Enough, Lucy."

A new potency radiated down from his eyes. Just like his father's hypnotic stare, it made her freeze while her heart galloped. She raised her brows. "My name is Camille."

"Is it?"

"Or Lady Godiva," she said. "But not a dead slave's!"

Jeff pinched her puckered nipple. " 'Never could I escape the sultry allure of my fair Lucy's bosom, as smooth and sweet as buttercream.' "

Camille pushed his hand away. "You're totally tripped out, Jeff! This house does something to you, something—"

"Cut!" Jeff made his hands come together like a movie director's slate. "Just so you know, honey, White Pines is the final act in your drama."

64

It was like a daydream as Ginger watched seamstresses wrestle huge bolts of sea-green and Easter-egg-blue fabric across tables in the sewing room on the floor above her store. The delivery guy handed her a palm-sized computer with a pen attached.

"Where's the metallic fabric?" Ginger rested a hand on the black knit dress over her burning stomach. "I mean, I paid for way more than this."

The guy checked his computer. "The truck, maybe. I'll find out."

At the same time, Lisa approached with a phone. "That publicist again."

"Maren." All the things Ginger had to do over the next month to get ready streamed through her head like that giant news ticker in Times Square. But every once in a while a surge of guilt would dim the lights. Especially when Maren called; she reminded her of Camille, when the hippest parties across Manhattan wouldn't overheat until the three of them showed up. But Ginger had to focus, even though the white walls looked as if they were shaking.

"Yeah, Ginger, listen, I've nailed down a couple reporters. Still trying to work my magic on *Vogue* and *GQ*."

Ginger motioned for the delivery guy to drop several more bolts on the tables. "Keep on it. That's why I hired you."

Maren huffed. "Another reporter pissed me off this morning. Said Ginger Roman is as *over* as the seventies."

"And I'm paying you to change that!" Ginger glared through huge bare windows facing the watch repair shop in the brick building across the street.

"Just letting you know what I'm up against."

Ginger flitted past sewing machines, reminding herself that she had hired Maren because she was the best, not because she was pleasant to work with.

"You only need to let me know," Ginger said, talking fast, "when every fashion critic in town is raving about my men's line. Anything else?"

"The printer has the invitations," Maren said. "The caterer—"

Ginger's chunky-heeled boots halted. The four male models strutting in were beyond gorgeous. Add Rand to the mix and it wouldn't matter what they were wearing.

"Are you listening?" Maren sounded annoyed.

Ginger rubbed her temple, wishing the dizziness would stop. "Yeah," she said as the models streamed past, toward a table loaded with bagels, coffee, and fruit. She covered the receiver and said, "You guys, I'll be over in a minute." Moving her hand, she said, "Maren, it's crazy here. Let me—" Whew, more spinning. Ginger slumped into a chair, let her hand crumple onto something on the table. A newspaper. And Nick's picture.

She gasped, skimmed the article. Nick was dead! He was never coming to get Camille's money. The money that, despite promising herself she would return more than a week ago if Nick didn't call, Ginger was already spending.

I'm horrible. Taking advantage of my best friend. And now a dead guy.

She looked around the bustling shop. What should she do now? Tell everyone to go home, then return the cash to Camille? No, Camille wanted Ginger's fashion star to shine again. And with Camille's life so weirded out right now, she didn't need this emotional burden.

Ginger headed to the food table, grabbed a bottle of juice, then feasted her eyes on the beefcake that would nourish her back into a fashion heavyweight.

65

Camille and Jeff tumbled into a pile of orange and yellow leaves, onto the mossy bank of the stream. She was still vibrating from the brisk horseback ride through the woods along the James River. And with Georgia and Jeff's shiny brown stallion, Master, standing beside the pine thicket, Camille was laughing, melting under the velvety heat of Jeff's lips.

"Remember this spot?" he whispered, resting on an elbow, stroking her stomach under her thick cream Shetland sweater.

"Mm-hmm." She tingled with the three-year-old memory of her first visit to White Pines: an innocent horse ride resulting in a panting tangle of limbs in the sunshine. "It was a lot warmer that day."

"I can heat you back up." Jeff's eyes glowed with tenderness as he bent closer, blocking her view of dark branches arcing over the clouds. His lips devoured her chin, mouth, and neck as he pressed into her body.

Combing her fingers through his hair, she savored the natural male scent wafting from his broad neck. As he slid a hand into her riding pants, she delighted in having her Jeff back, that life here at White Pines wouldn't be so horrible, after all. As long as she could keep him treating her like his princess. "Tell me how much you love me," she whispered.

"More than Pop loves politics," he groaned, pulling down his pants, then hers. He yanked her sweater off, then her turtleneck.

"Jeff, it's not fifty degrees out here."

"I said I'd warm you up." He slid through the leaves, on his stomach, planting his hot mouth where she loved it most.

"I can't believe . . . oh, Jeff." A hot sheen dampened the icy goose bumps on her bare flesh. The shock and speed of . . . oh, the way he sucked her like an overripe peach . . . The clouds seemed to swirl down and tickle her soul as her limbs trembled and she whimpered into the wind.

Then, in seconds, Jeff pulled her onto his lap, facing him. "Ride, Lady Godiva. Ride away." He unlatched her cream satin bra, then buried his face between her breasts, cupping her butt as she did her best stationary gallop. Within minutes, Jeff's moans joined the rustling leaves and gurgling stream.

She purred, "You like that, baby?"

"Yeah, Lady Godiva. Now take a real ride."

She pulled back, startled by his gruff tone, his hardened gaze. "What?"

"You made me fall in love with you right here. When you hopped on the horse and rode away naked. Now do it again."

"Jeff, it's freezing."

His fingers clamped her upper arm. "I said ride for me."

Camille brushed leaves off her sweater.

"No, nude." He pulled on his jodhpurs, sweater, and boots.

"Jeff—"

"Do it."

Camille's chest tightened. She wanted to run and cry and scream all at once. What was his deal? It made her feel as if she was tumbling into some psychedelic pit where the banker, Karen, the media, Mother, and Nick all morphed into a little goblin, sitting on Jeff's shoulder, whispering bad things about her. And she never knew which voice he was hearing, or what they were saying. But until she did, she would not let herself react. No, his moods could be spurred by something else entirely. So she would play along until she discerned exactly what.

Camille rose, ignoring her tight lungs and the biting wind. Wearing only a cloak of hair, she climbed onto the horse, splashed through the rocky stream, to the other bank, over crackling leaves, back to Jeff. That was exactly what she'd done three years ago, knowing it would drive Jeff wild because, one night when she'd met Dillon for drinks at a downtown bar, he'd divulged Jeff's Lady Godiva fantasy.

Now, Jeff grinned, shouting, "Lady Godiva rides again."

A few hours later, after making love in the claw-foot bathtub in the Victoria Suite, Jeff left to meet with his father down in the library. They were probably going to watch the football game, as opposed to talking business as he'd said they would, but Camille didn't care. She had some exploring to do.

As she dressed in an oatmeal denim and sweater set, she ached between her legs. She and Jeff had made love every day for the past two weeks, minus four nights he had stayed at his father's DC apartment. Either power was a true aphrodisiac or Jeff was collaborating with his mother's baby conspiracy. Fortunately, today, Mrs. Stone was in Charlottesville, attending a luncheon with Dixie for the Humane Society, where Dixie volunteered. Camille crept down the hallway at the time she knew Ida Mae or Hortense would carry up a lunch tray.

"Don't poke your nose where it don't belong," Ida Mae had said the other day after Camille asked whom the grilled ham-and-cheese sandwich was for.

No more questions. Camille would find out for herself, and she was right on time. Stopping just short of the landing, she had a clear view of Hortense, reaching above the door molding, retrieving a key, and voilà . . . unlocking the north wing. The maid picked up the white wicker food tray, then clicked the door from the other side. Twenty minutes later, she returned and headed down the back stairs.

In seconds, Camille was creeping down the dim hallway, following the tinkly music coming from the same door she and Ginger had tried the night before the wedding. Heart pounding, she gripped the brass doorknob. It turned. But she opened the door only a few inches, wondering if she would get attacked by some psychotic relative the Stones kept hidden away.

No, she had to know. Camille peeked in. The room was huge, its walls splashed with painted pink flowers softly lit by frilly lamps. To the left, gossamer fabric was draped from the ceiling over a butterfly-shaped bed. Straight in, by the windows facing the river, white shelves held rows of books and videos around a large television. There was a desk with a computer.

And a sweet voice was singing, "When you wish upon a star, makes no difference who you are . . ."

Camille stepped inside, closing the door. To the right, a bathroom with a daisy-shaped step stool at the sink. She crept toward the area hidden by the bathroom wall, where the voice was coming from.

She gasped.

There was a small white table. On it, a music box, with a tiny figurine spinning to "When You Wish Upon a Star." In the chairs were a giant red Elmo doll, a porcelain-faced baby doll, and a teddy bear with a pink bow.

In the fourth chair: a little girl with skin the color of butterscotch.

66

In the airy elegance of B. Smith's in Union Station near the Capitol, Karen told herself to stop letting lustful memories of her summer with Jordan Kyles interfere with their meeting. Because if she didn't convince him to lighten up his attack on Stone, then she might not get to reminisce with Sharlene at the Christmas party in four weeks.

She just wished, here at the window table overlooking an endless stream of yellow cabs and pedestrians, that Kyles's lips wouldn't make that enticing *O* shape with certain words. And it was so hard to discern just what he was thinking from those penetrating, smoky eyes.

"Karen, pardon my bluntness, but have you lost your mind?"

She tilted her head slightly. "Excuse me?"

"The Karen Bradley I used to know," he said, tapping a napkin to a bit of catfish finger sauce just under his pencil-thin mustache, "wouldn't work for a Neanderthal like Stone. Losing Franklin must've—"

"Get real."

"This feels surreal." His gold Northwestern class ring, on his wedding finger, glistened as he lowered the napkin.

"Jordan, take a look. This is me. And I want to talk about Stone." The slight hook of his nose reminded her how it had felt rubbing against hers when they kissed on the beach. She remembered feeling the baby-soft smoothness of his nutmeg cheeks, pressed against hers as they danced in the moonlight. And touching his black waves high-lighted by a few silver wires.

At the same time, Karen scanned the crowded restaurant for the diamond thugs. No matter what she did—whether moving into Freida's Georgetown apartment or driving to work—the fear of when they might strike again, if they did at all, kept her muscles knotted, her eyes sharp. And Jordan, second only to Stone, was the last person she wanted to know about her stalkers. "We can help each other, Jordan, without dwelling on the past."

The gray wool breadth of his shoulders shifted as he reached for a glass of iced tea, holding back his pewter tie with his left hand. He had come so far since his childhood in Chicago's terrifying Robert Taylor Homes. "You can't know where you're going until you know where you've been," he said.

"Then I'll map it out for you. Your prison education bill comes up for vote soon. Scale back your inquiry, and you've got a 'yea' from Stone."

Jordan stabbed his Caesar salad. "I don't negotiate who my com-mittee investigates, or the voracity with which we do it. Don't insult me—"

Karen smiled. "You know Stone could also help get you Repub-lican backing for your amendment to the Medicare reform package."

He chewed, his gaze on his plate.

"Jordan, there's something else," she said, drawing his stare. "Let's keep things behind closed doors. No open hearings. The press would—"

His eyes narrowed. "How dare you dictate my investigation."

"Just offering suggestions." Karen remembered reading about how this former Illinois state legislator's work on the Ethics Committee had sanctioned a lawmaker who used taxpayer dollars to finance a personal vacation, and another senator who bullied a BMW dealer into letting him drive cars for free.

But Karen refused to wither under his glare. *This is crazy. What am I doing here?* The image of Mama's twisted, swollen face, saying, "Ohlordhammercy, this headache," numbed Karen as much as the memory of Sharlene's icy blue eyes in her townhouse. *That's what. Anything to make Stone adore me and give me leverage to negotiate with my sister.*

"Excuse me, Ms. Bradley?" The waiter held out a card. "A gentleman at the bar said he had to leave but wanted to give you this."

"Thank you." Karen unfolded the note under the heat of Jordan's stare. It said: *"Cutie pie. We'll be waiting."* Karen smiled, folding the note, sliding it into the front pocket of her short black suit. "Men are so bold these days."

"An admirer?"

"They wish. Jordan, remember that night we went to the symphony? I can hear, clear as day, you saying, 'Everything I do is for the people.' Well, what I'm offering would certainly help pass your programs to help the people."

He rose from the table, bending behind her chair. With his hands on her shoulders, he whispered. "You're in deep water, sweetheart. And that bastard, he won't throw you a life raft when the storm comes. Then again, looks like Franklin taught you a master stroke."

Karen gently twisted forward. "I was beyond reproach."

"Like I said, you're someone else entirely now," Jordan said behind his own chair, reaching into his breast pocket.

Karen stood, stepping close. "A summer fling and you think you have deep insight into me."

"It wasn't a fling," Jordan said. Something tender radiated from his face, wrinkle-free despite his looming forty-third birthday.

"You ended it like it was."

"My campaign," he said, putting cash in the black bill folder on the table. "No time for a relationship back then. Now, Miss Bradley—"

She wrinkled her brow. "You're just up and leaving?"

He glanced around the crowded restaurant, then leaned down. "My best advice to you, Miss Bradley? Show your true colors and come work for me, or go back to Detroit before you read about yourself in the paper, too."

Karen's cheeks stung as Jordan strode away, stopping to rest a hand on the shoulder of a man at a table by the door. A vague, panicky feeling seeped into her stomach; she couldn't go back and tell Stone about this disaster. No, she'd just have to help Jordan understand the value of what she was offering. So she sat back down, pulled a small notepad from her burgundy leather shoulder bag, and wrote a strategy: How to cool Jordan Kyles.

67

Camille froze, staring at the little girl. Was her lack of sleep causing hallucinations? Otherwise, she did not want to believe her eyes. And maybe she could tolerate Mrs. Stone's baby mandate and Jeff's twisted mood swings, but never this. Suddenly Camille remembered the face in the window and that mysterious exchange about the doctor between Mrs. Stone and Ida Mae.

"Excuse me," the girl told the dolls around the table as she slid from her chair. Her frilly yellow dress swayed over white tights and patent leather shoes as she came toward Camille. "Rapunzel, Rapunzel! Let down your long hair!"

Camille's heart flipped as the child's enormous onyx eyes sparkled up through wispy black lashes. A tiny pink mouth—the same figure-eight shape as Jeff and Dixie and Rand and their father!—flashed two perfect rows of tiny white squares. She giggled behind painted fingernails.

Camille knelt on the carpet. "What's your name?"

"Arianna. But Nonnie says you aren't real."

"I'm as real as you are," Camille said.

"Then I want to meet the Little Mermaid and Cinderella, too," the girl said. "Gracious, my manners. May I offer you a bite?" Arianna waved toward the table, where tiny china bowls of chicken soup sat before Elmo, the bear, and the doll. Beyond the table, near the play sink, refrigerator, and stove against the wall, sat Hortense's tray.

"You have very good manners," Camille said. "And such pretty hair. I always wanted long hair when I was little, but my mother cut it all off. That's why, now that I'm big, I let it grow as long as I want."

Arianna pulled the yellow bow from her high ponytail, letting chestnut corkscrews spring around her shoulders. "I have long hair, but no mother."

Camille held her hands. "Sure you do. Everyone has a mother. And a father."

Arianna shook her head. "Not me." The longing on her diamond-shaped face clawed Camille's soul.

"Are you my mother?" Arianna asked.

Camille stroked her hand. "No, but whoever she is, she's very lucky to have a little girl like you."

"I won't be little soon, because I'm five."

"Wow, what a big girl."

The child sat on Camille's bent knee, then pushed a handful of curls into Camille's nose. "My shampoo smells like bubble gum."

Camille made a sniffing sound. "Mmmm. Can I borrow it sometime?"

"Only if you'll be my mommy."

Camille closed her burning eyes for a few seconds. "We should ask Nonnie first." Camille stood, holding Arianna's hand. "Let's go find Nonnie."

The girl snatched her hand back, eyes widening, forehead creasing. "No!"

"It's okay to come with me," Camille said, stepping toward the door.

Arianna stomped a foot. "Nonnie will be mad again!"

Camille squatted to Arianna's eye level. "You've been out before?"

The girl looked at the yellow bow on her waist. "To the horses."

"They're pretty, aren't they?" Camille asked.

Arianna nodded. "But Nonnie came yelling. She made me come back."

"Who took you?"

Arianna's face pinkened and crumpled; tears streamed from closed eyes. "Don't take me out again. Nonnie will be mad."

Camille hugged her, stroking her back. "Shhh, it's okay, Arianna. You can stay right here. Don't be afraid. Shhh."

The red cloud of sadness and rage burning inside Camille made it hard to concentrate on how to help this child. If Arianna were in fact a prisoner of White Pines, locked away from everyone but Nonnie, the maids, and whoever had taken her to the stables, was that against the law? It was no doubt cruel. But who were her parents?

And if Camille called Social Services, who would believe it? She wouldn't put it past Mrs. Stone to send the child away to some boarding school. Was that what Ida Mae had been arguing about on the phone that night Dillon came to the town house? And the child's facial features, except for the butterscotch complexion, clearly marked her as a Stone. Camille considered running away with the child, giving her a normal life. But even if they lived in a cave in Ecuador, Senator Stone would have some CIA roughnecks hunt them down, bring them back.

Camille rocked the little girl, whose sobs quieted to whimpers. Somehow, she would figure out a way to get her out of this pink prison.

68

As Karen watched the humming laser printer spit out press releases about the senator's speech tonight at the Black Republicans' Roundtable, the approaching jingle of change in Rollins's pocket made her stiffen.

"Ms. Bradley, Monty wants a word with you."

Karen held the warm sheets against the front of her brown pantsuit. After one month on the job, she was making progress, but three more meetings with Jordan Kyles had gotten her nowhere. And though she was happy to live with Freida, she was tired of hearing her talk every morning about her investigation into rumors about Camille Stone.

Maybe it wouldn't matter: in five days, Karen would be face-to-face with Sharlene under the Stone family's Christmas tree. For now, however, she had to keep the senator happy.

"Has he seen the paper?" She bit down a yawn. At the last minute, she'd extended her usual weekend with Daddy and Mama, opting for the seven o'clock flight out of Detroit this Monday morning instead of coming back to Washington last night. The time singing to Mama as she drifted to sleep was well worth it. Karen hadn't slept a wink, anyway. No, not after Lieutenant Sykes had called after church to say Wish Master was coming under federal scrutiny for the mysterious death of a secretary at its Atlanta headquarters. And, he said, she should take comfort in that because whoever was stalking her wouldn't dare make a move now. She'd told him to get real. Those gangsters would do what they wanted, when they wanted.

"Karen," Rollins said, "we got a mysterious call about you this morning. From a man who says you stole from him."

She let out a small laugh. "What a coincidence. The day the paper runs a half-positive story about Senator Stone, this happens."

"Monty still wants to see you," Rollins said, leading her down a hallway crammed with filing cabinets, bookshelves, and pictures of Stone with former President Bush, former British prime minister Margaret Thatcher, Hollywood actors who were staunch Republicans, and a prominent African-American senator from New York. "By the way," Rollins said, "have you prepared his notes for the Life for All luncheon? The late-term abortion issue coming up—"

"Done, ready to go."

"And the clippings on his opposition to gun control legislation?" Rollins asked. "We need it for his speech tonight with the black Republicans."

"Check," Karen said as they entered Stone's office.

Behind his desk, he was reading his daily packet of articles, copied from five newspapers and bound by the press intern. Among them: Freida's article in which critics called his new black female press secretary a PR bonanza. Stone glanced up, removed his glasses, turned down the Rachmaninoff playing on the credenza. "Good morning, sugar." He waved the clipping showing himself and Karen in front of the Capitol dome. "Let's keep this up."

"I'll certainly try."

"But what the hell is on Kyles's mind?" Stone tapped a lower article about Jordan proceeding with his ethics investigation and the possibility of open hearings. "Hasn't he heard a word coming out of your pretty little mouth?"

"It's taking persistence," she said. "But I'll make him come around."

"Time is a-wastin', sugar." The crease in his forehead deepened. "And what's this I hear about you might have a penchant for kleptomania?"

"Senator Stone, I can assure you, that was a crank call. I bet someone from the Jones camp saw today's article . . . Well, you saw how hostile that Kwame X follower was, at the interview reception."

"I'll be the first to admit, one's enemies know no bounds," he said, standing. "But, sugar, my gut told me you're too good to be true. So you'd do right to prove me wrong."

Karen smiled. "It's a deal."

"Now, first order of business. Tell that goddamn Kyles I'd sooner roast on a spit in hell than suffer some Clarence Thomas or Bob Packwood debacle on live TV." Stone pulled a cigar from his pocket, ran it under his nose. "Hell, if he subpoenas those biddies, no telling what the devil they might say. Now get on it! Get on him! Whatever it takes!"

Rollins, standing by the globe, polished his glasses. "The lawsuits are another story." His tone was rock-hard. "The depositions, the discovery period, that can all be kept private. But a hearing? Disaster with a capital *D*. And it's on you, Ms. Bradley."

Karen stiffened. The honeymoon was over. But she would not let those diamond thugs have Stone and Rollins handing over her separation papers so soon. No, she would call Wish Master directly, tell them to leave her alone so she could take care of business.

69

In her bedroom at White Pines, nothing about this conversation with Ginger was comforting Camille as she stared out past the covered pool, the browning gardens, toward the wide gray river. "I'm in Virginia, Ginger, not New Zealand. So if money is an issue, you can call me collect. But at least return my calls. Please."

"Money's not—"

"What's all that noise? Sounds like a herd of elephants is tromping through the store."

Ginger's laughter sounded hollow on the speakerphone on the table by the French doors. "A bunch of teenage girls just came in for satin jeans."

"Business is picking up?"

"Thanks to you."

"I miss you, Ginger. I'm so alone here."

"Rand and I will be there Friday, for the party. He's, like, the greatest person. One of his kids at Hugs and Hope got arrested, so Rand paid a lawyer to prove he was wrongly accused. I mean, without Rand's help, that kid woulda been totally screwed. But—"

"What?"

"The other night we were having tandoori chicken at that amazing Indian restaurant on Central Park South, and I mean, with all the beautiful lights out the window, and it smells so good."

"And?"

"This guy at the next table whipped out this boulder of a diamond, like yours. The girl screamed! But Rand said he never wanted to get married."

"Ginger, with your parents, you said the same thing."

"That was before—"

"You want to marry Rand?"

"I don't know. We'll be thirty in two years. And you're already married. I mean, it's got me thinking."

"Take it from me," Camille said. "Don't rush it."

Ginger exhaled loudly. "Sometimes, Camille, I feel like you don't want me to have as much as you have. Like, you're happy that I've had financial problems, while you can just come up with a half-mill on demand."

Camille glanced at the closed door. "Ssshhh! I can't believe you! But now that we're on the subject, you need to get over it."

Camille remembered moving into the apartment Ginger had bought right out of college when department stores were snatching up her designs. All while Camille toiled in that office with gum-popping Nan at World Wide Shipping for two years, saving money for law school. Because, while money for college had been a mere matter of checking the right box on her application, law school had been another story.

"You never saw me get jealous," Camille said, "when you were on every fashion circuit A-list in Manhattan with more money than you'd ever had! I was happy for you, Ginger, like a friend is supposed to be." Disco music, chatter, and a lot of feet on the wood floor came through the phone. "And I'm happy you and Rand connected, and the store is better. Ginger?"

"Yeah." Her voice cracked. "I hate that we're drifting apart, Camille. Without you, I have no one for the long haul. But—"

"Then why are you pushing me away?"

"I'm not, I'm just . . . I have to go."

Camille couldn't believe Ginger hung up. She'd never done that. Now they were both in the same position: alone, robbed of cherished confidants. And it couldn't have happened at a worse time. If they didn't get to talk at the Christmas party, Camille would fly up to

New York, look into Ginger's green eyes, and figure out what her problem was.

Camille flipped her left wrist; her gold watch said two o'clock. About the time Hortense or Ida Mae would be picking up Arianna's lunch tray. Camille snuck to her room, as she'd done every day since she'd found her. Arianna's two ponytails, sprouting above her ears from big lavender bows, were all Camille could see above the back of the little white rocking chair, facing the *The Lion King* playing on TV. "Arianna?"

The girl glanced back, then jumped from the seat, dropping Elmo as she dove into Camille's arms. "Rapunzel!"

"Hi, sweetheart." Camille held out a gold box of chocolates.

Arianna's eyes lit up as she said, "Nonnie says no candy."

Camille was pretty sure Nonnie was Mrs. Stone. For a week after the Dr. Zane ambush-exam, and the order to alert Mrs. Stone if her period was late, Camille had avoided her unless she was with Jeff, even if that meant skipping meals and spending long hours alone in her room, reading legal chronicles. But lately, she would join Mrs. Stone for coffee and toast in the morning, telling her she would love to get involved in some of her charities. Camille simply wanted to sugar-coat their relationship and then, at the right time, confront her about letting Arianna have a normal life. In the meantime, she was going to figure out who her mother was and shower this little girl with love.

"Chocolate is yummy," Camille said, biting a truffle.

Arianna pinched up a chocolate ball, took a tiny bite. "Mmmmm." She nibbled as Camille lifted her onto the wooden rocking horse.

"I like the real horses better. Will you take me to see them again?" The glimmer in her eyes reminded her of someone, but Camille didn't know who.

"Are you ready to leave with me?"

Arianna made her ponytails swing so hard they alternately hit her face and the back of her neck. "Let's play in the attic." In the closet, she led Camille through a waist-high door, up a staircase, where sunshine from high dormers sliced the dusty air.

"I come here sometimes," Arianna said, pointing to a bed, a cracked mirror, a wicker chair full of dusty dolls. "But I can't get dirty. Look!" Arianna dove toward a peeling, flowered hatbox next to the railing leading to the stairs. She pulled out handfuls of sparkling jewelry.

"Wow," Camille said, putting on chunky blue earrings. The dust made her fear an asthma attack, but she felt confident that her new inhaler would prevent one. "Let's put some on you," she said, closing a green bracelet around Arianna's little wrist as she chewed more candy.

Arianna froze, her eyes wide. "I hear Nonnie."

Since they had agreed not to tell anyone about their visits, Arianna dashed into her room while Camille watched from the closet.

"Nonnie!" She threw herself into Mrs. Stone's outstretched arms.

"How's my princess?" Mrs. Stone's gaze hardened. "Let's read so you'll be a smart girl. Gracious, were you in the attic?" She dusted Arianna's lavender dress. "What's in your teeth?"

Arianna clamped her mouth.

"Why on earth do they insist on—Come here, precious." She led Arianna to the ruffled pink couch by the window. While reading to Arianna on her lap, Mrs. Stone kissed her forehead, gazed at her with tender eyes.

Fear for Arianna's safety and a sudden heave rippling up from Camille's gut held her back from charging from the dark closet, screaming, "You're a prison warden, not a grandmother!" The dust was making her wheeze and sneeze, so she pinched her nose, vowing to use her inhaler back in her room.

Camille sneezed again, bumping a stack of shoe boxes. They thundered to the floor.

"Gracious, what's that?" Mrs. Stone rushed toward the closet.

70

Camille stared at the lengths of satin and sequins on the bed. She felt bloated and hungry for Hortense's fried grits, of all things, even though in just a short time she could indulge in a lavish dinner downstairs at the Christmas party. Her pulse still hadn't entirely slowed since that close call with Mrs. Stone in Arianna's room. Camille couldn't believe she'd dashed into the attic fast enough to evade Nonnie's closet search.

Now, if she could make Jeff relax, perhaps they could enjoy the party. He was at the dresser, inserting gold buttons on his tuxedo shirt.

"Jeff, help me pick a dress, please."

He faced her. "Pick a name, pick a life, pick a dress. Is it that easy?"

"Jeff, if I have one Christmas wish, it's that you'd get over this Dr. Jekyll–Mr. Hyde affliction. If you could just stay sweet and loving and—"

He came to her side, his face inches from hers. "Think about what you're saying. About how you feel right now."

"I'm mad, hurt, confused."

"Now you know how I feel."

"But why, Jeff? Tell me why."

The broad white back of his shirt was his answer. He returned to the dresser to fasten his bow tie. Then he retrieved a long white box from the closet and placed it on the bed. On top he set a small robin's-egg-blue package.

"Wear this, my early Christmas gift."

One glimpse of a Tiffany's box used to make Camille's heart flutter; now her stomach cramped. "I'm not opening anything with you looking at me like that."

He dug his fingertips into the underside of her wrist. "Open the fucking box!"

Camille squealed. As she stared into his eyes, finding only malice, he shoved the jewelry box into her trembling hands. She lifted the top. Through tears, a strand of red came into focus. Rubies. A necklace, bracelet, and earrings. It probably cost as much money as she had given to Nick. And it reminded her of the wedding tiara, whose rubies symbolized Stone blood. Was Jeff trying to convey some twisted symbolism here?

"Wear it with this," Jeff said softly, sliding the bigger box toward her.

She lifted the top: a lump of gray fabric, shredded and stained crimson. It was the dress Lucy had worn the night Randolph Stone whipped her to death.

71

Jeff could feel Camille's hand trembling as she grasped his elbow. They were descending the grand staircase, past the two-story Douglas fir perfuming the air, toward the carolers, into the crowd anchored by political and business heavyweights and their wives, glancing up at Camille.

"You look gorgeous," he whispered. Let her feel the pain of his own one-man play. So far, she was following his edict to act normal, preventing suspicion down the line when she would fall to her death down the stairs, or tumble into the icy river out back, or lose her way in the woods on a snowy night. Of course, he would wait until he'd squeezed out the last bit of love still scorching his senses, but cooling every day.

Camille smiled. "No. You, baby, are the gorgeous one."

At the bottom step, Jake Frisian stood with open arms. "The newlyweds! Jeff, you look more like your dad by the hour."

"I'll take that as a compliment," Jeff said as Jake kissed Camille's hand, in a red satin glove that matched her slinky strapless gown.

"Your bride defies the laws of nature," Jake said. "No woman should be so beautiful as to make a man deaf, dumb, and blind when she enters the room."

Jeff joined Jake in deep laughter. "My sentiments exactly."

He smiled down at his wife's hoisted-up tits. Her red lipstick made him want to eat her whole as he led her toward the tree's white lights and frosted angels, where his parents were greeting guests.

"Sugar!" Pop's eyes shone like silver dollars.

"Gracious, you are lovely," Mom said. "Jefferson, handsome as always."

Camille smiled, raising her wrist and pointing to her necklace. "Look what your charming son gave me for Christmas."

Pop puffed on his cigar. "Well, he is his father's son. Good taste in women, good taste in the things that tickle a woman's fancy."

Mom's eyes twinkled. "You will let me borrow that, won't you?"

"Sugar, I want your read on my press secretary. You'll meet her tonight."

"Sure," Camille said. "I don't think I've read one paper or watched TV the whole month we've been here. But Jeff says there was a nice article in—"

Pop raised the cigar. "My daddy's gonna flip in his grave, but I'm getting used to a colored face in the office. Just wouldn't want one in the family."

Camille tilted her head playfully. "You mean if Jeff had brought home a girl with an Afro and a nose ring, you wouldn't have approved?"

Pop roared with laughter.

"My gracious, I still have reservations. It's a matter of trust—"

"And loyalty," Jeff said. "Never know when she'll start thinking about the sins of the fathers and stab us where it hurts."

"Speaking of hurting," Camille said, "I almost didn't come tonight."

Jeff studied her unreadable face. If she was about to violate his order—

"I've been feeling so nauseous." She patted her stomach, amused eyes on Mom. "I'm nearly two weeks late. And that day I had cramps? False alarm."

Mom, the epitome of elegance in a shimmering navy-blue gown with Great-Grandma Stone's sapphire choker and earrings, flashed a megawatt smile. "Gracious. We'll have Dr. Zane come as soon as he gets back from Europe, after Christmas. I just don't trust those home tests."

Dark Secret

Camille beamed, flashing a defiant smile.

Jeff ground his teeth. He had the same out-of-control feeling when trying to guide *Miss Serenity* through a riptide: waves coming from opposite directions, hitting one another, upsetting the rhythm. He needed a strong gust to push him through, to help him map a course of action.

But if Camille were pregnant as Mom so desperately hoped, he couldn't possibly get rid of her. His mother had been through enough: Baby Monty, Jackson and Sue Ann's failure to get pregnant again, Camille's miscarriage. However, if the baby came out looking like Karen Bradley, that would be even more traumatic to Mom. And that was a risk he would not take.

Jeff kissed Camille's cheek. "The perfect Christmas gift, honey."

There was no doubt. He would proceed as planned.

72

Karen Bradley inched closer to the long bar in the corner of the ballroom. With its high chandeliers and white molding on the pale blue walls and ceiling, it reminded her of pictures she'd seen of the Versailles palace in France.

"The selection is downright ghastly," said a woman behind her with Armageddon-like somberness that clashed with the carolers' "Joy to the World." "We have more nouveau riche now—that is, worth ten million and up—than ever. Quite naturally that puts a drain on the pool of qualified butlers."

Karen couldn't wait to get out of here. After, of course, Stone introduced her to everyone, including his new daughter-in-law. A quick glance around . . . there was Sharlene, holding hands and huddling with a woman who looked like pictures she'd seen of Stone's daughter, Dixie. The white sister Sharlene had always wanted, with that same clean-scrubbed clear skin as the rest of the family. They both started laughing, Sharlene tossing her head back, the jewels around her neck sparkling. For a second, Karen remembered that moment in Franklin's den, jewels tumbling like flashes of the Grim Reaper's scythe.

No! Sharlene was looking this way, over rows of tables crowded with crystal and silver amongst mammoth poinsettias and evergreen boughs.

"I'll take one, please." Karen shifted behind a waiter offering pâté.

"Ms. Bradley!" Here came Senator Stone with three younger men. She smiled. "Senator, magnificent party."

His eyes glittered like tinsel as he scanned her short black dress with the beaded, scooped neck. "Sugar, you're the magnificent one. Now meet my other sons. Where the devil is Dixie? Debating my friends on conspicuous consumption, no doubt."

A man who looked like Jeff except for a dark ponytail and friendlier hazel eyes shook her hand.

"This is Rand," Stone said. "A bleeding-heart liberal who fled across the Mason-Dixon line first chance he got."

"Welcome to the plantation," Rand said with a wry smile.

Next, a kind of generic man with a firm handshake. Stone said, "Jackson will take the reins of the tobacco company when my brother retires."

The last one had youthful skin but spiky hair as gray as his eyes.

Rollins walked up. "Senator. We should get started."

Stone ignored him. "And this is Davis. Doing things his own way, luring money out of every nook and cranny from Chicago to Cairo."

"*Enchanté,*" Davis said, bending to kiss Karen's hand. His fingers were cold and damp. As he straightened, he smiled, but his eyes were like daggers.

"Excuse me," Stone said, walking away with Rand and Jackson.

"I understand," Davis said, "you've been calling my office."

Karen studied his smug stare. "I don't believe so."

"Yes," he said, a tiny diamond glistening in his ear. "Wish Master, just the other day. Were you calling to thank me for the letter of recommendation? It's obvious the new job is working out quite well."

Karen wanted to double over. This couldn't be real. Stone's son was Wish Master? The people she believed had killed Franklin and were terrifying her? If so, she couldn't tell the authorities; having Stone's son arrested or investigated would ruin her power play with Sharlene and the family Sharlene loved more than their mother. And certainly saving Mama was more important than . . . But if this guy was that sinister, would Karen be keeping her mother alive and sacrificing herself at the same time?

She locked onto his amused but frightening gaze. "What do you want?"

"Just watching for now," he said, lighting a cigarette. "DC is a helluva lot easier than Motown, you know?"

Karen stepped close enough to kiss him. "Davis, read my lips: I don't have what you're looking for. Never did."

But he blew smoke in her face.

73

Hypocrisy. That's what Davis saw in every direction here in the ballroom. If it weren't for Karen Bradley, he wouldn't have even come to the bloody affair. But after she called, he couldn't resist the rush of prodding her to fathom, live and in color, just who'd fetched her here. She'd parried so well an instant ago, but he knew she was as raw inside tonight as when she found that lying wisenheimer dead back in Detroit.

Davis sucked his cigarette, hating the image of Dad by the nautical ice sculptures on the seafood buffet, putting his arm around Mom as if he loved her. Yeah, his fists loved to bludgeon her. And Jeff, a Monty Stone in training, acting like some fucking diplomat, coating his rotten core with charm. If Camille ended up like Mom, she deserved it for joining the wretched clan.

One day I'll do something stupendous to show them what a sorry bunch of cretins they all are. Didn't they know the more they tried to conform to their bloody throwbacks, the worse off they were? Davis had, seemingly since birth. But that had only got him thrust onto the long couch of that cadaver of a shrink, claiming to help with the nightmares when he was just causing more. The counselors at school . . . the summer boot camp for "troubled" kids . . . That's what they got for naming their son after a Civil War hero.

Fuck them all to bloody hell!

Davis flicked his cigarette, grinding it into Mom's precious polished floor.

Sure, it was a tad diabolical to yank ropes behind the scenes, unraveling people's lives. But it was entertaining. And the family loot promised to make the underworld his playground ad infinitum.

Davis chuckled, remembering that night just a few weeks into his studies at the London School of Economics. Drinking dark ale at Beavers Retreat Bar in the Old Building with José from Madrid, Lucius from Cape Town, Mikko from Helsinki, Sasha from Moscow . . . a shitload of cash between them, devious intentions through and through. So when his pinko buddies asked him to pitch in some of Daddy's dollars on a risky hotel venture in Hanoi, he was dauntless. He could still feel the orgasmic euphoria, the *petit mort*, of bagging three times what he'd put in. And now he could only attempt to tame his ravenous need to toss trades in the air, stand way back, and watch the chips fall . . .

But it was maddening when things took a dive. Like Detroit. Soon, however, he'd get his bloody fucking diamonds back from Mademoiselle Bradley. And soon as he got a better grip on her intentions with his father, he'd have some strings to pull there, too.

74

Camille didn't know why Dixie was letting tears stain her silky plum tuxedo-style suit. But she needed to console Dixie and find out what was upsetting her, away from the nauseating Christmas pine smell and the too-loud carolers. So Camille led her to the powder room in the hall outside the ballroom. Dixie's wet face was stiff as she pulled a tissue from the gold box on the vanity, then sank into a white taffeta armchair.

"I loathe Christmas," Dixie said, blowing her nose.

Camille sat before her on a matching stool. "Why?"

"It reminds me—" Dixie tucked her curled-on-the-ends hair behind unadorned ears. "When I was sixteen, Mom sent me . . . to study in Europe."

If Dixie had a clue how fortunate she was—

"I hated every second of it," she said, raising her head. "Wasn't fair."

"Dixie, if I'd had the opportunities you've had . . . You should be thankful."

Her moist eyes widened; she hugged her abdomen. "I'm so empty."

Camille stroked her brown hair. "What was so bad about your year—"

"Six months. Mom made me go." Dixie drew her knees into her

chest, poking the seat cushion with *peau de soie* heels. She exhaled, wiping her eyes. "Get it together now, Dixie."

Squeezing her hand, Camille said, "Dixie, is there something you want to tell me? About what's really bothering you? Is it a man, school?"

Dixie shook her head, her amber eyes sharp. "I've made mistakes. And it's eating me up inside."

"I'm good at thinking of solutions," Camille said. "Can I help?"

Dixie's gaze lowered to the red satin expanse of Camille's stomach. "If you're pregnant like Mom said, let me be the godmother."

"I don't know for sure," Camille said. How odd that Dixie was steering the conversation this way. "But of course. Jeff and I would love that."

The sparkle in Dixie's eyes, and the quick smile parting her bow-shaped lips, reminded Camille of someone. Of Arianna. Suddenly a barrage of images and ideas—the overheard argument in the stable with Dixie, her mother, and Ida Mae; Dixie's stretch marks; being "sent away" five years ago; and her strange behavior regarding babies—glommed into a question.

Was Dixie Arianna's mother?

Camille pursed her lips to stop the words from gushing out. She also fanned gloved fingers on her lap to hold back a sudden surge of rage. If Dixie knew her own daughter was locked away upstairs, and was doing nothing to stop it . . . Camille curled her fingers into fists, squeezing. But no, Dixie was too conscientious a person to do something like that. Even if the child were the result of rape or some other awful circumstances. Unless Mrs. Stone was orchestrating the whole thing, somehow unbeknownst to Dixie . . .

No, I can't mention it yet. Don't want to jeopardize Arianna's safety and security. Because the child might well belong to Jeff or Rand or even Jackson or . . . if all those nasty allegations against their father were true . . . could it be Senator Stone's child? No—unless he or his sons, under the guise of some eighteenth-century master-slave fantasy, got a black maid pregnant and Mrs. Stone was keeping it, as she would say, "under wraps." Then again, Jeff and his Lucy fixation, and that fierce glint in his eyes upstairs before the party . . .

"Camille?"

She was shaking her head, staring toward the pearlescent and gold light fixtures over the sinks. "Sorry, I just don't feel so wonderful." She locked eyes with Dixie, plumbing her gaze for answers, finding none. No, Camille's determination to free that precious little girl overruled her closeness and compassion for Dixie. She would proceed with caution.

Camille stood, taking Dixie's hand. "Hope I said something to help."

Dixie squeezed back, breaking a tiny smile. "Just being my friend helps."

A short time later in the ballroom, Camille raised a hand to her mouth as Jeff led her toward a table with his family. She was sure she would heave.

"Here, honey," Jeff pulled out her chair, draped in red satin, a bow at its back. But it brought no relief to sit amongst the clank of silver on china, the carolers' somber "Silent Night," garlic and lobster smells wafting from giant trays on the waiters' shoulders. "Jeff, I don't feel—"

He kissed her cheek, saying, "Pop wants you here when he introduces his press secretary." He turned to shake hands with a tanned man and a woman in a slinky black dress.

"Get my daughter-in-law some saltines and tea," Mrs. Stone told a waiter. She was standing near Camille and Dixie, who was emitting somber vibes as Rand stroked her shoulder. He knelt between them, giving Camille an up-close look into his gentle hazel eyes, with the natural dark lining at the base of his lashes, enveloping her like velvet. They sparkled, as if he could hear her soul crying over whatever was going on with Jeff.

"I can't believe my friend stood you up tonight," Camille said.

Rand looked away, then back. "Ginger's starting to flake out on me. Her problems at the store, she's taking them out on me, as if I did something wrong."

"I hear you," Camille said softly. "She's basically cut me off."

Rand drew his brows together. "Not the way she tells it—"

"Ladies and gentlemen," Senator Stone called from a microphone in front of the hearth. Flanked by six sets of French doors and an enormous Christmas tree, the fireplace held a cloud of cotton dotted with white lights framing a life-size sleigh, Santa, and reindeer.

"A very Merry Christmas to you all," Stone said. "This year we—"

Blah, blah, blah. Camille glanced back at Rand in time to see him and Jeff exchange hostile glares before taking their seats. She wished she could confide in someone about the turmoil in her head—Rand, Dixie, Ginger—but there was too much risk. So she let her gaze climb the pine tree to Senator Stone's right, one red glass ball and glittery gold star at a time. Her fingers cupped her slightly rounded tummy, wondering if life were growing there.

If I'm pregnant, I'm trapped. She would not raise a baby without a father. Leaving White Pines with Mrs. Stone's grandchild—either of them, for that matter—would spark a nasty custody battle. And with Stone's power, they'd probably win. That was why she had to wait until the time was right to take Arianna away. And what about Dixie? Camille feigned a smile when Jeff grinned; Senator Stone was saying something about his new press secretary.

"And here she is," he said, holding out a hand as an attractive, caramel-colored woman in a short black dress and high heels joined him.

"Ladies and gentlemen, Ms. Karen Bradley!"

Rushing blood in Camille's ears blocked the applause.

No! She coughed into her red fist.

Her sister's stunning smile, her flowing hair . . . and the way Stone's gaze smouldered as he looked at her! No wonder, with half Karen's breasts exposed, just sitting there under his eyes like hot, buttered dumplings. They were a magnet for Jeff's gaze, too, as he clapped.

"She's beautiful," Dixie said, joining the applause.

But Camille wanted to scream. *This can't be happening.*

A few minutes later, Senator Stone led Karen to the table and said, "Camille, meet Karen Bradley. You girls are about the same age."

Looking into her sister's bright eyes, seeing amusement and determination, made Camille bite down a heave. But it pushed up anyway, propelling her past Mrs. Stone, past tables and tables of glittery gowns and expensive hairdos, men in tuxedos, out the ballroom doors. Down the hall, to the powder room. Seconds after locking the door, she lurched over the toilet, her guts turning inside out. All while a mighty fist squeezed her chest.

Dark Secret

On her knees, Camille scrambled on the cold tile floor, spit dripping from her chin, trembling hands clawing the spilled contents of her purse. Inhaler. She eked all the air she could from her lungs, sucked in medication. Finally, she could breathe. Until she gripped the pink toilet seat, spewing more.

She couldn't believe this. She had to warn her father-in-law that he was being deceived. But how could she say, "Mr. Stone, be careful because Karen is really my black sister who's out to get you or me or both of us." And Camille wouldn't even go near the infuriating thought that she had spent three years busting her butt to make Stone love her, while it seemed Karen had wrapped him around her pinkie in a month's time.

Camille wiped spit-up from her fingertips into a bunch of toilet paper. Damn Ginger for blowing her off when she needed her confidante most! Ever since Camille had hooked her up with Rand last Valentine's Day, on a horse-drawn carriage ride through Central Park, it seemed Ginger had been chattering about this party: what to wear, who would be here, what they would eat. But now, she didn't even show up. And as crazy as Ginger was for Rand—who defied every synonym for *gorgeous* tonight in his tuxedo—why was she flaking out?

More retching twisted her guts and burned her throat. Ugh, it tasted so disgusting. *Karen is here!* Could anyone see the resemblance in their eyes and brows, their jawlines? Did Jeff recognize her from the day at the town house, when Karen had worn sunglasses and a hat over her thick braid?

One thing was certain: this was Camille's family. This was where she had chosen to be. And despite the recent bizarre turn of events, Jeff would get over his moods, his mother was already starting to soften up, and all that would enable Camille to convince them to let Arianna out for a normal life.

No, she would not let Karen sabotage this or deceive her family.

Camille stepped to the counter, wiping black smudges from her eyes and cheeks. She ran a tissue over red smears around her mouth. Smoothed down the amber aura around her head.

Then, shoulders squared, chin high, she headed back to the party to defend her turf. Even though her husband, somehow, knew her dark secret. And her sister might be threatening to tell everyone else.

75

As Camille swung open the powder room door, a blur of brown curls, fitted black crepe, long legs, and spiky heels made her spin. Her sister hurried in. Camille locked the door, crossed her arms. "Karen, do you have a death wish? If Stone finds out about this little masquerade of yours—"

"He won't. Because you're going to help me." Desperation radiated from her dark eyes.

"If you're still trying to scavenge my kidney, this won't work." Camille stepped close enough to smell Karen's soft perfume. She was ready to do whatever was necessary to make her sister go away, just as she'd done with Nick.

Karen strode toward the door. "Then I'll go tell hubby and Massah Stone all about their beloved Camille."

Chin tilted upward, Camille said, "You have no right to be here."

"Neither do you. And it's time to come home."

"I *am* home."

"Then I'll tack up a big black eviction notice. Mama still needs you."

Camille stiffened. "I thought she already died," she whispered toward a vase of lilies on the counter. Some of the tension in her shoulders and neck dissolved; she hadn't killed her mother. So there was hope she could get a donor kidney from the registry. "Karen, what can I do to make you leave me and Senator Stone alone?"

"Come to Detroit for a tissue test. You wouldn't even have to tell the Stones. Just say you're going Christmas shopping in New York or something."

Camille wanted to interpret Karen's expression as sincerity. "Promise you'd leave me alone after that?"

"Only if there's a match and you agree to the donation."

For a second, Camille wondered if she were pregnant. "And how do you propose I have major surgery in another city without telling my husband?"

Karen shook her head. "No problem. The procedure only leaves a small scar, and you can be back on your feet in a week."

Camille raised her brows. "In the meantime?"

"We create a crisis. All of a sudden you're diagnosed with a terrible kidney condition. We tell Jeff the best specialist in the country is in Detroit. So you come, have surgery, and you'll be right back here in no time. No questions asked." Karen's shoulders rounded, and she lowered thick black lashes. "And you'd never have to see me again, if that's the way you feel."

Camille's cheeks burned. *She thinks I'm a total witch.*

Crossing her arms, she realized she was trapped. And, having felt the horrible shame and regret over thinking she had in fact let her mother die, Camille saw this as a possible chance to prevent such an awful reality from gnawing at her conscience for the rest of her life.

Camille took her sister's hand. "Okay, Karen. I'll do it."

76

Camille couldn't believe it was taking two hours to get a pregnancy test at this gynecologist's office not far from White Pines. Sure, they'd squeezed her onto the Saturday morning schedule, but how complicated was it to evaluate pee in a cup? She shifted on the exam table, not wanting to know what that silver machine in the corner was for, with its tubes and gauges against the watercolor flowers on the walls.

She yanked back the sleeve of her cream angora sweater set; next to her fingerprint bruises, her watch confirmed a good ninety minutes before the flight to Detroit. According to e-mails they'd exchanged throughout the week, Karen would be at the airport to take her for the kidney tissue test, and Camille would spend the night at a hotel there, just in case she didn't feel well afterward. Jeff and his mother wouldn't miss her; they thought she was holiday shopping in New York with Ginger. Wrong. Ginger hadn't even returned Camille's calls for ten days.

But she would deal with her friend after she confirmed, she hoped, that she was not pregnant. Dr. Zane was out of the country until next week, much to Mrs. Stone's outrage, but Camille had to know before going through with Karen's plan.

The brunette nurse in funky green glasses finally returned.

"Congratulations, Mrs. Stone. You're having a baby."

Camille felt like someone had hit the OFF switch on her lungs. She gasped.

The nurse sprang to her side. "Asthma?"

Camille nodded.

"Where's your inhaler?"

Camille pointed to her purse on a nearby chair.

The nurse grabbed it, found the inhaler.

"Try to inhale." The nurse held the yellow plastic tube to Camille's mouth. She depressed the metal canister, expelling the medicated mist. But it hit Camille's tongue. The nurse tried again.

Camille felt light-headed as she struggled to suck the drug into her lungs. They were still horribly tight. "More," she whispered.

The nurse delivered another spray.

At last, Camille took her first deep breath as the doctor entered and said, "I'm putting you on a steroid inhaler, twice a day."

Camille raised her brows. "Steroids? That sounds dangerous."

The doctor shook her head. "It's not. It's more dangerous for the baby if your asthma gets out of control."

The baby. Jeff's baby.

"I can't believe this," Camille whispered. For a moment, the tick of the second hand on her watch hypnotized her. Nine months. What would her life be like then? Would Jeff be back to normal? Would she have convinced Mrs. Stone to let Arianna out? Would Mother still be alive?

"Oh my God," Camille gasped. Now she couldn't help Mother. Even if all they did today was draw blood, it would be pointless. No way could she undergo surgery while pregnant.

Camille grabbed her purse; she'd call Karen on her cell phone, tell her she couldn't make the trip. But Karen would think she was just stalling, that she'd been lying at the Christmas party and every time they'd corresponded since. What could she do? Calling or not calling would only enrage Karen further, encouraging her twisted masquerade with Senator Stone.

"Mrs. Stone, are you all right?" The doctor handed over the white prescription slip.

Camille took it, rushing to the door. "Thank you."

She had only one ally in baffling situations like this one: Ginger, regardless of how bizarre she'd been lately. So, hurrying through the waiting room, Camille pulled out her cell phone and booked the next flight to New York.

77

At gate E7 at Detroit's Metro Airport, Karen read the red letters again behind the ticket counter as the flow of arriving passengers thinned. Yes, this was the correct flight, and her cell phone was on. But no Sharlene.

Damn her! Camille had never intended to get on a plane, or undergo the test, or share vitality with the woman who had given her life. Karen pushed past two girls in yellow snowsuits, hurrying behind their bag-laden mother like ducks.

Mama . . . How could Karen go home now and tell their mother that Sharlene had lied, that she just didn't care? Especially after Mama's predawn energy burst. She'd baked peach cobbler, ironed her favorite blue-flowered dress, and made sure Daddy shoveled snow from the front walk and driveway.

Rage propelled Karen back to her car, down I-94, through the side door into the kitchen. Mama looked up from the newspaper on the table, her apple-shaped cheeks poised to rise with a smile. But when Karen closed the door behind her, Mama's face flattened, the glimmer in her eyes faded.

Karen's throat burned. "I'm sorry, Mama. I tried."

"Commere, baby."

Karen threw her black wool coat onto the floor, sobbing into Mama's jasmine-scented shoulder.

"You hush, now. The Lord gon' take care of me."

"But I tried so hard, Mama. I thought Sharlene meant what she said. And I keep remembering her with Dixie. She replaced me with someone—"

"Shhh! Shhh!" Mama stroked her back. "Maybe this is a sign you need to come back home. Maybe the Lord—"

Karen shot to her feet. "If the Lord were on top of things, he wouldn't have made you sick in the first place!"

"You hush, now! Don't you talk about the Lord like that. They say he work in mysterious ways."

"Emphasis on the mystery." Karen picked up her coat. "I don't think—"

"So much for playing mission impossible in Washington," her father said from the doorway to the dining room. His eyes radiated tenderness and worry as he slid his hands into the front pockets of his Levi's. "Karen, listen to your ma. We don't want our daughter working for a man who'd just as soon make you his whore."

Karen rolled her eyes. "Daddy, unless you have a better idea, this is the only trump card in my deck."

He fingered his beard, which appeared even more silver over his burgundy turtleneck. "Christ, girl, you don't *have* a trump card if your boss's son and Franklin's enemies are one and the same. Scares me to death thinking about you out there alone."

"Ohlordhammercy," Mama whispered, cupping her forehead in her hand. "Don't let me lose both my babies to them folks."

Karen massaged her mother's shoulders. "Don't worry about me, Mama. I'm not giving up yet."

Her father carried the yellow tea kettle to the shiny countertop and made instant coffee in a peach cup scrolled with "Biscuits 'n Honey." "We know how wide-eyed you get around older men. Especially one who'd—"

"Maybe if I'd had one around growing up, I wouldn't have the need."

The spoon clanged inside Daddy's coffee cup. "My lawyer says the Windsor house is mine come the first of the year. Then the bakery—"

Karen kneaded Mama's tense shoulders harder. "We have more urgent matters, Daddy."

"Christ, what's urgent is for you to come back home."

Karen squinted. "You mean come back and watch Mama die? Never!"

Mama shot from the chair, making Karen's hands slide down her back. She pushed past Daddy, into the dining room, then around the corner to the living room.

The sudden sensation of Mama literally slipping through her fingertips made Karen grasp the countertop. She had to lift that heavy, hot feeling, as if some invisible force were pressing down on her shoulders. But what next? If confronting Sharlene at White Pines didn't work, what would? Coming right out and revealing the truth? No, that would only make Sharlene run away to another city with a new name and a fresh web of lies.

Karen would give Sharlene one more chance. But if her sister blew this one, Sharlene's third strike would be her last.

78

In New York, the guilt cramping Camille's stomach hardened into suspicion and hurt as the taxi pulled next to a row of limos. What in the world was going on at Ginger's store? It seemed like the old days, with the disco music, the blinking lights, and live male models in the windows . . . all the people lined up outside, snaking around the corner.

Camille jumped from the cab, surged through the crowd to the door.

"Hello! Where's your pass?" A pencil-thin twenty-something in shiny gold stretch jeans and a down jacket held up a black card in the shape of the male symbol. "Can't come in without it."

Camille had no pass, and no idea what was going on. But she was going to find out, right away. With or without a fucking pass.

"Move!" She pushed past the girl. Clearly, a fashion show was about to get started. All the clothing racks had been moved to the back, replaced by rows of chairs around a boxy black catwalk. Several fashion reporters sat in the front seats, notebooks in hand. Nearby, TV cameras aimed at the stage, over which hung, in the windows, a giant male symbol.

"That bitch," Camille whispered. "Why is it a secret?" The heels of her boots banged the hardwood floor leading to the dressing room.

"Turn around," Ginger said, kneeling in front of a male model in a slim-fitting canary ensemble on the carpeted platform. "That cuff is, like, all wrong."

Next to her stood Rand, in a shiny blue-gray suit. His angular face appeared taut with annoyance as he watched Ginger. Until he looked up and smiled. "Hey, look who's here."

Ginger leaned around the man's legs. She turned white as talcum powder, then flitted to Camille with outstretched arms. "What a surprise!"

"What's going on, Ginger?" Camille stared so hard, her eyes burned. She didn't care that the dozen-plus people dressing and primping were gawking. "I get you back on your feet, give you this idea, and you won't even talk to me!"

Ginger cast a nervous glance at Rand, who was watching with crossed arms. "Let's talk in private."

"I can't believe you, Ginger." Camille followed her into the office, where Ginger rushed behind the glass desk, flipping through a stack of letters, her hair hiding her face.

"Camille, you're going through so much. I didn't want to bug you—"

"You're trippin', Ginger."

"It's just, with all the heavy-duty stuff going on with Jeff—"

"All the more reason to talk to me." Camille bolted behind the desk, pulling Ginger's arm. "Look at me! And give me a straight answer!"

Ginger raised a newspaper clipping. "Look."

Camille read: CLUB OWNER FOUND DEAD. Beside it, a picture of Nick with two supermodels and a rock star, back when Pseudo was in its prime.

"I've been afraid for your safety, Camille, in case whoever hurt Nick might come after you, too." Ginger's face softened as she rested a hand on Camille's forearm. "That's why—"

"Wonder where he put my money," Camille said without looking up from the undated article. It said Nick's frozen body had been found in an abandoned meatpacking warehouse not far from here. He had apparently died after falling from a balcony.

Ginger perched on the desk, her shiny gold tube dress stretching over black boots resting on the chair. "Nick wasn't the type where you could call his money manager and ask for a refund for your investment. The snake—"

Camille shoved the article back at Ginger. "So this is why you haven't talked to me? What about the show out there, and the Christmas party?"

Tears dripped from Ginger's eyes, but Camille stepped away.

The door flew open; in barged a TV crew and Maren Connor, also wearing shiny gold. "Ginger, they need a quick sound bite." Maren turned to Camille, grinning. "Social climbing becomes you, Mrs. Stone."

Camille turned her back, picking up the article as they left the office. She balled the clipping in her fist as she slumped into the desk chair. What was that hitting her foot—

She gasped. Her black leather Chanel backpack, under the desk. With trembling hands, she snatched it up. She yanked it open: empty.

Camille pitched it, striking the wall. She imagined Ginger huddling with Nick, scheming to extort and split the money. No! Would the woman with whom Camille thought she shared a thicker-than-blood bond really use such a sharp sword to stab her in the back? Their friendship was blown, gone, just like the hundred-dollar bills and Jeff's trust and her only chance to finally help Mother. All gone . . .

In one noisy swoop, Camille used her arm to rake all the papers and picture frames and pens from Ginger's desk. She wanted to storm out and demand the money back from Ginger. Then she could return it to Jeff's banker, and possibly resolve that problem.

No, Ginger was a liar. The damage was done. With Nick, with Jeff, with their friendship. She was alone now, with no one to fully trust or love, except the life growing inside her and the little girl locked in a mansion in Virginia who needed Camille's help if she were ever to live a normal life. She would go shopping, cool off, focus on helping Arianna.

Camille picked up her purse, grasped the doorknob. But the door pushed open before she could turn it, and in stepped Rand, his face stiff.

"Hey, sister-in-law. What in the world happened with you and Ginger? I asked if everything was cool in here, she bit my head off." He glanced down at the doorknob. "Leaving?" Knitting his brows as his hair slid over his shoulders, he gently turned her hand palm-up. His shoulder twitched.

She let out a tiny laugh. "I went riding and slipped in the stable on a—"

Rand ran his fingertips over the purple-green ovals. His soft touch was the only soothing sensation she could remember all day. She inhaled his woody, musky scent, like incense, wishing Jeff still touched her like this.

"I won't let this happen to you," he whispered.

"I should've worn my boots—"

"Stop," he said softly. "I know what this is. I've seen it on Mom."

Camille wanted to succumb to the comfort of his knowing. And the affection in his hazel eyes seemed to reach out and caress her cheek. It sparked a sudden longing to feel him hold her, to hear him tell her he could smooth out all her life's entanglements. But the shame stinging her cheeks kept her silent.

"I'll kill him if he does this again," Rand said. "He's just like Pop—"

"Rand, I don't know what you're thinking, but Jeff did not do this."

"Mom always says her bruises don't come from Pop. But she's as graceful as a ballerina. I've never seen her slip and fall in my life."

Camille pulled her wrist back. "Rand, please. I want to ask you something else. Why does Dixie get so depressed around this time of year?"

His gaze softened, but confusion passed over his face. "She says she was scarred by six months with Europe's divas-in-training. And the extravagance of the season. You know how Dixie is."

"But there's something more," Camille said. "She really trips—" She probed his eyes. If Rand knew about Arianna, he would never allow what was happening. "You sure that's it?"

Rand examined her bruised wrist. "What I'm sure of is, you deserve better." His shoulder twitched as he strode toward the barren desk. "Where's the phone? I won't let Jeff do this—"

"Rand, no. I don't want you involved."

His gaze smoldered as he pointed to the S-shaped scar at his temple. "See this, Camille? My own father almost killed me. I was twelve, trying to defend Mom. So promise you'll call for help if you ever need it."

Camille closed her eyes, savoring the tenderness in his voice, the comfort radiating from his broad chest. And she wondered why someone as genuine as Rand was with her back-stabbing ex-friend.

79

"What, Rand?" Ginger shouted over disco music. "My show is starting!"

He hated the evasive glaze in her eyes. They were standing in the corner of the bustling dressing room, and he gave less than a damn that Maren was glaring at them, tapping her watch and pointing at the jam-packed store.

"What's going on with Camille?" he demanded. "Why is she so upset?"

"Rand, this, like, isn't the time—"

"Why are you shutting her out? You wouldn't have this, or me, without her." Increasingly, Rand wondered why he was with Ginger. At first he'd been attracted to her accomplishments and determination to succeed. And he appreciated her help at Hugs and Hope; besides reading and doing crafts with the kids, she'd taught some of them how to design and sew their own outfits. But lately she reminded him of a crab, scrambling over everything and everyone to get what she wanted. And he would not stand for her doing that to Camille.

Admit it, Rand, you're only with Ginger to get closer to Camille.

Ginger squinted up at him. "Rand, if you're so concerned about Camille, go find out for yourself! *After* you model that suit." She flitted toward Maren, then into the store.

Rand's shoulder twitched. Earlier, as Ginger bossed models and caterers and PR people, he had dismissed her behavior as nervousness about the show. But now he viewed it as downright rude. To him and everyone else. A relationship was supposed to inspire happiness and inner peace. That was how he felt when he thought about or looked at or talked to Camille, since the first time he'd met her at the town house. There on the terrace, during some event Mom was throwing for the family's just-say-yes-to-lung-cancer tobacco company, he had felt an immediate connection with Camille's karma. The mystery, the desperate yearning for love in her eyes, made his heart stop, then race. And his feelings were only intensifying every day, whether he saw her or not.

Now, the thought of her bruised wrist supercharged his pulse. He fingered his scar, knowing all too well the violent capabilities of his father and now, it seemed, his oldest brother.

No, I can't let that happen to her . . .

Rand peeled off the silky suit, tossing it onto the dressing room floor. All the while, the image of Camille's anxious eyes danced in his head. She wasn't ready to hear his amorous confession. But when the time was right, he would be there for her. In his faded jeans and sweater, he slipped out the alley door.

80

In a hallway outside an auditorium at Georgetown University, Karen stood at Senator Stone's side as a cluster of reporters peppered him with questions about welfare reform.

"As I said during the debate, I am not antipoor or antichild," Stone said. "On the contrary, my push to make able-bodied adults work will bring them into the mainstream of American life."

A male reporter in a weather-beaten leather coat asked, "What about prayer in school?"

Stone said, "That would muzzle the violence making bloodbaths of our classrooms."

"Then why not call for gun control?" another reporter demanded.

"Gun control would take away the constitutional right of law-abiding citizens to bear arms," Stone said, "while criminals continue to find weapons on the black market. And I believe—"

Across the hall, a woman in a floppy brown hat and long beige coat waved. Was she a Davis Stone assassin or the blend-into-the-background person who'd been photographing her? No, there was something familiar about her long jaw and jerky mannerisms. With Stone engaged for at least a few more minutes, Karen stepped toward her.

"I'm Vivian Newton." She fingered a tattered tissue. "Karen?"

"Yes." Stone would be furious if he knew Vivian were within a mile radius, especially if he caught Karen talking with her.

"Watch out for him," Vivian whispered. "He'll kill you with charm."

Karen drew her brows together. "Pardon me?"

"He ruined my life," Vivian said, turning her back to Stone. "Everything. My tires got slashed. My bank account? Haywire. Lost my home. Now I can't get a job anywhere, blacklisted."

A red flag fluttered in Karen's head. *This woman is crazy.*

"I admit, I went along with the affair for a while," Vivian said, twisting the tissue. "Even let him pay my son's medical bills. But when I called it off, he raped me. In his office."

The media pack was disbanding.

"I'm so afraid now," the woman said. "Even with the lawsuit, who's going to believe my word against Monty Stone's? I have no evidence—"

"Vivian?" Stone formed a navy-blue wall between them. His forehead crease deepened as he faced Karen. "Why the devil are you talking to her?"

The violence in his eyes, like sun reflecting off glass, made Karen shiver under her wool coat. At the same time, Vivian's accusations churned in her mind alongside the outrage still burning through her at the thought of Sharlene not showing up at the airport or responding to e-mails for three days. And something in Stone's expression reminded Karen of Biscuits 'n Honey, how his legislation had dried up the programs that could have helped keep it open.

An idea, like a tiny bubble popping, came to mind. Something that made her want to smile. But she would have to keep him happy in the meantime.

Karen widened her eyes. "Senator Stone, I had no idea it was Vivian—"

"She's trying to send me straight to hell," he said as they strode the corridor bustling with students. "And why did you step away just when that blasted reporter asked about the lawsuit? You are to remain at my side at all times, especially when the depositions start after Christmas."

"Yes, sir." At his side was just where she wanted to stay. For now.

Dark Secret

In the backseat of Stone's chauffeured Lincoln Town Car, Karen reviewed the day's schedule. She had to think of a new way to put pressure on her sister, or to exact revenge if that failed, too. In a navy blue cashmere coat, Stone was staring out the tinted windows, talking on a phone with Rollins. When he hung up, he turned to her, running a hand over the side of her head. "Sugar, I didn't mean to scold you back there, but that woman wants to take me to the devil's doorstep. The sight of her—"

She put her hand on his, returning it to his lap. "Senator Stone—"

"Monty."

"Monty," she said, "now that I know what she looks like, I promise never to talk to her again."

He nodded. "Rachmaninoff."

"Yes, sir," the driver said as music began playing.

Stone extended his arm behind her; Karen leaned slightly forward. "I have a confession, sugar."

Karen didn't want to fathom what he might say. "What's that?"

He turned, those X-ray eyes stunning her for a moment. "I lie in bed thinking about you. Ever heard of 'dusky Sally'?"

Karen nodded. "Sally Hemings. Thomas Jefferson's slave mistress."

Stone pulled a cigar from his breast pocket, held it lengthwise under his nose. "What do you think about that story?"

Karen smiled, remembering her father's warning. "I think Mrs. Stone would be highly pissed off."

"Millie would never know," he whispered, leaning inches from her face. His scent was a mix of spicy cologne and soap.

Karen ran her fingertips down his smooth cheek; his ruby lips parted. "Monty, I'm not ready for that."

He pressed his nose into her hair. "I'll get you in the mood."

Karen pulled back, closing her eyes. He would probably fuck her right here if she let him, or even if she didn't. But she would not let that happen. Despite all she had read about the lawsuits, she still felt immune to Stone's reputedly voracious libido. She was here on a mission, and until it was accomplished, nothing would get in her way. However, should she need to use it to her advantage, she wouldn't hesitate. Besides, the other women had no proof of what he'd done to them. Should it come to that, she certainly would.

Karen ran her fingers through his hair, which fell in feathery clumps.

"It's just not proper right now," she purred. "Maybe sometime, in your apartment. I'd make it worth your wait."

But only if she had to.

81

In the salon at White Pines, Camille sat on the couch as Mrs. Stone modeled a royal-blue crepe suit with matching hat and pumps. Two representatives from Christian Dior adjusted her collar and sleeves.

"Camille," Mrs. Stone gushed, "tell me what you think of this one. My gracious, you'd think I'd never been to an inauguration."

"Stunning," Camille said. It wasn't the dresses that were exciting Mrs. Stone; it was Dr. Zane's visit that morning. His confirmation of what Camille already knew had been like giving Jeff's mother a double dose of happy pills.

Camille smiled, too, because she was going to seize the moment to ask Mrs. Stone about her secret grandchild. Earlier, as part of Camille's quest to figure out just who Arianna's parents were, the little girl's onyx eyes had glazed when Camille asked if she'd ever met Dixie or Rand or anybody besides Mrs. Stone, the maids, and Dr. Zane.

"I want this," Mrs. Stone drawled. "Camille, pick something for the ball."

Camille tugged a red dress on the crowded rack. "This one's roomy."

Mrs. Stone scowled, taking Camille's wrist. "Gracious, Camille—"

"It's nothing." She pulled back her hand. "It's never happened before."

"He didn't mean to do it," Mrs. Stone said softly. "They never mean to hurt you. But something snaps. They lose control. It doesn't mean he doesn't love you just as much as he did on your wedding day."

Camille felt ill. She hated that Mrs. Stone was excusing their violent behavior and inviting Camille into a conspiracy of silence. Still, Camille did not think Jeff would go beyond bruising her wrist. After all, if he hadn't gotten violent when he found out the truth about her, however and wherever he had, then he wouldn't now. Especially if he were in on his mother's baby threat.

Camille had to stay composed and get on with her confrontation, despite the stinging tears.

With tenderness radiating from her blue eyes, Mrs. Stone caressed Camille's back the way Mother never had. She finally had the maternal affection she'd always craved, but it tasted bitter enough to pucker her heart. At least when she'd told her real mother that those cousins down in Mississippi had tried to touch her private places, Mother had had them spanked and warned never to try that again. And Mother, at least, had never locked her up for not looking like the rest of the family.

She let the tears drip down her cheeks as Mrs. Stone waved at the dress people. "You folks head into the kitchen for tea and shortbread cookies. We'll be just a few minutes." Then she turned back to Camille with tender eyes. "What is it, dear?"

Camille's heart jumped to her throat. "I know about Arianna."

82

Mrs. Stone blanched. "Who?"

"Don't play dumb, Nonnie." Camille locked onto her glassy gaze. "I met your granddaughter. Upstairs."

"Gracious, no."

"Yes," Camille said, arrows of rage shooting up from her heart. She wanted to run up to Arianna right now, hug her, pledge to be her mother.

Next to her on the couch, Mrs. Stone took her hands. "It's not what—"

"There's no sugarcoating this, Mrs. Stone. That little girl is a prisoner here. Just because she's brown."

"No."

"You could be reported," Camille said. "Not to mention the media—"

"No!" Mrs. Stone cried. "It's for her own good—"

"You mean for *your* own good. You're ashamed."

"Gracious, Camille. The irony of you speaking up about this, what with those rumors about your own background."

Camille shot to her feet. "Rumors. Unsubstantiated, or I would've been given my walking papers long ago."

Mrs. Stone fingered her daisy locket. "We've taken you in as one of our own. You're carrying our baby. Show some respect—"

"I'm showing respect for that little girl," Camille said.

Mrs. Stone pulled Camille down by the hands. "I adore that child more than life itself—"

"Then how can you do this?"

Mrs. Stone's shoulders slumped; her pouf of yellow hair shook. "I didn't mean for it to go on so long. When Dixie . . . oh, gracious. The adoption didn't go through."

Dixie. Camille's chest tightened, but she kept holding Mrs. Stone's hand.

"And I thought, what on earth—if Monty finds out Dixie got pregnant by a colored boy, he'd kill him! And it would ruin us. What with the press . . . especially Ida Mae's boy." Tears spotted the Dior suit. "Much as I despised him, his mother has been with us forever, and her mother before that. So we kept it under wraps."

Camille maintained a pleasant mask over blinding rage. "Does Dixie know the adoption didn't go through?"

Mrs. Stone raised her shiny beige manicure to her face, shaking her head.

Camille closed her eyes for a moment, summoning restraint from every cell. "Mrs. Stone, Dixie deserves to see her child. She's got so much angst. And Arianna deserves a mother, a normal life."

"Gracious, I know. Ida Mae and I kept the baby in the old nursery while I tried to figure out what to do. But the months turned into years, and—"

The image of Mother came to mind. Camille's years away were turning into a lifetime, a lifetime that could end without ever seeing her mother again. A sudden twinge of longing made her want to visit Mother, to ask why she hadn't seemed to love her, why Karen had gotten all the affection. And maybe Camille could understand Mother's anger at Daddy, but Mrs. Stone and Ida Mae were committing a far worse offense. Ida Mae . . . that witch! How could she?

"Why didn't Ida Mae's family take the baby?"

Mrs. Stone's head moved back slightly. "Heavens no! I want to provide the best of everything for my grandchild, even though she's"—her voice cracked—"colored."

Camille balled her fists to keep from shoving Mrs. Stone off the couch. She wanted to scream, *You stupid, selfish bitch!* or call the police or Social Services. But they would probably put Arianna in foster care. And if she was afraid to leave her room with Camille, it would terrify her to see police officers or social workers taking her outside to stay with strangers.

"Mrs. Stone," Camille said sweetly, stroking her hand, leaning closer to make their knees touch at an angle, "what if we say Arianna is a child I met at Rand's community center in Harlem, and she's coming to visit?"

Something bright flashed in Mrs. Stone's eyes, but dimmed just as quickly. "The girl looks just like me and Dixie. Monty would—"

Camille shook her head. "No, I think he would see brown and stop at that." After all, it seemed no one had noticed her resemblance to Karen. "Then we can tell Dixie the truth."

Mrs. Stone leaned back, staring blankly at the ceiling. "Gracious."

"I have an idea," Camille said, struggling not to let rage sharpen her voice. "Since having a black press secretary is helping Senator Stone's image, maybe taking in a black orphan might hush his critics even more."

The corners of Mrs. Stone's mouth curled up slightly.

"Maybe tell Mr. Stone," Camille said, "that Rand wants to bring a special little girl down for Christmas. Say the parents are on drugs or in prison. We take lots of pictures, send them to the local papers. Then we convince him to let her stay, so Dixie can get to know her daughter. How's that?"

Mrs. Stone wrapped her arms around Camille, kissed her cheek. "My gracious, Camille, you are creative. All these years, racking my brain . . . Well, let me ask Monty what he thinks."

83

After a teeth-grinding hour of watching Pop debate Kwame X on the live TV show *NightNews,* Jeff was finally home. He pulled off his suit and showered, relishing the idea of two weeks off for Christmas and New Year's: sitting around the hearth with the family, opening presents, eating home-cooked meals. And having a loving relationship with his wife. He wanted to forget the awful things he'd been considering. No, he could never go through with that. Not his Lady Godiva. Toweling off, he noticed on the bathroom counter a new, larger inhaler. The white and blue box promised the drug would prevent asthma attacks if taken twice daily. Was the Virginia air irritating Camille's lungs?

Nude, he dashed through the dark bedroom, lit only by the orange glow of the crackling fireplace. He slid next to Camille, spooning her, burying his face in her hair. Her arms, legs, and back were stiff as wood—until he pressed his open mouth to her neck. She moaned, turning over. "Hi, baby."

After a long, deep kiss, Camille said, "Your father was fabulous."

"Those radicals are loony," he said, remembering Karen Bradley in the green room, thinking, *That's what a mulatto is supposed to look like. So you can tell.* If Camille were pregnant, as she'd suspected back at the Christmas party—they hadn't discussed it since, as he'd spent almost every weeknight at Pop's apartment—would the baby keep their secret?

Jeff pressed closer into her curves, loving her scent.

"I missed you, baby." Camille's voice was as soothing as a lullaby as she slid his hand over her abdomen. "I have a special Christmas present for you. But the stork won't deliver until summertime."

He caressed her slightly rounded belly. "It's official?"

"You're going to be a daddy."

Jeff's hand stopped over her belly button. His fingers curved into a claw.

"Stop!" Camille leaped to her feet. She turned on the bedside lamp.

"Honey, why so jumpy?" he asked softly.

Camille pulled on a robe and left the room without a backward glance.

He hadn't meant to do that. Something just welled up from inside, surging out through his fingertips. His head felt like a teeter-totter: on one end, his mother's desperation for a baby; on the other, his rage over being tricked by a black whore who'd stolen his money and given it to that lowlife loser.

He wouldn't make a long-term decision tonight. No, he would rather allow his gut feelings to guide him moment by moment. So he went into the bathroom and studied Camille's new inhaler, which must have come from the doctor to keep things under control during the pregnancy. In the box was a pamphlet saying the inhaler contained 240 metered doses and, "You may not even feel the medication entering your mouth, but rest assured, that is how this aerosol system works."

So Jeff pushed the metal canister, counting upward with each "sssstttt!"

84

What a bastard! Bolting down the hallway, Camille couldn't believe what Jeff had just done. She hadn't read about that kind of reaction from a new daddy in any of her new pregnancy books. All she wanted was to hurry down to the kitchen—the staff should have left it dark by now—get some milk and oatmeal cookies, then sneak up to Arianna's room to watch her sleep in the glow of butterfly nightlights. The hallway was dim except for a sheet of light shooting from the slightly open door to Mr. and Mrs. Stone's bedroom suite.

"Monty, just tell me if it's true!"

Camille froze against the wall adjacent to the door. She could see a slice of the long oak dresser against the hunting scene mural extending around the room. Mrs. Stone, her face puffy and wet, set a lotion bottle on the dresser. "Did you have relations with those women?"

She must have watched *NightNews*, too, because some of the more lurid details of the lawsuit had been brought up.

"Millie, for the last time," he shouted, drawing near in his underwear, fists balled at his sides. "Why the devil would you believe those blasted liars?"

"But the articles," Millie said. "They identified your scar, the bedroom of your apartment. They couldn't have made it all up—"

Smack!

Mrs. Stone flew back, crashing into the dresser. An antique china clock shattered on the floor.

"I will not take this!" Senator Stone yelled. "Not from you, not from those feminist witches, not from the media! I will not!"

Mrs. Stone crumpled on the polished wood floor, holding her head with bloody hands.

"Never question me!" He kicked her hip.

She shrieked, curling into a ball.

Surely they could hear Camille's heart pounding. Did she dare seek a midnight snack? What if Senator Stone saw her there? Would he hurt her? And had Jeff grown up thinking this was all right? She imagined Rand—at twelve years old—trying to fend off more than six feet of brutality.

And she wished she could call him, to absorb comfort from his voice. Remembering the concern and anger in his eyes, however, when he saw her bruised wrist, she knew one call to him would send him flying down here in a heartbeat, only making things worse between her and Jeff, possibly adding another scar to that S on his temple.

Still, for a second, Camille wanted to dash into the room, pull Mrs. Stone to safety, then call the police. But Monty Stone was above the law. No wonder Mrs. Stone was terrified of telling him about Arianna. And after this, would she dare propose Camille's idea about bringing the child out of hiding?

Camille's heart ached. She sprinted to the landing, let herself into the north wing, to Arianna's room. Gazing at that peaceful little face, the dark crescents under eyes both shielded from and deprived of seeing the world. Eyes so full of longing for a real mother.

Poor Dixie. It all made sense now; Christmas five years ago would have been around the time she had started to show, so Mrs. Stone locked her in this room. But should Camille tell her right now? Then together, she and Dixie could convince Mrs. Stone to do the right thing. But what if Dixie flew into a rage and Mrs. Stone did something even more sinister to keep Arianna a secret? Or what if Mrs. Stone was lying about Dixie not knowing, just to trip up Camille, and Dixie *had* conspired to keep Arianna locked up?

No, I can't tell anyone until I figure out how to get her out of here.

Curling around Arianna, Camille stroked her hair, letting tears spill onto the satin comforter. And that filled her with a choking sense of longing for the mother's touch and loving gaze she had never had.

I need to see Mother one last time, ask why she didn't love me. In the morning, Camille would book a flight to Detroit for Monday. Jeff would still be home on holiday break with his father, but she would find some excuse to leave the house for the day.

Creak . . . Camille's heart raced anew. The hairs on the back of her neck prickled upward. She was too afraid to look. *It's probably Lucy, coming to warn me to get myself, the baby, and Arianna out of this house of horrors right away.*

85

Freida seethed when she read the green electronic message from her editor: "Needs more proof. The story's not strong enough to run yet."

Freida stormed to his desk.

"Ward, what do you what? A confession from Camille Morgan Stone herself? That's just not going to happen!" Everyone was looking at her.

Ward stood, glaring. "Bob says the story's not strong enough yet."

Freida squinted. "First you have me work every angle to the nth degree. Now you say it's not good enough!"

"You're right," he said. "It's not. So get back to work."

Freida trudged back to her desk. Next she would pound the pavement in Detroit and Cleveland, see what she came up with.

86

In Detroit, as Camille's father opened the front door, his expression stung as much as the ice pellets whipping her cheeks in the late December wind. He was just beyond her reflection in the glass window of the storm door; it looked like pictures of the same person superimposed on each other.

"Sharlene?" He ran a hand over silver chin whiskers.

She nodded, wondering if he would slam the door. For a second, she was tempted to run away, fly back to Virginia, and forget about her sudden maternal longing. "I . . . I came to see Mother."

He stared at her with the same disgusted expression she must have given him when he had finally come home on commencement day. After long moments, he opened the door; she stepped into a small but cozy living room, which smelled like pecan pie. But as he stood near the stairs, feet wide, arms crossed, she didn't know what to say. *Hi, I'm your daughter, remember me?*

"Never thought I'd see you again," he said, shoving fists into the pockets of blue corduroys that matched his sweater.

"Here I am." Camille's tone was flat. "Just wanted to come"—*home?*—"for a visit. Is Mother here?"

He stepped closer, jabbing a finger. "What kind of crap . . . showing up after all this time?"

Camille let her eyes project the loathing that was searing her insides. "That's exactly what I thought about you ten years ago. Is Mother here?"

He tilted his head toward the staircase. "Upstairs on her deathbed, thanks to you."

Looking into his eyes, Camille reflected on a childhood of wishing for him to come back and make their lives better. Of wanting hugs and encouragement for good grades and starring roles in school plays. Of having him there to light candles on her birthday cakes. But that had never happened. Bitterness heaved up from her soul, propelling her toward him. "Don't you *dare* talk about what happened because of *me!* Let's talk about what *didn't* happen because of *you!*"

"Don't raise your voice at me. I'm your father."

Camille raised her brows. "By genetics only. What were you doing all those years when Mother was raising us in that ghetto hovel?"

He stood mute.

"Look at me!" She held her hands near her face. "I look just like you! And for that, Mother hated me. I was a little white freak who got teased and rejected to no end."

Her father tilted his head downward at her. "Don't talk to me like—"

"Talk to you? I could only pray for that!" She lunged at him, pounding his shoulders. "I hate you! I hate what you did to my life!"

He grabbed her wrists.

"Let go!" she shouted.

But he pulled her to the couch. Camille focused on the tiny lights blinking on a ceramic Christmas tree on the table under the banister.

"Listen to me, girl!" he said, wrapping his clammy palm around her hands. "You don't know the pressure. Two babies at seventeen. I didn't—"

Camille took back her hand. "That's right, you *didn't!* Didn't stick around. Didn't provide for us. Didn't care! And I've just followed in your footsteps, making the very same mistake! Abandoning my family."

The sound of slippers on the carpet drew her attention to the stairs.

Mother . . . in a fuzzy pink bathrobe, moving slowly down the steps.

Her father dashed to guide her by the arm to the landing. There, she turned toward Camille, squinting over puffy, ashen cheeks.

The air felt thick enough to slice as Camille looked into the eyes she hadn't seen in a full decade.

I definitely shouldn't have come here. She probably still hates me . . .

87

Camille burrowed her backside into the couch as her mother's face unlocked something sad and raw in the deepest chamber of her heart. She shouldn't be here. No, it would have been better to leave matters alone, despite the visceral, abandon-the-family bond taking root in her father's presence. But Mother, she was a different story. The sharpness in her gaze broadcast she had no time for explanations about bygones.

"Sharlene." Mother coughed as she took two steps down from the landing. "Sharlene come home." Was that a chord of affection? Camille sat up straighter, prickling with sweat; she peeled off her heavy coat.

My mother. My real mother. Camille was breathing faster but smoothly; no trace of smoke hung in the air, no cigarette burned between Mother's fingers or lips as Mack guided her closer.

"My baby, after all this time," Mother whispered, her cheeks rising as she stroked Camille's cheek and hair. Her jasmine-scented body heat wrapped Camille in another dimension; she felt dizzy. Yes, this brown-faced woman had birthed her, raised her. Then why had Camille spent all these years wishing for Mrs. Stone's approval and affection, never suspecting the aberrations beneath the glitzy façade? *Now* where did she belong?

"I . . . I just wanted to talk to you—"

"Hush, now," Mother said, as they sat on the couch.

Mack tucked a tendril back into her braided crown. "Ernestine, don't let her just walk in and smooth things over lickety-split. She could've saved your life by now but——"

Mother's feline eyes narrowed. "Mack, this is my business right here. You don't like it, go on upstairs."

Her father shrank into an armchair by the window, facing them. His tense face became an annoying blur in Camille's peripheral vision. She took Mother's swollen hand, searching her eyes for clues. "I need to know . . . I mean, the operation. I wouldn't because . . . I thought you didn't love me."

"Ohlordhammercy." Mother waved a hand. "Hush, now. Your life with me was rough, girl. I know it, you know it, Karen knows it. I don't blame you for goin' off to start over. Almost expected it."

Camille stiffened. "Then why——"

"Don't look so sad, girl. You just wanted to get away from the folks who s'posed to love you, but hurt you the most."

Sourness in Camille's gut threatened to bubble upward. Part of her wanted to spend long hours painting Mother's fingernails and brushing her hair in exchange for unlimited hugs and heart-melting gazes like the one glowing in her mother's eyes now. But that urge shattered under the memory of her barking "ghost baby." Camille pulled back, sticking out her jaw. "Why did you love Karen more?"

Mother stared at her lap, smoothing her pink bathrobe. "I was young, in the ghetto with two babies. And you were the spittin' image of the man who left me there. Seemed like the sight of you pushed my mad button."

Through a blur of tears, her father strode toward Mother and adjusted the sofa pillows behind her.

"Is that why you kept smoking even though it made me sick?"

"I took you to the clinic," Mother said, her brown eyes glinting regret. "But you always had a fit. And you was scared of the medicine."

Camille tried to swallow the melancholy wad jamming her throat. "As if I trusted the doctors who killed Aunt Ruby. I thought those pills would leave me dead on the porch, too."

"Couldn't afford no other doctor," Mother said, staring at the carpet.

Camille's bottom lip trembled. "I wanted to help you . . . when Karen was supposed to meet me at the airport. But I can't now. I'm—"

Mother's eyes widened. "Don't say you diabetic, too."

"No, pregnant."

Her mother's eyes sparkled; her cheeks rose into a bright grin. "Mack, a grandbaby!"

He smiled slightly, but looked right back down at Camille's boots. At the same time, Mother took Camille's hands into her warm, fleshy palms. "You take good care of yourself and my grandbaby, hear?"

Camille nodded. *Mother will never see her grandchild.* She had to tell Dixie about her daughter, to save both of them from this heartache. Camille surrendered to her trembling lip, letting her face twist into a sob on Mother's soft shoulder.

"Shhh, baby. We all just as much to blame. Just like at the bakery, if I don't add enough sugar to the mix, the cake come out bitter. Even with frosting smeared on top."

Mother stroked her back. "That's you, Sharlene. Change your name, live in that fancy house, have all the jewelry and money you ever imagined. But I know, on the inside, you bitter. 'Cause I didn't sprinkle you with enough sugar when you was a girl." Her voice cracked. "Gave it all to your sister."

Camille's mouth turned downward. "But why? All I wanted was love."

"I didn't love myself," Mother whispered, rocking her. "Mama said if I got pregnant and dropped out of school, I wouldn't turn out worth nothin'. I believed her." Mother cupped Camille's cheeks. "I'm so sorry, baby. How I treated you, that's my biggest mistake in life."

Camille never wanted to leave the comfort of her mother's pink-ringed eyes. *But this moment is all we have.*

"You happy, Sharlene? With your life?" The pink bathrobe zipper under Mother's chin made her want to open up, describe all the ups and downs of the past decade, peel back all the layers of lies and pain and worry.

"Tell the truth, now. It can't be no cakewalk passing for white, period. But in a family like that . . . We seen that senator and his son on the news. They treat you all right?"

Camille shrugged. "Our child will have the best of everything."

Mother's eyes narrowed. "Does he know?"

Camille rode a wave of nausea. "I think so. Either from Karen or someone I used to know in New York."

Mother drew back one side of her mouth. "I wish that hardheaded girl would bring her narrow behind back to Detroit. Tonight when she come home for Christmas, I'll tell her this business with you is over and done with."

Her father nodded. "I'll go out there and bring her back myself if I have to. Before this whole thing blows up in her face. Yours, too."

Camille wanted to acknowledge the love in his eyes but was too distracted by his eerie resemblance to herself.

"You tell that boy," Mother said, pointing, "if he ever lay a finger on you, he'll have to answer to one crazy black woman from Detroit."

Camille smiled. "Mother, there's so much I—"

Mother lay back, closing her eyes. "Ohlordhammercy. This headache."

"Hold on, Ernestine," her father said, striding toward the dining room. "I'll get some painkillers."

Camille stroked her mother's hand, watching the pink in her cheeks turn gray. What should she do? Move back here to share Mother's final days? Try to make amends with Karen and her father? But that would mean raising a baby without its father, making it feel as rejected and unloved as she did.

I can't do that to my child. I don't want him or her to end up like me.

Camille kissed Mother's forehead and whispered, "I love you." Then she took a final look at the woman who had given her life, and stepped into the biting winter wind.

88

Freida Miller knocked on the door of a neat, colonial-style
house on Outer Drive in Cleveland, where Camille Morgan's college
application claimed she had grown up. Even though Freida was pretty
sure the senator's daughter-in-law was from Detroit, she wanted to
check out all leads.

"May I help you?" A woman with short blond hair called from
the doorway, smoothing her apron.

"Hi, my name is Freida Miller. I'm a reporter for the *Washington
News,* and I'm looking for Ella McCormick. Does she live here?"

The woman blanched, her friendly eyes narrowing. "Why, no,
Ella has been dead, what, twenty years now."

Freida glanced down at her notebook, making sure she had said
the right name. She had. "Well, I'm looking for the family of Camille
Morgan," she said, "and I understand she was raised by Ms. McCormick after her parents died, but—"

"Oh my," the woman said. "Please, come in."

She led Freida to a family room with a warm fireplace and plaid
couches. "Jane Morgan was my sister. After the crash, poor little Camille never woke up from the coma. She's been at Edgewood ever
since."

"Edgewood?"

"Yes, about twenty miles from here. We go every Sunday. Poor girl. Well, a woman now. Looks just like my sister, even though she's asleep."

Freida felt stunned. "What is Edgewood?"

The woman glanced down. "I'm sorry. It's a home, like a hospital. We couldn't possibly take care of Camille here."

Freida knitted her brows. "Then you don't know Camille Morgan Stone, daughter-in-law to a senator in Virginia?"

The woman's face went blank. "Pardon me?"

The next day, Freida headed into a marina in Detroit, looking for Mack Campbell. She'd found his work address thanks to her friend at Social Security, who had called her when he noticed some activity with Mack's Social Security number in recent months.

Freida stepped past a small motorboat in the front office, where the receptionist paged him. A few minutes later, a man who looked like the picture in the tabloid appeared. But when Freida introduced herself, he said, "You're wastin' your time here."

Freida didn't think so. So she waited in her rental car for three hours outside the marina. Then she followed Mack Campbell to a two-story Cape Cod on Detroit's east side. A short time later, she knocked on the door, hoping Camille Morgan Stone's black mother would answer.

89

"Hold on, Mama!"

But she kept gasping on the bed, eyes wide, cheeks gray.

Damn Sharlene! For coming here, upsetting Mama, killing her!

Mama let out a horrible groan as Karen punched 911 on the phone.

"What is your emergency?" a male operator asked.

"My mother," Karen gasped. "She can't breathe! And she's shaking."

On the other side of the bed, Daddy leaned over her, stroking her cheeks. "Ernestine, try to relax."

"Tell me what to do!" Karen shouted, her every muscle jittering.

The preacher on that Christmas Eve special Mama had been watching when the breathless convulsions started shouted "Hallelujah!" over organ music.

"Is she ill?" the operator asked.

"Kidney failure." Karen kicked the TV power knob.

"An ambulance is on its way," the operator said.

Mama tossed her head from side to side. Gasping. Chest rising and falling in violent heaves. Eyes wide with terror.

"No, Mama!" Karen flew to the side of the bed. "Hurry!" she shouted.

"Christ, Ernestine, slow down. Take it easy."

But she was getting more chalky; she grabbed Karen's leg, squeezing.

"Mama!" Karen held her gaze, refusing to let her soul slip away. "Hurry up!" she screamed into the phone.

"An ambulance will be there shortly, ma'am," the operator said.

Mama's thrashing slowed. Her eyelids closed halfway. Karen took her hand, squeezed it. *Please God, don't do this . . .*

"I love you, Mama," she whispered.

"Ernestine!" her father called, tapping her cheek. "Hold on."

Karen discerned a slight nod; a tear spilled from her mother's eye, rolling onto the peach-colored pillowcase. Her chest continued heaving.

"Hold on, Mama. Please."

Her mother let out a soft moan. A "shhh" sound.

"What is it, Mama? What are you saying?"

"Don't try to talk, Ernestine. Relax."

Sirens rang from the street.

Wild-eyed, Daddy dashed out of the room. "I'll let 'em in."

But Karen knew it was too late. In one adrenaline-charged instant, she pushed the pillows off the bed, climbed up behind her mother, laid Mama's head in her lap. Mama's glassy eyes stared straight up at her.

"You know I love you, Mama."

Her mother nodded ever so slightly, let out a long breath.

"Mama, don't go," Karen said, rocking back and forth. "Please don't go."

But Mama closed her eyes. And her chest became still.

90

A few nights into the new year, Camille crept down to the library, turning on the green banker's lamp on the desk. Wearing a thick white robe over her bathing suit, she was taking a quick detour en route to the indoor pool. With Jeff upstairs asleep, a swim would help her relax and digest how to act on the new warmth glowing inside her when she thought of Mother. She had no one to talk to about that, or about her growing sense that she should tell Dixie about Arianna. The only person who came to mind she could halfway trust was Rand. So she dialed him in New York.

"You sure you're all right?" His affectionate tone made her close her eyes, as if her rigid neck muscles were being massaged.

"Fine," she said. "I just—"

"Why haven't you returned my calls?"

"What calls?"

"I bet my *brother* is having them keep the messages from you."

"Just wanted to say Happy New Year," she said.

"Is it?"

"It has potential, I guess. What do you think?"

"Camille?" he said, over a woman's voice in the background. It was Ginger, shouting about him being on the phone with Camille while she was there.

"Ginger, cool it," Rand said. "Camille, if you're sure you're all right, I'd better go escort Ginger to the door."

Camille hung up, her heart aching. She still couldn't believe Ginger had been in on Nick's blackmail scheme. And now she was depriving Camille of the chance to confide in Rand about Mother, Dixie, and Arianna. It was exploding inside her; she dialed Dixie's apartment.

"Cripe, I couldn't get away from there fast enough," Dixie said, referring to her departure from White Pines after Christmas. "You okay, Camille?"

She would be as soon as she unloaded this secret. Camille's pulse raced; she could feel something squirm, like a small fish, in her pregnant belly.

"Dixie, I know where your daughter is."

Silence. "How do you—" Dixie gasped. "How—"

"I just figured it out," Camille said. "And your mom confessed."

"But . . . how do you . . . is she . . . tell me!"

"She's here. In the house."

"Since when?"

"Always," Camille said. "There was no adoption."

"That bitch!" The rage in Dixie's voice punched Camille's ear. "How could she . . . Wait, where at White Pines?"

Camille exhaled, then explained how she had found Arianna.

"I'll be there in a few hours," Dixie said.

"No," Camille said. "Don't get on the road this late. And she's asleep."

"I'm coming," Dixie said. The dial tone buzzed.

With trembling fingers, Camille hung up, then headed into the thick warmth of the glass-domed natatorium. Had she done the right thing? Surely this confusion and anger would propel her into swimming extra laps. She crossed the blue-tiled floor toward the row of chaise lounges facing the trickle of water from the tiled fountain at the corner of the Olympic-sized pool.

She untied her robe, eager to kick off her flip-flops and dive in. But a male voice said: "—one helluva day. The devil had me on his list of sons-a-bitches to kick in the ass. So chaos was king at the deposition." It was Senator Stone. His bare feet moved slightly, ankles crossed at the end of a white chaise lounge facing the pool. "The media lynch mob was tightening its noose on me, the catch of the day."

Camille's heart raced. As long as he wasn't looking up at the glass-domed ceiling, he wouldn't see her reflection against the black sky. After seeing how he'd hurt his wife, Camille had copped a less-is-best philosophy when it came to being alone with him. Even at Christmas dinner, she'd made sure to sit between Jeff and Dixie at the center of the long table rather than at the end near their father.

"No," Stone said. "The cute little thing's in Detroit, burying her mother. Died just before Christmas."

Camille's knees gave out; she grasped the back of a chair.

Mother's dead. And I killed her. She crumpled to the cold floor, unable to let out the sobs that felt like spears stuck sideways in her chest. Whatever twisted things happened from here on out under this roof, Camille deserved, because she had taken a life.

Now her only concern: save the one inside her, and the one in that pink prison upstairs, from a fate like her own.

91

Several hours later, Dixie rushed into the dark Victoria Suite. A night-light illuminated Camille coming from the bathroom, in a robe, her hair wild. Jeff's deep breathing resonated from the bed. Dixie wanted to hold her daughter, take her away, make up for Mom's cruelty. "Camille, where is she?"

Camille grasped Dixie's hand as they headed down the hall. Even in the dimness, Camille's eyes appeared wet and bloodshot. "The north wing. But—"

"The same room?" Dixie whispered. Her whole body hummed with rage. She was half tempted to yank Mom out of bed and slap her, scream at her, demand how she could ever do something so inhumane. But she didn't want to be like Dad, and she had to see Arianna first. *She's been here all this time . . .*

In the pink bedroom, Dixie marveled at a cloud of dark corkscrews on the satin pillow. *She looks just like me.* The only trace of Wilson: creamed-coffee skin and curly hair. Dixie knelt at the bedside, stroking her cheek. Camille watched from the other side near the night-light. "Will you wake her? I might scare her," Dixie said, tossing her coat onto the floor.

Camille nodded, perching on the edge. "Arianna, honey. Arianna . . ."

Dixie's heart flipped as those long lashes fluttered. "Rapunzel!"

the girl whispered, pulling Camille's arm as if to make her lie down with her.

"Arianna, someone's here to meet you," Camille said.

The little girl sat up, staring at Dixie with wide eyes.

"This is your mommy," Camille said.

Dixie wondered how she looked, in her jeans, turtleneck sweater, and ponytail. *I created her. She grew inside me. But I'm a complete stranger.* She ached for just a spark of affection in Arianna's jet eyes.

Arianna's brows drew together. In a flannel nightgown, she scooted onto Camille's lap. "No, she's not." She was shaking her head, rubbing her eyes.

"Yes, she is," Camille said. "And she's very sorry she's been away. Her name is Dixie. Can you please give her a hug?"

Arianna burrowed into Camille's shoulder. "I decided *you're* my mommy."

That sweet little voice stomped Dixie's heart. She wanted to shrink to the floor and scream. At Mom and Ida Mae for destroying the bond that had formed as she held her newborn before that family came from Fisher Island in Florida. All a lie! And now her sister-in-law was usurping her maternal status!

Yes, those nights with Wilson, pressed between his deliciously hard body and bales of hay out in the stables, had been inspired by rebellion against Mom's debutante dreams and rigid rules about how a girl *of her class* should behave. But the horrible longing, the not knowing where the product of her own flesh was eating and breathing, if she were happy or healthy, being treated right . . .

"Please," Dixie said softly, taking Arianna's little hand. "Just a hug?"

Arianna pulled it back, kicking the blankets.

That stabbed Dixie's soul so viciously, she fled the room in tears.

92

The computer beeps of the cash register had never sounded so wonderful as Ginger rang up the first of a half-dozen people in line. But somehow, she couldn't celebrate the great reviews of the men's line and the surge of holiday shoppers without her best friend. At least Rand was coming to take her to that actor's trendy new TriBeCa restaurant for a celebratory lunch. Then she could apologize for snapping at him so much lately; Ginger hated to admit sometimes she sounded like her mother, chewing out Dad for the most trivial offenses. It was as if the tone and words shooting from Ginger's mouth were the complete opposite of the adoration she felt inside for Rand.

"This place is kickin'," a woman said as she raised an armful of Ginger's second-skin stretch satin jeans onto the counter. "I walk by here all the time. But whoa, you got my attention with those guys in the window!"

Ginger smiled, just as the phone rang.

"Ginger Roman?" It was a woman.

"Speaking."

"I'm a buyer for a major department store chain in the Southwest. We'd like to purchase your satin jeans."

The huge windows, the bright racks of clothes, the exposed ceiling pipes . . . it all spun. This call could further resuscitate her career.

"Ms. Roman?"

"Let's see what we can do."

Rand appeared behind a woman in a red leather jacket and corn-rows. Something in his eyes was dim, somber. He tapped his watch and pointed toward the door. Ginger nodded.

"Ma'am, I have an appointment. Can I take your number and call back?"

A few minutes later, after Lisa took over the register, Ginger dashed over the snowy sidewalk, without a coat, and hopped into the red Dodge Durango at the curb. "Rand, I owe you a thousand apologies."

"Yeah, Ginger, we need to talk." The planes of his face were flaccid.

"Why do you look like you just found out there's no Santa Claus?"

"I need some time alone," he said over the blasting heat.

"What, you have the urge to go hiking in Tibet by yourself or something?"

"That was Peru," he said. "And I had a guide."

"Whatever. How does this affect me?"

"I'm not going on a trip. I just want to cool things off for a while."

Ginger twisted her thumb ring. The frosty yellow polish on her nails was chipping, and the winter weather was causing the skin to flake between her fingers. Her hands blurred; she closed her eyes to squeeze back tears.

"I'm sorry, Ginger. I don't think this relationship is going anywhere."

That voice, with its slight twang, was so masculine, so grounding. And his face . . . no, she couldn't look at him again. Her hands became a knot of flesh in her lap. "It's Camille, isn't it? She told you—"

"I'm turning thirty in February, Ginger. I need to assess where I'm going and who I'm with."

"I knew this was too good to be true." Ginger slid out, dashed back into the store, to the office. She slammed the door and dove into the couch, sobbing. This was fitting punishment for cheating her best friend. That call from the department store, it wouldn't have happened without the blood money. Nor would all the articles and glowing reviews or all the customers whipping out credit cards in the store. Now, whether Camille had told Rand anything or he was catching bad vibes on his own, Fate was stealing him, too.

I'm all alone. Just me and the store. And that means nothing now.

That was it. Even if she became the greatest designer since Versace or Gucci, she would always feel the dizzy guilt of knowing she had gotten there at Camille's expense. Was she really ready to feel "lonely at the top"?

No, she wouldn't have to. Ginger would win her friend back, find another man, and continue this upward trend with Mystique. She would have it all, and she would help Camille get back everything she'd lost, too.

Ginger wiped her smeared makeup, then started to pick up the receiver to call White Pines. But it rang.

"Ms. Roman, this is Freida Miller at the *Washington News*. I'm doing a story about Camille Morgan Stone. Do you—"

Ginger slammed down the phone.

That's it. That's how I can help Camille . . .

93

With a phone to her ear, Camille paced the Oriental rug near the giant burgundy velvet bed where she'd slept alone again last night. Now she savored the solitude, thankful that Jeff was in Washington so often, so she wouldn't have to ride the highs and lows of his roller-coaster moods.

"Hello?"

"Dixie, it's Camille." She'd been trying to reach Dixie at her apartment since their encounter with Arianna, but Dixie had not returned any messages left on her answering machine. Camille had to discern whether Dixie was plotting a scheme of her own to confront her mother or take Arianna away.

"What do you want?" Dixie's tone was hard.

"I think if you come visit a few more times, Arianna will warm up. She was probably startled by us coming in the middle of the night." Camille fingered the silky tassels holding back the drapes to show the gray river.

"She's my daughter, not yours, Camille."

"I'm sorry I'm the one who told you, but wouldn't you rather know?"

Dixie exhaled. "You waited long enough to bond with her be-fore—"

"I had no idea who her parents were!" Camille said. "Have you talked to your mother about this?"

"No," Dixie said. "I was afraid I'd . . . make things worse. But I'll get Mom back. Somehow. Someday. For doing this to me. And the baby."

"We have to be careful, Dixie, so she doesn't do anything crazy. And—"

"I don't need your help, Camille." Click.

Camille slammed down the phone. A panicky feeling seeped through her.

If Dixie confronted her mother, Mrs. Stone might send Arianna off to boarding school or do something vindictive, just to keep the secret from Monty and the press.

94

A week's worth of frustrations streamed across Rollins's face as Karen joined him on the couch in Senator Stone's office.

"My condolences," he said, nodding his more-tousled-than-usual head.

At least sincerity glinted in Jeff's eyes as he stepped close and gently squeezed her arm, saying, "Sorry about your mom." Then, taking a chair by the globe, he fanned his hands over the navy-blue wool of his suit pants, staring at his wedding ring.

Sharlene needs to feel this pain, this emptiness, too. Soon she will.

"Sugar, you're back," Senator Stone said, striding in from the Senate floor. "My heart goes out to you, but I've been to hell and back since you left."

Karen squared her shoulders. "I apologize for the timing, sir. But I'm eager to get back to work." No, she wouldn't be going back to Detroit as Daddy wanted anytime soon. She had business to handle here in Washington. The business of avenging Mama's death. And its success would hinge on her star status with Stone.

"Monty." Rollins had something to say; he was polishing his glasses with a polka-dot hankie.

"Yes, yes, go on." Stone did not look up from behind his desk. He was putzing with the stereo on the credenza.

Rachmaninoff began playing as Rollins turned to Karen. "We've gotten more calls from the fellow claiming you stole from him. If we don't clear this up, Karen, I'm afraid we may have to let you go."

"This was cleared up weeks ago," Karen said. "That caller simply has an ax to grind in the aftermath of—"

"We don't need any axes ground here," Jeff said, his gaze rock-hard. "Got enough to sweep up from everything else going on."

Karen stepped toward the desk. "Senator Stone?"

He glanced her way from adjusting knobs on the stereo. "Yes, sugar?"

"Do you have any reservations about my performance or character?"

He turned around, straightened. "I wish you'd whip that son of a bitch Jordan Kyles into line sooner rather than later. Especially on the issue of open hearings." He retrieved a cigar from the humidor. "And other than your unfortunate absence last week, no, sugar. You're exceeding my expectations." His gaze rambled down the curves of her black skirt suit, lingering on her legs and toe cleavage. "So you sit right down. Rollins is just blowing steam."

Through the corner of her eye, she could see Rollins checking his glasses against the light. She stifled the urge to face him and shout, "Overruled!"

"Now, down to business," Stone said. "Rollins and Jeff, share what you've told me."

Rollins put his glasses on, focusing on Stone. "We'll use your autobiography to set the stage for the presidential campaign. Come the second week of April when it's released, things should be really heating up."

"The publisher is booking a thirty-city tour," Jeff said. "Lots of media hype. Voters won't get past page one before they start singing 'The Star Spangled Banner.' "

Karen nodded. She had read a galley for Stone's book, *My Fore-fathers, My Future,* which traced his family's role in tobacco farming, politics, and law back to the 1600s. One thing was for sure; it cast a nostalgic haze over the gruesome reality of slavery down on the plantation.

Rollins said, "As for the publication party—"

"I want it in the ballroom at White Pines," Stone said.

"For a down-home, fireside-chat feel," Jeff said.

Karen raised an index finger. "May I add something?"

"Why, yes, sugar."

Karen strode toward his desk and perched on the edge. "We need to make this book—and you—stand out from all the other politicians and their memoirs. And what's the catchiest way to do that in this day and age?"

The men shrugged.

"Video," she said, holding up her palms and smiling. "Imagine the splash . . . a glitzy video of you on the Senate floor. Pictures of your family at work and home since colonial times. It would tug at the most patriotic of heartstrings."

Stone's eyes shone like new silver dollars.

Jeff stood, spinning the globe. "This video—we show it at the party?"

Karen nodded. "For the who's who of politics and an army of media."

The door flew open. "Senator Stone!" It was his deputy chief of staff, Kurt Smith, holding up a white envelope. "Bad news, sir. The Ethics Committee is calling for open hearings."

Stone slammed his palm on the desk. "What the devil—" For the first time in Karen's presence, his hair was mussed. The potency roiling in his eyes gave her goose bumps.

"I told you not to let this happen!" He stepped around the desk, pointing down at her. "I thought hiring you would do the trick. Now, if you have to get on your knees and express yourself to Kyles in a more . . . persuasive manner . . . then, sugar, get to it."

Karen's cheeks burned in the ringing silence. But she did not look away from Stone's flushed face. No, she was going to do whatever was necessary to preserve her status as his darling; that was the only way to execute the earth-rumbling revenge of Plan D.

She slid off the desk, stepped toward Stone. "Senator," she whispered in his ear, "you got yourself a deal. I'm on my way." She smiled, sauntering toward the door.

95

Karen hurried past several cubicles where aides talked on phones, tapped computer keyboards, and sorted mail. In the corner at her desk, she retrieved Davis Stone's business card from a pocket in her attaché. She propped it between a row of letters and numbers on her laptop, then typed the e-mail address.

She just wanted to tell him to stop tampering with her job, even if he had, for whatever reason, helped her get hired. Karen also wanted to pick up some high-tech tools necessary to execute Plan D. All before meeting Jordan Kyles for Szechuan prawns and another match of high-stakes sparring.

"Davis," she typed, "we urgently need to talk. If you're in town, let's meet. Or call me at home (202)"—Karen laughed—"you have the number."

She poised the cursor on the SEND box.

"Sugar, you ought to know better than that."

Senator Stone's deep drawl threatened to paralyze her and her plan and the message . . . if he knew Davis's e-mail address, or was even looking at the screen. Without flinching, she clicked the words into cyberspace, then spun her chair, facing his shimmering eyes. "Than what, sir?"

"Whispering in an old man's ear like that." Tiny lines around his eyes deepened as he smiled slightly. "Sashaying away in your little skirt."

Karen smiled. "I apologize. But I'm meeting Jordan Kyles for dinner to turn up the heat on my . . . assignment."

"Very well." With his back to the cubicle entrance, he bent slightly and whispered, "What about us?"

"Us?"

"In the car, you said—"

Karen trained her gaze on his lips. She stood, almost brushing her breasts into his lapels. "I'd like to share some of my ideas for the video, without Jeff and Rollins."

"I see. Perhaps Friday night, my place. In the meantime, you and Jeff fly down to White Pines, gather up any photos or documents you need."

Karen sat, clicking on her computer calendar. "Wednesday afternoon is open. But Friday we have Senator Parson's reception at five-thirty."

"Our nightcap will follow." The beige planes of Senator Stone's smooth face glowed. He nodded, then strode away.

A short time later, she headed to the Spy Supply Store, where a man approached at the glass counter full of surveillance devices. "May I help you?"

She described what she needed.

"Heya, take a look," the man said, holding up a brown leather purse. "You'd never suspect a thing, would you?"

Karen smiled. "Never."

"Heya, take one of these puppies for backup," the man said, holding what looked like a black tube of lipstick. "You'd fall over if I told you what folks do with these."

"I'll take it." Karen pulled out a credit card as the cash register rang up a figure that would surely blow a big crater in her bank account. "Ma'am, that'll be—"

"I'll handle this," a deep voice said. In the corner of her eye appeared a shock of silver hair, a long black leather coat. He smelled of cigarettes.

Karen turned; Davis Stone gave the man several hundred-dollar bills.

"I see you got my e-mail," she said, a sarcastic edge in her voice. He had grown a short beard and mustache that was jet black, accentuating the iridescence of his eyes. Karen shivered but did not stop looking up at the man who had probably ordered Franklin killed. "Guess your surveillance saves time deciding on a meeting place."

He took his change while looking down, flaring his sharp but slightly crooked nose. "Let's go." He glanced at the door.

Karen gasped. There in a red wool trench coat and matching pimp-daddy hat, feather and all, stood the man who had threatened her at Franklin's funeral, who had broken into her apartment, who had ambushed her at the post office. Who had probably pulled the trigger in Franklin's bathroom. She wished she could call the police, tell them to arrest him right here, right now. But that would interfere with Plan D. Karen crinkled her brow. "I'm not going near him."

Davis put his arm around her, leading her toward the door, but Karen would not move. "Listen, stop calling Rollins, telling lies about me."

"Then be straight with me. How 'bout I help you"—he glanced at the bag in her hand—"then I let you rest easy."

"You don't know what this is," Karen said, clutching the bag.

The man in red was on them in two strides. "Cutie pie. Look like you givin' my man too much lip, not enough sparkle."

That fruity cologne . . . she coughed. "Leave me alone!"

"Bright, get lost for a minute," Davis said.

The man went outside.

"Like I said, I'm here to help," Davis said.

"Is that what you said to Franklin Daniels?"

Davis's eyes glazed. "Let me do something or I'll have Rollins so suspicious of you, he'll have the FBI sniffin' up your skirt."

Karen turned toward a wall of TV monitors. Sweat soaked her blouse and suit despite the snow flurries outside the glass door. Her heart was pounding so loud she could almost hear it. And she hated that Davis and "Bright" were so mysterious and menacing. Yet part of her was bored with feeling afraid. She was treading treacherous waters, but she had a floating sensation, as if blind to what lurked in the darkness below.

But what did Davis know about what she was doing, and why would he want to help? However, if letting him assist would keep him off Rollins's phone line, then she'd toss a little assignment his way when the time was right.

Meanwhile, she was late for dinner with the finest man on the Hill.

96

Jordan Kyles was already sitting in a mauve booth at Mr. K's Chinese restaurant in Washington. A candle on the table magnified the concern in his eyes. He stood, helping remove her coat, as she set her unmarked Spy Store bag and purse on the seat.

"I need a martini," she said, sitting down. If nothing else tonight, she had to make him change his mind about the open hearings. She just wished she didn't feel so damn serene in his presence, and calmed by that look in his eyes that made her feel like a warm cloud was billowing around her.

His brows drew together; he took her hand. "Karen, you need some time off. Losing your mother so soon after Franklin—"

She pulled back her hand, studying the red-lettered menu. Egg foo yung or snow peas and chicken? "Work keeps my mind off things." No, anything Szechuan would be good.

"I don't want to talk work," Jordan said. "I want to talk about us."

Her stomach fluttered. She set the menu down. He was especially handsome in navy-blue pinstripes and a monochrome shirt-tie ensemble. "This meeting is strictly business," Karen said. "We got your calling card today."

Jordan sat back, his gaze hardening.

"You have to admit I made an enticing proposal," Karen said.

Dark Secret

"You do your investigation in private without open hearings; you get funding for your prison education program."

Jordan's jaw tightened. "My commitment to cleansing Congress of vermin like Stone is not for sale."

"Then think of it as barter," Karen said.

The waiter set two martinis on the pink tablecloth.

"To us," Jordan said, tipping his glass toward her.

Careful to hold the toothpick of olives at the edge of the glass, Karen took a generous gulp, loving the cool burn.

They set their glasses down simultaneously; he squeezed her hand. "Lately the only thing that entices me is you," he said.

No, she couldn't let her soul open up to him. But new feelings for Jordan were pushing up against those trapdoors she'd nailed shut over the part of her being where she could love a man. Besides, she had dangerous work to do, and didn't want Davis and Bright on Jordan's tail, too.

But the way he was looking at her, the way her body was suddenly screaming for him, she couldn't even remember the last time a man had held her, much less melted away her worries with endless waves of orgasm. And this electricity crackling over the table was more than mere lust; it was that she wanted to wrap herself in the warmth and strength of his karma and stay there. *Yes, Jordan can hold me and make me stop feeling so alone and sad.*

Karen lifted the toothpick holding three olives in her drink. She balanced it before her mouth, then licked a clear drop from under the middle olive. All the while, she held Kyles's smoldering gaze.

Within minutes, they were in his car, whizzing away to the sexy jazz of Peter White. At the first stoplight, Jordan turned to her. "Come home with me."

Closing her eyes, Karen almost moaned, even before Jordan placed his searing mouth on her lips. Her brain became a wonderful whirl; she thought of nothing. Nothing! Except the heat and flames racing through her, straining her nipples against her bra, making her squirm in the bucket seat.

He pressed closer, his thumb on her cheek, fingers in her hair, pulling her into him. She wanted to stay like this forever, intoxicated by—

Honk!

Jordan smiled, glancing at the green light.

Karen leaned back as he sped forward. "I can't do this. It would look like—"

"I'm the only one looking." He focused on taillights.

"If anyone found out—"

He turned, hardness flashing in his eyes. "You think people haven't seen us having lunch?"

He ran his hand over her jaw, parting her lips with his thumb. She closed her eyes. And when she opened them, she was stepping out at Jordan's house in Silver Spring, Maryland, into his bedroom. She barely noticed the soft lights, the sharp-angled wood furniture, the platform bed with crisp beige linens. No, she only wanted to look into those smoky eyes that were transporting her to another dimension where she couldn't remember . . .

They were slow-dancing, sort of. Her arms resting on his shoulders, his open palms on her ribs, their bodies so close, eyes locked. Already out of his suit jacket and tie, Jordan unzipped Karen's jacket, tossed it onto a chair.

Then, his full, parted lips came closer, closer . . . yes, so hot and soft. But just when she kissed back, his mouth trailed down her chin, to her neck. Something hot and tingly rippled below her belly button.

"You belong with me," Jordan whispered, peeling off her blouse.

Yes, right now, I belong here. But not tomorrow, when I face Stone . . .

Karen tilted her head to one side, giving Jordan a wider expanse of neck to tickle with his tongue. Hands at her waist, he did a Fred Astaire–Ginger Rogers spin, landing them gently on the bed. Smooth. As if he'd had too much practice. "Should I be afraid?" Karen purred.

"Yes, for me. Falling for you," he said, kneeling over her.

A lazy smile lifted her cheeks. He was like the sun beaming down, making her hot, mellow. And unafraid as he slowly unzipped her skirt, pulled it down, removed her stockings and blouse. Then, after drinking in every inch of her skin left bare by her burgundy satin bra and panties, he removed them.

Karen locked on his gaze as he stood, removing his shirt to reveal succulent hills and valleys of creamy chocolate. Her lips parted as his pants slid to the floor and a huge bulge in his beige boxers waved like a metronome. Jordan knelt over her, pressing her upper arms, one in each hand, into the bed. Meanwhile, he lowered that delectable O shape with his lips, right onto her nipples. In, then out. Up, down, up, down.

"Yeah, Jordan . . ." Karen squirmed downward, pressing the wet, burning flesh between her legs into his thigh. She imagined the aching strip glowing red-hot, like coils on an electric stove, then sizzling as she touched his skin.

"Ooh, I want all that," he whispered into her chest. Without warning, he rolled on his back, holding her above him. Then he pulled her down, plunging inside her.

Yes . . . The suddenness, the hugeness, stunned Karen. But the fire, the tingling, she was sure her insides would singe him. But, gripping her thighs, he hammered just the way she needed. Then, slowing for a second, his fingertips danced over a little fireball that melted her mind and spirit.

"We're one now," he whispered. "One. Always."

Affirming his statement was the vee of her caramel thighs on his smooth stomach, her slim fingers cupping the curves of his pecs, a fountain of sparks shooting up through her, their souls trembling in unison. She could never tire of this, of Jordan, of his commitment to helping others. She collapsed into the nook of his arm and chest. After a long kiss, Jordan pulled back, whispering, "Karen, I want you with me. At home, at work. And—"

The damp warmth of his chest suddenly felt slippery under her cheek.

"—whatever your eyes and ears have picked up in Stone's office would help my investi—"

Karen sat up, pulling the comforter over herself. "Is that why you brought me here?"

"Is that why you came?"

Disappointment burned through her like acid. She felt heavy and stiff as she contemplated jumping off the bed, throwing on her clothes, running out. How stupid to let emotion and some romantic fantasy interfere with her plan to avenge Sharlene. Now Karen must look like a bold-faced prostitute in Jordan's eyes. But she couldn't let a lovers' spat derail her mission.

So she laughed, walking her fingers up his stomach. "I came because I wanted you to fuck my brains out. Any objections?"

Jordan's gaze smoldered but his face was stiff. After a few moments, he grinned. "Then if I'm your boy-toy for the night, we've got work to do." He rolled on top of her for another searing kiss.

97

Late Friday afternoon, Jeff trudged up the royal-blue carpeted stairs at White Pines, eager to put on a pair of jeans, maybe work out, and have dinner with Camille. Every night this week in his room at Pop's apartment, he'd craved her warm curviness, the way her voice flowed into his ears like honey, the cute way she stuck out her jaw when miffed. That was why he'd taken the Gulfstream home for the weekend; he bit down the urge to sprint down the long hallway to her in the Victoria Suite. As Jeff turned into the south wing, that guy with his money came to mind, saying revolting things about Camille.

No, I'd rather pretend nothing has changed . . .

Yet he felt as if he was "in irons" while sailing *Miss Serenity*: when the bow faces the wind, the boat won't move because there's nothing to fill the sails. So he'd have to bring the sail cockeyed to force the bow out. As in, make a decision, soon, about how to hunker down and sail into the future, with or without Camille. Jeff pulled off his suit jacket, loosened his tie, walking faster. The book party was sure to draw a blizzard of media coverage. So acting on his initial urge to get rid of Camille would have to happen now, or wait until well after the party. Jeff stepped harder, almost stomping. He would never find another woman who aroused such intense verve, who made him want to spend a thousand lifetimes with her.

"I'm having new bedding designed for the crib." Mom's voice

wafted from the nursery. "Gracious, I love this window seat. What do you think, Camille?"

"Perfect," Camille said. "Let's find an adorable pattern in yellow—"

Jeff stopped. *Damn her for playing on Mom's emotions. Just like she played mine. I hate her!* It was time to end this charade, before Camille—or Sharlene or Lucy or whatever her name was—could hurt his mother.

Jeff strode across the creaky floorboards. "Sounds like big fun in here," he said, kissing Mom's cheek as she peeled a shred of blue paper from the wall by the bathroom. He hugged Camille, surveying the curtainless windows.

His mother pointed to the white brick hearth. "Jeff, how about the rocking chair over there? After all, you'll be using it, too."

"Knock yourself out, Mom," Jeff said, taking Camille's hand. "I just want to spend some time with my wife."

Camille squeezed his hand, smiled up at him. "I'd love that."

He bit down so violently, his teeth couldn't possibly withstand the pressure without cracking. Maybe that was why his gums were throbbing, his jaw aching, as he led Camille down the hall.

"Jeff, I can't believe how happy I am now." Camille looked up with eyes that had lied to him for so many years. "Your mother and I are having a ball. Even though, I admit, I didn't think I'd like it here."

Jeff stared straight ahead. *Wait until we get in the bedroom.*

98

The only time Camille had seen Jeff's nostrils flare like that, his eyes flash such malice, was the night of the Christmas party, when he had pinched her wrist and called her Lucy. She did not want to go into their bedroom with him; she had to cool him down first, make him forget whatever was infuriating him.

"Baby, Hortense made the most amazing lasagna," she said, taking his hand. "Let's eat first, then take a swim."

She got only a jaw-flexing profile, his jacket on a finger over his shoulder. Jeff pushed open their door. He shoved her inside.

The bottom of her wedding ring clanged as she grabbed the bedpost to keep from falling. His fingers stabbed her chest; she fell onto the damask bench, crouching under his hunched shoulders. With his chin down, eyes bulging, he reminded her of a bull about to charge.

"You tricked me! And my family!" His rage rang in her ears.

Camille could see her length stretched beneath him: in her amber leggings and thick sweater, her stomach was a small mound. One fistfall from Jeff and he'd quiet the tiny heartbeat that had brought her to tears during Dr. Zane's visit this week. And destroy her leverage over Mrs. Stone, which she needed to free Arianna.

"Jeff." The name squeaked from her constricting chest. No, she couldn't have an asthma attack. Her new inhaler was supposed to prevent this from happening. Why wasn't it working?

"I know about you, Sharlene!"

Camille gasped.

Jeff's eyes glowed with ferocity in the dim light of the vanity lamp.

"Nigger whore!" His eyes narrowed to slits. He huffed through an open mouth. Lips curled around glistening teeth.

Camille struggled to take in air.

Jeff pounced. Clawed her clothes, shook her, slammed her to the floor.

"The baby!" she squealed.

"I don't give a fuck!"

Hot, paralyzing pain radiated up from her hip and elbow. She whimpered. Camille stared up with pleading eyes. She coughed.

"You're a sick bitch!" His voice was demonic.

Dizzy, she squirmed. Had to get away. But he towered over her.

"How long did you think you could fool me, Sharlene Bradley?"

"No, Jeff," Camille wheezed, "let me explain."

"Shut up!" Jeff clamped his hands around her torso, lifting her. Screaming, she clutched his head. A grotesque scratching sound. Her stomach flipped as she sailed past the vanity.

"No!" Camille thudded against the wall, crumpled to the floor. Jeff dove at her, four lines of blood on his cheek.

She curled into a ball, forearms over her abdomen, face in her knees.

"This is for using sex to trick me!" Jeff snapped her head up by pulling her hair, slammed a fist into her face. Yellow swirls . . . horrible throbbing . . . pressure. She was too stunned to breathe, and when she tried—

"This is for stealing my money!" A blur of fist coming closer . . . burning lips, the taste of blood. "You fucking whore! Worse than Tabitha!"

"Jeff, please. Stop! I'm sorry!"

He pried her chest from her knees, aimed a fist at her stomach.

"No!" She kicked his shins, pulled his hair, clawed his bloody scratches.

He sat back, watching her cough.

Gotta get my inhaler . . .

"You know, Lucy, I loved you." His voice had the slow, steady rumble of a freight train. "With all my heart. Until I met your friend Nick."

Camille concentrated, willing her lungs to stay open enough to keep her conscious. She glanced at the nightstand, where she kept an inhaler.

"Have to give you credit," he said. "The way you remade yourself. Pretty clever. Never would have guessed . . ."

Through chattering teeth, her whistling breath was an eerie reminder that another life depended on her for oxygen. "Jeff, I can't breathe—"

"I don't give a fuck!"

There is no love here. No place for a baby. If I live I'll take Arianna away . . .

He knelt at her side. "You probably think I'll divorce you. No, no, Sharlene Bradley! You stay right here. Pay for what you did. You're so fucking good at pretending, let's see how you like this act."

He darted toward the nightstand, retrieved an inhaler, threw it at her.

With trembling fingers, Camille shook it, exhaled, pushed the canister—

It's empty! She glared up at him.

Jeff laughed. "How do you spell relief? D-E-A-D!"

"Please!" Everything was getting darker, shaking.

"No one will know the truth, Sharlene! Never!"

Camille laid her cheek on the cold floor, closed her eyes. *The baby . . .*

It sounded as if Jeff was undressing; fabric ripped. His shoes came flying into her shoulder and leg. "A thousand showers couldn't clean this filth!"

Rushing blood in her ears drowned out the running water in the bathroom. She throbbed, stung. "Please," she wheezed into the hard wood.

She was spiraling down a dark tube.

I deserve this for killing Mother.

99

Freshly showered, Monty Stone admired his still-firm and lean body in the bathroom mirror of his apartment. Karen was younger than any of the women he'd been with lately, and he did not want to disappoint her. Running a comb through his hair, he chuckled, feeling more alive than he had in years.

This reminded him of being a boy, sneaking behind the big leather couch in the library of White Pines, when the men retreated to smoke cigars, drink bourbon, and talk "business and bosoms" as his daddy would say. He could still hear the excitement in his grandfather's voice when he described how, on his fifteenth birthday, his own father had "given" him a mocha-skinned slave girl wrapped in nothing but bedsheets.

That was a normal part of life for southern gentlemen.

Hell, he'd practically blown a nut reading the journals as he worked on the book with the ghostwriter. The pleasures of colored wenches were one indulgence he'd resisted, fearing some blasted headline: CONSERVATIVE SENATOR HAS WILD AFFAIR WITH BLACK TEMPTRESS.

That would send Millie to her grave. Even though she hadn't had any stirrings since she went through the change. But that didn't mean she'd approve. And no doubt, he sensed Karen would be discreet. Not even the sneakiest reporter would know.

Dark Secret

Monty dashed into the bedroom to answer the phone.

"Pop."

"Son, did the storm delay your flight?"

"No, I made it fine. Let's meet for a drink."

"You're here?" Monty tightened the towel around his waist.

"No, in the car."

Monty knitted his brow, then smiled.

"Come on back, son. I want to share an old family tradition."

"What, Pop?"

"A surprise. What time can I expect you?"

"With traffic, probably eight-thirty, nine o'clock."

"Make it nine. And son, keep it under wraps."

100

Karen lifted a picture frame from the black grand piano, taking a closer look at Sharlene and Jeff. In her gown, his tuxedo, they were smiling in a flower-covered carriage. "Beautiful photo," Karen said, replacing it amongst dozens of family images. "How do you like having the newlyweds home?"

She turned to face Stone, catching his gaze on her calves. This rendezvous seemed the perfect opportunity to flirt, gather a little evidence, string him along with maybe a kiss or two—until she could pull the pin on the grenade to quake Sharlene's world. Karen smiled at him, behind the cherry bar, clinking glass and ice, running water, knocking around. Stone stilled for a moment, lips parted, eyes calling her close. She had to admit: he was very handsome, and exuded as mesmerizing a brand of magnetism as Franklin and Jordan.

"Hell, half the time Jeff's here. If he keeps it up, don't know how the devil they'll fill the house with babies like Millie wants."

"She's charming," Karen said over Rachmaninoff playing softly on the stereo in the wall of shelves stocked with leather-bound classics like *Moby Dick* and *Grapes of Wrath*. "She had all kinds of helpful information for the documentary when we got together earlier this week."

"Couldn't have asked for a more supportive wife," Stone said. In a hunter-green turtleneck sweater and dark blue wool slacks, he came around the bar, holding out a glass of white zinfandel. "Get cozy." He waved a tumbler of bourbon toward the brown leather club chairs and couch.

She could feel his eyes as she bent to look at pictures of Mount Vernon and Monticello in a glossy coffee table book, next to her new brown purse and a thick folder she'd started filling with book party documents.

"Senator Stone—"

"Ah-ah! Make it Monty or nothing at all."

"Monty," she said, "about the video. How much should we focus on the past, how much on the present?"

He patted the couch. "Karen, sit. You need to relax. Especially after losing your mother."

She held his gaze. *Yes, because your daughter-in-law loves you more than her own flesh and blood.*

"The reality is, work actually helps me cope."

"If there's anything I can do—"

Oh, there is, but you'll find out later. Karen slid next to him. "Dinner with Kyles was better than expected. Change is just around the corner."

Stone grimaced. "Lies. It's all lies. Why the devil does it matter if my best friend helps my campaign? And who the hell cares if my legislation to deregulate the poultry industry lines his pockets?"

Karen shook her head. "Even the appearance of impropriety—"

"Oh, hell, they've been doing this since time immemorial. You scratch my back, I'll scratch yours. Let's just come out in the open with it." He gulped bourbon. "Now they want to make a case of Jeff's honeymoon on Frisian's island. Blasted—" He set his glass next to her purse. "Enough about that."

He turned to her. "Sugar, having you around, I feel young again."

Karen smiled. "I'm flattered you hired me."

Something in the air jolted her.

"Sweet temptress." Stone dove into her neck.

"Stop!" She pushed him off as cold wine seeped into her lap. "We have to go over plans for your book party. Please?"

"Oh, hell."

"The seating arrangement?"

"Family and friends at the front," Stone said, sipping bourbon.

Karen scribbled into the binder. "How about big cardboard pictures of you, then autographing books after the documentary?"

"That works."

"And Monty, it would be more personal if I narrate live."

"I trust your creative judgment. Now indulge mine!" He grasped her lapels, ripped open her jacket. "Sweet black temptress." Stone buried his face between her breasts, sloshing his tongue across her skin.

"Monty, stop!"

But he pulled down the cups of her bra and noisily sucked her nipples. Shoving her back on the couch, he humped her leg.

"Monty, stop, please." Her palms pressed into the scratchy wool of his sweater, but he was too strong, too big to budge. He was shoving a hand up her skirt, ripping her stockings. Fingers squirming into her panties and beyond. He pressed his nose into her crotch, inhaling loudly.

"Stop! Please!"

"Sweet brown sugar. Daddy's coming home!" He pulled down his pants and boxers. Her skirt around her waist, he ripped off her panties.

"You're hurting me!"

"Daddy will take care of that." A stiff pink snake slithered up her leg.

He pried her legs apart, dove inside with his tongue.

Karen clawed his head, trying to push him off. But he gripped her legs.

Tears spilled from her eyes.

Without warning, he slid up, drilled into her.

She grunted; it hurt worse than losing her virginity.

"You love it! Brown sugar needs love from big daddy."

She turned to avoid his lips. He smelled raw. His shoulders jerked as his slimy worm . . .

"Stop!"

"I like it when you scream. Just like the black wenches screamed for my granddaddy. Now I've got my own pretty wench."

She pushed up on him, twisted her hips to escape.

"Work it, sugar."

Karen pounded his chest, twisting more. "Let me go!"

"Oh, Daddy's coming now. Coming home to his sweet nigger wench! Oooohhhh! Owwhhh! Aaaahhhh!"

His damp body spasmed. He collapsed. "Sweet temptress." Karen slid to the floor, where his belt buckle poked her hip.

She sat there, stinging, trembling, while he curled up like a baby after a warm bottle of milk: eyes closed, corners of his mouth turned up, his cheek melding with the leather couch.

Karen gasped. *Did this really happen?* Yes. And if Mama were looking down, she would be hurt and disappointed. How could she have gotten herself into this wicked web of deceit and danger? A case of temporary insanity. Yeah, caused by fear of losing Mama, frustration that Sharlene wouldn't save her, and the shock of her death.

But it's all wrong. I have to end it now. Before something worse happens.

Karen grabbed her purse and binder, then dashed on trembling legs up the staircase. For a second she thought of Jordan, what he would do . . . he would destroy Stone with his own hands, then lambaste him on live TV!

Running into his bedroom, she dropped her things on the dresser. Then, in a scalding shower, she scrubbed every inch from her tearing eyes to her trembling toes.

Mama, please forgive me.

101

Jeff let himself into the apartment at nine-fifteen, finding Pop behind the bar, smoking a cigar and pouring a drink. "Just in time," his father said.

Jeff tossed back a glass of Jack Daniel's. "What's the big surprise?"

His father stepped closer, examining his cheek. "Son, what—"

Jeff shielded the sting with a hand. "It's nothing."

"I'd make it clear, that kind of thing is not acceptable. Now go get a taste of what you might call a secret family tradition." His father glanced toward the staircase.

Jeff dashed up to Pop's bedroom, clinking ice in his glass, wondering if that was a hooker behind the bathroom door.

"Monty?" a woman called.

"No, it's Jeff."

The door opened. A woman in a white towel, with long wet dark hair, stepped out. Jeff gripped his drink. *She's trying to fuck her way to the top. Using Pop just like Camille used me. To take advantage of the power and privilege that's ours by birth. Not theirs.*

"What are you doing here?" she accused.

"I was invited."

Karen whispered, "Bastard."

"What?"

Dark Secret

"He's plastered." She walked toward the door. "He's had way too much to drink tonight."

Jeff grabbed her wrist, pulling her close.

"Let go!"

He shoved her toward the bed.

She rose, smacking his scratches. "You have no right—"

Jeff gripped her arm. "Maybe Pop'll play your game, but not me."

"Monty, help!"

"Shut the fuck up!" Jeff snatched off the towel. Brown nipples pointed right at him. "You're all whores! Fucking to get what you want."

As Jeff unbuttoned his jeans, Karen had that same scared-cat look as Camille. He shoved her head down. "Suck my dick!"

She did not move.

"Stop crying and shaking like a goddamn leaf!"

She tried to crawl over the bed, but he caught her ankle, dragged her back, facedown. Then he slammed inside the two perfect mounds of her ass.

"No! No!"

"Pretend to be all professional," he thrust, "trying to help my dad. But all you want is our money." Jeff pulled Karen's hair like the reins of a horse. Sweat soaked his clothes. "Sharlene, Camille, Karen! Black sluts!"

Karen looked back with wild eyes.

"Probably use this pussy to get whatever you want. Even with Pop."

"Stop! Please!"

He thrust even harder. "Sassy bitch!"

In an instant, all the rage he felt toward Camille, and now Karen, exploded in a blinding red flash. One final thrust, and he pulled out. She scooted onto the pillows, sobbing, as he pulled up his pants. All the while, Jeff savored the aftertaste of something his forefathers could enjoy anytime at White Pines: a family tradition he could easily get used to. But times were different now.

He glared at her. "One word about this and I'll beat the shit out of you, too."

102

Millie Stone tried again to focus on the *Newsweek* article about the ethics investigation. Curled up on her wicker chair in the solarium under the black sky, she couldn't shake the look in her oldest son's eyes as he'd led Camille from the nursery a short while ago. She set the magazine on the table, then hurried into the kitchen. Ida Mae was standing at the island, dropping a lemon wedge into Grandma Stone's steaming cup alongside a plate of gingersnaps. "Ida Mae. Have Jeff or Camille come down for supper?"

"No, ma'am."

"Gracious, come with me."

Upstairs, Millie's pulse quickened when she saw a slice of darkness through the slightly open bedroom door. Inside, moonlight poured past open drapes, onto the empty bed . . . a long silvery heap on the floor.

"Gracious, the baby."

Ida Mae flipped the wall light switch as Millie hurried toward Camille. This was another reason she'd opposed the marriage; someone like Tabitha would have known the importance of keeping family secrets. But an outsider might tell, and Monty didn't need yet another smudge on his reputation.

"Camille." She sounded hoarse with her throat burning so. Turning Camille from her side to her back, Millie gasped. One eye looked like a pink and purple golf ball.

Ida Mae plucked an inhaler from the floor. "I knew that asthma was nothin' to mess with. She dead?"

Millie knelt over her, checking for a pulse on her neck, putting an ear to her bleeding and blue lips.

"Barely breathing. Here, help me." They lifted Camille by the arms and legs onto the bed, faceup. With her blood-caked hairline and swelling arm, Camille was in far worse shape than she herself had been after even the most brutal nights with Monty. Perhaps this might teach Camille not to meddle in affairs where she didn't belong. Specifically Arianna. But for now, Millie had to make sure the baby was all right. The thought of a new life to nurture sparked a warm glow within the coldness that had taken root since the kids left home. She needed a little bundle to love, to occupy her mind and body around the clock. Millie let tears burn down her cheeks as she pulled Camille's hair from her face.

"Call Dr. Zane?" Ida Mae wiped her palms on her apron. "I know she got some broken bones."

"Not yet." No, even though it was Dr. Zane who had delivered Arianna. Then, as now, Millie imagined the talk, the headlines, the news shows, if Camille were sent to a hospital. And how furious Monty would be over the negative press. No, this was one family problem that Millie never, ever wanted unveiled. Her own shame—that she had put up with it for thirty-some years, or that she had raised at least one son who was carrying on his father's violent legacy—well, if anyone knew, it would kill her.

I can handle this on my own.

"Ida Mae, get me her purse." Millie pointed to the dresser. Finding another inhaler inside the bag, she sprayed some into her own mouth, parted Camille's bloody lips, and blew the medication inside. "Breathe, child!"

She did it again and again, not knowing whether the drug was even reaching Camille's lungs. Or how long she'd been unconscious. Or whether the baby was still alive.

"Breathe!"

But Camille just lay there, pale as chalk.

103

Karen was still trembling as she stopped her car at the gate outside White Pines. For the past two and a half hours, as she drove here from Stone's apartment, she'd been asking Mama to forgive her and help her get back on track to live a righteous life.

"Miss Bradley," the guard said. "We weren't expecting you."

Karen tapped her bag on the seat. "I have some things for Mrs. Stone."

The guard opened the gate.

Karen sped toward the mansion, eerily aglow in the moonlight. She cared about nothing but making sure her sister was safe. And alive. *I can't change what she did. But she's my sister and I love her. If I'm not too late . . .*

She remembered Jeff saying "Sharlene" and "Camille" and "black sluts" all in one breath. And those scratches on his face—had they fought? And the way he'd said, "beat the shit out of you, too."

He knows the truth about Sharlene.

She parked behind a car near the front door. Then, with a trembling hand, Karen knocked. But what would she say? "Hi, is my sister home?" No, revealing their double deception might endanger them further.

Ida Mae opened the door, raking her gaze over Karen from hair to boots. "Senator Stone at a reception tonight. Won't be back 'til morning. Girl, you a mess."

"I just saw him," Karen said, "and with the tight deadline for the documentary, he said I could browse the pictures and journals in the library."

"I better check with Miss Millie."

Karen stepped inside. "Please don't trouble her. I know where everything is. Even brought my laptop to write the script." She patted her bag.

Finally, Ida Mae led Karen into the library, where Karen sat at the desk, flipping through boxes of pictures. But as soon as Ida Mae left, Karen crept up the staircase. She had no idea where Camille's bedroom was as she headed through an open door leading to a long hallway. If she found her sister, she would take her away. Tonight.

At the far end of the hall, Mrs. Stone and a man appeared, then closed a door. And they were coming this way . . .

"Millie, now that she's breathing better," the man said, "check on her every hour. If the spotting gets worse, call me and we'll go to the hospital."

"Gracious, no." Mrs. Stone's voice was getting louder and closer.

Karen slipped through the nearest door, waiting a good twenty minutes after the voices had passed. Then she dashed to the room Mrs. Stone and the man had just left. Inside and to the right, beyond a draped archway to a sitting room, was the silvery glow of a television. There sat Sharlene in a wine velvet chair, her back to the door.

"Sharlene?" Karen whispered, creeping close. She hoped Jeff and Monty were still in Washington.

"Sarah Jane." The voice came from the television. It was a brown-skinned woman, the mother in the movie *Imitation of Life*. And Sharlene was speaking softly into the telephone. Without turning around, she hung up and said, "They should've named this *The Sharlene Bradley Story*. Sarah Jane gets beaten up by her boyfriend. And by the time she realizes how stupid she is, her mother's already dead."

Stepping closer, around the chair, Karen said, "Sharlene, I—" She gasped. "What did he do!" God only knew what was beneath the thick white bathrobe. And the bag of ice on her left arm.

"I got what I deserved," Sharlene said in a slow monotone, staring at the screen. "I'm sorry. To you and Mother. Our father, too."

Karen knelt, looking into Sharlene's open eye. "The baby?"

Sharlene shrugged. "I'm spotting."

Karen took her sister's bruised hand. "We're going to the hospital now."

Sharlene shook her head. "No, I'm going to hell. Because I wouldn't help Mother. This pain is nothing compared to—"

"Sharlene, get real. You need a doctor."

She lay back on the chair, her hair twisted into a ball atop her head. "Karen, tell me why you're with Senator Stone."

Karen shook her head. "I'm going back to Detroit tomorrow. And if you have any sense you'll come with me."

Sharlene's swollen mouth curled down into a sob. "Why do you care? Why don't you hate me?"

Karen carefully wrapped her arms around her trembling sister. "We're blood, Sharlene. And if Mama can forgive you, so can I. We have to stick together."

"I am so sorry," Sharlene cried.

Part of Karen wanted to scream back that Sharlene's sorrow was a day late and a dollar short. That Mama was already dead, that Karen's revenge plan had backfired, leaving them both battered and hurt. But Mama would want her to show forgiveness, too. So she hugged her sister, taking comfort in the fact that Sharlene was finally realizing what she'd done. What they'd both done. And that perhaps they could spend the rest of their lives making up for it. She took Sharlene's arm again, pulling her up.

"Let's go home," Karen said.

104

Karen had to get her sister out of here, but Sharlene wouldn't budge. "If I leave, Jeff'll have me hunted down and killed."

"Get real, Sharlene. You stay here, and next time he *will* kill you! I saw that demonic look in his eyes," Karen's voice cracked, "when he was raping—"

Sharlene cringed. "What?"

Karen made fists to still her trembling fingers. "Jeff and his father—"

"No!"

"Yes, tonight. That's how I knew something happened to you. But I'm taking it as a sign. I should've just left you and them alone."

Sharlene's eye widened. "What were you planning to—"

"First I wanted to pressure you into helping Mama. But when she died, I wanted revenge. So I decided to destroy—" Karen sobbed, explaining Plan D.

"Do it," Sharlene said.

"No, tonight showed me how dangerous this whole charade is," Karen said. "And look at you. That's what happens when they—"

Sharlene squeezed Karen's hand. "I'll help you."

Karen shook her head. "No, it's—"

"Karen, I said let's do it together."

"Only if you let me take you to the hospital. And we have to keep it a secret that we're sisters. What about Ginger?"

Sharlene drew her brows together. "What about you going back to work for Senator Stone?"

"I bet he'll breeze into the office Monday acting like I enjoyed what happened. But can you stand even one more day here?"

"Jeff won't do anything worse than this. With the book party coming up, he wouldn't dare. He wants his father to be president so bad it makes his dick hard. Believe me." Sharlene wiped her bloody nose.

"Sharlene, we have to go to the hospital."

"No, Mrs. Stone will take care of me," Sharlene said flatly. "And I have to stay long enough to take care of a little girl here."

"You can have the baby in Detroit."

"No," Sharlene said, "there's a little girl, like us, here."

"What do you mean? Mixed?"

"They keep her locked up. She's never been off the grounds."

Karen squinted, leaning closer. "What did you say?"

"She looks like you," Sharlene said. "Dixie's the mother. The father is black. Ida Mae's son, but I've never seen him around."

Karen pulled out her phone. "I'm calling Social Services and the police."

Sharlene grabbed her hand. "No! I've thought about it. But I don't want Arianna placed with strangers. She'd be terrified."

"That's barbaric! Where is she? I'll take her now."

Sharlene shook her head. "No, she doesn't know her life isn't normal."

"We have to do something!"

Sharlene grimaced, clutched her abdomen.

"What is it?" Karen asked.

"Cramps. Ow, it hurts."

"You need a doctor, now," Karen said, lifting her sister out of the chair.

But the bedroom door opened.

A deep voice called, "Camille?"

Karen's heart leaped to her throat. It was Jeff.

If he sees us together, and figures out we're sisters, he'll kill us both.

105

Camille stared at the television as Jeff approached, reeking of whiskey. She wished he would leave, so Karen could come out from behind the curtains and take her to the hospital.

"I thought sure you'd be dead by now, Lucy." He chuckled.

Camille glared up at him. "Monster," she whispered. Her rage was like lidocaine, numbing the throbs all over her body.

"Honey, I'm sorry I hurt you," he said with wet lips and glazed eyes. "But you hurt me. You hurt me worse than I've ever been hurt. I would have died for you. I loved you that much." He crawled toward her, groaning into her lap.

She coughed on the alcohol and cigar odors.

"Lady Godiva, why? I gave you everything. My family, your job, love. I gave you love. Goddamn real love. And you turned around, stole my money, gave it to that lowlife, and you—"

Sharlene felt nothing. *He raped my sister. Tried to kill me and our baby.*

"I gave you all that and then I find out that . . . you're a nigger whore."

His words slapped Sharlene's bruised face.

Jeff cried those two vile words over and over. "Ask me how much I love you, honey. I love you less than horseshit on my riding boots."

She stood, ignoring the red-hot throb in her hip.

Jeff tumbled to the floor.

"My blood is red, just like yours." Her tone was hard, shooting down at him. "But you think I'm not good enough because of some part of me that you can't even see. If you loved me before you knew I'm black, that proves it shouldn't matter."

He rose, towering over her. "But you tricked me!"

Camille wanted to scream that his mother was deceiving him, too, by hiding her beloved granddaughter . . . and the fact that his sister had gotten pregnant by a black man. But no, she didn't want him to hurt Arianna, too.

She held his watery blue stare, her body humming with hatred. For him, for herself, for a life that had guided her down this despicable path. But what could she do now to rectify the situation? Help Karen.

If Jeff didn't kill her first.

"I need some air," he said, striding toward the curtained doors.

106

"Baby Boy!" Ida Mae burst into the room. "Your mother is looking for you. And she in a real tizzy." Like a tugboat behind a barge,
she pushed Jeff from the room. Camille locked the door, then limped
toward the curtain where Karen was hiding.

"Is there a way down from the balcony out there?" Karen asked.

"No, but follow me." Camille cracked the bedroom door, listening. Nothing. Grimacing, she led Karen down to the third bedroom
suite on the left. Then into a closet, through a waist-high door, to a
dark shaft with a ladder.

"You go down," Camille said. "At the bottom, there's no light,
so you have to feel around for a latch. It'll open a door inside the
bookcase in the library. I'll meet you there."

Jeff was calling her from the hall.

"Go!" Karen descended the ladder.

Camille closed her eyes. She had to move, despite the arrows of
pain shooting up from her hip and abdomen. Even though she'd re-
gained consciousness as Dr. Zane peered down at her, saying the baby
was all right, Camille didn't trust him. She had to get to the hospital
to make sure. And despite the horrible turn her existence was taking,
she was not going to let it cost the life inside her.

"Lucy!" Jeff was banging on doors. And it sounded as if he was
stumbling. Camille decided to wait until he passed, so she could some-

how hurry down and meet Karen in the library. Finally, in the silence, Camille limped into the hall. Covered with goose bumps, she was getting closer to the front stairwell. She hoped Jeff had gone to the their room and passed out.

A hand shot from the darkness. Squeezed her throbbing arm.

"Where the hell are you going, Lucy?"

Jeff's eyes glowed with malice.

"I . . . I'm going down for some milk."

"No, I'm not through with you yet."

A shriek, then a thud, made Camille jump. It was Jeff's parents.

"Jeff, go check on your mom."

"No, Pop was so miffed over this." He pointed to his scratched cheek. "He came back with me tonight. What he and Mom do is not my business. You are." He pulled her toward their bedroom.

Karen is going to spend all night in that dark ladder shaft . . .

107

The adrenaline and rage pumping through Rand as he bolted into the mansion was as potent as it had been the second he had heard Camille sob into the phone last night. His arms, legs, and chest literally burned with the need to protect her, then beat the bully who was his older brother into next year.

The faint medicinal scent, and the too-silent stillness in the house, scraped up so many morning-after memories . . . Mom limping into the kitchen, wearing gloves or sunglasses or long sleeves to hide purple splotches. Rand sprinted to the Victoria Suite, not caring if Jeff was inside. The curtains drawn over the winter gloom cast enough light to outline Camille's form in the plum-colored sheets and satiny bedspread.

At her bedside, Rand fell to his knees, breathing fast and hard.

"Camille," he whispered. His fingers hovered over her head; he wanted to stroke her, but feared touching the scarlet-purple swirls.

Her long lashes fluttered.

The hot pangs rippling through him punctuated something he was ready to admit: *I love her.* And he'd only been with Ginger because it gave him more chances to be near Camille. With feathery softness, his fingertips found a place on her cheek to touch. "It's me, Rand."

She moaned softly; the corners of her mouth raised slightly.

"Have you seen a doctor?"

Camille nodded. "Last night."

"Dr. Zane or the hospital?"

"Both."

"The baby?"

"Fine."

"Come to New York with me."

She opened the eye that was not swollen and purple. "I can't."

"I know what my brother is capable of."

She shook her head slightly. "Your mother won't let him—"

"Did she stop this?" He kissed a tear rolling into her hair. "Camille, I promise you, I will never let him hurt you again."

She squeezed his hand. "I need help." Slowly, she explained the truth about herself, her sister, their plan. It confirmed the source of that alluring air of mystery about her. But it did not matter what her real name was, who her parents were, what race or profession they might be. And sure, she was wrapped in a beautiful package, but so were a lot of women. It was her essence that enamored him: the invisible aura around this woman that rippled around him like a satin ribbon, stroked his soul, made him want to purr. It was also the tenderness he saw in her eyes when she read to the children at Hugs and Hope in Harlem. *I'll give her unconditional love. The kind she's always wanted.*

"There's something else," Camille said softly. "You have a niece. But your mother keeps her locked up here." She explained the Arianna saga.

Rand bunched his fists so violently it hurt. "Damn this family!" He started to rise, but Camille grasped his hand.

"Rand, will you call Dixie, tell her what happened to me? We can't let your mother know. We have to wait. Then we—I mean, I'd like to take her."

The idea of letting a little girl stay a minute longer in some locked-away room here made Rand want to storm the place. At Hugs and Hope he'd seen so many cases of abuse, of children living in savage conditions. How could something like that happen here in the so-called lap of luxury? As easily as the brutality that had sliced open his forehead as a boy.

He leaned over her, nuzzling her hair, wanting to wrap his bulk around her as a human shield until she could get out of this place.

"I'll help you," he whispered. "But if it backfires, I've got a plan of my own. And maybe we can work out something together."

"Rand," Camille sighed, her eyes closed. Her mottled hand gripped his. "Thank you."

"You got me now," Rand said softly. "All the way."

Minutes later, he shot into the library. Pop was behind the desk, his glasses on, reading something to Jeff, who was in a chair facing him.

Rand grasped two handfuls of Jeff's blue sweater, yanked him up, shoved him toward the fireplace. Jeff's head slammed into the shiny wood floor. In a red blur, Rand pummeled his brother's chest and stomach.

"Randolph!" He barely felt his father's hands on his shoulders, or Jeff's attempts to punch back.

"I told you!" Rand shouted. " 'Like father, like son' will get you killed!"

108

Monday morning, Karen settled at her desk, first opening an
e-mail from Davis: "Remember my offer to help. Anytime. Anything.
We'll settle your debt later." But right now, the way she and Camille
had mapped out a plan, there was no space for Davis. And how could
she trust a thug like him?

All she wanted was to get through today and the next couple of
months, keeping herself and Sharlene safe, never giving Stone a clue
about his impending demise. Then, perhaps, she could lead the police
to Davis and Bright, and succumb to the quivers whenever she thought
of Jordan Kyles.

Karen composed an electronic message to him, asking when they
could resume the "heated discussion" they'd begun last week. He'd
been in Chicago for ceremonies opening new housing for the poor,
so she hadn't spoken with him since their torrid tryst. As she typed,
the phone rang.

"Karen, I didn't sleep a wink last night," her father said, "worried
to death about you and your sister and this kamikaze mission."

She stiffened. This was his fourth call since Saturday, when she'd
asked him to help execute their plan. "Daddy—"

"Let me talk to the senator right now," he said. "If stopping you
means telling him what you're doing, then that's what I'll do."

"That would hurt us both," she said. "Please just help us, Daddy."

Dark Secret

Her father's tone was softer when he said, "Your ma wouldn't like this. Now I'm late for a meeting with my lawyer about the house. I'll call back."

Almost immediately, the receptionist buzzed: "Ms. Bradley, Freida Miller is here to see you."

Karen rolled her eyes. What could Freida want that she couldn't have asked over muffins and coffee this morning? Karen hurried out to the reception area, glad Stone hadn't yet arrived back from that Republican breakfast banquet.

"Girl, I have a question," Freida said, her tone as somber as her high-necked black dress and military-style boots. "About a story for tomorrow."

Karen led her to the long, polished wood table under a chandelier in the conference room.

"Let me apologize now, girl, as your friend," Freida said. "But I found out Camille Morgan Stone is your sister."

"Get real, Freida. That's crazy."

Her braids shook, but her sharp gaze did not waver. "I have proof. And we're running with it."

Karen rolled her eyes. "There's no proof; that's absolutely untrue."

Freida tapped a blue pen on a small notebook. "I tracked down Ginger Roman in New York. And I just got off the phone with your father. He told me everything. You've been lying to me—"

"I don't know what man is claiming to be my father," Karen said, "because my father is in Canada right now for his job."

"Mack Campbell," Freida said. "In Detroit. On Chandler Park Drive."

"My father's name is Anderson," Karen said. "Harold Anderson."

"Well, I met Mack at your mother's house," Freida said.

"Mack is my crazy uncle. Ask him if the moon is green, he'll say yes."

"He seemed pretty coherent to me," Freida said.

"I said he's not my father, and you can quote me," Karen shot back, "in court, when I—and Senator Stone—sue you for printing malicious lies!"

Freida chuckled. "Girl, you sound just like that old bastard."

Alarm prickled Karen's skin. She held Freida's stare, reeling with self-digust. But she had to stand her ground: a newspaper article about Sharlene's deception of the Stone family could send Jeff into a rage, perhaps prod him to finish what he'd attempted Friday night. "Freida, I have a huge scoop, if you can be patient."

"What?"

"Just trust me," Karen said, standing. "It'll blow everyone out of the water. But I'll take it elsewhere if you run with these lies."

Freida followed her to the door. "I told you my editor latched onto this story like a pit bull. And he won't let go until it bleeds all over the paper tomorrow morning. So whatever scoop you have, I still need a reaction from you, and Stone, before five o'clock."

Karen hated her friend's defiant tone. "I'll have a reaction for you, all right. But you won't like it."

She led Freida to the door, then hurried back to her desk. No way was she going to let her friend obstruct Plan D. So she e-mailed her new buddy Davis again, asking if he knew any janitors over at the *Washington News*.

109

As a maid led her into the solarium at White Pines, Ginger raised shaking fingers to her open mouth. The trees and leafy plants became a swirl of green; she grasped the doorway, unable to walk toward Camille, sitting in a floral-print wicker chair with her feet propped on an ottoman. Sunshine streaming through the glass illuminated her bruised face, a cast on her arm, a swollen belly under an ankle-length gray cashmere dress.

I did this to her. My jealousy, my selfishness. How can I make up for that?

"Camille, honey," she whispered, grasping her heavy shoulder bag.

Camille looked up from the latest copy of *Vogue* with no expression.

Ginger rushed to her side. "I'm so sorry, I—"

"Leave." Camille's tone was as pitiless as her one-eyed gaze.

"You wouldn't return my calls, so I just—"

"Leave now."

"Let me apologize," Ginger said softly, shame stinging her cheeks, making her sweat under her wool coat. "I was afraid. And jealous."

Ginger perched on the ottoman, bending to look up into Camille's face. But her friend pushed with her right arm, grimacing, rising from the chair.

"You stupid, selfish bitch," Camille said through tight, swollen lips.

"Please, Camille. I'm so lonely."

"You've got Rand."

"No, not anymore. The only thing I have now is the store. But—"

Camille raised her cast. "Ginger, I don't care. About you. Or your store. I can't believe, after all we went through, you and Nick—"

"No!" Another swirling sensation made Ginger clutch the ottoman's piping. Then she pulled the bag off her shoulder, extended it. "I wasn't in on it. I mean, he just showed up with the money. And"— her silver thumb ring on her other hand felt slippery as she turned it in the sunshine—"I kept it."

Camille slumped back in the chair, exhaling. "You're pathetic."

Ginger grasped her hand. "Camille, I'll do anything to show I'm . . . I mean, worthy of being your friend again." She placed the bag on the ottoman.

Camille fingered the wavy end of her long braid. "It's beyond repair."

Ginger covered her face with her hands. She was worthless as a person, even though on page 224 of the *Vogue* on Camille's lap was an article about her newly booming business, thanks to her men's line. Camille's idea. And the past few weeks, since the show, had drawn a head-spinning succession of customers and party invitations. But she had never felt so empty.

"Camille, please believe me. I'll spend my life making it up to you."

Camille picked up the magazine, flipping through.

"Starting with this reporter who keeps calling me," Ginger said.

Camille looked up. "About what?"

"You. But I'm about to send her flying into media hell."

110

Freida glanced at the clock, thinking about the "huge scoop" Karen had promised. How much bigger could it be than this? She clicked open the computer file holding notes from her conversation with Mack Campbell this morning, confirming Karen and Camille were sisters.

More than two months, living with me, telling me this isn't a story! But why would Karen want to cover it up? And as for waiting a few weeks, Karen could forget that. It had taken long enough to substantiate this story. Freida was running with it, today. Whether Karen called back or not.

The phone rang: the lobby security guard. "Ms. Miller, Reba Vargo from Cleveland is here to see you." But Freida was not expecting any visitors. Even one from Cleveland, where Camille Morgan Stone claimed to be from.

Freida hurried downstairs. The guard pointed out a thin woman, late twenties, with straight auburn hair skimming the padded shoulders of a lime-green wool overcoat. Black eyeglasses sat on her tiny, freckled nose.

"Can I help you? I'm Freida Miller."

"Oh jiminy, it's you," the woman said, talking fast and holding Freida's hand. "I'm so glad I found you. That sweet girl who answers the phone said you're the one to talk to about Sharlene Bradley."

Freida focused on the woman's green eyes. "What about her?"

"Let's sit down." Reba pushed her glasses up, flashing a silver thumb ring. Her thin legs moved so fast under her coat, she looked like a green beetle scurrying toward the lobby's sitting area.

"Now, jiminy, I can't believe I'm here," the woman said at lightning speed. "But I seen a report in a tabloid, then I heard some rumors, and I said I need to just go down there myself and set the record straight. My convention is in Washington, so I—"

"Convention for what?"

"Birdhouses," Reba said. "I own a flower shop. We sell birdhouses."

Freida held back her first impulse to think this woman was a quack.

"Well, jiminy, where do I start? All these rumors that Sharlene is black. It's a crock!" Reba's parakeetish laugher almost made Freida jump. "When I saw the *People's Inquirer,* I nearly fell off the chair behind my cash register. Jiminy, I haven't talked to Sharlene in years, but I know for a fact she's as white as I am." She pulled back her coat sleeve to flash a milky arm. "And that article, it said she had kin from Detroit. If she did, jiminy, she never mentioned it to me, and we were best friends. Here." The woman reached in a lime-green purse with a silver handle, pulling out pictures.

"That there's me and Sharlene at the prom," the woman said as Freida examined a photo of what looked like Camille, Reba, and two white guys. "There, that's us at an Indians game. We were about ten. Oh, and here's us with her parents, before the crash. Poor girl never recovered."

Freida studied the picture of a little girl with honey-colored hair on the lap of a white man in the cockpit of a small airplane. Waving from the passenger seat was a white woman with brown hair. The dates printed in the corners corresponded with Camille Morgan's identity.

"Jiminy, the things people will say!" Reba said. "The Sharlene I knew loved Led Zeppelin and riding horses on our farm. I mean, does this girl look black to you? Gadzooks, no! I wish those media people"—Reba rested a hand on Freida's arm—"not you, but those other media people, I wish they would just leave her alone. We're not in touch anymore, but Sharlene deserves happiness as much as you and I do. It's jealousy—"

Freida probed Reba's face, finding no nervous twitches or shifty eyes.

If Reba is for real, then what about my sources from the Riverfront Academy of the Arts in Detroit? Who were they talking about? And who's telling the truth?

After thanking Reba, and taking her phone numbers to check her out, Freida hurried back upstairs. She was glad to see the janitor leaving her desk, dumping the trash can into a larger bin that he wheeled away.

Sitting down, she punched in her phone code to check her voice mail: no messages from Karen or anyone else. So she decided to review her story and her notes, to see if Reba's information synced with anyone else's. But her computer screen was flashing: SYSTEM ERROR. And the tiny box at the upper right that used to flash 389 FILES now said 0 FILES.

Freida went numb. All her hard work was gone.

111

Karen was hoping to hurry down to the video editing studio in the basement of the Senate building before Stone and Jeff returned to the office. But one step into the hallway, and there they were, laughing with Rollins about some Democratic representative caught picking up a prostitute.

"Sugar, where are you off to in such a blasted hurry?" Stone smiled, patting her back, making her cringe.

She pointed to her burgundy shoulder bag. "The videographer and I are matching pictures to the script for the documentary."

Rollins cleared his throat but did not look at her when he said, "We've been thinking. It'd be better to have this professionally done."

Karen cast a pleading look at Stone. "Monty, you said I could do it."

He nodded. "Until Rollins convinced me otherwise."

"You couldn't possibly do as glossy a job as someone who does this all the time," Jeff said, reaching for her bag. "So let's have all the pictures and documents you got at White Pines, so we can hand them over to the new guy."

A bruise ringed his left eye; and those scratches on his cheek must have come from Camille.

"You already hired someone?" Karen asked, gripping the bag.

"Rollins got a referral from Senator McDonald," Stone said.

Karen glared at Rollins, who started the glasses-polishing routine without looking up. Bastard.

"But one thing I would like." Stone leaned close to whisper: "After the book party, we'll celebrate again. Plan to spend the night at White Pines."

Karen's stomach cramped. *In the slave cabin. No, thank you . . .*

She smiled. "What about my idea to narrate?"

Jeff shook his head. "If your timing is the least bit off—"

"It wouldn't be." Karen stared into Jeff's eyes, wondering how he felt. Karen remembered her sister grimacing as the ER doctor bandaged her broken arm, stitched up the torn skin by her eye. Thank goodness the baby was all right, but that little girl . . . Karen stiffened.

Repulsion slithered through her; she felt ice cold. Here was a man acting as if nothing had happened, yet he had raped her! Both of them had raped her! The violence of their actions contrasted in her head to a brief memory of Jordan's gentleness. But the sting between her legs made her wonder if she could ever share that again with a man, Jordan or anyone else. They had stolen a part of her, squashed it under their selfish, blind brutality. For that, they would pay.

And neither Rollins nor Jeff would interfere as she sketched a new battle plan.

"Just let me know who this new video person is, and I'll hand over all the materials," she said, hurrying away. She took the elevator down to the basement, where she hopped on the "subway," a red-leather-seated tram that whisked her through a tunnel to the Senate building. Alone except for the conductor several seats away, she dialed her father at the marina in Detroit.

"Daddy! Did you call a reporter this morning?"

"Christ!" Mack said over machine shop noises. "She left her business card in the mailbox. Wouldn't talk to her then, but maybe she'll help me stop this cockamamie plan of yours."

"Don't you realize," Karen whispered, "you could put us in danger?"

"I just don't like the sound of what you're doing."

"Daddy, you owe us both," Karen said. "This is the least you can do."

Silence.

"Daddy?"

"Yeah," he said, his voice cracking. "I have to think on this one."

A few minutes later, Karen headed into an editing booth with video whiz Mike Bergen. He pushed buttons, retrieved snippets of videotape, cut and spliced, until he had achieved the desired sequence of pictures for the documentary.

"I'll probably work some late nights because my days are so hectic," she said.

"Just call me," Mike said over the electronic gibberish of rewinding tape.

"I was hoping you might let me have a key," she said.

"We don't usually do that," Mike said.

Karen leaned over the keyboard. Pushing buttons and turning knobs, she retrieved thirty seconds of video, spliced it, and played it back.

Mike chuckled. "Well, I guess you know what you're doing in here," he said, watching the perfect segue of Stone walking down a long corridor, then standing at the podium.

"I used to edit PSAs all the time back in Detroit," she said.

"Obviously," Mike said, pulling a key off his keychain. "Here. But keep it quiet. My boss would kill me."

So would mine, if he knew what I'm about to do.

112

Camille answered the knock at the bedroom door, relieved that Dr. Zane had finally arrived to remove her cast. Then she could visit Arianna, whom she had only seen at night, as the child slept, fearing the cast and bruises might frighten her. And Dixie had called this morning; besides being hysterical over what Jeff had done, she was finally ready to start visiting Arianna with the hope that familiarity would breed love and affection. But she wasn't supposed to arrive this early.

Camille swung open the door. She gasped. It wasn't Dr. Zane hurrying into the room; it was Rand, the nylon sleeves of his red down jacket swishing as he strode in. "Did anyone see you?" She quickly closed the door.

"I had to check on you," he said, peeling off his jacket to reveal a thick brown sweater and corduroys.

Camille let his presence swaddle her as softly as her white sheared mink coat. But he had to get out of here. During one of their frequent, late-night phone conversations, they had agreed he would stay away until D day. Especially since his father had barred him from the house after he beat up Jeff. If he were caught, it would only complicate things. "Rand—"

He pulled her into his broad chest. Camille closed her eyes, pressing her ear over his pounding heart. The safety and serenity she felt there . . . she could stand like this, pressed into Rand, forever. After a few minutes, she looked up into his tender gaze. Rand's lashes lowered; he was staring at her mouth. "Can I kiss you?"

She nodded slightly, parting her lips. His mouth skimmed hers so softly, it was like a tickle. But it still made her insides hum. He kissed her again. More forcefully, and longer, his still-cold nose brushing her cheek. His embrace ferried her to a realm where . . . she laughed.

He pulled back, alarm in his eyes. "What?"

"I'm pregnant and married to your brother."

"I don't care." He stroked her round stomach. "He doesn't appreciate the jewels he's been given."

Camille smiled. "Then kiss me again."

He did, long enough to make her feel light-headed. His lips plying hers set something aflame deep down. She let out a soft moan, tossing her head back as he kissed her throat. It took a moment to realize that, yes, the door was open, and yes, Mrs. Stone and Ida Mae were standing there watching.

"Randolph Stone!"

Rand pulled back, facing them. "What."

"Gracious, where are your—"

He glared at his mother. "Where are yours, Mom? You might think it's okay for Dad to do what he does, but I will not let Jeff do that to Camille. Especially not pregnant." Rand grabbed his jacket, storming past them. "If that means I have to move here to play body-guard, I will."

Camille wanted to disappear. Rand's good intentions could potentially short-circuit Karen's plan. He needed to cool off, realize she would be fine until D-day. Meanwhile, she had to appease Mrs. Stone.

"You got yourself in a bad enough spot," Ida Mae said, wiping her hands on her apron. "Don't need to come between brothers, too."

Camille glared down at Ida Mae, balling her fists to keep from exploding with rage that this woman would go along with such a sick plan to imprison her granddaughter. Camille's lips tightened. Her neck tilted. "As my mother used to say, Ida Mae: God don't like ugly!"

Ida Mae's short brows drew together. "You ought not even go there, girl."

Mrs. Stone stepped between them. "Gracious," she quavered.

"We're going to erase this here scenario from our minds. It never happened." She took Ida Mae's hand, leading her to the door, glancing back. "Camille, you will not commit adultery under this roof."

Camille held back the urge to scream about all the things already being committed here. That would have to wait.

113

Karen hurried into the bustling Senate reception room, handing
a note to a congressional page, asking her to carry it to Senator Stone,
who was on the floor to tout the merits of a bill that would block even
more restrictions on tobacco advertising. It seemed the phones were
ringing off the hook today, with a half-dozen media requests for interviews about his rumored bid for president next year. Now Karen
had to let him know about an invitation to a live news show this
evening.

Through double doors, the page walked onto the floor, then returned. "Senator Stone says yes, he'll do it."

"Thank you," Karen said. She spun back, hurrying down the stairs.
Walking briskly through the cream-painted brick tunnel, she reviewed
a mental checklist of things to do. She barely saw the blurs of navy-
blue suits and ties in various shades of politician red, as senators and
staffers rushed past. But a familiar, darker face above a striking brown
pinstripe suit made her focus: Jordan Kyles, walking right toward her,
a tense set to his jaw.

Karen's stomach cramped. She wished she didn't have to face him
at all. No, her heart was involved now, and if he thought she'd slept
with him to convince him to soften his attack on Stone . . . then she
would have to immerse in a steaming bath for hours to feel clean again.
He nodded at two aides, who hurried on as he stopped.

"Karen." Why did he have to exude so much sexiness with that one downward glance, focusing on her with those smoky eyes? "I thought you'd matured past the dating game."

She crossed her arms. "You were out of town."

"I want to see you again."

"It was a mistake," she said. "Mixing business and—"

"You could at least return my calls. It's been weeks."

All the people walking past became a fluorescent blur; Jordan was her singular focus. The faint spice of his cologne, the broadness of his chest, sent a sizzling bolt of longing through her. But only for a second. In her head, she could still hear her skirt ripping, her screams, as Senator Stone stabbed his thing into her; then Jeff, pulling her hair, making her sting even worse . . .

"Karen? Do you feel all right?" Jordan's glowing complexion came back into focus. Concern radiated from his eyes; he placed a hand on her arm.

"I can't see you anymore," she murmured. At least not for a few weeks.

His gaze hardened. "It's rather crass of you, Karen," he whispered, nodding to a passerby who called his name, "to toss some pussy my way, then move to the next victim when you don't get what you want."

Karen closed her eyes. No! Of all the men in the world, she didn't want the man she was falling in love with to hold that licentious opinion of her. Someday, she could explain what she was doing. Not yet, however. But she could not spend even the next minute with this cheek-burning humiliation.

"First, Jordan, there is no next . . . victim, as you say." She remembered the heartbreaking weeks following their last tryst on Martha's Vineyard on Labor Day weekend three and a half years ago. He'd returned none of her calls or letters; she had felt so empty she wondered if she'd dreamt up all their cheese-and-wine picnics and long bike rides. "Maybe I just wanted you to see how it hurts when someone picks you up and puts you down at their leisure."

Jordan narrowed his eyes. "Maybe I don't ever want to lose you again."

A floating sensation, spurred by her fluttering heart, made Karen want to let a smile bloom up from her soul. But she couldn't fall for him now, not with Stone breathing down her neck, telling her to put herself in situations that stained her stature just to save his. And Stone could never know her feelings for Jordan were making her back down from her campaign to make him soften his investigation. Putting her energy, instead, into the bomb that would blast the House of Stone.

She acknowledged she and Jordan were standing at a respectable distance, but the electricity humming between them was surely sending sparks all around. She projected a pleading look up at him. "Jordan, please understand, I—"

"Don't let me interrupt, sugar."

Karen's heart seemed to stop, then race. It was Stone, his silver eyes burning a hole right through her.

114

An ominous shiver tore across Camille's skin the instant she swung open Arianna's bedroom door. Something was very wrong: the stillness, the silence, the absence of the faint scent of bubble-gum shampoo. Behind Camille was Dixie, alternately beaming and frowning over how this first daytime visit would go. "Arianna?" Camille called, her voice quavering.

Dixie stepped into the room, arms crossed. "Cripe, Camille, you think she's hiding from me?"

"No, she should be here. Arianna?" Camille shook her head to stop all the horrible images of where the little girl might be. But the bed, the table and chairs, the rocking horse . . . no sign of her. They were so close to D day, and things were moving so smoothly, with Camille corresponding with Karen via e-mail about how things would unfold to set them all free. She couldn't help wondering: had Rand's kiss prompted Mrs. Stone and Ida Mae to think they were conspiring to do something?

"Where is she?" Dixie's voice echoed from the bathroom.

The attic. Camille dashed upstairs. But it was dark and silent. Back into the bedroom, Dixie looked under the bed, behind the shelves holding the TV, books, and toys. "My God, Camille, I thought you said she never leaves!"

"She doesn't," Camille said. Adrenaline pumped through her; the baby stirred. *I should've taken her away the day I found her. What was I thinking?*

"Those witches!" Something primitive and blinding exploded inside Camille. Dixie's eyes, radiating fear and disappointment and rage, were like seeing her own feelings flash in a mirror. But where was Arianna? Had her grandmothers hurt her? Sacrificed her safety for the sake of a secret? No! She and Dixie had to stop them at all costs, even if it jeopardized Karen's plan, which Camille had yet to reveal to Dixie for fear she might object.

Camille grabbed Dixie's hand. "Come on. Your mother—"

"My God," Dixie gasped, following Camille as she waddled full speed to the south wing. Dixie ached as intensely now as she had that night when Camille had led her to the beautiful little creation of her own flesh and blood. Rage seared her senses at the thought of her own mother. This whole revelation was so stunning, Dixie had refrained from confronting Mom for fear she might act on the primitive maternal urges shaking her limbs.

"Camille, we have to find her," Dixie said. "We have to."

"We will," Camille said, her tone hard as she shoved open Mom's bedroom door. "Where is she"?

Dixie took long, hard steps toward her mother, who was laying dresses on the spindly four-poster bed. "You're a monster, Mom! How could you do this to me?" Dixie could see her own denim shirt rising and falling in violent heaves. She bunched her fingers at the sides of her jeans.

Mom slowly turned to face her and Camille.

"Dixie, what on earth are you doing home?" Mom said in a soft monotone, her eyes glazed as she fingered a yellow dress.

"I saw her, Mom! She looks just like me! And Camille said—"

"My gracious, girls, calm down."

Camille stood inches from Mom, shouting, "Where's Arianna?"

Ida Mae came out of the bathroom, setting a glass of water and a white pill on the dresser. She finger-combed a lock of Mom's hair and wiped her clumpy black eyeliner with a tissue. "Millie—"

Mom ignored her, holding up a green cocktail dress. She turned in the long, antique mirror that reminded Dixie of the night Dad had shoved Mom into it, cracking the glass and making a bloody zigzag along Mom's eyebrow.

"I haven't worn this dress in years," Mom said cheerfully. "Dixie, remember the cruise when we wore those matching gowns with—"

Dixie wanted to grab her, shake her. But images of Dad doing that held her back. "Mom!" she screamed. "Where's my baby?"

Her mother cast glassy eyes on her. "Why, in Florida. You know that."

"No, I saw her. Here! Camille took me to the room where you locked me up, too."

Mrs. Stone smiled, laying the dress on the bed. "Gracious, Camille's not adjusting well to life here at White Pines. Don't pay her a bit of mind."

Ida Mae pulled Mom back, sitting her on the bed, stroking her hands. She glared at them. "Y'awl bes' leave now. This ain't none a your business."

Dixie squinted at her mother's partner in crime. "You're just as sick as she is, Ida Mae. How could you let her brainwash you! You're both sick!"

Mom pulled a beaded blue pantsuit onto her lap, fingering rhinestone buttons down the front. She glanced up at Camille. "Gracious, I thought about running away, too, the first time Monty did that to me. But, Camille, you and our babies belong here. We wouldn't want you and Rand to do anything foolish. Putting yourself and others in danger."

"Where's Arianna?" Camille bent over her big belly, her eyes huge with rage as she glared at Mom. Her hair created a honey-colored aura that swayed as she shouted. "Tell us now!"

Dixie sat next to her mother, squinting. "Mom, don't play dumb."

"Gracious, girl. Your father would kill Ida Mae's boy. You know that. Arianna is doing just fine."

"She's mine! And I want to see her!"

"When is she coming back?" Camille demanded.

"I don't know, dear," Mrs. Stone said.

"Did you ever ask Senator Stone about letting her out?"

"My gracious, no. He would never—" She picked a loose sequin off the suit. Then she buried her face in her hands.

Ida Mae put her arm around her, stroking her back and saying, "Millie, shhh."

"You're crazy, both of you!" Dixie screamed.

Camille snatched the phone off the bedside table. "If you two don't tell us where she is, we'll drive to Washington right now! We'll tell Monty Stone there's a little black girl—"

Dixie stepped to Camille's side. "We'll do it, Mom!"

Mom sharpened her gaze. "Lower your voices, girls."

"I'll call the police, too!" Camille screamed.

"The media," Dixie shouted. "Everyone!"

115

"What kind of exclusive interview?"

Freida Miller met Ward's skeptical expression with her chin high, even though she had no idea what Karen planned to deliver at White Pines.

Ward crossed his arms, staring down at her. "It's bad enough you can't handle what could be one of the hottest stories of the year, Freida. But now you're talking in riddles. Give me more information."

"If we can just hold off a while, I'll have exclusive interviews with the key players in a story that will rock Washington," Freida repeated. "It involves Senator Stone. That's all my source will say. But I can feel it in my gut. This is for real."

Ward tugged at his mustache. "Your gut, huh? And I suppose you've checked your horoscope, too?"

116

Monty Stone's blood heated to a slow boil as he took stock of the way Karen was looking up at his nemesis here in the Senate tunnel. Why the devil was she giving Jordan Kyles that love-swept stare? A look half as intense from her Sophia Loren eyes could persuade the fiercest general to scale back his battalion.

Why, the little coquette! Was Kyles conspiring with her, appealing to her black sympathies, to bring him down? *No, Karen wouldn't let that lustful ape sway her judgment.* He had to get her away from him, warn her that her bid to save his reputation allowed no room for authentic romance or betrayal.

Kyles nodded. "Good afternoon, Senator."

"Ms. Bradley," Stone said as her expression hardened into a businesslike mask, "we need to prep for that show." He touched her arm, leading her back toward the Russell Building. Next to her in a red seat on the underground trolley, he said, "Karen, Kyles is still coming at me with all the might of Grant's army. Which suggests either you're distracted or you're not trying hard enough. Which is it?"

Her crossed leg, the knee bending just so over the thigh, stoked flames of longing that soon he would quench with even more gusto than the last time.

"Honestly?" Her big brown eyes took on a piercing stare. "I've been concerned about the ethical ramifications. At my last job I got caught up in—"

"Blasted lies! Why the devil did I believe your problems back there in the Motor City wouldn't follow you here?"

"They haven't."

"First the allegations of theft—"

"He stopped calling," Karen said.

"Now you and Kyles—"

"I'm only doing what you told me to do," she said as they disembarked. "And if that means using the power of female persuasion, I thought you would be perfectly amenable. I apologize if"—she lowered those dark lashes—"seeing it for yourself was upsetting."

He didn't want to acknowledge the twinge of jealousy at the thought of Kyles tasting her sweet brown sugar, too. Had he? Stone admitted he'd encouraged her to do whatever she had to do, but that was before he got a sample himself. He certainly didn't want to share her with the man who was trying to dig his grave. Stone waited for the elevator doors to close. "Sugar, I don't know if I want you in my camp anymore."

Karen tilted her head, making her hair move to one shoulder. "Perhaps we're both too emotionally involved in our work. If my execution of your orders is too intense, then—"

"You will not throw this back on me."

Karen crossed her arms, a sassy glint in her eyes as the elevator doors opened onto the fourth floor. "I'll pack my things as soon as we get back."

Stone followed her into the hall, watching her succulent backside through a red cloud of rage. He could not shake his daddy's voice saying, "I told you so" or the suspicion in Jeff's eyes as he questioned a colored girl's loyalties. But this was what Rollins and the consultants wanted. And it was working, to a point. What the devil should he do now? If he fired her he wouldn't get to see her, dream about their next liaison. And if she were being straight about her dealings with Kyles, it would all be for naught. No, he couldn't let her go, but one more strike and she'd be out of this ratings game.

"Sugar, wait."

Karen stopped, facing him.

"Stay. A crotchety old fellow has his moments. Come into my office. Let's talk." He led her inside, closing the door as she sat on the couch. The way her legs crossed made something primitive well up from his gut; the thought of Kyles touching her, tasting her, drove him mad. He had to sample her again. Now.

Stone half sat, half dove into her, his lips finding their way to her mouth. She pushed up to no avail as he nuzzled her hair, her neck.

"Monty, stop!"

"Admit you want me again." He had to caress every inch of her, running his hands over her breasts, her hips, those legs. He wanted to follow suit with his mouth. It was the same wild, unstoppable feeling that overtook him when Millie sassed or asked too many questions . . .

"Stop!" Karen shoved him, her dainty hands in his chest, knocking him clear off the couch, onto the floor. A deep gurgle escaped his throat. The globe, the chandelier, the mantle blurred.

And when he stood, she was gone.

117

Karen bolted from Stone's office. She dashed into the press room, grabbed her coat, flew on legs like pistons into the hallway. Panting, she tried to appear calm as a cluster of people walked past. This was out of control, crazy, and dangerous. And it would only get worse.

But could she make it? Just two more weeks to the book party. Two more weeks and it would all be over.

"Karen!"

She jumped. Was Stone coming after her? To rip off her clothes, rape her again? With Jeff and the other brothers, too?

"Karen, are you all right?"

She glanced back through a curtain of curls. Jordan was dashing toward her. No! Stone would go ballistic if he saw them together again. But Jordan caught up, rage flashing in his eyes. "What'd he do? Spank you for talking to a nigger?"

Karen shook her head, stopping at the elevators. She stared into his comforting eyes, not wanting to lie, but refusing to tell Jordan what happened. Not as her lover. And certainly not as chairman of the Ethics Committee.

"Jordan, soon. I'll tell you everything."

"No, I want to know now," he said, blocking the elevator. "I'm already investigating your boss because four women claim he raped them. Now you come running, looking like this. Why are you trying to protect the sleazy bastard?" He pulled a phone from his pocket. "Tell me, or I'll call the police."

118

Mack Campbell blinked away tears as he turned the key, opening the back door at Biscuits 'n Honey. Walking into the dark, cold kitchen for the first time in seven months, he could almost feel Ernestine and hear her wooden spoon beating against a bowl of batter. Or Betty, yakking and moving too slowly while Karen smoothed over the fiasco-of-the-day.

"Christ, Ernestine, why'd you leave me?" The lights flickered on. All he wanted now was to make the mixer hum again, the oven blast sweet-scented heat, the cash registers ring. He had to make Ernestine proud. He was sure she was looking down, watching him, helping his lawyer convince that judge to give him the Windsor house, providing the cash to reclaim her dream. His plan was to surprise Karen, as soon as she was done in Washington.

Ernestine, just help me get the girls out of that crazy mess, and we'll be home free. Their cockamamie plan had him thinking about swigging down his worries with peppermint schnapps or at least a beer during all those lonely nights at the house. Or forgetting everything with the deep rumble of horses' hooves and the cheering crowd at the track, the rush of adrenaline or defeat numbing his grief. So far, he'd resisted. If he could just make it a few more weeks . . .

Mack found a notebook in the office. Had to make a checklist of things to get this place back in business for spring. Pulling open the desk drawer, his finger caught on a jagged edge of metal.

"Christ!" He sucked the gushing blood. Hurrying into the bathroom, he opened the knotty-pine cabinets. Ernestine had to have left some Band-Aids in there somewhere. He rifled past antacid, aspirin . . . there . . . a box of . . . what was that? A dark blue velvet bag. Mack ignored his bleeding finger, pulling the satin strings to peer inside. No, that couldn't be.

He turned toward the light above the sink.

"You're shittin' me."

A bagful of diamonds twinkled up at him. Franklin . . . the day he'd stayed in the bathroom for so long . . . when Karen was in New York. The sneaky bum, putting her and all of them in danger by hiding his loot here.

The pawnshop. He could get a mint for this, then blow his mind with trifectas and perfectas.

He was trembling, his knees wobbly, pulse racing. No, Ernestine wouldn't approve. And Karen needed this to get that thug off her back. So should he call her? The police? Gripping the bag, his palms oozed even though he could see his breath. His bleeding finger dripped, but he couldn't take his eyes off the pretty sight in the bag. And it was only six o'clock. The pawnshop over on Gratiot would still be open . . .

119

Dixie sank to her knees on the pink carpeting, just inches from her daughter. Something warm fluttered through her; she wanted to spend the rest of her life staring into that little face and those dark, sparkling eyes. But apprehension paralyzed her, stifling the urge to hug Arianna for fear of startling her. Not to mention Mom glaring down at them, and the anxiety Dixie felt that Arianna would dash straight to Camille at any moment.

Now all she wanted was the chance to get to know this little girl and get her out of here safely.

Arianna, in an oversized apricot sweater with velvet leggings, and a matching ribbon around her high ponytail, glanced up at Mom.

"Nonnie, don't make me go back to boarding school," she said. "I like my room. With my toys and—"

"Gracious, it was only an open house," Mom said, "to see if you liked it. And you won't have to go back if Dixie and Camille obey the new rules."

Dixie glared at her mother, as did Camille, who stood with crossed arms near Ida Mae, who was putting fresh sheets on Arianna's bed. In a matter of hours, after threats from Dixie and Camille, Mom had brought Arianna back, presumably by sending Ida Mae in a chauffeured car to Foxbury to pick her up. Having gone on an open house sleepover there as a five-year-old herself, Dixie figured Mom had registered Arianna with Ida Mae's last name rather than Stone.

"What rules?" Camille asked, scowling at security cameras aiming at the door, Arianna's bed, and the play area. Leave it to Mom to have all that equipment installed so quickly.

Mom pulled a plastic key card, the kind that hotels used, from her pocket. "Anyone who wishes to visit Arianna will have to get this from me first." She pointed toward the door, which had a new brass box under the doorknob with a slot for the card, along with tiny red and green lights.

Arianna reached for the card. "What's that, Nonnie?"

Mom shoved it into the pocket of her pleated blue silk slacks that matched her blouse. "Nothing you need to concern yourself with, sugar."

"Mom, this is ridiculous," Dixie said, not wanting to say or show too much in front of Arianna. She noticed Camille was looking at the cameras, then the closet. "We don't need—"

"I decide what you need," Mom said.

Dixie wanted to scream at her, but knew that would not get one of those passkeys into her hand. Maybe she and Camille could swipe one from Ida Mae's or Mom's room in the middle of the night. Or perhaps she and Camille should have gone through with calling Dad and the media. But what would her father do? With his book party coming up, and his ravenous ambition to become president, surely he would not want this kind of scandal leaking out. His response might be even more sadistic than Mom's. And considering his still-smoldering rage over his own father's unsolved murder, Dad would surely have Wilson tracked and riddled with buckshot.

So for now, Dixie decided to comply with Mom's new rule while calculating how to detach herself and her child from this highly dysfunctional situation. In the meantime, she held her arms out to Arianna, praying for a smile and spark of warmth in those eyes. "Can I be your new friend, please?"

Arianna studied her for long moments, then glanced at Camille, who nodded. Little fingers wrapped around Dixie's hand, pulling her toward the computer. "Let's play my new numbers game," Arianna said as the screen became a blue blur beyond Dixie's tears.

On the couch in the Victoria Suite's sitting room, Camille held Dixie's quivering shoulders as she sobbed into a wad of tissues.

"Dixie, listen," Camille said, stiff with anger and determination. "I have some things to tell you." Now was the right time to divulge how the secret D day plan could benefit Dixie, too. So Camille proceeded to explain the truth about herself and the plan to free Arianna with the help of Rand and Karen. As Dixie's hazel eyes widened with shock but not scorn, Camille prayed her sister-in-law would respond with enthusiasm.

"The security cameras and key card will complicate things," Camille said, "but we'll figure something out."

Dixie's gaze sharpened. "You can't take her away."

Camille slid a stiff mask over the panic punching her gut. "You'd rather she stay locked up?"

"I'm her mother. You're not." Dixie glared at the mound bulging under Camille's long pink angora dress. "You'll have your own soon."

"I know that, Dixie. That's why we need to do this together. We'll work out something for all of us once we get her out."

Dixie wrinkled her nose. "You've been lying and scheming to my family all this time. I could never trust you. Especially on this."

Camille cringed inwardly. "Your family has been lying and scheming to you, too, Dixie. Mine cost a life, and theirs did, too. So let's do this together."

Dixie stood, glaring down. "I won't let you take her away from me." She strode into the bedroom.

Camille followed, taking her hand. "Dixie, wait. This is a lot for you to deal with all of a sudden. Just think about it." Camille could feel desperation welling in her eyes as Dixie stared with an odd expression.

"Cripe, this is insane," Dixie whispered. Then she left.

Trembling, Camille sank onto the vanity stool. They were too close to let Dixie sabotage the plan. Because while Camille wanted desperately to get away from Jeff and his twisted family and the tangle of lies she'd made of her life, her heart would break if she had to forfeit the chance to watch Arianna blossom in the real world. In school, with playmates her age . . . eating at McDonald's . . . going to the mall and amusement parks . . . playing outside!

Suddenly Rand came to mind. "Yes, Rand." Camille glimpsed her full face breaking into a smile in the vanity mirror. That was it. She would ask Rand to convince Dixie this was the right thing to do.

120

Strapped into the soft beige leather on Stone's jet, Karen flipped through her burgundy attaché without letting Rollins, next to her, or any of the other half-dozen staffers see its contents. The bastard. At the end of the day, when she dropped her bomb, he'd be out of a job, too. Now if everything would just go smoothly until then . . .

"Sugar, come back here." Stone was standing in the doorway of the back room, which had a double bed and a desk and a table and chairs.

No! I will not let him rape me on the way down to the plantation.

At least Jeff was already there. Karen rose, smoothing her skirt. The last time she had defended herself, after that run-in with Jordan, Stone had responded the next morning by calling her "a feisty little thing," then asking her to fax the press release about his support of prayer in school to the media in time for his floor debate.

Karen fastened her bag, then shoved it under the seat. She hurried back, past Stone; he closed the door. She breathed deeply.

"Sugar, next week, with the hearings—"

"Monty, I apologize, for not stopping him." Thank goodness Jordan had backed off, stopped calling her, when she'd insisted he not phone the police that evening by the elevators, because she was just having a particularly hard day with grief. "But they have no evidence."

Monty pulled a cigar from a polished mahogany humidor with

the Stone crest carved into a gold oval on top. "Sugar, tell me what you think of me."

Noticing an unusual tenderness in his gaze, she joined him at the table. "Pardon me?"

He nodded. "I need to hear what a woman of your disposition sees when she looks at me or hears the name Monty Stone. And don't mince words."

Karen smiled. "I really couldn't begin to—"

"Out with it." He ran the cigar under his nose, holding her gaze.

"I think your charisma can deflect any accusation those women make."

"You play up that charisma, hear? Stick with me through all this and I'll reward you handsomely." He put a hand on hers. "You've done something to me, sugar. Softened me up. Helped me see your people in a better light."

"But Kyles is still—"

"Hell, it's more than that. You in action, I have to say, gets me here." He tapped his chest. "I've grown . . . attached to you."

Karen did not look away from his affectionate expression, because it seemed surreal. And sickening. This man had no clue that he'd committed a criminal act against her and who knew how many other women. Perhaps tonight she would help him evolve to a new level of comprehension.

Several hours later, Karen drove to the same bed-and-breakfast near White Pines where she, Mama, and Daddy had stayed for Sharlene's wedding. In the upstairs suite, she found Rand, Ginger, and her father.

"I just talked to Sharlene," Karen said, addressing the group in the glow of a Tiffany lamp around a lace-draped table. "She knows her cue to leave the party. Then, Rand, the two of you will get Arianna and—" Rand looked so much like Jeff. Would he sabotage their plan, get them killed? Even if Sharlene said they were in love. She'd said that about Jeff once.

Rand held up two keys. "Ginger, this is for the SUV. Mack, the speedboat."

Mack nodded. "I'll have the engine running, ready to go. But what if there's a glitch? Say Karen or Sharlene can't get out in time."

Karen shivered. "There's no room for glitches tonight, Daddy."

121

Camille was pulling on her black velvet dress when she caught Jeff's hot-tempered stare in the full mirror. "Is that my brother's pickaninny?" His gaze lowered to her basketball belly.

"I can't believe you, Jeff. Would you like a DNA test?"

"Not necessary." He fastened his tie. "You ever fuck him?"

Camille rolled her eyes, stuffing her inhaler, lipstick, and tissues into her little black purse, which she set on the bench next to her black patent-leather flats. Thank goodness Rand had convinced Dixie to help tonight; he told her this would be best for Arianna and would facilitate the growth of a mother-daughter relationship.

Now if Jeff would just calm down . . .

"Answer!" he shouted, storming toward her.

Camille immediately turned her back, wrapping her arms around her stomach. "Jeff, calm down. You can't go to your father's party like this."

He spun her around. "I'll tell you what, Lucy. You're right. Tonight means everything to him. But the sight of you makes me want to spit."

He opened the door, jerked her into the hallway.

Camille shrieked. But no one was around; Mr. and Mrs. Stone were already downstairs greeting hundreds of politicians, supporters, and media crews. "Jeff, stop!"

"I tried to love you, Lucy. But I can't do it." Jeff pulled her down the hall, to the dark wooden door leading to the attic.

No! Her kicks, punches, scratches did not stop him. He pulled her up the narrow steps. Pushed open the creaky door, shoved her into the blackness.

"Enjoy the party!" He slammed the door.

"No!" Camille screamed.

She imagined Karen frantically scanning the ballroom for her. Arianna spending the rest of her life locked in the north wing of White Pines, despite Dixie's protests.

And me . . . pregnant and dead in the attic.

122

Karen tapped the metal mesh of the microphone, making a scratching sound echo from speakers over the sea of people laughing, sipping drinks, and nibbling shrimp throughout the ballroom.

Everything and everyone was in place to execute Plan D. Except Sharlene. Jeff was there, grinning and shaking hands with the Republican Speaker of the House. In a navy-blue suit, his hair stylishly tousled as he gripped an amber-filled tumbler, he was at ground zero: the black platform holding the projection equipment, the launch pad where Karen had, before the party, secretly loaded her missile. But now, she needed Jeff to tell her where his wife was, if she could get past the moat of media around the podium.

"Excuse me." Two camera operators parted, but it would take forever to squeeze through all the reporters, fuzzy boom microphones, and tripods situated to capture the huge screen over the fireplace and French doors.

"Hey, girl!" It was Freida, notebook and microcassette recorder in hand.

"Freida, if you see Camille, let her know I'm looking for her, will you?"

"As long as we're still on for tomorrow morning."

"Exclusives just for you."

"Girl, I don't know what you're up to, but I can't wait."

Karen squeezed her hand. "Just pray."

The chandeliers flickered.

"Ladies and gentlemen," Rollins announced, "please take your seats."

Karen reached Jeff, standing next to his parents as well-wishers streamed past their table with Dixie, Rand, Jackson, Sue Ann, and Davis, who kissed her hand. He had an important task tonight that Karen had finally, via e-mail, agreed to let him carry out, even though she only half trusted him.

"Hello, everyone," Karen said. "Are we missing your lovely wife, Jeff?"

"She's moving slow these days. Being pregnant and all. Give her a few minutes." Jeff's jaw flexed as he glared at Rand.

Mrs. Stone crinkled her brow, jangling bracelets as she picked lint from Jeff's lapel. "Gracious, I should check on Camille. She cannot miss this."

"Mom, she's fine," Jeff said sharply, turning to watch his father, bathed in the silvery light of a TV camera, as a reporter interviewed him.

"Rand." Karen shook his hand, connecting with the worry in his eyes. "You made it down from New York."

"Wouldn't miss it," he said.

Karen nodded ever so slightly, with a glance at the doors. He took off.

123

Camille's eyes were open so wide in the blackness, they ached. The wind howling in the rafters and the thick air swirling dust were already making her lungs rattle. *Mother, please help me . . .*

Camille shivered. The tiny hairs on her body stood on end. But the image of Karen and everyone else waiting in terror for her to show up inspired her to get her bearings and find her way out. As she took a step forward, tiny splinters pierced her stockinged feet. She banged the wooden door. Surely the lock was so ancient she could shake it open.

She tugged at the doorknob.

Crack!

She flew back, crashing onto rough floor planks.

In her hand was the doorknob, broken.

She lunged to the door, finding a long, square screw protruding from where the knob had been. And it would not budge. But they had to have noticed her missing by now.

"Help me!" she screamed, pounding on the door.

That only stirred up more dust.

She coughed. *My inhaler is in my purse, in the bedroom.*

"Please! Mother, don't do this to me!" The baby was kicking more forcefully than ever.

Maybe she could find her way to the north wing, to the staircase leading to Arianna's closet. But it seemed impossible to navigate the old furniture, the different rooms, in the blackness. She felt around the door. She needed a flashlight, a candle, a kerosene lamp. Anything!

Were the ghosts of White Pines listening, watching? And did they see her as one of them, or a selfish fool who was getting what she deserved?

124

Icy-hot tremors wracked Karen as she scanned the crowd, not finding her sister. She was standing next to Rollins at the podium as he said, "Ladies and gentlemen, I have the distinct honor of introducing one of this country's greatest leaders."

Just beyond all the media, at the Stone family's table, were two empty seats. Where Rand and Sharlene should have been. The way Mrs. Stone kept glancing around, her face taut, she must have been looking for Sharlene's black velvet dress and ponytail, too.

Jeff's placid expression as he sat there with legs crossed only intensified her alarm. She had to make sure Sharlene was in a position to escape once things heated up, in just a few minutes. But Rollins, with Stone at his side, was saying: "—and now, I introduce to you, Senator Montgomery Stone!"

The crowd rumbled to its feet. *No stopping this train now. God help us . . .*

A lightning storm of cameras flashed on Stone as he said, "The Commonwealth of Virginia is the birthplace of presidents because she's cradled the likes of George Washington, Thomas Jefferson, and James Madison. Now I'd like to join the list. Ladies and gentlemen, you are the first to know: I am officially making a bid for President of the United States."

The crowd chanted like an ominous drum: "Stone! Stone! Stone!"

"Thank you very much," Stone said. "I hope you're cheering because you want me in the White House, not because you're getting a free salmon dinner."

The crowd roared.

"Now I want to get to the good part," Stone said, drawing Karen closer. "I'm going to put you in the talented hands of Ms. Karen Bradley. Karen?"

During his tender moment on the plane, she had felt triumphant after winning back permission to narrate the video. But now, as she tried to step to the microphone, her leg muscles trembled so violently she couldn't move.

125

The light was dim, but the flashlight Sharlene had found by the door was enough to navigate around the hulking armoires and chandeliers crammed into the web-covered attic. Which way was north? South? It could take an hour to get past all this stuff. But she had to. All their lives depended on it.

Her rattling lungs joined the wailing wind and beating rain on the roof. So far, since the beating, she had resumed taking a new, twice-a-day steroid inhaler that prevented attacks. And she could only pray that it would hold up under this terror and cold.

The flashlight cut swaths in the dusty air as she pushed past old trunks, couches, boxes of china. Stumbling around a corner, she came to a long rectangular area. The main house. Now, to the left, the north wing. To Arianna.

Moving faster, she reached a wall. With no door in sight.

126

In the glare of television cameras and flashing bulbs, Karen tried to project cool confidence from the podium.

"Hold on to those name cards, ladies and gentlemen," Karen said, terror threatening to crack her smooth voice. "You'll need them to pick up your STONE FOR PRESIDENT hats and T-shirts. If we could please dim the lights."

Now I'll never see if Sharlene is here.

The ballroom darkened as the orchestra played "The Star Spangled Banner" just loud enough to quiet the murmuring crowd. Light shot from the projection stand, splashing video on the huge screen above her. "This documentary is titled the same as the book," she said, *"My Forefathers, My Future: Fourteen Generations of the Stone Family."*

Mama, help us . . .

"Senator Montgomery Stone," Karen began, her voice booming through the ballroom as the screen showed Stone on the Senate floor. "Lawmaker. Korean War veteran. Husband and father of five. Soon-to-be grandfather."

Cameras illuminated patches of the audience and the silver-dollar glow in Stone's eyes at the table just past the media. Still no sign of Sharlene.

"Montgomery Stone has played a vital role in government for

nearly five decades," Karen said as the video showed Stone greeting citizens among pink apple blossoms near the Capitol.

"Now, as this great man bids to become commander in chief, you should understand the rich history behind him." A stark drumroll played over the thunder and rain blowing past the huge windows. "In 1637, Randolph Stone set sail from England for the colony named for the Virgin Queen. Here in Virginia, he joined the House of Burgesses." A picture of Queen Elizabeth I flashed, then men constructing White Pines.

"Mr. Stone started building this spectacular house . . . where he married Isabelle Smith. And with the help of ten children, he sowed the seeds of a tobacco, sugar, and rice empire stretching thousands of acres on several plantations throughout the Tidewater region."

A succession of pictures showed men in colonial attire. "Mr. Stone's descendants participated in the Virginia Convention in 1775, when Patrick Henry said, 'Give me liberty or give me death.'"

The worry clawing Karen's gut grabbed her vocal cords. She coughed. "Excuse me," she said, as the screen showed painted battle scenes. Karen wanted to scream "Sharlene! Where are you?" She cleared her throat.

"Stone men fought in the Revolution, and were part of the Continental Congress when it ratified the Declaration of Independence in 1776. They fought in the War of 1812. And two years later witnessed the burning and rebuilding of the White House and Capitol."

Karen pressed trembling fingers on the podium.

In minutes, she would run for her life. With or without her sister.

127

Rand stood in the upstairs hallway, heart pounding, mind spinning with all the terrible things Jeff might have done to Camille. Still gripping her purse and shoes, which he'd found in their bedroom, he called her name.

He froze, holding his breath. There! The ceiling creaked. Rand dashed for the attic steps, grabbing a powerful flashlight from a linen closet. At the door, he turned the rusty lock, heard it click. Jammed!

He stepped back, kicked it open with a loud crash.

"Camille!" He whipped the flashlight around, cutting yellow beams in the dusty air.

"Camille!"

Was that pounding to the left? He shot the light to the floor.

Yes! Footprints in the dust.

128

Camille ignored the pain shooting up from her bleeding feet. Her toes throbbed from kicking open the door to the north wing. It seemed she'd been running for hours, her heavy stomach bearing down on her bladder.

"Please," she wheezed, her throat dry as sandpaper. "Please help me."

Imagining her sister and Rand crazed with worry downstairs only made her heart race faster. And nothing looked the way she remembered. Where was that railing leading to the staircase in Arianna's closet? There were so many—

The flashlight darkened. "No!" Darkness closed in on her. She threw the flashlight, crumpling to the floor, sobbing. But . . . the tinkle of music.

Yes! She listened hard despite the thunder and rain.

"I'm almost there," she whispered. "The corner. The stairs were in the corner." Holding her hands before her, she crept through the blackness. Her shoulder crashed into a wooden post. Something hit her knee. The bed.

A handful of dusty fabric . . . something cold and smooth like a mirror . . . a chest with rough iron hinges. A railing.

Sobbing, she made her way down the steps, into the closet, into the soft glow of the pink bedroom.

"Arianna?" Camille squinted in the light.

But Ida Mae glared back from Arianna's bed. The child was on her lap, holding the jewelry box ballerina. In a pink flannel nightgown, Arianna scrambled over Ida Mae, throwing her arms around Camille's leg. Giggling, she said, "You're dirty!"

Ida Mae stormed toward them. "You full-fledged crazy now!"

Camille picked up Arianna, who clung to her neck. She wasn't supposed to lift anything heavy, being pregnant, but this was an emergency. So she waddled toward the door.

But Ida Mae body-blocked her. "You crazy if you think you gon' take that child outta here!"

129

Stone felt as if a Fourth of July fireworks display was lighting up his insides. Nothing would stop him from riding this wave of patriotism straight to the White House. And Karen—why the devil had he doubted her? This here idea for a video was brilliant. No doubt the afterglow, with the media finally taking a positive spin, would surely melt the negativity of next week's hearings.

Hell, bring it on. I can handle anything now.

Karen's sweet-as-honey voice droned on as he imagined his presidential duties. There would be foreign dignitaries to meet. Important military decisions to make. Hard-hitting legislation to sign into law. Legions of Americans to lead into the twenty-first century in the Stone tradition. Observing his family around the table, Stone envisioned Jeff taking his seat in Congress; the baby would arrive just in time for publicity pictures.

No trouble from Jackson and Dixie. Davis, I'll have him straightened up. And Rand . . . Camille . . . how dare they miss this?

"Millie!" he whispered.

"Yes, Monty. Karen did a wonderful job. I never should have doubted—"

"Where are Rand and Camille?"

Millie's gaze hardened. "I'm worried about them."

Stone's euphoria resumed. He throbbed; in a few hours they

would share a celebratory tryst. And he'd heard the script so many times, it lulled him into a brain-gasm about what tonight, and the future, would bring.

"The Stone family was so wealthy, they owned hundreds of slaves in the early nineteenth century," Karen said over pictures of rolling fields, buggies, and black people working in the sunshine. "The Africans were bought at slave auctions in Richmond, then brought to White Pines, living in log cabins behind the mansion. One tidbit you won't find in the senator's book is . . . Stone men made it their duty to plunder the bodies of slave women."

The audience gasped, but to Stone, lost in his thoughts, it sounded like more oohs and aahs at Karen's outstanding production.

"From these trysts, mulatto children were born, some so fair they looked white," she said over pictures of white and light-brown people and documents. "Now, ladies and gentlemen, you also won't read that Randolph Stone helped Virginia pass a 1644 law deeming mixed-race people slaves, and the 1662 law banning interracial sex and marriage. And any white woman who had a mulatto child would be enslaved with her baby."

"Pop, what the hell is she doing?" Jeff's furious tone made Stone focus.

"Gracious! This is blasphemy!" Millie cried over the audience's gasps.

Stone struggled to decipher Karen's words: "The Stones maintained high moral ground in public, depravity in private. For example, one tradition passed through generations was, and is, the mulatto mistress."

"What the devil is she doing?"

"But these trysts spawned brutality. When Master Stone discovered romance between his mulatto son and his white daughter, he lynched his own son! And when Amanda Stone found her husband in bed with a mulatto named Sarah, she strangled Sarah and hung herself in the attic."

The audience buzzed as the screen flashed pictures of Stone men and their wives in white gowns, then Camille in her wedding dress and tiara.

Dark Secret

"These lurid customs still vex the minds of Stone men," Karen said.

Jeff bolted from his chair as Davis left the table.

"Stop her!" Stone shouted, standing. He stepped toward the projection screen, but stands holding soiled dinner plates blocked the aisles along with extended legs and pulled-out gold-bamboo-backed chairs.

"Many of you attended Jeff and Camille Stone's garden wedding." Video showed the couple feeding each other cake. "But none of you know the bride's interracial family"—a picture of an interracial family filled the screen—"was banned from the wedding. You see, ladies and gentlemen—"

"Stop her!" Stone shouted. A TV camera blinded him. "Stop this!"

"—that woman with Camille's parents outside White Pines is me. I am Camille Stone's sister. That means Camille Stone is half black. Thus she embodies a violation of the racist laws that the Stone family helped create three centuries ago here in the Commonwealth of Virginia."

A huge fist of rage squeezed Stone's chest. He clutched his lapel. Hell no! He would not let this ruin him. Never!

130

Rand tracked the footsteps down the glowing staircase to the north wing's old nursery.

"Let us out!" Camille screamed at Ida Mae, who was making an *X* with her body over the door. Camille pushed her; Arianna screamed.

Adrenaline propelled Rand toward them. "Ida Mae, move!"

All three froze, facing him. *Good God, what a precious little girl.*

"Millie gon' kill me if I let my grandbaby go! Specially tonight."

He glared down at Ida Mae. "You're just as heartless as the rest of my family!" He pushed her, hating the terror in Camille's bloodshot eyes. Dust streaked her face; cobwebs danced around her head like tiny ostrich feathers.

"Is there time?" she wheezed.

Rand pulled her purse from his back pocket, reached in, and handed over her inhaler. As she took a puff, he picked up Arianna, who was still crying. He stroked her head. But she screamed as Ida Mae tugged her arm.

Camille, closing her eyes and breathing deeply, pulled her shoes from his waistband. She slipped them over bloody, dirty feet. Then she swung open the door, looked both ways, then back at him.

"Can you do this?" Rand asked.

Camille nodded.

"Miss Millie gon' kill you both," Ida Mae screamed, "for takin' that chil' 'way from here!"

Rand shoved her with one hand, making her reel to the carpet. And they bolted down the hall.

131

Millie Stone was numb. She had never fathomed such horror.
How could she ever show her face again? It would be impossible. But
for now, she had to hold her head high, get through this without
expiring from humiliation.

*Gracious, we're ruined. I knew about Camille. But I didn't care. I took
her into my home and my heart to protect her. And now this . . .*

Why wasn't anyone stopping that scheming colored traitor Monty
had been so simpleminded to hire? "First," Karen said, "let me tell you
what happens when black blood comes into the Stone family mix."
Video of Arianna filled the screen. "This is Senator Stone's secret
granddaughter."

The audience roared.

"Gracious, no!" Where was Dixie? Her seat was empty.

"Yes, little Arianna is half black, just like me," Karen said. "But
you've never seen her, because the Stones are so ashamed their precious
daughter Dixie got pregnant by a black stable hand at age sixteen that
they keep this five-year-old girl locked up here like an exotic bird!"

Everything slowed as if Millie had taken a Valium.

Gracious, this can't be happening.

"And this," Karen said, "is how Jeff Stone reacted to news that
his wife is half black." Camille's purple-splotched body filled the
screen. "All while pregnant with his child. But you can't entirely blame

Jeff. He learned this in utero. When Senator Stone beat his own wife when she was pregnant."

All the eyes on her . . . the shocked chatter . . . that blinding camera.

Gracious, I'll die of shame, right here in the ballroom.

132

Where the devil had she gotten that video? The sight of his own bare behind frantically humping Karen made his chest constrict further. Why weren't the security guards tackling her? Where was Rollins? And damn these chairs, all the reporters and cameras blocking the way.

"I like it when you scream," Stone heard himself say through the speakers. "Just like the black wenches screamed for my granddaddy. Now I've got my own pretty wench."

No! Stone clawed his squeezing chest. Bullets of sweat drenched his trembling body. A glance back at Millie—deathly pale, eyes huge. *This will kill her . . .*

"What you're seeing, ladies and gentlemen, is Senator Montgomery Stone, the presidential hopeful, raping me," Karen said.

"Oh, Daddy's coming now. Coming home to his sweet nigger wench!"

Stone was hot. Cold. Blinded. He fell to his knees, welcoming the silent blackness that engulfed him.

133

Sweating and panting, Jeff pushed like an angry bull.

"Watch it, man!" A cameraman pushed him as a tripod tottered. "I got a hundred grand worth of equipment here!"

Those two conspiring black sluts won't make it out alive.

Karen's dark eyes burned with defiance. "The Stone family believes in keeping family traditions alive. No sooner had Senator Stone raped me than his oldest son—my brother-in-law!—repeated the violent act."

The audience moaned. Two cameras aimed point-blank in Jeff's face.

"Get the fuck out of my way!" Jeff forged forward, hearing himself shout: "Suck my dick! Stop crying and shaking like a goddamn leaf!" There he was, larger than life, pushing Karen on the bed. He tripped over a tangle of black cords, crashed to the floor. Cameras closed in above him.

"Ladies and gentlemen, this occurred just hours after Jeff Stone brutally beat my sister." Cries of "oh!" and "no!" from the crowd.

Jeff got to his feet. Karen Bradley was about to take her last breath.

134

Now! As Jeff's recorded shouts continued to fill the ballroom, along with the clamor of the crowd, Karen spun around. The security guards and police hadn't pushed her away, thanks to Davis. Now all she had to do was shove open the French doors and flee into the night.

"Get her!" Jeff shouted to the beefy security guard to her right.

Trembling, Karen fumbled with the door. A hand grabbed her hair. Her arm.

"No!" Karen twisted, kicked. Until Jeff let go of her hair.

Someone was on his back—Davis! "Go!" he shouted.

The security goon still had her hand. She raised her high-heeled foot, kicked him in the crotch. But two state troopers lunged.

So she threw herself into the door, shattering glass. The ground swallowed her heels; she ran on stockinged feet.

"Stop!" Two burly state troopers flanked Jeff. A mob followed.

Would they draw guns and shoot? Karen ran faster. But the dock, and the tiny lights on the boat, looked a million miles away.

135

Camille followed Rand as they shot down the stairs leading into the kitchen, bustling with caterers carrying trays of plates and mounds of food. Dixie stood by the island, a strange glint in her eyes. Would she help as she'd promised, or would she try to keep Arianna here?

"Boy, what you doin'?" Hortense hurried toward him, reaching for Arianna. "Put that girl down. Must be crazy!"

An ominous rumble came from the ballroom; people raced across the lighted patio. *Karen did it. Now the lynch mob is after her.*

"Back off!" Rand shouted, surging toward the glass doors. "Move!"

Hortense tried to tackle him, pushing him into a counter, shattering dozens of crystal goblets on the floor.

Arianna screamed. And Ida Mae came bolting down the steps, pulling Camille's hair, clawing her dress, screaming, "Oh no you won't!"

Then Dixie lunged toward them all with a huge knife.

136

Ginger revved the motor of the Dodge Durango on the grass behind the guest cottages. *I hope this works . . .*

She turned the windshield wipers to a higher speed. Parked behind a cluster of trees, facing the water, she hoped to evade the patrol of the groundskeepers and security guards.

Shouting people and barking dogs made her look in the rearview mirror. There was Karen, running. With Jeff on her heels. Policemen and hounds followed. Ginger opened the door, leaned out. "Karen! Get in!"

In seconds, Karen dove into the vehicle, clutching the backseat as Ginger sped away. "Did you see Sharlene?"

"No sign of her or Rand," Ginger said. "And I've been here an hour."

Karen trembled anew. She glanced back. Jeff and the cops were getting closer. Climbing into the front seat, she said, "Turn into those woods." Karen looked back toward the house. "There they are! I see Sharlene's hair!"

But a police sport utility vehicle blocked their path.

"Shit!" Ginger shouted. She shifted into reverse, floored it.

The mob parted. She slammed on the brakes, hoping the wheels would not get stuck in the muddy grass.

Karen opened the door. "Get in!"

Rand, Sharlene, Dixie, and Arianna climbed in. They were drenched. Panting. And the child . . . her big beautiful eyes were wide with terror.

Karen's heart melted. *How could they . . .*

"We're almost there!" Ginger said, speeding down to the dock.

But the wheels made a feeble *whir* sound.

"Stuck in the mud," Rand said, glancing back.

Bright lights from police cars shone inside the Durango.

"We can do this!" Karen shouted.

Everyone dashed from the vehicle: Rand carrying the little girl. Sharlene waddling in fifth gear. Dixie darting. Ginger's skinny legs moving like scissors. Karen hardly feeling her bare, cold feet hitting the ground.

And they ran for their lives.

137

Karen's bare feet sloshed through mud, onto the slippery dock. The cold air stung her throat and lungs. But she didn't let go of Sharlene's arm. No, she had to help her sister and everyone else onto the boat, so Daddy, standing at the captain's chair, could whisk them to safety.

If Jeff and the police and the dogs didn't get them first.

The agony in Sharlene's eyes made Karen ache to her bones; she was gasping, holding her stomach, slipping on the wood planks. Dixie and Ginger slid into the rocking boat, gripping a silver rail next to red leather seats.

"Here," Dixie said, taking Arianna from Rand. The girl hugged Dixie.

Rand hopped in, taking Sharlene's trembling hands. But Jeff pounded onto the dock, lunging at Sharlene. "You won't get away alive, Lucy!"

"No!" Karen shouted.

Rand jumped out, blasting a fist into Jeff's nose. Jeff fell backward, splashing into the dark water. The cops and dogs scrambled onto the dock just as Rand lifted Sharlene, set her in the boat.

"Now, Daddy! Go!" Karen dashed toward the captain's seat.

The boat roared. Rand helped Mack steer through blackness to another dock, where a car would take them to the airport. Finally—

Davis darted up from the cabin. Wearing all black, with a knit cap, he waved a silver handgun. Karen gasped. Behind her shrieked Sharlene and Ginger, sitting with Arianna on the leather seat across the back of the boat.

"Davis, what are you doing?" Dixie yelled.

"Hey, take it easy, man," Rand shouted over the roaring engine. He raised his hands. "We got women and children!"

"Shut up!" Davis shoved Mack, then steered in the other direction. His silver eyes glowed with violence. "Karen, I obliged you. Now reciprocate." The boat lurched; she grasped the captain's seat. "Or I take us for a thrill ride on Chesapeake Bay."

"Davis," she cried. "I never had your—"

Her father stepped between them, reaching into his pocket.

He held up a dark blue velvet bag.

Karen's eyes widened. "Daddy!"

Davis snatched the bag, opened it. "Whee-hoo!"

"Found it at the bakery," Daddy said, "in the bathroom, last week when I bought it back. It's all there. Every last rock."

She wanted to throw her arms around Daddy's neck and kiss him. But Davis still had the gun, sideways, balancing the jewel bag on it.

Rand rammed his shoulder into Davis's waist, making him drop the gun and the diamonds. He knocked Davis to the floor, face-first. Ginger wrapped his wrists and feet with red nylon rope. Then Rand dragged him into the cabin.

Karen sank to the floor, sobbing with relief as her father took the wheel.

"Thank you, Mama!" she whispered over the roaring engine.

Epilogue

Baby Ernie's plump legs wrapped around Camille's hip as she held a match to the last of six candles. The soft yellow glow illuminated the sparkle in Arianna's eyes as she licked a fingerful of frosting from her Minnie Mouse birthday cake. Perched on a stool at the long table in the kitchen of Biscuits 'n Honey, Arianna leaned close enough to wish over the flames.

"Smile pretty for the camera," Karen said as a flash froze the moment.

Camille smiled, too, as Rand approached, his wedding band glistening. "Have I told you today," he whispered, "how much I love you?"

She tingled down to her soul, knowing that Mother was smiling on them. It had all been a happy blur since they'd escaped White Pines: Senator Stone recovered from his heart attack, hiring a super spin doctor to deflect the book party scandal before running for president but failing to get the Republican nomination. Mrs. Stone moved to Charlottesville with relatives; during the divorce, the police started probing Jeff's possible role in the death of Nick Parker; and a federal grand jury was close to indicting Davis and Bright for Franklin Daniels's murder.

"Happy birthday to you," Ginger began singing, prompting everyone to join in. Camille had forgiven Ginger, whose trip here had also enabled her to meet with Detroit department stores eager to buy her men's line. And Karen's friend Freida Miller was here, stopping by on her tour to promote her book on the Stone scandal.

But Dixie was singing loudest, smiling the widest. Now that she was studying veterinary medicine at Michigan State University, she visited Arianna every weekend. Camille still couldn't believe Dixie had agreed to let her and Rand have temporary custody of Arianna, saying because the child was so attached to Camille, and Dixie wanted to finish school, this was the best arrangement for now. Camille still had some anxiety about what Dixie might decide in the future, but she was trying to live in the moment and cherish her blessings.

". . . dear Arianna, happy birthday to you!" Beyond the cake lay a glossy brochure for the bakery, which Karen had produced at her public relations firm in Detroit. She also did promotions for the community center Rand had opened in the neighborhood where Camille and Karen had grown up. Across the table, Karen's engagement ring sparkled. She spent frequent weekends in Washington with Jordan, but they had not yet set a wedding date.

"Let's celebrate," Daddy said. "Not only is Arianna the big six years old and here to stay, but I've been sober and haven't gambled for five years."

"Congratulations, Daddy." Sharlene kissed his cheek. Stroking Arianna's hair, she said, "Now make a wish, sweetheart."

"I already got a double wish," Arianna said, her eyes sparkling up at Camille, then Dixie. "I got two mommies."